Praise for Anna Durand's Books

"[*Notorious in a Kilt*] is the book I have been waiting for! A great second-chance romance and one of my favorites in this series."
The Romance Reviews

"I loved the Scottish in Ian and the strength of Rae, but the love of one little girl makes [*Notorious in a Kilt*] something to behold."
Coffee Time Romance

"I have enjoyed this whole series, but Emery and Rory [from *Scandalous in a Kilt*] have stolen my heart and are now my favorites!"
The Romance Reviews

"[*Scandalous in a Kilt*] is beautifully written with a heavy emphasis on the actual romance and sensuality experienced by [the] two characters. [...] I've found each of the [Hot Scots] books to have entertaining and original plots and marvelous characters."
Readers' Favorite

"An enthralling story. [...] I highly recommend the writing of Ms. Durand and *Wicked in a Kilt*, but be warned you will find yourself addicted and want your own Hot Scot."
Coffee Time Romance & More

"*Dangerous in a Kilt* by Anna Durand delivered! [...] It was the journey, characters, and smoking hot sex scenes that kept me turning the pages."
The Romance Reviews

"There's a huge hero's and heroine's journey [in *Dangerous in a Kilt*] that I quite enjoyed, not to mention the hot sex, and again, not to mention the sweet seduction of the Scotsman who pulls out all the stops to get Erica to love him."
Manic Readers

Other Books by Anna Durand

Fired Up
Dangerous in a Kilt (Hot Scots, Book One)
Wicked in a Kilt (Hot Scots, Book Two)
Scandalous in a Kilt (Hot Scots, Book Three)
The MacTaggart Brothers Trilogy (Hot Scots, Books 1-3)
Gift-Wrapped in a Kilt (Hot Scots, Book Four)
Insatiable in a Kilt (Hot Scots, Book Six)
The Mortal Falls (Undercover Elementals, Book One)
The Mortal Fires (Undercover Elementals, Book Two)
The Mortal Tempest (Undercover Elementals, Book Three)
The Janusite Trilogy (Undercover Elementals, Books 1-3)
Willpower (Psychic Crossroads, Book One)
Intuition (Psychic Crossroads, Book Two)
Kinetic (Psychic Crossroads, Book Three)
Passion Never Dies: The Complete Reborn Series
Reborn to Die (Reborn, Part One)
Reborn to Burn (Reborn, Part Two)
Reborn to Avenge (Reborn, Part Three)
Reborn to Conquer (Reborn, Part Four)
The Falls: A Fantasy Romance Story

NOTORIOUS
in a Kilt

Hot Scots, Book Five

ANNA DURAND

NOTORIOUS IN A KILT

ISBN: 978-1-949406-03-0 (paperback)
ISBN: 978-1-949406-04-7 (ebook)
ISBN: 978-1-949406-05-4 (audiobook)
Library of Congress Control Number: 2019931413

Manufactured in the United States.

Jacobsville Books
www.JacobsvilleBooks.com

Publisher's Cataloging-in-Publication Data
provided by Five Rainbows Cataloging Services

Names: Durand, Anna.
Title: Notorious in a kilt / Anna Durand.
Description: Lake Linden, MI : Jacobsville Books, 2019. | Series: Hot Scots, bk. 5.
Identifiers: LCCN 2019931413 (print) | ISBN 978-1-949406-03-0 (paperback) |
    ISBN 978-1-949406-04-7 (ebook) | ISBN 978-1-949406-05-4 (audiobook)
Subjects: LCSH: Man-woman relationships--Fiction. | Scots--Fiction. |
    Americans--Fiction. | Highlands (Scotland)--Fiction. | Texas--Fiction. |
    Families--Fiction. | Romance fiction. | BISAC: FICTION / Romance /
    Contemporary. | FICTION / Romance / Romantic Comedy. | FICTION /
    Romance / Later in Life. | GSAFD: Love stories.
Classification: LCC PS3604.U724 N68 2019 (print) | LCC PS3604.U724 (ebook) |
    DDC 813/.6--dc23.

Chapter One

Rae

The sun burned low in the sky, weary from holding itself up all day, a condition I understood all too well. My skin was coated with dried sweat, and my clothes sported dirt smudges and—What was that? I picked at a stain on my jeans that swiped across my thigh. Sheep shit, naturally.

No, I would never pose for the cover of *Glamour* magazine.

I braced my boot on the lowest board of the wooden paddock fence, my toe twanging the woven wire affixed to it. The sun painted the sky with stunning shades of salmon and gold, the colors streaking across the heavens on the tails of fiery cirrus clouds. On the far side of the paddock, in one of several fenced pastures, my sheep grazed amid the gently rolling grassland of my ranch. I held my hand over my eyes like a visor, scanning the land for any signs of trouble. The coyotes had gotten bolder this year, but so far, my perimeter fencing had kept them at bay.

Last year, I'd lost three sheep. My daughter, Malina, had been devastated—and we'd cried about it together. Not for long, though. We Everhart women knew how to suck it up and keep going. Life had thrown a lot of obstacles in my path over the years, but every time I doubted whether I could keep going, I'd look at my twelve-year-old daughter and realize she was the proof I could survive no matter what. In a way, she had saved me. I might never have built this ranch into a profitable business without the motivation of caring for my daughter.

Profitable now. But for how much longer? My income had decreased for the past three years. What would I do if the wool market didn't turn around? *Ugh.* I really shouldn't think about finances at the end of a very long day. Besides, I always got a little maudlin whenever my daughter was away. Right now, she was in California visiting my mom.

I turned away from the pastures to face the gravel driveway and the house on the other side of it. My gaze wandered to the driveway, following the track it carved through the grassland, half a mile to the paved highway.

Movement caught my eye, and I blinked rapidly, lifting my hand to shield my eyes again. Was that a person traipsing down the driveway toward me? Nobody walked all the way from the road. Nobody. It was a half-mile hike.

The figure drew closer and closer.

Surely, the stranger would stop and turn around when he got to the metal gate and the fence that enclosed the house and barn.

The figure kept coming.

I squinted, slipping a hand into my pocket where I kept my cell phone, and shuffled forward two steps. The figure approaching the gate looked like a man, based on his sturdy frame and the way he strode toward the gate with masculine purpose and certainty. A hat squatted on his head, its brim casting his face in shadow. No, not just a hat. The nearer he came, the more detail I could see. He wore a felt fedora just like the one Indiana Jones wore in all those movies. The stranger's T-shirt was blue and short-sleeved. His khaki pants hugged his hips and clung to his thighs, getting looser below the knees and flaring slightly around his hiking boots. Over one shoulder, he carried a brown duffel bag. He kept his head down, so I couldn't make out his face even as he reached the gate.

He lifted the latch, swung the gate open a few feet, and stepped through it. After replacing the latch, he marched in my direction.

I started to pull out my phone, to call nine-one-one, but hesitated. Something about the man seemed oddly familiar.

"Hey!" I shouted. "Stop. This is private property."

The man halted, removed his hat, and plopped his bag down in the dirt. He ran a hand through his light-brown hair. The glow of the sunset illuminated his face in golden tones tinged with pink.

I drew back, frozen in place. It couldn't be. No, no, no, I had to be hallucinating. The heat had gotten to me, and my brain decided to harvest a memory from the distant past and bake it into a bizarre hallucination.

The man resumed his leisurely, purposeful stroll toward me. His mouth curved into a casual smile.

My feet refused to budge. My vocal cords refused to function. My tummy fluttered, my pulse sped up, and a ridiculous anticipation zinged through me at the sight of the six-foot-two Highlander with broad shoulders and thick biceps sauntering toward me. My former college professor. My onetime lover. The only man I'd ever loved.

Iain MacTaggart halted an arm's length away. His smile failed to crinkle any lines around his eyes, and no one would ever have guessed he was...How old now? He must be fifty.

And of course, he looked as hot as ever. Young. Virile. His hook nose had never detracted from his appeal, rather it had always given him a dangerously seductive air. That and his easy smile. And his voice. Oh dear God, his voice. That Scottish brogue. He hadn't even spoken yet, and my body had already come alive at the memories.

"Rae Everhart," he said as if savoring the syllables. "It's been a long time, but I found you."

My throat had gone dry and tight, but I managed to squeeze out one word. "Iain?"

Duh. Like I wouldn't have recognized him in an instant even after thirteen years. My brain seemed to have shut down, though, leaving me to fend for myself in the presence of the only man who'd ever made me weak with desire. Hearing his voice again after all these years, that deep and smoky timbre, my body flashed back to the last time I'd seen him. Felt him. Kissed him. And oh, so much more.

Slack-jawed and immobilized, I stared into his pale-blue eyes. The breeze knocked a wavy lock of his hair over his left eye, but he seemed not to notice. His gaze was fixated on me.

"I've waited thirteen years for this," he said. "Can't wait a second longer."

He closed the distance between us, wrapped an arm around my waist, and pulled me into his hard body.

"Wha—"

His warm, soft lips silenced whatever the hell I'd been about to say. No clue what that had been, but it probably would've come out breathless and idiotic. He pressed his mouth to mine, holding his lips there without trying for more. Just lips on lips. His mouth. My mouth. The light stubble on his face rasped against my skin, the sensation tantalizing and erotic. The fluttering in my belly melted into a heat that pooled low, and when he slid a hand into my hair, I fought the urge to sag into him and moan. Sense memories, nothing more. Ghosts of the distant past.

Still, I could not break away.

He peeled his lips from mine with aching slowness, deliberately letting the contact linger for as long as possible. Once our mouths had separated, he kept his arm around my waist and his hand in my hair, his fingers caressing my scalp and his palm binding me to his body. Holy shit, he'd grown more muscles since the last time I'd seen him. Hard, powerful muscles.

Why was it so dark? Had the sun vanished?

Of course not. I had my eyes closed. *Idiot.*

I forced my lids to part, blinking to clear my gaze.

His blue eyes seared into mine. In that outrageously sexy voice, he murmured, "You have no idea how happy I am to see you, Rae. You're even more beautiful than the last time I saw you."

The last time. The last night. *Armageddon.* Memories assailed me, shattering the sultry spell he'd woven around me.

I shoved away from him, wiped my hands on my jeans, and straightened my shirt. "What on earth do you think you're doing? You can't waltz up my driveway, invite yourself through the gate, and then kiss me."

"But I did, and you let me." He plucked his hat off the ground where he must've dropped it when he pulled me into his arms. Dusting it off, he said, "I came a long way to see you."

"And that gives you the right to barge into my life?"

He sighed, ever the patient professor. The Unflappable Iain MacTaggart, that's what he'd been to me. To the rest of the student population at Nackington University, he'd been nicknamed The Notorious Dr. MacT, Professor of Fuckology. Every girl had wanted to crawl into his bed, and some of the boys too. The rest of the guys hated Iain because he had the kind of mature sex appeal only a man over thirty could hope to achieve. He'd been thirty-seven, two years older than I was now. I'd been twenty-two and awestruck by the sexy Scotsman who made archaeology and Celtic history sound like the hottest thing ever.

So naturally, I'd slept with him. Once.

And my entire life had blown up.

I locked my arms over my chest. "Go away, Iain. I'm way too busy to accommodate whatever midlife crisis you're suffering from. You are not welcome here."

My body disagreed, still pliant and steamed up from that kiss. The passion I'd felt for him so long ago seemed to have lain dormant inside me, just waiting for an opportunity to erupt again.

Oh hell no. I had a life of my own these days, one I'd fought hard to create—for myself and for my daughter. No man, not even a sinfully hot one, would trample on my carefully crafted life.

"Iain," I said, striving for calmness, "go home. Turn around and walk back the way you came."

"Afraid I can't." He slapped the Indiana Jones hat back onto his head, tilted at a sexy angle. "I'm not leaving until you've heard me out."

I stared at him for several seconds, fascination and annoyance warring inside me, making acid boil in my stomach. He was as pigheaded as ever, but I had no time for this.

Spinning on my heels, I stalked across the driveway to the front door of the house and slammed it behind me. Maybe a teeny bit of fear had spurred my flight.

Footsteps thumped on the roofed porch.

Iain's voice rumbled from the other side of the door. "I'll wait out here until you change your mind."

And I knew, without the slightest hint of a doubt, he would do exactly that. For days, probably, if I left him out there that long.

Thirteen years. What did he expect after so much time? That I'd throw my arms around him and praise God for sending him back to me? *Like hell.* But he wouldn't go away. In the ten months I'd known him back in college, I'd witnessed his stubborn streak on many occasions. Once he set his sights on a goal, he did not give up.

Shit.

Talking to him would be a mistake. Letting him into my house would be begging for disaster. Iain could never know the truth, not after all these years and all the pain he'd caused me. He'd lost the right to know when he abandoned me in the midst of a life-altering scandal. What might've been had evaporated the day after I said "yes" when Iain MacTaggart invited me back to his apartment.

Nothing mattered more to me than my daughter. I would do anything to protect her from the kind of hurt I'd endured when Iain left me without a word, without a trace, without a fucking forwarding address or phone number.

Iain could never know about Malina. Our daughter.

"Rae," Iain called through the door, "I'm asking for a few minutes, that's all."

Part of me—the remnants of that stupid, silly college girl who'd adored this man—urged me to let him in. A few minutes, nothing more. Hear him out, send him on his way.

Maybe I should confront my past, so I could lay it to rest once and for all.

I swung the door open, stepping aside and waving an arm. "Get in here and say whatever it is you think you need to say. I'll listen, but you will leave once you're done. No arguments. When I say go, you go."

The pigheaded man tipped his hat to me. "Whatever you say."

He ambled into the house, hat in hand and duffel bag slung over his shoulder. The fading sunlight lit him from behind. He dropped his bag on the wood floor. It thunked like it weighed fifty pounds.

I shut the door, feeling like the dumbest supposedly mature woman on earth.

"What I have to say," he told me, "is simple. I never should've let you go without a fight, and I won't make that mistake again. I've come to win you back, Rae."

Chapter Two

Iain

I watched Rae's jaw drop as she shook her head slowly. I'd shocked the poor lass. Considering how long I'd waited to find her, I couldn't blame Rae for thinking I was daft. All those years ago, I had never intended to seduce her. For ten months, I'd done nothing except talk to her, spend time with her—and not once had I held her hand, much less kissed her. Until that night. We had, well, fallen into each other's arms.

No, not fallen. We slid gradually down that slippery slope, the professor and the undergraduate, convincing ourselves we were friends until, on the night that changed everything, we'd given in to our true feelings for each other.

I couldn't resist drinking in her appearance one more time. She was bonnier than ever, her body more mature and with new curves that enhanced her sensual beauty. I loved her breasts, her voluptuous hips, that sun-kissed skin. Her hair that had once hung midway down her back now bounced just above her shoulders, the red tones in the auburn color more intense than ever. Her dark-blue eyes sparkled in the rays of sunset streaming through the thin lace curtains of the window beside the door to her home. She wore blue jeans that looked well worn by work, not by stone washing or some other trendy process. Her long-sleeve denim shirt hung open to reveal the yellow T-shirt beneath it. Black boots made of rubber and fabric, and splattered with mud, covered her feet.

We stood inside a short hallway, and I couldn't see what awaited deeper inside the house.

An odd smell wafted past me now and again, something familiar I couldn't quite place. It reminded me of my uncle's farm. He'd fertilized his garden with manure. Well, if Rae worked with livestock, she might well get a bit of shit on her boots.

I gestured at her denim shirt. "How can you wear long sleeves in this weather? It's bloody hot out there even with the sun almost down."

She glanced down at her shirt. "It's treated with insect repellent. Didn't you get bitten up out there? The mosquitoes are bad this summer thanks to all the rain we got in the spring."

"They must not like me. I don't taste as good as you."

Rae rolled her eyes.

When I'd walked up the driveway, the first thing I'd seen was Rae. The only thing I'd seen was Rae. Not until after she fled into the house had I noticed the surroundings. The country was beautiful here. She seemed to own sheep, if the flock I'd spotted belonged to her. The network of fenced areas had been confusing, but a paddock enclosed an area directly behind her red barn. I'd noticed a three-sided shed attached to the barn's backside. Her home, a simple white structure with two stories and a roofed porch, seemed older but well cared for.

Ah, I had something in common with this house. I was getting older too, though I didn't have a woman like Rae to care for me. I didn't expect her to do that. My plans involved me taking care of her the way I should have done years ago. If she would let me.

Rae slammed the door behind me, eying me with suspicion.

My plans might require a wee bit more work than I'd expected.

"Are you high?" she said. "Because I can't see any other reason why you'd say such an insane thing."

"Why is it insane? I loved you then, I love you now, and I'm not leaving until you're mine." It sounded simple enough to me and rather reasonable under the circumstances.

"Yours?" She reached for the doorknob. "I don't belong to you or anyone."

The instant she turned the knob, I settled my hand over hers. "That's not what I meant. Could we sit down and talk? I've had a long slog up your drive."

I let my hand linger on hers, enjoying the feel of her skin, its warmth and the softness that seemed incongruous with her apparently rugged lifestyle. How long since I'd touched her? Not counting a few minutes ago outside, more than a decade had gone by since I'd touched her.

Far too long.

Questions about her new life reared up in my mind, but I tamed them. Interrogating her would not make her trust me again.

I withdrew my hand, rubbing my jaw. "Could I at least have a drink of water before you toss me out? I'm parched."

She glanced around with jerky eye movements, seeming almost frantic. "Um, I…"

My eyes had become gritty. I ran a hand over them, yawning. Borrowing my cousin Rory's private jet had spared me the hassle of going through security, but after a six-hour flight from Scotland, I'd endured a long journey to reach the end of Rae's drive, a journey that involved three taxi cabs. My walk to her house had left me knackered.

One side of her generous mouth crimped. She flitted her gaze over me, her lips turning down at the corners. She shut her eyes briefly, then sighed. "Though I probably should, I can't kick you out when you're exhausted and dehydrated."

"Thank you." I didn't believe she wanted me out, but I wouldn't argue the point.

"Wait here," she said, and held up a hand. "Don't move. I'll be right back."

I admired the view of her backside as she hurried down the hallway.

At its end, she hesitated and jabbed a finger in my direction. "Don't move."

"Still bonnie when you're bossy, just the way I remember."

Her mouth fell open again, but she snapped it shut and disappeared into the rest of the house. I heard noises of someone knocking about, rushing from room to room from the sound of it. What on earth was she doing? I'd asked for a glass of water, not a tour of her home. She had no need to tidy up the entire house for me.

She was flustered and anxious, and I couldn't blame her. After so long apart, we needed time to acclimate to each other.

Our kiss a few minutes ago had affected us both. She'd kept her eyes closed for a moment after I'd pulled away, giving me a breathtaking view of her face, those delicate features relaxed, her cheeks dusted with pink, her lips parted. I'd fought a powerful impulse to take her mouth again, dive in deep, satiate myself with the taste of the woman I'd dreamed about for so long. Shame had kept me from searching for her. Recent events in my extended family had shown me the folly of my ways. If I wanted the kind of life, the kind of love, my cousins had found...

I had to risk everything for it. For her.

My mobile phone jingled with the chime of a new text message. I pulled out the mobile and glanced at the new text. *Where are you?* it said. *He's gone and I'm lonely without you.* I quickly tapped out a response. *Told you it was the last time.*

A clattering issued from deeper in the house.

I shoved the mobile back in my pocket. What was Rae doing in there? I opened my mouth to shout that very question when Rae appeared at the end of the hallway.

"Come on," she said. "We'll go to the kitchen. It's through the living room."

"No need to be anxious," I said. "You'll get acclimated to having me around soon enough."

"You won't be here that long."

She ushered me through the living room so swiftly I had no chance to examine its contents. A sofa, I noted. Everything else flew by in a blur as Rae grabbed my arm and hauled me onward into the kitchen. I caught a glimpse of photos hung on the walls. A much-younger Rae with two older people, a man and a woman who must've been her parents. Rae in cap and gown. Rae holding a lamb. Rae riding a horse.

More questions surfaced, but once again, I repressed them. For now.

She half dragged me into the kitchen and gestured for me to sit down in one of the chairs arranged around the rectangular wooden table.

I chose the chair at the end in front of a window, lowering myself onto the seat with a groan of relief. Seated at an angle in the chair, I stretched one arm over the back and smiled slightly at Rae.

Sunlight poured through the window, softened by lace curtains identical to the ones in the entryway. The light bathed her in a warm glow that gilded her skin. Though she sported a faint tan, the creamy color of her skin and the tiny freckles that speckled it showed through. Beautiful as ever. I'd longed for this woman for thirteen years, and I couldn't give up without a fight.

A magazine lay facedown on the table. I picked it up, and my brows cinched together when I read the title—*Sheep Ranchers Quarterly*. As I'd suspected, she raised sheep. I couldn't figure out why, though, since she'd had a bright future ahead of her in academia. Ah well, she'd tell me when she felt more comfortable in my presence.

Sweat dribbled down my temple. I fanned myself with the magazine. "No central air?"

"There is, but I turn it down when I'm going to be outside for a while. I cranked it up a minute ago, so it'll get cooler soon."

"You've gotten frugal."

"I'm not a cheapskate." From her position between the doorway and the end of the table opposite me, she said, "I'm trying to conserve energy."

Something in her tone of voice and the slight hunching of her shoulders gave me the idea she wasn't being frugal out of concern for the environment. "I meant no offense."

Rae grunted, scratched her cheek, and shifted her weight from one foot to the other. Her frown mutated into a pucker, then flattened out.

Since she seemed to be having an inner struggle of some sort, I decided to ignore it and let her struggle on in private. Not my business—yet.

I lifted my brows. "Water?"

She jerked, her eyes flaring wide. "Oh, I forgot. Sorry, I'll get that for you."

While she retrieved a glass from the cupboard and filled it from the tap, I watched her. As a nubile college student, she'd captivated me. As a mature woman, she entranced me. The way she moved with purpose, even while flustered. The way she challenged me with her words and with her body language. The way she'd let me kiss her.

The Rae I'd known before would've blushed if I'd dragged her in for a kiss like that. The woman bustling about in this kitchen today had not only permitted the kiss, she'd reciprocated.

Rae spun around and thrust the glass at me.

Water splashed onto my shoulder.

"Sorry," she mumbled, snatching a dish towel from the counter and mopping at the wet spot on my shirt.

Her breasts rose and fell on quick breaths while her delicate fingers probed my flesh. I wanted to pull her onto my lap for another, more forceful kiss. I wanted to devour her from head to toe. I wanted... everything with her.

Take it slow, ye dunderhead. Help her trust you.

I laid my hand over hers, stilling her fingers. "Easy, Rae. I won't bite."

She stared down at me, her pupils large, her lips pinker than before.

Desire. Oh aye, the signs were unmistakable. Sex might be my way in with her.

And since sex was the one thing I knew I could succeed at, unlike my nonexistent relationship skills, I should rely on my strengths. Seduce her into bed to seduce her into loving me again.

The fact I would enjoy seducing her had no relevance to my new plan. No, none at all.

I set down the magazine and withdrew my hand from hers, taking the glass. "Thank you."

"You're, uh, welcome."

"Don't suppose I could trouble you for a wee piece."

"A what?" She hesitated for only a moment before realization dawned on her lovely face. "You want a snack."

"You remember what 'piece' means."

"Mm-hm. You really want a snack?"

I sipped my water. "If it's not too much trouble."

"You did walk half a mile to get here. Sure, I can make you a sandwich."

"Don't go to the trouble for me." I waved toward a clear glass jar on the counter and the cookies stacked inside it. "One of those will do."

"Peanut butter cookies?"

"Sounds good. Protein and sugar, my two favorite food groups."

"Uh-huh." She looked dubious but carried the cookie jar to the table and set it down in front of me. "Knock yourself out."

I lifted the lid, leaned in, and closed my eyes while I inhaled deeply. Nutty, sweet, inviting. My stomach growled. I couldn't help the smile of ultimate satisfaction that tightened my lips. "Ahhhh, the scent of heaven."

"Never thought of peanut butter as heavenly."

I plucked a cookie out of the jar. "Don't you like these cookies?"

A half-stifled laugh snorted out of her. "Yeah, sweets and I have a love-hate relationship."

"Why is that?" I offered her the cookie.

She accepted the offering and dropped onto the chair next to mine. "I love to eat them, but I tend to go a little overboard and get an upset stomach."

"Ah," I said, grabbing a cookie and leaning back in my chair. "I was thinking you'd say sweets are bad for your figure. Most women have a complex about gaining weight."

"Not me." Rae snapped off a large bite of cookie, gnawing on it with a delightful lack of concern for being ladylike, relishing the peanut-buttery goodness with a little moan. "Most women either have a man or are looking to get one. This makes them obsessed with staying thin. I don't give a hoot about my weight since I'm not interested in men anymore."

I froze with a cookie raised to my open mouth. "What?"

"I'm not a lesbian or anything," she explained, "but I have responsibilities that make dating way too complicated."

The woman I planned to seduce claimed to have no interest in men. I sensed a story behind her statement, and this time I would ask.

I took a bite of the cookie, chewing while I studied her. Swallowing, I tipped my cookie in her direction. "What sort of responsibilities?"

"This is a working ranch. I own it and run it by myself, except for one ranch hand."

"A sheep ranch." I nodded at the magazine on the table.

"Yes, sheep. I raise them for the wool and sell some of them to people who want them for pets or for the wool. I'm looking to branch out into other avenues of income, though."

"Interesting. Not seeing the relevance to celibacy, though."

"Running this ranch takes a lot of time."

I swept my gaze around the room. "You live here alone?"

"No." She wolfed down another massive bite of cookie. "I have a daughter. The rest of my time is devoted to raising my child."

I cocked my head, afflicted with a sudden fascination with every aspect of her life. "How old is your daughter?"

Her face went slack, and she stopped blinking. "Old enough to be a handful."

"Where is she? It's summer, so I'm assuming she's not in school."

"Ma—" She bit down on her lower lip, held it for a heartbeat, then released it. "She's visiting her grandmother."

I opened my mouth to ask more questions.

She held up a hand. "Enough prying into my life. Why are you here?"

"To win you back."

Rolling her eyes, she scarfed down the last piece of her cookie. "That's not an answer. Not a complete one, anyway. It's been a long, long time, Iain. Why now?"

I polished off my own cookie, wiped my hands on my pants, and sighed. "A friend of mine got married recently. For several months before that, it seemed like he'd lost the woman he loved for good. He'd hurt her badly, and she didn't trust him not to do it again. But he vowed to do whatever it took to earn back her trust and her love even though it meant humiliating himself to please her overprotective brothers." I laid a hand on the table, fingers bent. "I thought if he could win back the woman he loved, I might have a chance too."

"Right." Arms folded over her chest, she scrutinized my face. "Did your friend wait a decade and a half?"

"No." My lips twisted into a rueful smile. "Only I am that much of an eejit. Which means I'm an idiot."

"Yeah, I remember that word. You used to call the frat boys eejits." Her toes tapped on the wood floor. "When everything hit the fan, you bolted for Scotland. I needed you, and you abandoned me."

She'd needed me? Of course she had. I'd thought of nothing but my own shame, fleeing to avoid a fate I'd feared all my life—becoming a criminal. How could she understand that? I'd have to tell her everything, eventually. For today, I could offer her an honest answer to the unspoken question in her statement.

With my elbow on the table, I raised my hand to plant my forehead in my palm. "I didn't mean to abandon you. I wanted to stay, more than anything."

"You accidentally stumbled onto a plane to Scotland."

"No." I lifted my head to gaze at her, a chill washing through me as those events replayed in my mind. "I wasn't only fired, Rae. I was forced out of the country."

Chapter Three

Rae

"Forced out?" I searched his face, but he showed me nothing more informative than a bland look. Iain had two modes of facial expression—casually bland and casually cheerful. Nothing got him riled up, nothing made him let loose a belly laugh, and nothing stripped away his calm demeanor even during sex.

The frat boys may have nicknamed him the Notorious Dr. MacT, but to me, he would always be the Unflappable Iain MacTaggart.

"I'll tell you the story later," he said, his voice as bland as his face. "After we've gotten accustomed to each other again."

"Accustomed, acclimated, whatever. None of that is happening."

He took a long drink of water, keeping his hand around the glass when he set it down on the table. "I'm not asking you to forgive me. All I'm asking for is a chance."

"To do what, exactly?"

"We had a good thing once. Let's find out if we could have that again."

I spread my hands on my thighs, whisking them up and down to wipe off the clamminess. Once upon a time, he'd made me nervous in a deliciously fluttery way. Now, he made me antsy in a very unpleasant way. Keeping secrets sucked. "We didn't have a thing, good or bad. We hung out for a while and then we slept together once. It was a fantasy, not a relationship."

Which one of us was I trying to convince?

His fingers tightened around the glass, then relaxed. Tightened, relaxed.

"Deceive yourself if you like, *gràidh*," he said, his voice soft and warm like a silky bubble bath, "but we had a relationship. It was good. It was real."

Gràidh. He'd called me that several times during our...acquaintance, but I'd never asked what it meant or what language he was speaking, too infatuated to think about such things. My foolish heart had overridden my common sense. For all I knew, he'd been calling me "moron."

No, he wouldn't do that. Whatever his faults, Iain was never cruel. He came with an arsenal of qualities designed to make any heterosexual woman fling herself at him, and those qualities had only intensified since the last time I'd seen him. The light stubble on his face, the hint of a scar on his nose, the more-chiseled physique...How was I supposed to react to all of this? Charming, sexy, determined, and he'd traveled thousands of miles solely to find me.

Dressed like freaking Indiana Jones.

I gave myself a mental slap upside the head. Getting rid of him was the only prudent option. Once, I'd thought I loved him. That had been a lifetime ago. I would not fall for him again. Nope. Not falling. Not even if he called me *gràidh* again in that soft, rumbly voice.

Malina had left for California three days ago and wouldn't come home for another eleven days. Maybe I could—

Stop right there. My foolish heart, or maybe my libido, had almost canceled out reason.

My fingers curled into my thighs. "Probably wasn't as good as we remember. Memories get glossed over until all you see is a pretty fantasy, not the gritty reality."

"Please stop calling it a fantasy. I loved you, Rae. I still do."

Though I made a somewhat rude noise, butterflies awakened in my tummy and excitement zinged over my skin yet again. Would I never learn? Letting this man into my life the first time had nearly destroyed me. Letting him in again might hurt more than my heart and soul. It might hurt my daughter too, and I could not allow that.

Iain aimed that easy smile at me. "You don't believe me yet. I understand. A few days is all I'm asking for, only a few days."

Faced with his smile—so casual and yet infused with languid sensuality—I dissolved on the inside and the outside, slumping in my chair as I permitted myself precisely five seconds to relish the bliss of being enveloped in Iain MacTaggart's full attention. He looked so good, too good, like he'd stepped through a time portal from thirteen years in the past. No one should be so unchanged after all these years. He should've had the decency to grow some flab or at least sprout a few wrinkles.

Oh, he had changed a little. His physique had become tougher, more muscular, and his hair sported a smattering of gray strands, especially at the temples. His hands, once smooth, had become rough and callused, and his skin had been toasted by the sun. He hadn't gotten older. He'd gotten hotter.

So unfair.

I leaned in, squinting at his face. "How many facelifts have you had? You don't look any older."

"Natural youthfulness," he said with a teasing tone. Then he leaned in too, our faces a breath apart. "You don't look any older, either."

"I have a wrinkle." I tapped the corner of one eye. "Here."

He brushed his thumb over the spot. "That's not a wrinkle. It's dirt. You are eternally beautiful and youthful."

"And you are so full of it."

With that thumb, he traced a line down my cheek to the corner of my mouth, skimming the pad across my bottom lip. "Even your name is beautiful. Rae. The English version means 'doe,' which I suppose is appropriate since female deer are elegant and bonnie. But I prefer the Scottish meaning—grace. It suits you best, even if Rae was originally a man's name in Scotland."

"You always were obsessed with the meanings of names."

"Not obsessed. Interested. In history, and in you." He dragged his thumb down to my chin, fanning his fingers over my cheek. "Everything about you fascinates me."

I cleared my throat, which had suddenly gone tight. "Don't think you ever told me what your name means."

He tapped my chin with his thumb. "Gift from God."

"Of course that's what Iain means." I shook my head, but that only made his fingers scrape across my mouth, and I tasted a hint of the salty flavor of his skin. "Does that mean you are a gift, or you received a gift?"

"What I gave you, in the end, wasn't a gift, but I'm hoping you'll bestow one on me now in spite of that. The gift of days."

Bestow? Only Iain could make the word sound erotic. "Are you suggesting I let you hang around because of what your name means?"

"No. My middle name means 'follower of St. Columba,' after all, and I doubt that would convince you."

Iain Malcolm MacTaggart. I'd always loved his name, the way it rolled over my tongue. I'd wanted to name our daughter after him, so I chose the feminine version of his middle name—Malina, for Malcolm. He would figure it out if I ever told him her name, so I would never speak her name in his presence. He'd figure out she was his if he ever saw a picture of her, so I'd rushed around the living room, hallway, and kitchen stripping out every photograph of her.

Malina had his pale-blue eyes, his honey-brown hair, his aquiline nose, and his disarming smile. Every time I looked at her, I saw him.

I had also spirited away every one of the books about Scotland I'd kept on the now-empty shelves in the living room. The books currently lay in a pile in the corner of my bedroom. If Iain saw those books, he might figure out I'd become obsessed with his native land. He might wonder why. I wondered why sometimes.

Had I really gotten over Iain? Could I get over him with our daughter reminding me every day? No matter what happened, I would forever have a piece of him with me.

I used to like that. Today, sitting beside him in my kitchen, I worried about that unbreakable bond, the one he knew nothing about. Maybe I should tell him.

No way in hell. Iain had abandoned me once, and I would not give him the chance to do the same to our daughter.

I squinted at him. "Why are you really here? I don't have anything worth stealing if that's your game."

Why I said it, I had no idea. Desperation, I supposed. I needed him to give up the crazy notion of winning me back.

Iain snapped his spine straight, his jaw tight. "I am no thief."

The razor edge to his voice surprised me. I'd hit a nerve, though I had no idea why. I considered asking, but I didn't want to know him better. I wanted him gone, to preserve my sanity and the life I'd fought so hard to carve out for myself and my daughter.

He seemed to shed the tension with a heavy sigh, relaxing back into un-flappable mode with his Buddha smile in place. The crack in his affable facade had sealed up again.

Strange, but irrelevant.

Pushing up out of my chair, I gave Iain a decisive nod. "I'm driving you into town. Then, you can make your way back to wherever you came from."

"You'd leave me homeless in a strange place?" That smile broadened just enough to dimple his cheeks, and his eyes twinkled with humor.

"Don't you have a room at a motel?"

He shrugged one shoulder. "Didn't think beyond tracking you down. Find you. See you. Talk to you. That was the extent of my plan."

I let my head fall back and groaned miserably.

He rose and stretched, yawning. "I'll find something in town."

"No, you won't." I rubbed my forehead. "There are only two motels in Ricksville. Plus, this is Twine Festival week, which means if you didn't book ahead, you won't find an available room."

Iain's forehead crinkled. "Twine Festival?"

"We have the world's fifth-largest ball of twine. It's behind the town hall."

"And there's a festival to celebrate it?"

He looked so adorably flummoxed I couldn't help smiling. Another crack in his serene mask.

"Yep," I said. "Texans are weird, in an endearing way."

Rubbing his neck, he grabbed the glass and swigged the rest of his water. He swiped the back of his hand across his mouth, stretched again, and swept his gaze over me. The interest in his eyes, heated and yet gentle, made a warmth blossom in my belly.

"I'm driving you into town," I said, and whirled around to snatch my keys off the hook beside the sink. I flapped a hand toward the door. "Let's go. You can catch a bus to the airport."

Disappointment flashed on his face, but he ambled out the door and through the living room. I hurried after him, and within minutes we were heading down the driveway in my Ford F-150, dust pluming in our wake, visible in the red glow of the taillights. The sun had set, plunging the world into a darkness speckled with the glittering diamonds of stars, things that had died out eons ago but their ghosts lingered.

No, that wasn't a metaphor for me and Iain. Not at all.

I focused on the road ahead revealed by the spray of the headlights and asked a question that had occurred to me. "Why did you walk up my driveway? How did you get here if not by car?"

"No rental cars were available, so a taxi brought me to your mailbox, but the driver refused to come down this way. He claimed your driveway is a 'potholey mess' that would destroy his car." The dashboard lights cast a strange green glow on him. "I haven't noticed any potholes."

"I have the driveway graded every spring." I drummed my fingers on the steering wheel. "Did you by chance call Long Star Taxi Service?"

"Yes," Iain said, sounding surprised. "It was the only service that would come out this far. I caught one taxi from the Austin airport to Llano, then took another one to Ricksville, and a third to get here."

"Yeah, I live in the boonies. But I've got great Internet."

"At least you have the essentials, then." He gazed out the windshield, seeming lost in thought. "Shouldn't it be Lone Star Taxi, not Long Star? Thought that was the state's nickname."

"Yeah, it is." My hands tightened around the wheel. "The guy who runs the taxi service thought he was being clever by naming it Long Star. It just confuses people, though, because it looks like a typo. And what's a long star, anyway?"

"I'm getting the idea you have history with the taxi driver."

The Unflappable Iain MacTaggart could also be the Impossibly Perceptive Iain MacTaggart. Way back when, I'd loved that about him. I'd loved everything about him. Tonight, I wished to hell he'd stop poking his perceptive nose into my business.

Maybe if I shared one tidbit about my life with him, he'd lose interest.

Not likely, my rational brain warned. But my rationality had said "adios" the second Iain kissed me.

"I sort of dated him," I told Iain. "Grayson Parker. He worked for me as a ranch hand for a while, part-time. We got involved briefly. When I suggested he should have dinner with me and my daughter, to get to know her, he skedaddled. Said he wasn't interested in taking over someone else's family. He wanted his own kid, not some deadbeat dad's castoff."

"The scunner said that? Castoff?"

"Not sure what a scunner is, but yeah, he said that. I don't think he meant it. He got defensive because he was embarrassed about not having the nerve to get into a real relationship."

"A scunner is a bloody annoying person. A jackass." Iain grunted. "Better off without that ersehole."

"At least he said goodbye before he took off." I glanced at Iain sideways. "Unlike some people."

He flinched so minutely I almost missed it.

"Go on," he said in that infuriatingly even tone, "insult me all you like. I deserve it. But I am not skedaddling ever again."

How odd to hear the word skedaddle spoken in a Scottish brogue. A deep, sexy brogue. The kind that transformed a rather goofy word into something decadent. Made me want to skedaddle with him anytime, anywhere.

I bit my upper lip so hard I winced. Nope, I hadn't learned a frigging thing in the past thirteen years. One hot guy could make me act like a twenty-two-year-old drunk on hormones. Grayson had been good-looking, but nowhere near as sizzling as Iain. No man I'd ever known compared with Iain MacTaggart.

"Tell me," Iain said, "is this Grayson really out of your life? He refused to come down your driveway."

"He lives in town. I see him sometimes at the feed store or the grocery store, but he pretends not to notice me." I sighed, my shoulders sagging. "In a small town, you can't get away from your past completely. Grayson is as out of my life as possible."

We lapsed into silence, the only sounds the rumble of the truck's engine and the ticking of gravel on the undercarriage. At the end of the drive, I braked to check for traffic—not that there ever was traffic way out here in the boonies. I was just letting up on the brake when I made the mistake of glancing at Iain.

He was watching me. Eyes soft and gentle. Mouth curved into the barest smile.

The wistful expression shivered a tingle over my skin and made my heart do an idiotic *thump-thump*. I was too damn old to get nostalgic about a college crush. Oh, but if he'd been a simple crush and nothing more, why had I cried for days after he left? Why did I name our daughter after him? And why, goddammit, had I enjoyed our brief time in my kitchen more than I'd enjoyed anything in years?

His words from earlier replayed in my mind. *Deceive yourself if you like, gràidh, but we had a relationship. It was good. It was real.*

I shoved the gear shift lever into neutral and twisted sideways to face him with the folded-down middle seat between us. "Here's the deal. I have a guest bedroom. You can stay there for a few days, but my daughter comes home next Sunday, so you have to be gone before then."

He nodded, his face brightening even as he kept that subdued aura, nonchalant as ever. "That gives me ten days. Thank you, Rae."

"Don't thank me yet. You haven't heard the rest of the deal."

"Go on."

I twisted around further, bending one knee. "This is a working sheep ranch. I don't have time to entertain you. My life is not glamorous or sexy. I work my butt off all day and then, at night, I sit through Disney movies and teen-pop concerts on TV to spend time with my daughter."

He slanted toward me across the barrier created by the folded seat and laid his arm over the back of my seat. "Your child isn't here. You could watch something more...adult. With me."

"Not watching porn with you, Iain."

The blasted man chuckled. "I didn't mean pornography. Interesting that you thought of it, though."

"Iain—"

"Relax, I'm not seducing you in this truck." He eased a little closer, his fingers grazing my shoulder. "I'm happy to help out around the ranch. Anything you need done, I can do it."

"You're a college professor, not a ranch hand."

The smile faltered for a split second. "I haven't been a professor for thirteen years. These days, I work construction and odd jobs."

Hmm. Well, that did explain the muscles and the suntan and the calluses.

"Fine," I said, "you can help out. But there will be no fooling around, MacTaggart, absolutely none. Work. Talk. That's all."

"Yes, ma'am," he said in the best fake Texas twang I'd ever heard. "Your cowhand is rearing to go."

"Please drop the accent. And they're sheep, not cows. Fuzzy-wuzzy wittle sheep."

He chuckled again. "Fuzzy-wuzzy? I think you're in desperate need of adult conversation."

"Yeah, probably." I turned the truck around and headed back toward the house, with Iain's arm still draped across my seat back. "Remember, Iain. Work. Talk. And that's—"

"That's all. Yes, I understood the first time." He tickled my shoulder until I glanced at him and then he winked. "We'll see how that goes, *gràidh*."

Fluttering tummy. Fluttering chest. Tingling skin.

I may have made the worst decision of my life.

Chapter Four

Iain

I would've offered to cook for Rae, but I'd never developed a talent for it. My mother tried to teach me, but as a lad, I'd been more interested in girls than braising beef. I managed to feed myself with simple meals, but bangers and mash wouldn't impress Rae. Since I couldn't help with the cooking, I acted as Rae's assistant, gathering ingredients for her and getting out the various pots and implements she needed. Despite her repeated attempts to convince me she had nothing to offer beyond a week or so of hard work and conversation, I grew more and more determined to prove my worth to her.

Was I being stubborn? She rejected me, so I resolved to change her mind. She'd made it clear she thought that was the reason behind my commitment to winning her over. I knew what I felt, though. From the moment four months ago when I'd resolved to find her, I'd felt more alive than ever before. This quest felt right. Now that I'd found her and spent time with her, I realized I could never give up. I still loved her, whether she believed it or not.

After an amiable meal during which we discussed nothing in particular, I settled onto the sofa in the living room while Rae dropped into the armchair positioned nearby at an angle to the sofa.

I patted the sofa cushion beside me. "Plenty of room over here."

She puckered her lips briefly. "I prefer the chair."

"Afraid of me, are ye? Maybe you're worried you'll be overcome with desire and tear my clothes off." I smirked and winked. "I wouldn't mind that."

Rae propped her feet on the coffee table. "Thought you wanted to convince me I can trust you."

"Sex can be a very enjoyable way to engender trust."

"Not in my experience."

She grabbed the TV remote and hit the power button. A cartoon came on, one even an old bachelor like me recognized—*Snow White and the Seven Dwarfs*. It was in the midst of a musical number with birds flitting around a fairy-tale princess.

I set an elbow on the sofa's arm, propping my chin on my raised hand, one finger tapping my chin. "Where is your husband?"

"Don't have one."

"You're divorced?"

"Nope. Never married." Though she aimed her face toward the TV, her eyes kept flicking to me as if she couldn't quite let herself meet my gaze head-on. "What about you?"

"Married once. It was a mistake." One I didn't want to talk about tonight. "Where is the father of your child?"

She didn't want to answer, but that only made me hunger for the truth more. I craved every bit of knowledge about her I could get. Besides, I despised men who fucked women without a care for whether they might get them pregnant, then bolted when they learned they'd done just that.

Rae gnawed on her lip, still facing the TV. "She's never known her father."

"Do you at least get financial support from him?"

She punched the power button, and the TV went dark. Chucking the remote onto the table, where it hit with a *thwack*, she turned toward me. "Why are you being so nosy? I take care of my daughter fine without anybody helping me."

"Easy," I said. "I didn't mean to offend you. But I can't fathom how a man could abandon his child."

She crossed her arms over her chest, a sign I now recognized as defensiveness. "I'm sure you would never, ever do that."

The sarcastic tone of her voice contradicted the fear I saw in her eyes. Something was going on here, something I didn't understand. Suddenly, I needed to know.

I dropped my hand to tap my fingers on the sofa's arm. "What are you implying? I don't have children, but if I did, I would never run out on them or their mother."

Her gaze shifted to her feet. Shoulders bunched, she tucked her hands under her thighs.

I sat forward, wanting to touch her but knowing I shouldn't.

Before I could speak, she raised one hand in a staying gesture. "I don't want to talk about this anymore."

"All right." I'd let it go, for the moment. If I ever met the bastard who'd left Rae and her daughter alone, I'd skite a sledgehammer on his face. "What can we talk about?"

She tucked her hand under her arm. "You still haven't told me how you were forced out of the country. Tell me—"

A huge yawn interrupted her statement. She covered her mouth with one hand. As soon as she began to lower that hand, another yawn overtook her, and she shielded her mouth again.

The lass was exhausted. Did she honestly work this ranch alone all day? One helper, she'd mentioned. One man, I presumed. A stab of jealousy speared my chest, but I had no right to feel envious of any man in her life. Not her ranch hand, and certainly not the taxi driver who'd tossed her away because she had a child. If I ever met Grayson Parker again, I'd batter him for certain.

Rae yawned a third time.

I sprang off the sofa to bend over her chair, one hand on the arm. "You're for bed, *mein Liebling.*"

She angled her head up to squint at me. "First, I'm a *gràidh.* Now, I'm a *Liebling.* No clue what any of it means."

Both were endearments, one in Gaelic, the other in German. I doubted she would appreciate the sentiments, so I told her, "Never mind that. You're exhausted, and I'm taking you to bed."

"Excuse me?" She pulled her head back, her eyes narrowing even more. "I am not having sex with you."

"No, I meant I'm taking you to your bed so you can sleep."

She choked off a panicked noise. "No. You can't. Not my room."

Christ, she wouldn't let me near her bedroom. I had a long, bumpy road ahead of me to earn back her trust.

She cleared her throat, seeming to regain some composure. "I'll show you to the guest bedroom."

"All right." I swept her up in my arms before she had a chance to complain with anything more eloquent than a squeak. "Where am I, then?"

"In Texas."

"Cheeky woman. I meant where am I to sleep?"

"The guest bedroom, upstairs." She leaned forward in my arms to point toward the hallway. "The stairs are that way."

She turned her head to look at me, and her lips nearly brushed mine. Those stunning eyes, the color of sapphires, gazed into mine with surprise. I heard the little hiccup as her breath caught in her throat. Her lips parted, and I burned to kiss them, burned like I never had for any other woman. The years had done nothing to lessen my passion for her, but seducing this woman required subtlety and patience—and tenderness.

I'd hurt her, more than I'd realized until tonight. Other men had clearly compounded the damage, but I was the root of it. I had to make this right.

Patience. Subtlety. Tenderness.

I marched down the hallway to the stairs.

Rae

I locked my arms around Iain's neck while he took the stairs two at a time. His biceps flexed against me, but his hold on me never wavered. Holy cow, he had impressive strength and agility. He'd said he worked construction and odd jobs these days. Physical labor had made him strong and dexterous and scorching hot. I longed to run my fingers through his hair, to touch those few strands of gray and caress his scalp, but I'd probably fall out of his embrace if I did and tumble us both down the stairs.

No, Iain would stay standing. He might even catch me.

A flash of heat rushed through me. Maybe I could enjoy having him around for a week or so. Maybe I could enjoy having him, period.

Sex with Iain. Yes, I could handle that.

No, no, no. Responsible adult, remember? Mother and role model to a twelve-year-old girl, that was me. Business owner too. Neither of those titles meshed with the idea of giving in to my carnal desires for the man carting me up the stairs.

But maybe...

We reached the upstairs hallway, and Iain turned right to head down it. The hallway dead-ended at the stairs, so he hadn't needed ESP to guess which way to go. Partway down the hall, he stopped to glance at the four closed doors before us. On the right lay the door to my office and the one for the storage room. On the left, two doors led into the guest rooms, one of which had an air mattress instead of a bed.

His brows crinkled in the cutest way. "Which door?"

I resisted the urge to trace my fingers over his brows and instead told him, "You can put me down."

"Which door?" he repeated with a touch more emphasis.

Stubborn as ever, of course. Some things about him seemed different, but a lot seemed unchanged.

I pointed to the first door on the left. "There."

He carried me to the door and tried to grasp the knob, but his hold on me slipped and he gave up the knob in favor of clasping me tighter. The warmth of him around me, the firmness of his body, the scent of dried sweat and manly spice...Damn, it was intoxicating. Sure, I could blame him for my total loss of maturity and common sense. All Iain's fault. He had no right to be so delicious.

"A little help?" he said, nodding toward the doorknob.

"Why don't you put me down now?"

One corner of his mouth kicked up. "Open the door and I might."

I stretched my arm down to twist the knob and push the door inward. "Okay, you can put me—"

He strode into the guest bedroom and set me down, letting his hands drift down to my hips.

"The only bathroom is downstairs," I said. "It's the first door on the left when you come down the stairs."

"Good to know." He removed one hand, but the other lingered on my hip. "The bed is rather large."

"So are you."

"Do you entertain many large guests?"

I shook my head, trying not to smile but failing. He sounded almost jealous, but Iain never got jealous. "My stepbrother is six foot seven. I got this bed for him, for when he visits. He plays for the UCLA basketball team."

"Are your parents divorced?"

"Yeah, but I'm too tired to talk about family drama."

I tromped over to the closet and got out two pillows, then tossed them to Iain. "The ones on the bed are decorative, not comfy."

He tossed the pillows onto the bed. "Thank you for worrying about my comfort."

"Do the same for all my guests." Like I had many of those. My stepbrother and stepsister, my stepfather, my mom. That was it. "Your bag is still downstairs, isn't it? I'll go get it."

I moved toward the door, but Iain laid a hand on my arm. "Don't bother. I can get it in the morning."

"Don't you need your pajamas or whatever you sleep in?"

He leaned a little closer and said, in a husky voice, "I sleep in the nude."

And there was an image I did not need flashing through my mind right now. Naked Iain. Nothing but a sheet concealing all that lickable flesh. I could sneak in here in the dead of night, crawl under the covers with him, and—

Just thinking about it made me wet. Which meant I needed to get away from him.

Something behind the open door caught his attention, and he wandered over to peer back there. His brows ticked up a smidgen. With one finger he hooked the object of his curiosity and held it up. The fuzzy pink robe swung from his fingertip.

"Not my best color," he said.

"That's mine. I repainted my bedroom last month and slept up here while the fumes cleared out."

"Ah." He replaced the robe on the hook behind the door.

"Good night, Iain." I scurried toward the doorway. When I reached the threshold, he stopped me with a single, earnest question.

"May I kiss you good night?" he asked.

Kiss me? My rational brain urged me to consider the consequences, but I was getting damn sick of thinking. What the hell? He'd be gone soon, anyway.

I leaned back against the doorjamb. "Okay."

His brows flew up like he couldn't believe I'd said yes, but then a sensual smile curved his lips. He sauntered up to me, planted a hand on the jamb above my head, and slanted in until his mouth hovered a breath away from mine. Ice-blue eyes captured my focus, their glacial color a contrast to the heat of his hooded gaze. I stopped breathing. He grazed his lips over mine, the barest hint of contact, like the touch of a feather skating over my skin again and again, soft and yet wickedly arousing. The steam of his breaths tickled my skin. My eyes drifted shut, and I sagged against the jamb. He skimmed his lips over mine again, tormenting me with a promise of what I craved, more of him, all of him. When his free hand closed around my hip, I couldn't resist tipping my head up, exposing my throat to him, all but begging for him to take me in a ravenous kiss.

"Rae," he purred, his lips ghosting over mine, "you're bloody perfect. The way I remember, only better."

I couldn't speak, move, breathe, think.

His hand on my hip grasped me more firmly, and he pressed his mouth to mine. We hung there in a suspended moment, lips to lips, neither of us moving for what felt like forever. I hungered for him to thrust his tongue inside my mouth, to haul me into his hard body, to consume me in every way imaginable.

With a groan, Iain stepped back, the distance between us measured in inches but gaping like a giant crack had opened up in the house between us.

"*Gute Nacht, mein Liebling.* That means good night, Rae."

I stared at him. "Don't you want to kiss me deeper?"

"Yes, but not tonight."

My mouth opened, but I clapped it shut again. He was doing this on purpose, and I didn't care. Maybe just for a few days…

"Good night, Iain," I said for the second time tonight and walked out the door.

Only when I'd reached my room on the first floor and shut the door did I permit myself to consider that kiss. I must've lost my mind. Twice today, I'd let Iain kiss me. He showed up on my doorstep after more than a decade and acted like nothing had changed, like we could pick up right where we'd left off.

I slumped against the closed door. We'd left off with catastrophe. After our one and only night together, he'd kissed me goodbye and walked out of my apartment and out of my life. I'd never seen him again. Never heard from him. I tried to find him, but I'd had no idea where in Scotland he lived. Maybe if I could've afforded a good private investigator, I might have tracked him down. Maybe I'd waited too long to try. For the first two months, I'd been in shock over the catastrophic scandal that had erupted around me, too stunned and ashamed and in grief over losing the only man I'd ever loved to think about trying to find him. Besides, I couldn't help wondering if he'd left willingly. Why would a thirty-seven-year-old professor, a worldly man who'd dug up relics all over the world, fall for a college senior? It was a dream, and I'd finally woken up.

Two months after Iain vanished, I'd found out I was pregnant. I had hired a cut-rate private investigator, the only kind I could afford, to hunt for him. Nothing came of it. I searched the Internet but found nothing. I'd even searched online white pages to get the phone numbers of MacTaggarts in Scotland and called several of them before the international phone charges got too expensive. I'd had to give up, having found no trace of Iain.

But here he was. In my house. Sleeping upstairs.

In the nude.

Maybe if I slept with him, I'd realize it hadn't been as good as my memory insisted it had been. One roll in the hay, nothing more. Satisfy my curiosity and get him out of my system for good.

"Ugh," I moaned, shuffling to the bed and flumping onto it. "I am insane."

I chewed on the inside of my cheek for a minute, my gaze nailed to the dresser. The bottom drawer. My secret hiding place.

Not going there.

Without glancing at the bottom drawer again, I retrieved my nightie from another drawer and changed into it.

My gaze wandered to my secret hiding place.

With a heavy sigh, I gave in to the impulse. I retrieved two items from the bottom drawer, sat down on the bed cross-legged with my back to the headboard, and allowed myself two minutes to wallow. First, I picked up the plaid scarf. The fabric was blue and green with orange lines threaded through it. I held the scarf to my chest, petting the soft fabric, indulging in a memory.

"It's the MacTaggart clan tartan," Iain had told me on the day when I invited him into my apartment for pizza and pop. I'd expected him to say no, but he'd agreed with a subdued smile that represented excitement in the language of Iain. He'd explained, "My mother made the scarf for me. I want you to have it."

"Me? Why?" I took the scarf he held out to me, fingering the smooth plaid and the fringe at either end. "Won't your mother be upset you gave it away?"

"No." He plucked the scarf from my hands and draped it around my neck. "Please accept this as a token of…friendship."

Right. Friendship. Back then, I'd been naive enough to believe that.

I hugged the scarf to my chest, dipping my head to inhale the dusty scent of the garment I'd kept in a drawer for thirteen years. The day my daughter had been born, the day after Valentine's Day a little more than twelve years ago, I'd asked my mom to bring me the scarf so I could wrap it around Malina's little body. I'd held her like that for a long time, tears streaming down my cheeks. Tears of joy for my daughter's birth. Tears of grief for the father she would never know.

But she could know him now.

Setting down the scarf, I picked up the other item I'd retrieved. The four-by-six photo album had a plain white cover. I flipped it open, examining the first of many pictures I'd taken over the years. No one knew about this album. I'd made it for a secret purpose, spurred by a stupid and hopeless need to document the moments in Malina's life.

For Iain.

Chapter Five

Rae

I closed the album, running my hand over the smooth cover. Why had I taken these pictures and preserved them for him if I didn't have the nerve to tell him he had a daughter? I couldn't tell him. Yes, I worried he'd take off again and leave Malina heartbroken like I'd been. But I had another obstacle too. I'd told Malina her father died before she was born.

Yep, I'd done that.

When she got old enough to start asking questions about her father, I'd panicked. How could I tell her about Iain without admitting he'd abandoned me? That would lead to more questions about things I could never confess to my child.

So, I lied. I said her father died and refused to discuss it any further. Parental prerogative.

A coward, that's what I was. I'd dug myself in too deep to explain my way out of it. Iain could not be here when Malina got home. End of story.

I wriggled forward until I could lay back on the bed and roll onto my side with my head on the pillow. A powerful urge gripped me, and I thumbed through the photo album.

A long, skinny piece of thick paper tumbled out.

My fingers caught the paper on instinct, and I turned it over to see the glossy surface. It was a strip of pictures from one of those photo booths in malls. The images showed me and Iain smiling and laughing, his arm around me, our cheeks pressed against each other. My God, I'd forgotten he actually smiled that day. An honest-to-goodness grin. Suddenly, I remembered that he'd smiled a lot on our one perfect day together, so much so I'd been shocked by his exuberance. Shocked and exhilarated.

How could I have forgotten? I supposed it had been easier to downplay how wonderful that day had been instead of remembering it, reliving it, pining for it, pining for him. I'd moved on, yes, but my heart had clearly clung to the memories.

In the last photo, Iain was kissing me.

That moment. I remembered it like yesterday, as vivid and clear as when he'd kissed me good night a little while ago. The photo I held preserved the moment of our very first kiss. The day everything changed. The day before the disaster.

Holding the photo strip to my chest, I closed my eyes and indulged in the memories. That day with Iain had been perfect. We'd done all the frivolous, romantic things we hadn't allowed ourselves to enjoy before because I'd still been a student. That morning, I'd informed Iain I had received my grades and had passed all my classes. I was no longer a student, technically.

All it took was "technically." He'd swept me away for a day of romance. A picnic. The photo booth. Our first kiss. More kissing in the back row of a movie theater. Lots more kissing in the car, at a smokily lit restaurant, in the car again. Eventually, he'd taken me back to his apartment.

There on his sofa, we'd made out for half an hour. Still, he didn't touch me in any sexual way. I'd begun to worry he had no interest in making love to me, that after ten months of waiting, he would push me out the door.

When he lifted his head, tearing his lips away from mine, I'd grunted my displeasure.

Oh, the look on his face. Tender and hungry at the same time. He'd combed his fingers through my hair, his thumb tracing circles on my cheek, and then he had spoken the words that forever altered both our lives.

"Stay with me, Rae."

How else would a lovestruck girl answer? "I'd love to."

Iain swept me up in his arms and carried me into the bedroom, like a knight straight out of a fairy tale transporting his bride to the nuptial bed. We weren't married. I worshiped Iain, but he'd never suggested he felt anything but friendship for me—until this day when he'd revealed his lust. I had no idea if he loved me the way I loved him.

The way he'd undressed me had left me boneless in his arms. Slowly. Sensually. His hands always on me, his fingers always exploring. He laid me on the bed, stripped himself, and lay down beside me to run his hands over me from head to toe. His mouth followed, kissing and licking and nibbling until I was squirming and panting, and God, so wet for him. When he drew my nipple into his mouth, I clutched his head and arched my back.

When he kissed me, it was wild and deep and intoxicating.

He settled his body on top of me, the weight and heat of him so delicious I could've died from the sheer pleasure of it. The sensation of his lips on mine, his hands sliding up and down my sides, his firm chest rasping against my nipples, and God, the pressure of his cock filling me, his hips pumping, his—

I flopped onto my back and groaned. The memory had seduced me, drawing me back to the past and the most incredible night of my life. But indulging in a reverie of Iain had made me yearn for the real thing. My nipples had puckered, the tips swollen and achy. With every little movement, the slick softness of my nightie tormented my skin and made my nipples ache even more. My clitoris had gone stiff. My sex, drenched with wetness, pulsated deep inside.

Shit. I would never get to sleep in this state.

I could trot upstairs to the guest bedroom. No, absolutely no. Bad, bad, bad idea.

A few hours in Iain's presence had thrown me backward in time and transformed me into my college self again. He might have afflicted me with this thirst for pleasure, but I did not need *him* to quench it for me.

I flung out a hand to the bedside table, yanked the drawer open, and fumbled inside until I located the tool I needed. With the vibrator in my hand, I settled the other palm over my breast, kneading it in the slow and sensuous way Iain had done that night. I skimmed the vibrator along my inner thigh. Iain had moved his hand that way, up my skin until he found my slick flesh. Biting down on my bottom lip, I flicked my finger over my nipple and pinched it, mimicking the sensation of Iain's teeth nipping me there. God, the way his erection had scraped over my belly. I slid my nightie higher until it mounded against my breasts and raked my nails over my belly, then I switched the vibrator on.

The sound seemed loud in the silence of my bedroom, but I was beyond caring.

Visions of Iain consumed me, his naked body hovering above me, his face tight with need. I played out the memory, slipping the length of the vibrator between my folds the way Iain had glided his cock up and down, the pace slow and relentless, driving me mad. Just as I had that night, I bucked my hips into the movements, but instead of gripping Iain's shoulders, I gripped the headboard with one hand. The leverage let me lift my hips higher. Though Iain had made love to me at a leisurely pace, the more I succumbed to the fantasy of that night the faster I moved the vibrator and the harder I panted. Couldn't wait. Couldn't stop.

I plunged the vibrator inside me.

My back arched, my mouth flew open on a silent cry. I thrust faster, deeper, harder.

"Oh God," I breathed, hardly able to speak at all.

My fingers clenched the headboard tighter, my nails scraping the wood. Iain thrusting. Iain gripping my hips to raise them and plow into me so deep I'd been certain our bodies became one for that single instant.

"Rae? Are you all right?"

I froze, teetering on the verge of orgasm. Breathless, on fire from head to toe, I struggled to puzzle out what I'd heard. Iain? Was this part of the memory? No, he hadn't asked if I was okay while he was making love to me.

A tentative knock on the door at last evaporated the haze of lust.

Well, it at least thinned the fog a bit.

"Iain?" I called. "Is that you?"

"You have another man sleeping in your house tonight?" he said with amusement tinging his voice. "Aye, it's me. I came down to the bathroom and heard an odd noise in your room."

He'd heard the vibrator.

And with a jolt, I realized I still had the thing wedged inside me, vibrating away.

"I'm okay," I said, but my voice came out strained.

"Ye donnae sound fine."

My heart racing, my head growing light, I tore the vibrator out of my body, switched it off, and dumped the thing on the bed beside me. Then, I fought to regain enough equilibrium to speak to Iain. I damn sure couldn't go over there, open the door, and look him in the eye.

A couple slow, deep breaths helped—but only a smidgen.

"Really, Iain," I said, "everything's fine."

He said nothing for a moment, and my heart raced faster as I wondered what the hell he was thinking. I got my answer when he cleared his throat and spoke again, his voice huskier.

"I have heard a sound like that before," he said. "Were you by any chance self-pleasuring with a sexual wellness device?"

The damn man was teasing me. Sexual wellness device, my ass. He knew exactly what kind of "device" I'd been using.

"Go to bed, Iain."

He chuckled. "Wouldn't you rather I come in there and—"

"No thank you." Yes, I absolutely wanted that, but it was far too dangerous.

"Have it your way." He sighed with no small amount of sarcasm. "At least finish yourself off so you can get a decent night's sleep. The sheep need you well rested."

"Thank you for the concern," I said with my own dollop of sarcasm. "Now, scram."

His footfalls pounded up the stairs.

My body throbbed and tingled and burned. He was right, of course. I'd never get to sleep unless I dealt with this…situation.

I grabbed the vibrator, switched it on, and held the tip against my clit.

The orgasm hit so fast I gasped. My entire body went stiff, frozen in that moment of pure pleasure when the first spasm gripped me. My free hand clenched the sheets. I caught one breath before the pleasure seized me again, convulsing my body until my ears rang and my abdominal muscles ached from the intensity of the spasms.

I lay there, limp and spent, for ten minutes before I could summon the energy to move. I stashed the vibrator in the drawer.

My cell phone rang, making me jump and yelp.

I fumbled for the phone and mumbled, "Hello?"

"Oh no, did I wake you? Sorry, baby, sometimes I still forget you're two hours ahead."

"Mom?" I hadn't even noticed the caller ID on my phone. Pushing up on one elbow, I said, "No, I'm awake."

The big yawn interrupting my words belied my claim. Rather than sleepiness, however, this was the languor following a major orgasm.

"I won't keep you long," Mom said. "Just wanted to give you the daily update. Malina is fine. Ty gave her a surfing lesson today, and she's currently watching *Beauty and the Beast* with Zoey. She misses you, but we're keeping her busy."

"Glad she's having fun." Malina had always gotten along with my stepbrother and stepsister, and so did I.

My mother paused, then said in a suspicious tone, "Aren't you going to quiz me on what she ate and what her state of mind is?"

"You said Malina's fine." I bolted upright. "Unless there's something you're not telling me."

She laughed. "There's my suspicious girl. No, I was testing you. What's got you distracted, Rae? There's obviously something going on out there."

A big, tall, sizzling-hot something.

Lying to my mother had never worked for me. She seemed to have a sixth sense about it, which had stopped me from sneaking out to meet my boyfriend in high school. Recognizing the futility of keeping any secrets from Cheryl Raines, I confessed. "I have someone staying with me."

"A man?" she asked with more enthusiasm than a mother should show upon learning her daughter was shacking up with a virtual stranger. But then, Iain wasn't exactly a stranger.

"Yes, a man." I fingered the photo strip where it still lay on the bed, my gaze shifting to the last image where Iain was kissing me. A pang ached in my chest. "It's Iain MacTaggart."

Silence. Only a faint hum in the background of the call indicated she hadn't hung up.

After a few seconds, Mom said slowly, "You mean the Iain MacTaggart who got my baby knocked up and abandoned her."

"That's the only Iain MacTaggart I know."

"Have you been—No, you would've told me if you'd kept in touch with him."

I growled out a sigh. "Mom, if I'd known where Iain was thirteen years ago, I would've told him I was pregnant. I couldn't find him, you know that."

"Yes, I know. Of course I do. I'm shocked, that's all."

"Me too." I stuffed the photo strip into the little album and clapped it shut. "He says he wants to win me back."

"Have you, um, told him anything about…"

"Malina? No way. He left me high and dry once already, and I don't know if I can trust him not to do it again."

"But you're letting him stay in your house."

"You think *you're* shocked?" I slapped a palm on my forehead. "He waltzed up the driveway and kissed me. Dressed like Indiana Jones and looking hotter than ever."

"Hm, yes, I can see how that would knock you off kilter. The man you love suddenly reappearing."

"*Loved*, Mom. Loved, past tense."

My mother clucked her tongue. "Oh Rae, it's not past tense when you describe him as hotter than ever and tell me you let him kiss you. Unless after that you smacked him?"

"No, I…sort of let him kiss me good night later on." And then I got off to thoughts of him. My mom didn't need to know *everything*.

Cheryl Raines laughed at her daughter. Laughed. Loudly.

"Sweetie," she said in her best motherly tone, "when you let a man kiss you twice, that's not a past-tense emotion."

I sighed. "Too tired to argue with you."

As if my body wanted to support my claim, I yawned again.

"You should rest up," Mom said, "for when you let Iain kiss you good morning."

"Honestly, Mom. You're supposed to encourage me to behave responsibly."

"You are an adult. It's about time you cut loose and had some fun."

All I could muster in response was a frustrated groan.

"Good night, Rae."

She hung up on me. While chuckling.

I returned the photo album to the drawer but kept the scarf with me. As I fell asleep with it lumped up and clutched to my chest, I wondered if I'd made a huge mistake inviting Iain into my home. I trusted my child. I trusted my mother.

But could I, should I, trust Iain MacTaggart?

Chapter Six

Iain

In the morning, I woke early and made my way down to the first floor to retrieve my bag. My sleep had been fitful, plagued by dark dreams of the past—the disaster that took me away from Rae, the self-inflicted pain in the years after that, and the lifelong worries I'd never quite shaken. How could I shake them? After a lifetime of fighting to become a better man than my father, I'd committed far worse transgressions than he ever had. If Rae knew…

Maybe she didn't need to know.

I halted at the bottom of the stairs, bag in hand, my gaze wandering to the closed doors in the downstairs hall. Behind one of them, Rae slept. Even a sheep rancher didn't rise before dawn, apparently. I'd peeked out the living-room window, but the barn stood dark in the moonless, predawn blackness. Coming for Rae might've been the most selfish thing I'd ever done. One day, I would need to confess everything to her.

After I won her. Only then.

I winced. So much for honesty and integrity. *A better man than your father, are ye?* Maybe not, and maybe I didn't deserve Rae, but I needed her.

Up the stairs I slogged, one at a time instead of two by two. Why I'd felt compelled to show off for Rae, I couldn't fathom. The look on her face, a mixture of lust and appreciation, had made it worthwhile. I'd need more than displays of physical strength to earn back her trust.

In the guest bedroom, I dropped my bag on the floor. I started to reach for my mobile phone on the table beside the bed but stopped. My gaze fell to the bag. I knelt to unzip it, plunging a hand inside to dig out one item—a small, square velvet box. The velvet was worn and slightly faded, a testament to the years it had spent in a drawer in my bedroom back home. I rubbed a finger over the velvet, wanting to open the box but knowing I shouldn't. Too many memories. Too many lost dreams.

Shoving the box into the bag again, I grabbed my mobile.

I dialed my mother's number and sat down on the bed. She answered on the fourth ring, her voice as bright and cheery as ever. How my mother could stay cheerful after everything Da had put her through, I couldn't understand, but I admired her fortitude. Though she might seem a bit flighty at times, the woman had the heart of a lioness.

After the usual pleasantries, I got on with the reason I'd called. "How is Da?"

"Donnae worry, Iain. Your da is keeping busy. Cousin Aidan hired him to do some carpentry work, and you know how your da loves making things."

I'd learned everything I knew about carpentry from my father. My fondest memories of my childhood revolved around the workshop behind our house where Da and I would spend rainy days building shelves or cabinets, sometimes even furniture.

My worst memories centered on lawyers and courts and backroom deals.

"So, Da isn't... ah..." I scratched my cheek, grimacing. "He isn't getting up to anything he shouldn't be?"

"No, love, no. He's behaving." She sighed. "Ye worry too much. Everything's been fine since ye made those discoveries. Your da has no need of getting up to anything anymore."

It had been years since his last... incident, but after a lifetime of Da's escapades, I had trouble accepting he'd retired. As if anyone retired from that sort of thing. I couldn't expect my young cousin Aidan to keep my father distracted forever. Aidan had a wife and a baby, with another child on the way. Sooner or later, I would have to take over minding my father. Again.

"How are ye liking America?" my mother asked.

"Texas is different than I expected, but then I'd thought it would look like all those John Wayne movies Da made me watch." I managed a genuine laugh, remembering those evenings throughout my childhood when we ate fish and chips in front of the TV. "His obsession with American westerns led me astray. I was fair devastated to see no desolate canyons or tumbleweeds anywhere in sight."

"But ye lived in America before."

"Not in Texas. America is a big country."

She fell silent for a moment, then said, "Your Aunt Sorcha will be here anytime. We're going to see Rory and Emery."

My other cousin, the second-oldest son of my Aunt Sorcha, had twins on the way. His wife, Emery, had seemed about to burst when I last saw them a few days ago. Lachlan, Sorcha's oldest child, had a baby on the way too—a sibling for Nicholas, the toddler son of Lachlan and Erica. Even my youngest cousin, Jamie, was up the duff. Her husband, Gavin, fussed over her like she'd become an invalid, insisting on doing everything for her. If she reached for a book on a shelf at eye level, he jumped in to get it for her. Rory was worse with Emery, and he would've been happy if she stayed in bed until she gave birth. With Aidan and his wife, Calli, expecting too, I'd begun to feel a bit out of place among my favorite cousins.

I said goodbye to Ma, asking her to give my best to Rory and Emery, then set my mobile back on the table. Would Rae and I have children together? She had a daughter already, but the thought of making babies with her gave me an oddly warm sensation in my chest.

Jumping ahead again, I was. A bad habit I'd developed since I caught sight of Rae yesterday. Everything I'd felt for her years ago had flooded back as strong as ever.

I glanced down at my clothes, the same things I'd worn yesterday. Sweat-stained, dusty clothing.

This wouldn't do at all.

Stripping off my clothes, I rushed downstairs for a quick shower, then hurried back upstairs to dress.

Rae

I woke to the patter of rain. Yawning, stretching, I gradually realized it wasn't rain. The shower was running. My houseguest must've helped himself to the amenities. Well, I couldn't expect him to ask my permission when I was asleep. What time did he get up, anyway? I rolled over to grab my little digital clock and blinked until I could comprehend the numbers. Five forty-eight. I always woke up by six, but Iain was already in the shower at five forty-eight.

Sitting up, I yawned and stretched again. Iain in the shower. Naked. Wet. My mind created vivid images of him slathering suds all over his muscular body.

An ache started between my thighs. A lovely, slippery ache.

I pushed up off the bed and whipped my nightie off over my head. I didn't own a sexy nightie, just a plain white satin thing with broad straps and a hem that hung down to my knees. What did a sheep rancher need with racy lingerie? Iain's presence in my home, and his current activity in the bathroom, made me curse myself for not buying at least one measly teddy.

He hadn't seemed to care about my utilitarian wardrobe—or the smear of sheep shit on my jeans.

Why did I care either way? Had I already decided to sleep with him?

No. I let him stay out of curiosity. Besides, he'd offered free labor.

Sure, it was the free help I'd wanted, not the hot body that came with it.

The shower shut off, and a moment later, footsteps thudded up the stairs.

How had he dried off and dressed so quickly?

I rushed to pull on a clean pair of jeans and a T-shirt, plus socks, then suffered a brief moment of panic when I couldn't recall if I'd put on underwear. A quick peek inside my shirt and jeans assured me I was wearing the appropriate undergarments. I hurried into the bathroom to wash my face and brush my hair. Did I own any makeup? Uh, somewhere in the closet, maybe. Giving up that idea, I trotted upstairs to the guest bedroom.

The door hung wide open.

I froze in the doorway, incapable of speech or movement thanks to the vision before me. Iain stood completely nude in front of the dresser, his back to me. And my oh my, what a glorious backside the man had. Broad shoulders. Thick, muscled biceps. Taut ass. Thighs that looked strong enough to withstand driving those hips into a woman over and over and over, for hours on end.

Just like he had on that night when we spent hours in bed together, our bodies entwined.

From my position in the doorway, since I still couldn't muster the willpower to move, I cleared my throat. "Most people shut the door when they get undressed."

He threw me a sideways glance. "Do they."

"Yes." I managed to brace my shoulder against the doorjamb, needing the support what with Iain's back and ass flexing as he sorted through his bag, which he'd set on the dresser. "And why are you changing clothes? Are you a diva who can't pick an outfit?"

He paused in selecting his clothes, turning his head to eye me with confusion. Slowly, the confusion melted into that easy smile. "Ahhh, I see. You're assuming I was dressed when I came upstairs after my shower."

"You weren't?" More visions assailed me, thanks to my annoyingly active imagination. Iain dashing upstairs in the buff. Water dribbling off his body.

"I dried off in the bathroom," he said, returning his attention to the duffel bag, "but I was naked when I went downstairs."

"You traipsed through my house naked? I have a kid, you know."

"Who is not here at the moment."

He half turned toward me, though not enough to let me glimpse the part of him I'd seen and experienced long, long ago. Maybe his dick had shriveled up with age. He had to have one flaw somewhere on his body. I couldn't tell, since he held a shirt in front of him, shielding his groin.

"You and I," he said, "are the only ones in this house."

"True, but you still shouldn't walk around—" I gave up chastising him. This conversation, and the sight of his bare backside, was making me a little crazy. Too long without sex had made me a little crazy. "Never mind. Just try not to drip water all over the wood floors."

He angled away from me again and pulled on a pair of boxers followed by blue jeans. They molded to his ass, and I caught my lip between my teeth as I wondered if the fabric clung to his groin the same way.

Iain faced me at last, holding the T-shirt in one hand. "Like what you see?"

As if he didn't know the answer.

What I'd wondered about a minute ago became an undeniable reality. Yep, the jeans molded to his front as snugly as they molded to his back, highlighting the outline of his penis. The more I studied that bulge, the more I longed to know the answer to another question. Did my memories of his nude body, etched into my mind so long ago, exaggerate his endowments?

"I'm taking that as a yes," he said, a faint smirk tightening his lips.

"Huh?" I said oh-so-eloquently, distracted by thoughts of his dick.

With one big hand, he cupped the bulge. "You're staring. Why not come over here and feel it for yourself?"

My God, he'd gotten brazen since the last time I'd known him. Back then, he'd been tender and sensual, so unlike the naughty man standing before me. His old self had seduced me into bed without much effort, though he'd waited ten months to do it. The new Iain…I wasn't at all sure I could hold out for long. He really had gotten hotter than ever, with just enough rough edges to make him irresistible. And that body, oh lord. More muscular, more sculpted, more powerful…

Designed to drive a woman to the heights of ecstasy and beyond.

"Speechless, eh?" Iain said with a teasing lilt. "I'll take it as a compliment and a positive sign."

"You're very sexy, Iain, and I'd love to get naked with you." I tore my focus away from his bare chest. "But it's a bad idea."

"You paused before saying it's a bad idea." He pulled the shirt on over his head, and of course, it clung to every chiseled line of muscle on his torso. "That means you want me. And considering how you were dealing with your desire last night, alone in your bedroom, I don't need to be omniscient to see the truth. We'll be naked. Soon. And I'll be buried inside your luscious body all night long."

My sex felt empty, aching for exactly what he'd promised.

Iain strode to me, took my face in his hands, and hovered his mouth a breath away from mine. "A good-morning kiss?"

My heart pounded, and I couldn't catch my breath. Would he kiss me deeply this time? I needed him to, needed it so badly.

"Yes," I whispered.

He pressed his lips to mine, the touch soft and warm. He pressed more firmly, but still, he did not take more. I opened my lips, begging for a soul-searing kiss, but instead, he took my bottom lip between his teeth and released it little by little.

Without a word, his expression neutral, he stepped back and leaned against the jamb opposite me.

Despite his casual posture, the bulge in his pants—much larger and stiffer than a moment ago—assured me our good-morning kiss had affected him too. I'd loved the feel of his big hands on my cheeks and burned to feel them on other parts of my body.

My gaze flicked to his bag where a glimpse of plaid snagged my attention. "Is that a plaid blanket in your bag?"

"No," he said with a faint laugh. "It's my kilt. I remembered how much you liked it before."

"You wore it once." And damn, I had liked it. A lot. Iain in a kilt with a dagger strapped to his hip, marching across the campus of Nackington University and straight into the lecture hall, had been a sight to see. When he'd stood tall and proud on the platform, chin lifted, no one had dared mock him. Recalling that day, I couldn't help admitting the truth. "I always liked you best in a kilt."

He perked up, seeming like he hadn't expected me to say that.

"The dagger was cool too," I said.

"Not a dagger," he said. "It was a replica of a medieval *sgian dubh*."

"I remember you telling the whole class that when one frat boy called it a steak knife." I couldn't stop myself from smiling at the memory, but then another item in his bag caught my attention. "What is that box there?"

He plucked the cardboard box out of his bag and held it up.

Condoms. The arrogant man had brought a box of condoms.

With that easy smile on his lips, he reached his other hand into the bag to pull out a second box of rubbers.

I shook my head. "Two boxes of condoms? A little overconfident, don't you think?"

"Not at all." He tossed the boxes into his bag. "*Semper paratus*. It's my motto."

"Which means what?"

"Always prepared."

"Overprepared, I'd say." Men usually tried to wiggle out of using condoms, particularly once I told them I was on the pill, but Iain brought two frigging boxes of the things. "I'll be in the kitchen getting breakfast ready. I hope you like eggs, pancakes, hash browns, and sausage links."

His lips quirked as he raised his brows. "A large breakfast."

"We'll need the protein to power us for the day ahead." I hooked my thumbs in the belt loops of my jeans. "Unless you were lying when you said you'd work for your room and board."

"It was no lie. Whatever you need, I'll do."

"Good." I pointed one finger at his bare feet. "Might want some socks and shoes."

He headed for the dresser and picked up a pair of sneakers.

"Um," I said, gesturing at his shoes, "do you have any boots? I mean something more durable than the hiking boots you had on yesterday. Steel toed would be best. Sheep and horses can step on your feet."

"Are yours steel toed?" He eyed my sturdy boots.

"Yes, they are."

He dropped the sneakers. "My boots aren't, and I brought only these shoes, the boots I wore yesterday, and another pair of boots that won't be any more appropriate. I wasn't expecting this to be a sheep ranch."

"That's okay. I'll call Ben and ask him to bring an extra pair of boots for you. You guys are probably the same size."

"Ben?" Iain's eyes narrowed the tiniest bit, and his jaw tensed. "You have a—boyfriend?"

I tried to suppress my laugh, which turned it into a wet snort. I must've misread his facial expression because the Buddha MacTaggart did not get jealous. Back in college, when everyone realized I was spending a lot of time with the hot Scottish professor, spiteful boys had hit on me in hopes of ticking off Iain. The tactic never succeeded. Iain didn't care if they marched right up to me when I was standing beside him and asked me out on a date. Maybe he'd been certain I'd reject the idiots, which I did, but he could've shown a little irritation about it.

The closest he'd ever gotten to jealousy was when he'd told a particularly persistent young man, "You're interrupting our lunch, laddie."

Naturally, Iain had spoken those words in a calm and unperturbed tone.

Iain of the present day shook off whatever it had been and gave me his trademark relaxed smile. "He's not your boyfriend, is he?"

"No. Ben is my ranch hand. Part-time. I can't afford full-time help."

He rolled his shoulders back and lifted his chin again. "Good thing I'm here, then."

Okay, I was confused again. Did he feel the need to outperform Ben in the ranch-duties department? No, that implied jealousy again. Several times yesterday and today, I'd thought he showed a hint of envy. I must've been interpreting his actions based on my own desire for him to at long last show some real, raw emotion.

I shook my head and tromped downstairs with a sock-clad Iain close behind.

"You're in luck," I said as we reached the bottom of the stairs. "You got
here in time for the big event."

"What event?"

I slapped his arm. "Deworming day."

Chapter Seven

Iain

*I*clasped my hands over the tip of the shovel's handle, one foot braced on the metal blade, having stopped in the middle of cleaning out a horse stall. When I'd asked for a pitchfork, Rae had informed me the shovel was easier—and she'd been right. My limited experience with farm animals came from spending time with Uncle Ross helping him with his pigs. He'd used a small bulldozer with a front-end loader to clean out their pen, but even if Rae had one of those, it wouldn't have fit inside this stall.

Rae's gelding, Sunny, had nuzzled my face for a good minute before he ambled outside to leave me to my task. The smaller horse, Ariel, belonged to Rae's daughter. The two animals shared one large stall, which Rae had told me used to be two stalls. She had taken out the wall herself using "a sledge-hammer, a lot of well-placed kicks, and some help from Mom."

She wasn't afraid of manual labor. I loved that about her.

Of course, I loved everything about Rae.

Gazing out over the stall's half door, through the barn, I could see Rae and her ranch hand engaged in an animated discussion. Rae grinned and touched Ben's arm. He smiled in return, shrugging.

Rae threw her arms around Ben.

My spine snapped straight. I squinted at the pair outside, at the way Rae hugged him fiercely and—

I ground my teeth. She'd just kissed him on the cheek, then finally took her arms off the young, blond Viking.

Ben hunched his shoulders, his gaze averted, and shambled off in the direction of the paddock beside the barn. Rae and Ben had gathered the sheep into the paddock while I toiled inside the barn. She'd chosen him to assist her but kept me out of sight. Though she claimed Ben was not her boyfriend, I had my doubts.

Had she ever said he wasn't her lover? No, I'd suggested he wasn't her boyfriend, and she'd agreed, but he could still be her lover.

My jaw ached, and I realized I'd been grinding my teeth harder. Rubbing my jaw, I forced myself to take several long, slow breaths. Nothing had gotten me this agitated since before I met Rae more than a decade ago. Too many years of feeling adrift on a stormy sea had changed my outlook on life. After years of practice, I'd become rather adept at maintaining an even keel.

Yet here I was, glaring at a man because Rae had hugged him.

Outside, Rae turned and headed for the barn.

I got back to my task, determined not to let her see my reaction to Ben. I stabbed the shovel into a pile of manure.

"That's not how you do it," Rae said.

"I bloody know how to use a shovel."

"Jeez, you're snippy all of a sudden."

Sighing, I leaned the shovel against the wall and met Rae's gaze. She had her arms folded on the stall's half door. And she was smiling. A closed-mouth little smile that suggested she'd discovered one of my deepest secrets.

Not that it was a secret. I was failing rather spectacularly at concealing my resentment.

Her eyes sparkled with humor when she said, "What's your deal with Ben? You've been snippy with him ever since I introduced you. He did bring you boots, the good kind with steel-reinforced toes, and he's letting you keep them."

"I thanked him for that."

"Mm-hm. Right before you started giving him the evil eye." She flashed me a sly smile. "Maybe you're laying a curse on him. You are an archaeologist. You'd know all the good old curses."

"I'm not cursing anyone." I stabbed my fingers through my hair. "Not qualified for that anymore."

She watched me for a moment, her mood unreadable.

I cleared my throat and scratched my neck.

"Since we're all working together today," Rae said, "you'd better figure out how to get along with Ben. He's a real sweetie, you know. What is your problem with him?"

Ben was a sweetie? She'd never called me that.

"He's after you," I said.

She clamped her lips between her teeth while little snorting noises emerged from her nostrils. Her eyes sparkled again with a humor that had started to annoy me.

Like a typical man, I reacted in the least appropriate way.

I stomped to the stall door, inches from Rae. "Why did you kiss him?"

"Who?"

"Ben. The laddie you keep touching and hugging."

Rae stared blankly at me for a second, then burst out laughing. "He proposed to his girlfriend last night, and she said yes. I was congratulating him."

I unlatched the stall door and swung it open, yanking it out from under Rae's arms. She stumbled sideways a step. I stalked toward the open barn door.

"Where are you going?" she asked.

Halting a good two meters from the main door, I half turned to glance at her. "To skelp your ranch hand."

"Oh come on." She approached me, hands on her hips. "You can't be jealous. Iain MacTaggart never gets jealous."

And yet I was ready to assault a young man who did seem like a decent bloke.

I sighed and rubbed my eyes with my thumb and forefinger. "I'm sorry. Whether or not Iain MacTaggart ever gets jealous, he's acting like a fucking plonker."

Her soft laughter teased my senses. "Talking about yourself in the third person is weird, but 'plonker' sounds like downright nonsense."

Lowering my hand, I looked at her. "A plonker is a foolish, stupid man."

"Don't be so hard on yourself." She frisked her hands over my chest as if wiping dust off my shirt. "You're not stupid."

"I notice you haven't disputed the term foolish."

"Kind of like seeing you acting like a green-eyed fool." She laid her palm on my chest. "But for the record, I am not and never have been involved with Ben, sexually or romantically. He's my employee and friend. Period."

She liked my foolish, envious behavior. Another good sign.

I placed my hand over hers on my chest. "I promise not to be a green-eyed ersehole again."

"Stop calling yourself that."

"An *arschgeige*, then."

She wrinkled her nose. "What language is that? Gaelic?"

"German. I thought you might prefer a more exotic term for the kind of dunderhead I've been today."

"Okay, dunderhead I can agree with." She moved back, creating a gap between us I didn't care for at all. "But none of those bad words apply to you."

Bad words? She really was a mother, avoiding curse words. A good mother, I'd wager. No, I didn't need to bet on the possibility. It was a certainty.

I fought the urge to haul her into me and ravish her mouth. The lass had always triggered my most primal desires, but I had resolved to seduce her gradually, tenderly, not like a rutting buck. If I didn't kiss her soon, kiss her the way I'd wanted to since first seeing her yesterday, I really would turn into a bleeding *arschgeige*.

"No more Dr. Snippy," she said in a stern voice only a mother would use. "Right?"

"Agreed, no more." I frowned at my own behavior. "Had a wee bout of anxiety since I found you again."

"Sure, I'll let you get away with calling it a *wee* bout." She fixed those sharp, blue eyes on me. "How did you find me, anyway?"

"Hired my cousin Rory to help me. He's a solicitor and knows a private investigator here in America as well as having other sorts of connections." Noticing the suspicious tilt of her head, I added, "Legal connections, nothing shady."

"Good to know." She hooked a thumb in one of the belt loops on her jeans. "How long did it take you to find me? I mean, how long were you looking?"

"I thought about you every day for the past thirteen years, but I didn't think I had a right to track you down. Not that I would've had the vaguest idea of how to go about it, anyway." My shoulders slumped as I reflected on the events that led me here, to her. "I told you about my friend Gavin and his problems with my cousin Jamie. That inspired me to want to find you, but I needed two more months to work up the courage to do it. When I asked Rory for help, he took charge of the search. That was in February. The fifteenth, to be precise."

"You started your search on February fifteenth? How bizarre."

"In what way?"

Her eyes widened with a shock that seemed to make her stop breathing. She shook it off with a dismissive noise and said, "It's the day after Valentine's Day, that's all."

My brows rose a touch at her odd reaction, but I shrugged off my statement—literally, by lifting my shoulders. "Should've set things in motion on the fourteenth. Would've been romantic, eh?"

"Sure, whatever," she said. "How long did it take this investigator to find me?"

"He called two days ago with the news. Took him a good while since your name isn't on the deed to this property. It's in the name of Cheryl Raines."

"My mom, yeah, she owns it." Rae gave me that suspicious look again. "You found out where I was two days ago and waltzed up my driveway yesterday. What did you do, charter a plane to get here fast?"

"No, I borrowed my cousin Rory's jet."

She blinked once, slowly. "Your cousin owns a private jet?"

"A Gulfstream G600, yes. Rory and Lachlan share the jet."

"Oh." She spoke the single syllable with her lips forming an O, her eyes large but not as wide as a moment ago when I'd told her my search for her began on February fifteenth. "Are all your relatives stinking rich?"

"No," I said with a light chuckle. "Only Rory and Lachlan. And also Evan, but his fortune makes the rest of us combined seem like paupers."

"I see." She blinked several times, shaking her head. Clearing her throat, she squared her shoulders and said, "Just to be crystal clear, you've agreed not to beat up Ben."

With a growl, I threw my hands up. "I won't touch the whelp."

She tsked. "Now-now, that's no way to start your no-jealousy campaign."

"Not a blasted campaign. It's..." I flung up one hand this time.

"Anxiety, I get it. You're worried I'll hook up with somebody else before you can seduce me. I told you I'm not interested in men."

"In men other than me, you mean. Can't look at me the way you did this morning and claim to have no interest."

"Oh, I may be interested, but I won't act on it." Rae smiled, dimpling her cheeks. "It's nice to know the Unflappable Iain MacTaggart does flap a little now and then."

"Unflappable who? Ye cannae mean me." If she knew my thoughts, she wouldn't call me such a thing.

"I'm talking about you. The Unflappable Iain MacTaggart is what I've always called you in my head." She stuffed her hands in her pants pockets and rocked back on her heels. "You never get upset about anything. I've always liked your equanimity, but sometimes, I really wish you'd express a stronger emotion."

"Saying I love you isn't strong enough?"

"Not when you say it in that easygoing voice and smile that Buddha smile."

I couldn't help chuckling. "Buddha? I'm no pacifist."

My burning need to batter her ranch hand proved as much.

"No," she said, "but you've got the inscrutable, serene smile down pat."

I couldn't decide if that would help my cause or hurt it. Never had I met a woman who dreamed of going to bed with the Buddha. The serenity she saw had come at great cost and been borne out of necessity. If she wanted raw, she'd get it when I let loose the full force of my desire for her.

In light of my plan, I needed to keep her thinking of me, of us, naked and hungry for each other.

I wrapped an arm around her waist and dragged her into me, forcing her to slant her head back to look at me. "Don't worry, sunshine. I'm planning to show you very strong feelings."

With one thrust of my hips, I made my meaning clear.

She sucked in a breath.

I let my hand wander down to her buttock, cupping it possessively.

"We have work to do," she said, though the hitch in her voice told me she hadn't forgotten about our encounter in the guest bedroom earlier.

"I'm yours, sunshine. Command me."

"Stop calling me sunshine. It's a goofy pet name."

"Maybe it is." I trailed a fingertip down her cheek. "But you always blush when I say it."

Rae wriggled out of my grasp, smoothed her shirt, and lifted her chin. "It's time to deworm the sheep."

My gaze wandered to the various supplies and equipment piled on the dirt floor, up against the wall opposite the stalls. Two saddles rested on old wooden barrels with bridles and halters draped over them. Everything else lay on the ground.

"You need shelves," I said, "at the least. Hooks and saddle racks would be good too."

"I used to have shelves, but they got old and broke." She eyed the mess and sighed. "Tried to make shelves, but it turns out I suck at carpentry."

"Maybe I can help."

"Shelves are a low priority." She spun on her heels to face the doorway. "We've got more pressing work to do."

Before I could speak, she marched out the door.

I followed, admiring her bonnie erse even as I wondered how one dewormed a sheep.

The answer became clear a few minutes later when my humiliation began.

Anything for Rae, I reminded myself over and over. *Anything to win her.*

Chapter Eight

Rae

Who knew deworming sheep could turn into great entertainment? Maybe I shouldn't have found humor in Iain's plight, but the man had brought this on himself. Ben and I had both offered tips and assistance. Stubborn as ever, Iain had refused our help. That explained why he was currently flat on his ass on the ground, scowling at the sheep that milled around him sniffing and baaing at him. His hair had gotten severely mussed—it looked good on him, though—and his clothing had gotten smeared with dirt and grass and a good dose of manure.

I'd given him five sheep to wrangle. The rest of the flock hung around in the adjoining small pasture where I kept them at night. The pasture connected to the shed attached to the back of the barn that provided shelter for the flock.

Some sheep might get easily spooked, but mine had grown up with a little girl who loved animals. Malina had never mistreated the sheep, but the way she used to run around and squeal had desensitized them. As she'd gotten older, she had taken to hanging out in the paddock with the sheep whenever I needed to corral them for hoof trimming, deworming, or any of the other tasks I performed to keep my flock in good condition.

At my suggestion, Iain had spent a couple hours hanging out with the sheep in the pasture while Ben and I made some repairs to the shed. The critters had gotten used to him. Even in his frustration, Iain did not shout or throw his arms up. He somehow pulled off an air of calm exasperation.

Of course, he hadn't met my llama yet. Ben had locked her in the smallest pen, the one hidden behind the shed, for the duration of the deworming event.

"Why couldn't you give me one at a time?" Iain called out, his squinty gaze aimed at me.

"Sheep don't like to be separated from their flock." Standing at the paddock fence, on the outside of the enclosure, I folded my arms on the top bar of the wooden fence. "You said you wanted to do everything the way I do."

Oh yes, his stubbornness and male pride had gotten him into this debacle.

Ben, standing a few feet to my left, spoke to Iain over the fence. "Rae offered to catch the sheep so all you'd have to do was hold on to them one at a time."

I nodded. "When I do it, I get all twenty-five sheep in there with me."

"Yeah," Ben said, "she wrangles 'em like a pro."

"She is a professional," Iain said. He clambered to his feet and dusted himself off as best he could. "The pair of you could try a wee bit harder not to laugh at me."

I shook my head. "We offered to help, and you said no."

He turned in a circle, eying the sheep with grim determination. "I can do this."

"You're flapping again, Iain."

The harried Scot flashed me a sardonic, twisted-mouth look.

"Flapping?" Ben asked, his brow furrowed.

"It's a private joke," I said.

"Private?" Ben smiled with knowing satisfaction. "You like him. A lot."

I pretended a sudden interest in the grass at my feet, kicking at it with the toe of my boot. "We have history, that's all."

"A history of you being in love with him?"

The humor in his voice made me flatten my lips. "None of your business, Ben."

My friend-slash-employee chuckled and resumed watching Iain flounder.

Was I in love with Iain? Years ago, I'd thought I was. So much had happened in the intervening years, and I hardly knew the man who'd barged back into my life yesterday. I could not fall for him after less than a day. Even if he made me feel good. Even if he was gorgeous and sexy and totally adorable when he tried in vain to snag a sheep.

Iain lunged at a sheep, but the woolly girl dodged him. He lost his footing and fell face-first onto the ground. *Splat.* The Buddha MacTaggart lifted his dirty face and scrunched his mouth.

He clambered to his feet and strode toward another sheep.

Sproing. The sheep evaded him with a sideways hop.

The Scot stumbled and fell to the ground on his ass. *Whump.*

I waved at him. "Sure you don't want some help?"

"Rae's an expert," Ben said, grinning.

"You're both laughing at me," Iain said, slapping his palms on the ground. "The little fuckers are slippery."

"We're not making fun of you," I said. "You're being unreasonably stubborn."

"Aye, maybe I am." He bent his knees to rest his wrists on them. A sheep sniffed his cheek, and he gusted out a sigh, his head drooping.

Oh, poor Iain. How could I let him go on suffering? After ten minutes of struggling with the sheep, he'd had enough.

I climbed over the fence and landed in the paddock on both feet. Wending my way between the sheep, I reached Iain and offered him both my hands.

He accepted them, and I gave him a little support in getting up.

A smear on his cheek caught my eye, and I instinctively tried to wipe it away.

Iain shied away from the touch. "I think that's sheep shit."

"Probably is." I lifted the hem of my shirt, spat on it, and used the wet fabric to wipe the smear off his cheek. "There, all better."

His gaze had veered to my chest, where my bra was now exposed because I'd raised my shirt high to reach his face.

In a soft voice, he said, "Do you lift your shirt for every man who gets shit on his face?"

"No." I dropped my shirt, tugging it into position.

"Only for me?" he said with a hint of a smirk.

"Ben doesn't get manure on his face."

Iain sighed, but it came out more like a growl. "He's an expert at catching sheep, is he?"

"Thought you weren't jealous of him anymore."

"Ahmno jealous."

"Whatever you say." I patted his chest. "Relax, Ben doesn't get as dirty as you are because he lets me catch the sheep."

No doubt about it this time. Iain growled.

He stepped back, spreading his arm in an expansive gesture. "Have at it, mistress of the sheep."

"I'm a shepherdess, not a mistress."

"Haud yer wheesht and catch the bloody little fuckers."

"I have no idea what you're telling me to do first, but the sheep part I got."

With those brawny arms barred over his chest, he said, "It's simple. 'Haud yer wheesht' means keep your lovely little mouth shut." His attention swerved to my lips. "Or I'll keep ye quiet mah own way."

His way? That involved teasing me with chaste kisses he somehow turned into foreplay. If he planned on kissing me deeply this time, I might keep yammering just to make him do it.

"Are you two gonna deworm the sheep or what?"

Ben's question ripped me out of my fantasy of Iain ravishing me with a bone-melting kiss.

I glanced around. "Where's the drenching gun?"

"No idea," Iain said. "I dropped it somewhere."

With an effort to remain casual and relaxed, I meandered among the sheep until I spotted the drenching gun on the ground. The big syringe featured a bent metal tip for administering the deworming liquid. I'd loaded the syringe, but Iain had insisted on doing the job himself.

I returned to Iain, who hadn't budged an inch. "Got it."

He grunted, his gaze on the sheep.

"Sorry," I said. "I shouldn't have let you run around flailing at my sheep for so long."

One of the sheep nuzzled Iain's palm as if apologizing for being so difficult to wrangle. He grudgingly scratched the critter's chin.

"Making friends?" I said.

"Surrendering is more like it. They won the battle."

"Hold this," I said, handing him the drenching gun.

I approached the sheep nearest me and took the animal's jaw in my hand while exerting the lightest pressure to lift it. My other hand on the critter's shoulder kept her from backing away.

"Good sheepie," I murmured. "That's a good little sheepie. It's time for your medicine, that's all."

Swinging one leg over the sheep's back, I straddled her. To Iain, I said, "Bring me the drenching gun. And try to channel your inner tranquility."

With amazing calmness and ease, considering the debacle moments ago, he approached the sheep and me, handing over the drenching gun. I slipped the tip into her mouth and injected the deworming liquid.

Iain gave me an appreciative nod. "You make it look easy."

"Experience is on my side."

"You catch them, and I'll squirt the medicine into their mouths."

I released the sheep, and she scampered away. "Sure you're up for this?"

"Yes."

We treated the rest of the flock together with no more incidents. Iain even started calling them "sheepies" and whispering foreign phrases to them. I was pretty sure he'd called some of them "*gràidh*," but I couldn't decide if I should be offended by that. When I brought in the last five sheep, Iain set his hands on his hips and studied the animals with a crease deepening between his brows, right over his nose.

After a moment, he waved a finger at the sheep. "Am I wrong, or are all these sheep female?"

"Bonus points for the Scot," I said. "They are all girls. Rams are a real pain to have around because you have to keep them separated from the ewes unless they're breeding."

"I see." He scratched his chin. "How do they, ah, make bairns if they're all female?"

"Simple. I lease a ram."

"You—" His forehead wrinkled, but then he laughed softly. "You hire a male prostitute to service your sheep."

"I suppose you could describe it that way." I gave his shoulder a light shove. "If you're a Scottish man with a dirty mind."

"Fortunately, I am." He smoothed hair away from my cheek. "You'll be glad of it when I have you naked."

Since I had no response to that, other than my sudden urge to climb up his body, I let the comment go.

We released the flock into the pasture, and Iain had just turned away from the field when he got nudged by a large body. He stumbled forward, caught himself, and spun around.

He stumbled backward this time, straight into the paddock fence. "What is that?"

My llama, Lily, edged closer to inspect him face to face. The top of her head was only a couple inches below the top of Iain's. She stretched her long neck to sniff his nose.

Iain held stock-still, not even blinking. Barely moving his lips, he muttered, "What is this thing?"

"Oh come on," I said. "A world traveler like you must've seen a llama before. Lily's a sweetie. And look, her eyes are almost the same color blue as yours. No wonder she's smitten."

He rotated his eyes to glance at me without moving his head. "I've seen llamas, but not this close up."

I took pity on him and shooed Lily away. The llama trotted off to join the flock.

The big, strong man huddling by the fence slumped against it. "You could've warned me."

"About Lily? I forgot. We put her in the pen behind the shed while we're deworming the sheep." I walked to Iain. "Ben must've let her out. Sorry she scared you."

He straightened and rolled his shoulders back. "Not scared. That creature surprised me."

Okay, I'd let him get away with claiming surprise.

"Why do you have a llama?" he asked.

"She guards the flock. I got Lily after I lost three sheep last year. I thought about getting her a llama buddy, but she became instant friends with the horses, so I didn't bother."

After we, with Ben's help, completed the rest of the tasks for the day, I made us all a hearty dinner. We enjoyed casual conversation while we ate, laughing about Iain's travails with the sheep and talking about the differences between Scotland and America. After dinner, the three of us sat on the porch sipping iced tea by the light of the single bulb stationed by the front door. Iain and I occupied the porch swing while Ben had taken one of the two padded chairs. Iain had chosen to sit at the opposite end of the swing from me, leaving a gap of a couple feet between us, and I couldn't decide how I felt about that.

Ben set his tea glass down on the floorboards of the porch. "Think you two can handle this place by yourselves while I'm gone?"

"Gone?" I stared at him like he'd spouted foreign phrases the way Iain often did.

"Yeah," Ben said. "Told you, I'm leaving for my sister's wedding tomorrow. This was my last day."

Oh shit. I'd completely forgotten. Me and Iain alone for nine more days? I'd thought I'd have Ben as a buffer in the daytime, but now I'd have nothing and no one to keep me from giving in to my lust.

I had willpower. What else did I need?

The mere thought of nine days alone with Iain had my inner voice asking, *What's the harm in having a little fun?*

Maybe I should sleep with him—purely to satisfy my curiosity. Even my mom had sort of encouraged me to do it.

"You forgot I'm leaving," Ben said. "It's only eleven days, then I'll be back. Besides, Iain seems plenty strong enough to get the job done while I'm gone."

I felt Iain watching me even before I noticed it in my peripheral vision. Get the job done? Oh yeah, Iain could do that for sure.

"Better get going," Ben said, rising from his chair. "Got packing to finish."

After wishing Ben a safe trip and giving him a quick goodbye hug, I claimed the chair Ben had vacated. The seat was still warm. If Iain had sat here, I would've relished having his heat under my bottom. Ben had no such effect on me. No man other than Iain had ever affected me this way.

But I had other matters to discuss with him.

I crossed my legs, angling them away from Iain where he sat on the swing, and folded my hands over my belly. "It's time you told me about that day."

Chapter Nine

Iain

That day. Rae wanted the truth, deserved the truth. I braced one ankle atop the other knee, striving for a serenity that, for once, I didn't feel. Rae's nickname for me, the Unflappable Iain MacTaggart, described me well enough but discounted the deeply hidden parts of me. She'd glimpsed those parts, the things I'd learned to control and ignore, when I let my envy show today. If I wanted a future with her, I had to be honest about everything.

Could I show her the darkest parts of me? Would she understand and forgive?

When I had asked my cousin Rory for help in tracking down Rae, he'd assured me everyone deserves a second chance. I'd believed him then, but now I wondered. Small steps. I wouldn't throw everything at her at once. Giving Rae time to adjust to each revelation seemed the most prudent approach. Revealing the whole picture to her little by little had nothing at all to do with fear.

Bloody liar.

I rubbed my eyes, and avoiding Rae's inquisitive gaze, I explained. "That day, when I arrived at my office three security guards were waiting for me. They'd dumped all my files into trash bags. I asked what was going on, and one of the guards informed me I was to go with them to the president's office at once. The guards escorted me across campus to the office of the university president, but he wasn't the only one there. The dean of the humanities department, my superior, was there. And so was Conrad Bremner-Ashton, the father of your charming roommate."

Rae huffed. "Cecilia Bremner-Ashton, aka Cece, aka the Wicked Witch of the Midwest. I had no idea how obsessed she was with you."

Cece had been Rae's roommate for the full ten months during which I'd known her. Cece's family had owned the town of Nackington, Wisconsin, and the educational institution that bore its name—literally owned it as in having purchased most of the land and businesses early in the twentieth century. Conrad Bremner-Ashton had been the school's single-largest donor during my time there. That fact, along with his shady connections and shadier business practices, had made Conrad the de facto leader of his unofficial mafia. No one dared cross the Bremner-Ashtons.

"I didn't realize at the time," I said, "how nefarious the Bremner-Ashtons were. I'd had little contact with them until that day. Conrad did the talking while President Schaech and Dean Milton sat by and watched. I was informed I would be deported by force unless I agreed to leave the country and never return. Whether they could have me deported or not, I had no idea. But Conrad also threatened to punish you unless I complied."

Though I hesitated, Rae did not speak. When I glanced at her, she wore an impassive expression.

"I didn't want to abandon you," I said. "But the choice was simple. I could stay and try to fight the most powerful family in the Midwestern United States, or I could leave and spare you from their wrath. I wanted to call you, to let you know, to say goodbye, but they took me into custody like they were their own police force. I was escorted to my apartment and allowed to pack one bag, then I was escorted to the airport."

Still nothing from Rae. No words. No movements. No reaction at all. Her gaze stayed on me, but her mood was still unreadable.

The swing's seat felt harder suddenly, and I shifted my body to find a more comfortable position. No luck with that. The discomfort originated inside me, not with the cushion under me or the wood beneath that.

At last, she lay her arms on the chair and spoke. "That's what you think. You spared me."

"I'm not claiming to be a hero, but I did what I had to do to protect you." I bent forward, elbows on my knees, and stared at the boards of the porch floor. "Every day since, I've regretted not fighting for you, for us. But if I had…I don't know what the Bremner-Ashtons would've done. Cece accused me of sexually harassing her. They brought her in just before the guards took me away. She gave a fantastic performance, crying and stammering. She said I seduced you and then I tried to do the same to her. What could I do? Leaving spared you."

Rae pursed her lips, one toe tapping on the floor. "You didn't spare me, Iain. They announced I'd gotten an A in your class strictly because I was putting out, so they changed my grade to an F. That left me one credit short of graduating. I was also expelled from Nackington. I tried to get into another college, any college, to finish my degree, but anyplace I applied to had to request my transcripts from Nackington, and they'd see the F in Celtic History and the expulsion. They'd want an explanation, and I couldn't give one. So, they'd call Nackington and hear the whole sordid story. I gave up on college."

The full force of what she'd just said slammed into me. I couldn't speak, and the only part of me that would move was my eyes. I swiveled them to her, overwhelmed by a coldness that penetrated to the core of my being. It couldn't be true, but Rae wouldn't lie.

"Rae, I—" Unable to move, I flapped my jaw a few times. A tactic certain to make her swoon with desire for me. "They said if I—"

"You took the word of people who threw you out of the country."

Goddamn eejit. She was right, and I was being a numpty of the first order. How could I explain why I'd fled without a fight? If she knew my family's history, she might not want to get tangled up in it. If I didn't tell her, she would never understand my actions. Either way, I'd lose her.

I ran a hand over my mouth and looked straight at Rae. "I shouldn't have believed Conrad and his minions, but I had…reasons for the way I behaved. It's complicated, and I'd rather not go into it yet. Believe me when I say I've regretted abandoning you every day of the last thirteen years, and I will never leave you again."

Her lips twitched downward, quivering faintly, but her expression had turned defiant—her voice too. "It doesn't matter. I am never getting involved with you again, not the way you want."

"Why am I here, then? You've agreed to let me stay until next Saturday."

She went still and stoic again, and I swore I could hear the engine of her mind grumbling as she struggled to form a response. Either that or she was grumbling softly at me.

Those beautiful eyes narrowed. "How did security get to your office so fast?"

"What?"

"You dropped me off at my apartment, which was five minutes from the campus. Cece didn't go nuclear until she saw you kissing me goodbye, and she railed at me for a good ten minutes, calling me all sorts of names before she stormed into her bedroom and slammed the door. I assume that's when she called her father to make her ridiculous claim that you'd sexually harassed her. I heard her shouting for another ten minutes, at least. It had to have been an hour before security would've gotten to your office."

Ah, the time gap. I'd hoped she wouldn't notice. Telling her why I'd been delayed would bring on more questions, and I doubted she would appreciate the answers.

Of course she'd noticed the discrepancy. Rae was too canny not to notice.

I laid my arm across the swing's back, running a finger over the smooth wood. "I had errands to run."

"Errands? That's not good enough, Iain." She leaned forward, her razor-sharp gaze cutting into me. "Where were you?"

"Running errands," I said carefully, emphasizing each syllable. "Leave it, Rae. Please."

She scrutinized me for a long moment, then collapsed back against her chair. "Fine, have your secrets. Just don't expect me to trust you as long as you're keeping things from me."

"Have you told me all your secrets?"

She clamped her lips between her teeth, glanced away, and then hugged herself. "I told you everything related to the day that ruined my life. The rest is none of your business."

I tapped my finger on the swing. "Why don't you want me to meet your daughter? You were prepared to introduce her to the plonker who owns the taxi service."

"That was a test. One he failed."

"A test of what?"

"His commitment to the relationship."

My turn to fall silent and study her. Her arms rested on the chair again, but her fingers tapped in a restless rhythm. Though she frowned, her eyes evinced fear. I couldn't describe the look in her eyes. I sensed the fear in them.

"Listen," she said, "I tried dating after my daughter was born. But I realized pretty quickly my daughter's well-being had to be my number-one priority. I would not bring a parade of men into our home, only to have each of them leave. Kids don't understand why adults go away, and I would not put my kid through that over and over just so I could have a boyfriend. I tried a few more times over the years, going on dates while my daughter was in school. I lost interest. Protecting my child is my top priority, and that is why you will never meet her."

She might as well have stabbed me in the chest. The pang that radiated through me originated there, though it was a phantom pain. Rae didn't trust me at all. Her words told me as much. And yet, she let me sleep in her house, let me kiss her, let me handle her sheep. Not that my activities in the paddock had qualified as handling. The wee creatures had seemed to find it as humorous as Rae had.

I hadn't come this far, traveling thousands of miles and spending significant sums of money to find her, only to turn and run back home with my tail between my legs.

Once, I'd done that. *Never again.*

"All right," I said, scratching my jaw, "I won't ask about your daughter again or ask why you seem to have hidden every photograph of her. Since I'd rather not tell you all my secrets yet, I can't expect you to share everything with me. You know why I left before. You know I want to make it up to you and have a fresh start. But—" I pulled in a deep breath, not wanting to say the words but knowing I had to. "— if after nine more days you want me to go, I will. Give me, give us, these days to get reacquainted. I will tell you more, eventually. All I'm asking for is time."

She squished her lips into a tight pucker, then exhaled a long breath that deflated her shoulders and softened her features. "Fine."

The tension in me sifted away too, and I relaxed into the swing. A change of subject seemed in order. "I have you all to myself for nine days."

Her lips tightened and twitched upward at the corners as if she repressed a smile. "Ben is only here three days a week, anyway. I already knew I'd be alone with you for most of the time."

I rocked one foot to make my seat sway. "You'll have to restrain your lust for me for nine entire days and nights with no one else around to make you behave."

Her lips curved up into a faint smile. "You're confusing me with twenty-two-year-old Rae who salivated at the sight of you in a kilt. I'm a mature single mother these days, and men in skirts don't impress me anymore."

"A kilt is not a skirt." Damn if I hadn't sounded irritated. This new and improved version of Rae made me lose my grip on the calm demeanor I'd spent years perfecting. It wasn't an act, but I had needed practice to come to terms with my da's behavior and find an inner peace. Rae erased all my work with one word—skirt.

The cheeky lass knew what she was doing with that statement, and I adored her even more for it. Feisty, clever, determined Rae was utterly irresistible.

Her self-satisfied smile proved she'd done it on purpose. "I remember the time you came to class in a kilt, with those big old boots and that sky-blue dress shirt, not to mention the big knife. You walked all the way across the campus dressed like that. Frat boys must've been harassing you the whole time, but the Unflappable Iain MacTaggart didn't care."

I scoffed. "Why should I care if acne-ridden eejits taunt me?"

"All the girls loved getting a glimpse of your legs."

My foot stopped rocking, stilling the swing. "I wore the kilt for you."

Her head jerked back. "What? You said it was a visual aid for your lecture on the clan system of medieval Scotland."

I shook my head. "That's what I told the class. But I wore it for you, because you'd once mentioned you thought kilts were sexy. And that's how I know your skirt comment was nothing more than your attempt to make me angry."

"Why would I want to do that?"

"So I won't try to seduce you." I smiled when she rolled her eyes. "Don't worry. I wasn't planning to seduce you...tonight. Only when you come to me and ask for it."

We gazed at each other for a moment, the heat between us evident in the glossy look in her eyes and the way she kept licking her lips.

Rae shifted her attention to the ever-darkening sky. "What makes you think I'll ask you to have sex with me?"

I laughed softly, not mocking her but enchanted by this wonderful woman. "You've let me kiss you more than once. And you masturbated to thoughts of me."

"Maybe I was thinking about someone else."

"No, it was me. Thinking of you fucking yourself with a vibrator had me rubbing one off twice that night." I slid across the swing to get closer to her chair. "We want each other. It's no crime. You're not my student, and I'm not your teacher. We are mature adults who don't need to hold back anymore."

Her breasts rose and fell with each breath, and the stiff peaks of her nipples jutted through the fabric of her shirt and bra.

My mouth watered with a hunger to devour every inch of her, starting with those nipples.

"Don't you have a job to get back to?" she asked. "Construction or whatever."

"I work when I want to because I want to, not because I need to."

"What, are you rich or something?"

"Yes."

Her eyes bulged, and her mouth fell open on a sound that wasn't quite a word.

Before she could formulate a question, I said, "Rather not talk about that tonight."

"Fine." Rae hopped up from her chair, feigned a yawn, and said, "I'm exhausted. Good night, Iain, see you in the morning."

As if I'd let her get away with that.

She tried to breeze past me, but I caught her around the waist and hauled her down onto my lap, where she wound up sideways across my thighs, her feet dangling. I tugged her closer until only millimeters separated our faces. She stopped blinking, her deep-blue eyes fixated on me.

Her tongue darted out to wet her lips.

Maybe I couldn't convince her to trust me yet, but I could give her one thing she'd complained about more than once.

"What are you doing?" she asked.

"Giving you what you've been wanting."

I dived a hand into her hair, cradling her nape. She splayed her hands on my chest but made no effort to pull away. *There she is, my passionate Rae of sunshine.* I took her mouth hard and fast, allowing no time for her to change her mind. She opened to me, welcoming me into the soft, slick heat of her mouth, moaning when I thrust my tongue deep. The sweet taste of her, the determined strokes of her tongue, the way her fingers clutched my shirt, all of it overpowered my good sense—if I'd ever had any of that—and I couldn't stop myself from delving deeper, taking more, gorging myself on the woman I'd longed for all these years. I wrapped both arms around her, crushing her lush body to me.

She latched her arms around my neck.

The feel of her body intoxicated me, the way her breasts mounded against my chest and her hair fell around my face, tickling my skin. Her soft palms found my nape, her fingers questing into my hair. And her erse, the way it hugged my hardening cock…

With a ravenous little moan, she wriggled and flailed one leg until she straddled me.

I groaned into her mouth, wrecked by the sensation of her hot cleft rubbing against my cock, with only two layers of denim and maybe her thin panties between our flesh. Years ago, I'd wanted her. Now, I craved her like a man who'd gone without food or water for weeks, and she was the sustenance I needed. To have her, to consume her, to brand her as mine…

Bloody hell. What was I doing? Rushing things to satisfy my cock.

Taking hold of her upper arms, I peeled her away from me.

Rae gazed at me with unfocused, desire-heated eyes. She blinked slowly. Her kiss-swollen lips had turned a bonnie shade of dusky pink, and a faint flush tinted her cheeks. She breathed hard, her breasts heaving, those nipples looking even stiffer than before.

I spread a palm over her cheek, skimming my thumb across her chin. "That's enough for tonight."

"Enough?" she said, her voice a husky whisper. She shut her eyes briefly, taking a slow breath and exhaling it between her puckered lips. When she looked at me again, her gaze had cleared. "You're right. That was enough. I don't want you getting the wrong impression and thinking I'll hop into bed with you after one day."

A smile tightened my lips, but I managed to keep it subdued. "That's right, sunshine. Don't let me have the wrong idea after you glued your body to mine and rubbed yourself on my cock."

She tried to frown, but it was ineffectual. "Sex is a bad idea."

"You keep saying that, but you also keep looking at me like you want—"

Rae sealed two fingers over my lips. "Stop talking. Say good night and leave it at that before you ruin this by getting cocky."

I rocked my hips up and tipped hers forward, letting her feel how *cocky* I was.

She hissed in a breath. "Honestly, Iain."

"Afraid you'll need to speak a complete sentence, or I might misunderstand." I slid my hands over her hips to her waist. "Was that 'honestly, Iain, please make love to me sweetly' or 'honestly, Iain, please fuck me hard right here on the swing'? Need to be sure I'm giving you what you want."

"What I want," she said, giving my chest a light slap, "is for you to stop being obsessed with sex."

"It's not me that's obsessed, it's you." I cradled her rump in my hands and stood, carrying her with me, to set her down on her feet. My hands lingered on her perfect bottom. "You're the one who begged for a deep kiss."

Her mouth opened and closed—twice.

I kissed her forehead, took her hand, and led her into the house.

Chapter Ten

Rae

I let Iain shepherd me into the house, down the hall to my bedroom. It stood closed, hiding from view all the evidence of my daughter and her uncanny resemblance to her father.

Guilt coiled in my gut, a tight wad of barbed wire that pricked me every time I thought about Malina and the father she'd never known. Maybe I should've told Iain about her, but I still didn't know if I could count on him to stick around. I believed it when he said he hadn't meant to abandon me. Believing didn't erase the pain of losing him or the shame of being labeled the campus slut.

That wasn't his fault. I'd never blamed him for what others said, but the fact he'd taken off left me wondering if he'd ever really cared about me. His determination to seduce me did not silence the small voice in my head that kept asking if he wanted a relationship with me or if he wanted only sex.

Did any man travel halfway around the world for a roll in the hay?

I turned toward him, my back to the bedroom door. "Thank you for helping out today."

"Don't thank me. I'm working for my room and board."

"And the chance to get in my pants." I flattened my back against the door, arms crossed over my chest. "I'm not a lovestruck college girl anymore. I have responsibilities."

"So do I, but I still find time for relaxation." He braced a hand on the wall beside my head. "As for getting in your pants…" He hooked a finger inside the waistband of my jeans. "I can do that right now."

He undid the button of my jeans, and I just stood there, immobilized by the look on his face even as my heart raced. His hooded gaze never wavered from mine, his lips had parted a hair, and the whispers of his breaths seemed to echo between us. I dropped my arms, plastering my palms to the wall, helpless to move or speak as he tugged my zipper down, down, down.

"What are you doing?" I asked, though I thought—hoped, maybe even prayed—I knew what he was planning. My breaths came faster and shallower, and my skin tingled with anticipation.

He bent his arm and ducked his head near mine, those pale eyes shimmering in the low light. "Shhh."

"I—oh…"

His hand slipped inside my jeans, inside my panties, cupping my mound. "No need for a vibrator tonight."

Blue eyes seared into mine. How could irises the color of glacial ice burn with a scorching heat? I remembered that look from the one and only night we'd spent together. I'd seen it right before he thrust into me for the first time.

Iain shoved his hand between my folds.

My clit throbbed, and my sex pulsated with a need for more of him. Inside me. Deep. Claiming me.

His thumb found my nub and stroked it mercilessly. This was no gentle seduction. He intended to make me come, hard and fast, and I had no willpower left to say no. I wanted this. I wanted more than this, but for tonight, I'd indulge in one moment of sheer pleasure.

Because he was right. I wasn't his student, and he was not my teacher.

Screw responsibility. I'd done nothing but behave like a responsible adult for so damn long. I could have this one moment of reckless passion. Relaxing into Iain's touch, I let myself drown in those gorgeous eyes and the sensation of his rough palm on my flesh. His thumb kept rubbing my clit, and his long fingers stretched down my cleft to—

"Unh." The sound burst out of me at the instant one of his fingers dived inside my sheath. While he pumped it in and out, I crooked my fingers into the wall. Just as my neck arched, he thrust another finger inside me, and then another. I moaned, sagging against the wall.

Thumb rubbing. Fingers thrusting. Me panting.

When my mouth fell open on a gasp, he sealed his open mouth to mine. The kiss was insanely deep, ravenous, wild, like we couldn't get far enough inside each other. I hooked one leg around his, granting him full access to my body, and he plunged a fourth finger inside me. The heel of his hand scraped along my cleft while he pumped his fingers and raked his thumb round and round my clit. I came with his fingers buried inside me and his tongue ravaging my mouth. My body went rigid, the muscles inside clenching around his fingers and releasing, clenching and releasing, over and over until the exquisite pleasure at last relinquished its hold on me.

Iain pulled away, though not by much.

Limp and breathless, I could do nothing more than gape at him.

He removed his hand from my pants, raised his fingers to his face, and drew in a long breath. Eyes half closed, he seemed to be…relishing the scent of my wetness on his skin.

A new desire flickered inside me.

Iain wiped his fingers on his jeans and smirked. "I got in your pants."

How could I argue with that? He had. I'd let him. And damn, I'd loved what he did to me.

But I had to make the parameters clear. Again.

"Pay attention this time," I said. "You can't stay past next Saturday, and we will not be having a relationship."

He patted my hip. "Not yet. First, we'll have a good poke or two, or three, or four. With a passionate woman like you, who knows."

"A poke?"

"It means a fuck."

"Sex is not the way to earn my trust."

He touched my hip again, then slid his hand around to my bottom. "Sex is the gambit, not the endgame."

My mouth crimped at one corner. "You still play chess, I gather."

"And I imagine you still refuse to learn it."

"Chess is too slow and complicated."

We were talking about chess right after he'd given me a fantastic orgasm. Oh no, this wasn't weird at all.

"You didn't mind slow," he said, "when I made love to you."

"That was in another lifetime. I'm not twenty-two anymore." I squirmed, but rather than relieving the lingering ache between my thighs, the movement only served to push my butt into his hand. "Look, you should know what I'm like. I don't make noise. The most you'll get from me is a few gasps and moans, no screaming or wailing or hollering about how much I love your gigantic dick and oh please do me all night long, you're the best I've ever had."

He stroked two fingers along the cleft of my ass. "I don't care if you make noise. I'll know you enjoy it by the look on your face and the way you come. That's how I know you liked what I did to you a moment ago."

How did he have an answer for everything? A hot answer that made me want him even more. It was so irritating.

Iain massaged my behind. "You said you'd love to get naked with me."

"I…" Had no idea what to say to that. Yes, I'd spoken the words. "Iain—"

He dragged me into his body, possessing my mouth with a blistering kiss.

No breath. No thoughts. My pulse thundered in my ears and through my veins. My skin tingled from my scalp to my toes. The delicious feeling of his lips on mine coaxed my eyes to flutter closed and my body to melt against him, longing for more of what he'd given me a moment ago.

He pushed me away. His voice rough, he said, "Good night, Rae."

And then he strode down the hallway. I listened as his footfalls clomped up the stairs.

That man was going to ruin me. Again.

And I didn't give a damn.

I'd learned nothing in the past thirteen years. All the struggles to make a new life and take care of my child, none of that mattered anymore the second Iain MacTaggart had stormed back into my world. Would he bring nourishing, warm rain or destructive lightning and hail?

Once his footsteps faded away, I retreated into my bedroom. Seated on the bed's edge, I dug my phone out of my pocket and dialed my mom's number in California. The call was picked up on the second ring, but rather than my mother's mature voice, a bright young voice greeted me.

"Mom!" Malina almost shrieked. "You won't believe it! I caught a wave today! Ty showed me how yesterday, but I wiped out. Today, I got it!"

"That's great, sweetie. You'll be a surfing expert in no time."

Since my daughter had turned from little girl to preteen, I'd discovered twelve-year-old females often spoke with invisible exclamation points at the end of every statement. I swore sometimes I could see those exclamation points hovering in the air.

"And guess what," Malina said, "Zoey's taking me to a museum tomorrow. She says there are dinosaurs and everything."

"Sounds like fun."

"Yeah, it's cool. But I miss the animals. How's Ariel?"

"He's fine, sweetie. Tomorrow, you'll have so much fun you won't even think about home."

"Museums are awesome, but I wish you were coming with us."

"With Ben leaving for his sister's wedding, I had to stay home." We weren't the lots-of-hugs type of family, but her forlorn tone made me want to crawl through the phone and throw my arms around her. She'd never been away from home without me except for the occasional one-night sleepover. "When you get back, we'll go to the museums in Dallas and Fort Worth together."

Her voice brightened. "Cool!"

A knot tightened in my gut. I loved that my kid had a thing for history, but her love of all things old and decaying had always reminded me of Iain. Last year, when Malina had asked for an archaeology book for Christmas, I'd suffered a pang in my chest behind my ribs. It was so dumb. I hadn't seen Iain in years.

Yet here he was in my house. Malina's father. Maybe I should tell him—

Uh-uh, no way. Whatever mysterious "reasons" he might've had for leaving me, I would not risk him hurting our daughter the same way.

My daughter, not our daughter.

I slapped a palm on my forehead. Jeez, if I was thinking of Malina as *our* daughter, that could mean only one thing. I was developing feelings for Iain all over again.

Developing? Had I ever stopped having feelings for him?

"Mom, are you okay?"

Yanked out of my melancholy thoughts, I said, "Sure. Why wouldn't I be?"

"Because you made a weird noise. Like a moany groan or something."

If she said I'd made a noise, I must've made a noise. *Damn.*

"Just tired," I said. "It's two hours later here. Which reminds me, isn't it your bedtime there?"

Malina moany-groaned this time. "Mom, it's summer vacation."

"You still have a bedtime."

"I'm twelve. Only babies go to sleep at nine o'clock."

Ah yes, twelve was the new thirty. Not in my book.

"You're on Texas time," I said, "which means it's eleven o'clock. You got to stay up late, so it's time for bed."

"Mom," she whined.

"Now, Malina. Go. To. Bed."

She sighed with all the melodrama of a preteen girl. "Okay, fine."

"Good night, Leenie."

"Aw, Mom, I'm too old to be called a baby name."

I stifled a laugh. "Yes, of course. Good night, Ms. Malina Everhart."

A voice in the background at her end called out, "Let me have the phone. I want to talk to your mother."

"Okay," Malina said. "Grandma wants you. Night, Mom."

"Night, sweetie."

Shuffling indicated Malina had relinquished the phone.

"Well, well," my mother said, "how are things there? Are you behaving yourself?"

"Have I ever misbehaved?"

"You were the perfect child." She paused—for dramatic effect, no doubt. "But you did have that incident in college when you did the horizontal mambo with a sexy foreigner old enough to be your father."

"Iain is only fifteen years older."

"Teenage boys have sperm, you know."

"Ech, Mom." Now I sounded like my daughter. *Terrific.* Not only had I reverted to my college self, but I'd regressed further into the preteen years. "I was an adult when I slept with Iain. And hey, why are you talking about sperm and the horizontal mambo in front of my kid?"

"I'm not. Malina's in her room with the door closed."

"Oh. Well, that's different."

"You certainly are—" Silence interrupted her sentence. "— tonight?"

"Mom, are you walking around? You know your phone cuts in and out when you do that. I didn't catch whatever you said."

"I'm walking into the living room." Her voice came through clearly. "Is this better?"

"Yes."

"Sitting on the couch now, not moving anymore. What I said was you certainly are touchy tonight." She sighed. "Is that man harassing you?"

I tried to stifle a laugh, but it came out as tiny snorts. "No, he's not like that."

"Have you slept with him yet?"

My mouth opened, but I couldn't speak. Mom and I had never talked about my sex life, mostly because it had been virtually nonexistent. She'd always been frank about sex, giving me instruction in the use of condoms when I was sixteen and had my first official date. Still, I wasn't sure I could handle talking to my mom about the things Iain and I got up to together.

Guess what, Mom? Iain shoved his hand down my pants and gave me the best orgasm ever in the history of orgasms. I'm seriously considering sleeping with him.

No, I did not want to discuss this with my mother.

"Well?" she said. "Have you?"

"Slept with Iain? No."

Engaged in sexual activities with him, yes. Fantasized about sex with him, absolutely. Done the deed, no. Not yet. But maybe…*No, no, bad idea.* Explaining to myself why it was a bad idea kept getting more and more difficult. Two consenting adults, alone in a remote house, free to explore our every carnal fantasy…

"You want to, don't you?" Mom asked. "You did call him hotter than ever."

"Um—well—" What was the point in lying? I stank at it, anyway. "Yes, I've thought about it. No heterosexual woman on the planet could meet Iain MacTaggart and not have even a fleeting thought about getting naked with him."

My mom fell silent for a few seconds. "You should do it."

"I—what?"

"Have sex with Iain. You're a grown woman, and you deserve to have a little fun."

I held the phone away from my face, staring at it like the device might pop up a message explaining to me how my own mother could suggest I have a casual affair. She'd suggested it twice, once yesterday and again tonight. When I lifted the phone to my ear again, I said, "You're kidding, right?"

"No."

"Parents aren't supposed to tell their kids to have casual sex."

She made an impatient noise. "For heaven's sake, Rae, you're an adult. The father of your child, the man you love, is back in your life. Nothing about this is casual."

And that was exactly why sex with Iain was a horrible idea.

"I can't do it," I said. "This is way too complicated, and he's already asking questions about Malina, about why I hid all the photos of her. I've been careful not to say her name. If I sleep with Iain, he'll have more questions. He'll want us to…bond or something. Share our secrets."

"Maybe you should tell him he has a daughter."

"If I do that, he'll want to meet her. What if he takes off again? Malina would be devastated."

"Yes, it's a risk. Life is full of those." She hesitated, then said, "I know you love him. So, ask yourself how much you're willing to risk to have what you wanted all along. Malina's stronger than you think, and even if you and Iain don't work out, she deserves to know her father."

What could I say to that? Malina had dreamed of a perfect family, with a mother and a father, all her life. She used to draw pictures of the three of us. She didn't even know Iain's name.

"I can't tell her," I said. "For years, I've insisted her father is dead."

"She'll understand. Besides, if Iain is as smart as you've always said, he'll figure out what's going on."

Oh shit. Mom was right. Iain already sensed something was up, and he wouldn't stop probing until I cracked and told him. I should give him the boot this instant. *Adios, Iain, scamper back to Scotland.* Just thinking the words set off an ache in my chest.

I could keep this one secret. I would keep it. No way in hell would Iain seduce the truth out of me.

"You think about it," Mom said, "and get some sleep."

"Uh-huh. I'm not telling him, not ever."

"We'll see."

"And what does that mean?"

"I want what's best for you, even if you can't see what that is yet."

We said good night and hung up. While I changed into my nightie, my attention kept drifting to the bottom drawer of the dresser. The photo album. The one I'd made for Iain. Could my mother be right? Had I never stopped loving him?

Resisting my feelings got harder every day.

But oh dear heaven, resisting the urge to crawl into bed with him had become almost impossible.

Chapter Eleven

Iain

The next day, Rae tried to act like nothing had happened between us, as if I hadn't made her come for me right there in the hallway without removing a stitch of her clothing.

I couldn't let her get away with dismissing our first sexual encounter in thirteen years. The woman was stubborn and determined to keep me at a distance. I couldn't understand how she meant to do that when her desire was evident in her every movement and every little noise she made.

I couldn't have hidden my lust for her if I'd wanted to. The sight of her hips swaying when she walked in that purposeful manner, like a woman who knew where she needed to be and what she needed to do at every moment, made my balls ache and my cock stiffen. The Unflappable Iain MacTaggart spent most of the day suffering with an erection that wouldn't stop. Not until I had her. Not until I'd slid myself inside that warm, supple body and—

"Are you coming?"

Rae's voice yanked me out of my fantasy, and I stared dumbly at her. Coming? I'd been close to doing that all day. No wonder the sheep looked at me with suspicion.

"Hey!" Rae called from the barn doorway, clapping her hands. "Are you done mucking out the stalls? I have to do some stuff in my office, so you can take a break in the house if you're done. We can have a quick snack first. Are you coming?"

That word again. She should be the one coming—under my hand, under my mouth, with my cock deep inside her.

Rae frowned at me.

"I'm coming," I said, leaning the shovel against the wall. I'd forgotten I had it in my hand, lost in my daydreams of making love to her. "Stalls are clean. You could eat off the floors in here."

She wrinkled her nose in the most adorable way. "No thanks. But I'll send your dinner out here if you want to lick it up off the dirt floor."

No, I'd much rather lick her. Drop whipped cream all over her body and lap it up, working my way down to her slick folds, and deeper…

"I'm going inside," she said, giving me an exasperated look. "If you're having a stroke, old man, let me know so I can call an ambulance for you."

"Not having a stroke." I strode up beside her and tugged her tight against me. "If you're trying to annoy me by calling me an old man, save your breath. You'll need it for screaming my name when we're naked."

She rolled her eyes. "You sure are obsessed with sex."

"No," I said silkily, slipping my free hand into her hair, tipping her head back at the perfect angle for a deep kiss, "ahmno obsessed with sex. Ahm obsessed with yer body."

She puckered her lips in a halfhearted attempt to seem irritated. "Sex is a bad—"

I silenced her overused excuse by covering her mouth with mine. Her lips remained tight, her body tense, until I flicked my tongue out to tease the seam of her mouth. She exhaled a long sigh, her body softening, and opened fully to me. I seized the advantage, delving into her sweet mouth, and raked my tongue over hers again and again, urging her to respond, demanding she respond. She breathed out a soft moan and coiled her tongue around mine. We devoured each other without reservation, thrust for thrust, glide for glide, not relenting until we'd lost our breaths and had to stop to inhale oxygen.

The faint blush on her cheeks made me smile.

With one finger, I traced the line of her jaw. "You are beautiful when you're aroused."

"But not any other time?" she said between quick breaths.

"Always." I fanned my fingertips over her mouth. "You, Rae Everhart, are the most beautiful woman in the world, whether you're clean and fresh from a shower or sweaty and covered with sheep shit."

She glanced down at herself. "Please tell me I don't have sh—manure on me."

"You don't." I crooked a finger under her chin and compelled her to look up at me. "Why do you work so hard not to curse? If you want to do it, go on. I don't mind."

"Let go of me and I'll tell you."

I considered not letting go, since I enjoyed holding her body against mine, but I wanted to know the answer to my question. With a sigh, I unhanded her.

Rae took a step back and straightened her shirt. "I taught myself not to swear so I would set a good example for my daughter. If I have a foul mouth, how can I tell her not to swear? It's a necessity, not a hang-up." Her mouth twisted into a sardonic slant. "You should hear the things I say in my head."

"Love to hear them." I scratched my chin. "I understand why you watch your tongue around your daughter, but you and I are alone here. Curse like a sailor, I donnae care."

She glanced around as if checking for eavesdroppers.

"Afraid of corrupting the sheep with your foul language?" I asked.

"No, I…" She hunched her shoulders. "I've never slipped up before, like I keep doing when I'm around you. Almost swearing, barely catching myself." She wagged a finger at me, though her lips kinked into a saucy smile. "It's all your fault. You make me want to curse like a sailor."

"Hmm." I moved closer to cup her cheek. "You know I'm not easily offended. I curse all the time, in several languages. You have my permission to stop censoring yourself."

"Well, okay then." She straightened. "This bitch is going into the fucking house to have a goddamn snack. Are you joining me, asshole?"

I couldn't stop myself from laughing, louder than I had in a long while.

Rae laughed too, with more subtlety than I had. "Happy now?"

"Glad you stopped holding back. But I'm not certain 'asshole' is the label I want you to give me." I tapped the tip of her nose. "Something sexier would be my preference. With a keen mind like yours, I have no doubt you could talk dirty with the best of them."

"If I ever talk dirty, it will be with you. Only you."

Only me? I liked that. A good sign. The best sign yet.

Rae seemed to realize what she'd said, and she cleared her throat loudly, averting her eyes.

I tucked a stray lock of hair behind her ear. "I look forward to hearing everything you want to say to me."

"Didn't mean—Oh to hell with it. Think what you want." She whirled around and sauntered toward the house, glancing at me over her shoulder. "You coming?"

I trailed behind her, admiring her bonnie backside.

Fifteen minutes later, after consuming a snack of graham crackers with melted marshmallows and chocolate sandwiched between them, Rae and I moved into the hallway to go our separate ways. She had planned on going upstairs to her office, but the way she kept licking her lips suggested she wanted something else, something more decadent than the food we'd shared.

I skated a finger over her lower lip. "Wouldn't you rather relax on the sofa with me?"

Her eyes had gone soft, her voice too. "Maybe later."

She went upstairs, and I stretched out on the sofa to watch television. After a while, I called my cousin Lachlan, then my cousin Rory, and finally my friend Gavin. Rae stayed upstairs even as the sun sank lower in the sky, and I watched bearded men building log cabins on TV until I couldn't stand it anymore. I was about to run upstairs and throw Rae over my shoulder to get her out of her office when she came downstairs. Night had chased away the sun by the time we finished a late meal of hamburgers and potato crisps.

Rae surprised me by asking, "Is your offer to relax on the sofa still open?"

"For you, it's always open."

We settled onto the sofa side by side a few minutes later, but relaxing wasn't what either of us wanted. We kissed. Deeply and slowly. Groping and fondling. Rae wound up straddling my lap, and I wound up kneading her rump, hungry for everything her body offered.

I broke the kiss, lifting her off my lap to set her down beside me.

Her lids fluttered several times. She whisked her tongue over her lips, swollen from our ardor. "Why did you stop?"

"Because I'm on the edge here, Rae." I sat forward, my cock throbbing for her. "Unless you want to have sex here and now, I need to leave the room." I turned my head to look at her over my shoulder. "Are you ready?"

"I—don't know."

"Then I'll go." I rose and glanced down at her. "I'll be in the shower."

A very, very cold shower. Not that cold ever eased my lust, especially not for her. But at least the shower would give me time to recover from our passionate encounter.

I kissed the top of her head and stalked to the bathroom.

Rae

Ten minutes after Iain announced he was taking a shower, I gave up on TV and padded down the hall toward my bedroom. Might as well get some sleep—or try to. After what he'd done to me last night, and the way we'd made out on the sofa, I doubted sleep would welcome me with open arms tonight. If and when I did drift off, I had no doubts I'd dream of the naughty man sleeping upstairs.

Iain had asked if I was ready for sex. In that moment, I'd wanted him more than I had ever wanted any man, even more than I'd wanted him years ago. My body urged me to say yes, but my head insisted on staying calm and rational. Sort of. I hated my rational brain right now. Kissing Iain made me so hot and wet I longed to succumb to my lust. Just this once. Be reckless.

After changing into my nightie, I cracked my bedroom door open to check if Iain had left the bathroom yet. My teeth needed brushing. Yeah, that was the reason for my voyeurism. Not that I was hoping for a glimpse of Iain in the buff. The man loved to mosey around the house naked.

The bathroom door hung all the way open, and light spilled out across the wood floor in the hallway and the wall on the other side. I didn't hear the shower running, so maybe he'd forgotten to turn off the light.

I tiptoed to the bathroom door, turned, and froze.

My heart thudded. A delicious shiver swept through my body, tightening my nipples.

There he stood, drying his hair with a towel, eyes shut, completely nude.

I stopped breathing. The soft-white bulbs in the bathroom bathed his naked body in their warm glow, the light glistening on the droplets of water that clung to his skin. A bead rolled down his chest between his pecs, following the center of his torso down to the trail of hairs that pointed straight to his cock. The water droplet stalled there, glued to the hairs. His penis hung between his thighs, impressive even when not hardened by desire.

Yesterday, I'd seen Iain naked from behind. Only once before had I witnessed him nude from the front. The night we'd made love.

The night I'd realized how much I loved him.

Even as I let my gaze roam over the sight of Iain nude here in the present, my thoughts spiraled backward in time to that other night. It had been beautiful. Tender. Perfect. Or so I'd thought. Admiring him tonight—appreciating the new-and-improved version of Iain, with harder, more powerful muscles and an even hotter sensuality he exuded from every inch of his incredible body—I knew sex with him now would prove far more pleasurable than I could imagine.

And I could imagine a hell of a lot.

"You're staring at me like you want to be fucked."

His voice, that deep and erotic rumble, snapped my attention to his face. I couldn't have torn my gaze away from him if I'd wanted to, caught in a dual dilemma, ensnared by memories of our first and only night together and electrified by the sight of present-day Iain.

Something tickled my chest. I glanced down to discover my hand rested between my breasts and my fingers flittered over my thin nightie, teasing my skin with a feathery sensation. I cleared my throat, lowered my hand, and tried to appear unaffected by his nakedness. My mouth literally watered at the sight of him. Christ, I was too old to be drooling over him like a teenager.

"Well?" he said, smirking. "Do ye want to be fucked, *gràidh*?"

"Maybe I do, but I don't give in to every passing urge."

"Passing urge?" He chuckled, and the vibrations sent droplets drizzling down his chest. "You stare like that when I've got my clothes on too."

Yeah, I couldn't deny that, though my obsession with his body had skyrocketed into unabashed lust the second I spied him standing there, wet and naked. I could walk over there and lick every drop off his skin one by one, working my way down to that impressive cock.

"Now you're licking your lips like ye want to devour me," he said, his voice smokier to match the hunger on his face. "Ahm wanting to taste ye too."

"It's a b—" *Bad idea*, I'd meant to say, but I couldn't finish the sentence. For two and a half days, I'd told him repeatedly sex would be a bad idea. Faced with the very real possibility of us getting it on within the next thirty seconds, I could no longer deny how much I wanted this. With him. Only him.

His attention flew to my breasts, his lips parted, and he slid his tongue over his bottom lip. "Ahm starved for those wee nipples. If ye donnae come here, ahm going over there to suck on them."

I glanced down. My nipples poked through my nightie, so stiff the slightest movement glided the fabric over them with exciting effect. "I should go to bed."

"Yes, with me."

Our gazes intersected, pulled together as if magnetized to each other. With his hair damp and tousled, his body relaxed, he was the most tempting thing I'd ever laid eyes on.

He dropped the towel. It slumped to the floor. "What do you want, Rae?"

Good question. I couldn't claim to not know the answer. I wanted him. This was crazy and reckless, and I should not give in to the urge.

Why shouldn't you? a naughty little voice whispered in my mind. We were both adults, both free of commitments to anyone else. He would leave next Saturday. In the meantime, why shouldn't I take advantage of the chance to explore this attraction between us? I wouldn't fall in love with him. Just sex, nothing more. Purely grown-up fun to satisfy my curiosity. After one night, two or three at most, I'd get him out of my system.

After thirteen years apart, I hadn't gotten him out of my system.

"You've got about three seconds," Iain said, his voice rough with a need that made my body tingle in the most wonderful ways, "before I walk over there and show you what I want. Make up your mind."

The naughty part of me won the argument.

I sashayed across the bathroom and settled my palms on his damp chest. Angling my head back, I leaned in. "I want you."

"You're sure? Because I mean to take ye to the nearest bed and defile yer sweet body for the rest of the night."

"Defile away." I plastered my body to his, the wetness on his skin moistening my nightie and pasting it to my torso. "I'm sick of pretending I don't want this. I do. We're adults, and we can do whatever the hell we want."

I dragged one hand down his body, my fingers spread wide, relishing the way his breaths shortened and his chest began to heave. His dick swelled while I explored his body. My palm on his chest roved in slow circles while my other hand glided onto his thigh. I slid that hand to his inner thigh, careful to avoid his growing erection for the moment. I had plans for that glorious cock. It was thick and veined, curving up less than when he was younger but no less enticing.

"Rae…" He hissed in a breath when I took his sack in my hand and tugged. "Ah God, woman."

I dropped to my knees, his shaft in my face. A bead of moisture poised on the head, and I couldn't resist lapping it up. His choked groan encouraged me, so I dragged my tongue up his inner thigh, nipping along the way while I scraped the nails of my other hand down the inside of his other leg. I licked and cupped his balls until he groaned loudly and threw his head back. I'd grown so hot and slick, and my nipples had grown so stiff and achy, I couldn't wait a second longer.

With one hand, I gripped the base of his shaft and pumped slowly. His flesh was smooth except for those veins, and I closed my mouth around his head, buffering my teeth with my lips.

He thrust a hand into my hair, groaning loudly.

"Mmm," I moaned. "Gotta taste your cock, Iain. I want you to come in my mouth, and I can tell you want it too."

"Aye, but—"

He let out another choked sound as I took him into my mouth, sucking and licking while my other hand worked his shaft from the base. He gently rocked his hips toward me every time I took him deeper. I kneaded his inner thigh, then glided my hand up to scrape my nails through the hairs on his lower belly.

His hand in my hair tensed. His balls retracted, a sure sign he was close.

Iain stumbled backward a step, pulling his dick out of my mouth.

"What's wrong?" I asked, gazing up at him from my kneeling position.

"Get up," he growled. "If ye make me come, I'll have to wait to take ye, and I cannae wait a second longer."

I'd thought those exact words. He needed this as much as I did, and so I obeyed his command. I rose and shed my nightie, moving closer, our bodies inches apart. "Maybe next time you'll let me finish. I'd love to have your flavor in my mouth."

"Christ, Rae, I had no idea you're so…dirty."

"Not twenty-two anymore, remember?" I leaned in as close as possible without touching him. "You wanted me to talk dirty."

"And I love it." He pulled me snugly into his body and closed his other hand around my ass. "Still think I was overconfident to bring two boxes of condoms?"

"Not at all." I ducked my head to pinch his nipple with my teeth. "You were right, I want to be fucked. I need it. I need you inside me, that thick, hard cock filling me up and making me so wet for you."

"Yer wonderful, Rae."

His mouth descended on mine, his lips warm and soft. The kiss began tenderly, our lips exploring each other, but soon the kiss heated up until our tongues were tangling and our hands were groping. I plowed my fingers into his damp hair, twining my fingers in the locks to drag him closer, and made soft grunts every time he plunged his tongue deep. Both his hands grasped my ass, lifting up to elevate the heels of my bare feet off the floor.

A groan vibrated in his chest.

I swung a leg up to hook it around his hip.

He hefted me higher, encouraging me to raise my other leg, and I latched my ankles behind his taut ass. His arms whisked up to my back, clasping me to him, just as my arms wrapped around his neck with my hands still buried in his hair.

Iain rushed forward until my back slapped into the wall.

And we never stopped kissing.

Naked, mashed between his body and the wall, I threw my head back and rocked my hips into his erection. Its length rubbed along my cleft. Breathing hard, I glanced down and almost came right then and there. His shaft glistened with my juices, the tip red and peeking out between my folds. The sensation of his cock nestled against my sex rippled through me like a warm-up orgasm.

"Don't come yet," he hissed. "Not till ahm ready for ye to."

Another pulse of pleasure unfurled inside me. "Don't say things like that if you don't want me to go off. Probably shouldn't tell you this, but your over-confidence gets me so hot."

He growled. Like an animal. Like a beast about to ravage me. "Ahmno good at making love anymore. This may be rough and wild."

"Don't care." Panting, I clung to him, so close to the edge I couldn't stand it. "Hurry up, I can't take this much longer."

Iain set me down, crouched in front of me, and lifted one of my knees to hook it over his shoulder. "Donnae worry, ahmno the sort to leave a lass hanging."

His mouth kinked into the sexiest smirk I'd ever seen.

The wicked man slanted forward until his mouth hovered a breath away from my clitoris. He stretched out his tongue and lapped at the rigid nub, his pace leisurely but his movements infused with a purpose and determination that jacked up my arousal to the point of pain. The instant he closed his mouth around my clit, I came with a strangled whimper. My back flattened into the wall as my body went rigid, every muscle frozen except for the ones pulsating inside me. The feel of every spasm inside my empty womb made me crave him even more, despite the fantastic release he'd given me.

He kept suckling me, licking me, until at last I fell limp against the wall, gasping for air, held up by my leg slung over his shoulder.

"Sorry," I said. "Couldn't stop it."

"Donnae be sorry." He eased my knee off his shoulder and rose, locking his arms around my waist. "I wanted ye to come under my mouth. And ahm…awestruck by yer passion."

"Awestruck? Oh come on. Don't feed me cheesy lines."

"No cheese, and it's not a line." He scooped me up in his arms. "It's the truth."

I linked my hands at his nape, feeling a bit awestruck myself. He meant everything he said. Iain would not lie to me.

Did that mean I trusted him?

He carried me down the hall to my bedroom, and I knew one thing for certain. I wouldn't have time to think about anything because this man was about to ravish me for hours and hours.

Chapter Twelve

Iain

As I lay her down on the bed, amid the covers she'd already pulled back, I marveled at this sudden turn of events. I'd hoped to have her soon, but she kept telling me it was a bad idea. If I'd known all I had to do was take a shower and leave the door open, I would've done it two nights ago. This was better, though. She'd made the decision. I hadn't pushed her to want this. She wanted it because she wanted me.

I climbed onto the bed and dropped to my knees at the foot, sitting back on my heels to admire the vision before me. Rae was more than beautiful, she was a goddess incarnate. Though she had stretch marks on her belly, no doubt from pregnancy, her imperfections only made her more beautiful. They spoke to her life experience, her maturity, and the fact she'd raised a child on her own.

"You're staring at my stretch marks," she said, "like they're the most fascinating thing you've ever seen. Most men try not to look at them."

"*Mon trésor*, you've no reason to be ashamed. I appreciate the way a woman's body changes with age and experience."

"Not ashamed. I've never felt bad about my body." She squinted at me. "Did you call me your treasure in French?"

"I did." I bent over her to skim my fingers over the longest stretch mark, then traced the line with my tongue. "Learned French from a fiery mademoiselle who happened to be an archaeologist. We dug up medieval bones in the daytime and enjoyed the pleasures of the flesh at night."

Rae squinted at me harder. "Do you really want to talk about your ex-bedmates while we're naked in bed together?"

She was right. What the hell had I been thinking?

On all fours, I crawled up her body until my face hovered above hers. "No more talk of anyone but you."

"And you."

"Naturally." I settled my body on top of hers. "You can say dirty things anytime you like."

"Mm, I'll keep that in mind."

I glided a hand down her side to her hip. With her soft curves pressed against me, I couldn't help sighing with contentment and wondering if I did remember how to make love—to her. "You are even more luscious than I remembered, and a fair sight naughtier. I love your body, your passion, your maturity. I love you, Rae."

"Please don't say that." She wriggled, pinched her face, and cleared her throat. "Are we going to have sex or have a heart to heart with you squishing me?"

"*Merde*," I hissed, and pushed up to kneel astride her thighs. "Didnae think—Are ye hurt?"

Her eyebrows lifted while her lips twitched like she was struggling not to smile. "I know *merde* is French for shit, but that's not exactly the dirty talk I was hoping for. And no, you did not hurt me." She folded her arms over her breasts. "You haven't answered my question."

Question? What had she asked me? Crouched here, drinking in the vision of Rae's glorious body spread out before me, I had trouble concentrating on anything she'd said since she announced I was "squishing" her.

Ahhh, the question. It came back to me in a flash.

I bent to capture one of her nipples between my teeth, lashing my tongue across it until she gasped. I released the taut peak. "We're fucking."

"Get on with it, then." She spread her thighs. "You led me to believe there'd be mind-blowing sex."

"I never mislead a woman."

The blatant invitation of her open thighs beckoned me, but I wouldn't rush the first time I'd been with her in thirteen years. I lay down on my side, nestled against her body, my head beside hers. She huffed her irritation. I chuckled. Her impatience was endearing, and I planned on taking advantage of it.

"We can't do it like this," she said.

"Hush, *mo gràidh*, we have all night."

She started to complain, but I covered one breast with my hand, kneading it and flicking my thumb over the stiff, dusky peak. Her body was perfect, to me. I'd loved her when she was twenty-two, but I could love this mature version of her so much more. Rae was my sunshine, the light that banished the darkness. I would worship her all night and pay tribute to the woman who made me forget the things I'd done.

I ran my tongue over a stretch mark on her breast, then laved another one on her belly, all the while fondling her breast. Her breaths grew heavier, and the scent of her desire tantalized me. Though I'd gorged on her intoxicating flavor only moments ago, I burned to do it again.

Time to take advantage of her impatience.

"*Ma chérie*," I murmured against her belly, moving my mouth lower with each word, "you're sweet and warm and the most decadent dessert a man could devour."

"Cut the cute foreign endearments and do something. Do me, you infuriating Scot."

Her last word ended on a gasp when I pulled her clitoris into my mouth. Bent at the waist, I had my chin on her mound and my forehead between her thighs. She opened her legs more, bending her knees, rocking her hips up each time I suckled her taut bud. I stretched my arms out to loop them under her thighs and ease them up, her knees above my head.

"This is an odd position," she said, "but I like—oh God."

A moan transformed those two syllables into an expression of pure pleasure. She thrust her fingers into my hair, clenching it tight. Her breaths had shortened into pants, and she grew slicker every second. I moved my hands under her hips to raise them slightly, just enough so I could lap up more of her cream. She gasped and moaned, her nails scraping my scalp. I nipped her clit, slaked my thirst for her with long, languorous strokes of my tongue along her folds, and suckled her bud until her whole body went rigid.

I sat up.

She tried to scowl at me, but she couldn't manage it while teetering on the edge of orgasm. Instead, she slapped my chest. "Why the hell did you stop?"

"That was enough for me." I feigned a yawn. "Good night, Rae."

"What?" She gawped at me for a second or two, then her eyes narrowed, and she clasped my cock in her hand. "You are so full of *merde*."

"I'd almost forgotten you studied French."

"You can fool me with German and Gaelic, but I'm wise to your *français*." She stroked my cock, her hold firm and her skin soft. "Sex, Iain, now. Your dick. Inside me. *Comprende*?"

I hissed in a breath when she ran her thumb over the tip of my cock. "Understood. If you know any dirty French, use it now."

"Sorry, they didn't teach us that at Nackington."

Rae released me and lay back on the bed, arms above her head. The position lifted her breasts enough to make me groan. She was taking advantage of my need now, tempting me into giving her exactly what she wanted. Despite her claims that sex was a bad idea, she had no shame when we got down to it.

Her gaze wandered to my erection. "Do I need to take you in hand again to get you motivated?"

"No, I'm fair crazed with motivation." A quick glance at my naked cock jolted a realization through me. "*Verdammt nochmal.* I wasn't expecting this. Don't have a condom."

"Ver-what?"

"It's German for dammit. *Verdammt nochmal.*"

I jumped off the bed.

"Wait," she said, pushing up on her elbows. "Don't worry about it. I'm on the pill."

She wasn't thinking clearly thanks to the way I'd tortured her with a near orgasm.

I shook my head. "I always use a condom. Always, even if the woman is taking birth control pills."

Rae made an odd face, biting down on her lower lip. She had seemed about to speak but silenced herself.

"Something wrong?" I asked.

"No, nothing," she said a bit too quickly. "Go get your condom but hurry the hell up."

I ran upstairs, taking the steps three at a time, retrieved a box of condoms from my bag, and rushed headlong down the stairs again. I arrived in Rae's bedroom out of breath and tripped over the rug that encompassed the bed, biting out a mangled curse in German. I caught myself before I tumbled into the bed headfirst.

"Jeez," she said, "I didn't mean you had to give yourself a heart attack. Sounded like a herd of elephants stampeding through the house."

I held up the condom box. "Got it."

"Uh-huh. Better take a minute to catch your breath and your equilibrium." She lay back again, her arms over her head, and raised one knee to grant me a full view of her pink, glistening flesh. "But don't take too long. You owe me an orgasm, Dr. MacTaggart."

"So I do."

I tore open the condom box, ripped a packet open, and covered myself as fast as possible without tearing the condom. Tossing the box away, I knelt on the bed at her feet. She writhed like a feline soaking up the sun, catching her lip between her teeth and releasing it slowly. *Bod an Donais*, she was... everything. The sun, the air, the sky, the moon, the ground beneath my feet, the oxygen that filled my lungs. I would've spoken all those words to her, not giving a damn if she thought I was a fool, except I couldn't speak. Couldn't think anymore when she arched her back, elevating her bonnie breasts.

"Cannae do slow and tender," I said, "not when I've been wanting ye for so long."

"Told you, I don't care how you do it." She writhed again in that feline way. "Fuck me, Iain."

A string of curses in various languages spilled from my lips. I walked forward on my knees, lifted her legs, and knelt between them. She bent her knees to hook them over my shoulders as if she'd read my mind and knew what I intended to do with her. I slapped my palms on the bed at either side of her body. She clenched the pillow under her head, her lips parted, her pink tongue sliding along the bottoms of her upper teeth. We'd both stopped breathing, the anticipation an electrical current in the air, crackling between us.

I drove into her.

Chapter Thirteen

Rae

I gripped his arms, hanging on while he thrust into me again and again, each stroke powerful and all-consuming. His biceps bulged with his movements, and he grunted every time he plowed into me. My back bowed up with each thrust, my neck too, and my mouth fell open on whispering moans. He filled me up, stretched my body in ways that made me crave even more of him. I'd grown so wet we made sucking sounds as our bodies merged and separated. My moans turned sharp and short along with my panting breaths, my breasts bounced whenever he punched into me, and my nails dug into his arms, but it was the look on his face that made me wild with the need to come, to feel his cock inside me when I hit that peak and plummeted off the cliff.

His face. God, he looked at me like he'd die if he couldn't stay inside me forever. Though sexual hunger tightened his features, giving him a pained look, a different kind of need softened it. Something I didn't dare examine too closely. I tried not to, really I did. But then he spoke.

"I love you, Rae," he said, his voice rough, his words punctuated by sharp exhalations and the slapping of our bodies. "Yer the only one fer me, the only one. I need ye, Christ, I need ye."

"You're supposed to—oh God—talk dirty. Mm, uh, Iain, please." What was I doing? I never, ever talked during sex. Never. Tonight, I couldn't stop the words from pouring out of me between gasps and moans. "Don't stop, I—oh yes, God, yes."

He shifted his hands to either side of my shoulders, forcing my knees closer to my face. With a feral growl, he accelerated the pace, pistoning into me so hard and with such ferocity the headboard knocked against the wall and the bedframe squeaked. I clenched his arms tight enough it must've hurt, but he seemed not to notice anything except me. He nailed his gaze to mine, that odd tenderness morphing into an expression of near awe as my body tensed and I stopped breathing, paralyzed with my mouth open on a silent cry.

The breath locked in my lungs exploded out on a whimper. My body convulsed around his cock, and just when I thought my climax would subside, he captured my mouth and plunged his tongue deep, and I came harder. He swallowed the strangled cry that erupted out of me, devouring my mouth while his shaft consumed my sex. The muscles inside me milked him with a strength I'd never experienced before, and he grunted into my mouth, still pounding into me.

When he ripped his mouth away, I threw my head back and shouted wordlessly, until one coherent word spilled from my lips.

"Iain!"

His entire body stiff, he lunged into me with one punishing thrust and erupted inside me. He roared and thrust again, twice, three times, before he went still above me, gasping for air. Sweat beaded on his forehead, a drop trickling down his temple to fall onto my chest. His shaft lingered inside me, still slightly firm. He shrugged one shoulder, then the other, to let my legs fall away from him.

I lay there, my legs straddling him, in shock from what we'd done. Iain had never taken me like that before. But me...holy shit, I'd made noise. I'd shouted. I'd virtually screamed his name. The last time we'd been together, the only time before tonight, I had moaned and gasped but nothing else. He had made love to me slowly and tenderly that night, several times, but it had been nothing like this. We'd both turned into rutting animals.

And I'd loved it.

No man had ever touched me the way he did or pushed me to the highest peaks of pleasure. No one else could make me feel so...decadent and wild. But always, he made me feel cherished. *Mon trésor*, he'd called me. His treasure. God, he made me feel that way.

Iain pulled out of my body, divesting himself of the condom. He lay on his side next to me, one hand on my belly, and kissed me with an aching sweetness.

"Wow," I said, "you didn't do it like that before. Rough and wild, like you said."

"Thirteen years has changed us both." He fanned his fingers over my belly. "How do you feel about this version of me?"

"I like it. Couldn't you tell? I've never made that much noise for anybody else."

"My fault. I denied you an orgasm, which made you crazed with lust." He kissed my breast. "Do you forgive me?"

"Forgive you?" I exhaled a throaty, breathy laugh. "I loved everything you did to me. Everything. You gave me the best orgasm ever. I should be down on my knees offering thanks and worshiping you in any way you want."

He arched a brow. "*Any* way I want?"

"Yes, anything." I tunneled my fingers into his hair, pulling his face closer. "So, if you'd like me to finish what I started in the bathroom…"

"Not sure I could be, ah, up for it anytime soon."

"I can help with that." I pushed against his chest. "On your back, Dr. MacT, Professor of Fuckology."

One side of his mouth kinked upward. He rolled onto his back and linked his hands under his head.

I climbed astride him with my knees at either side of his thighs. His cock had softened but wasn't quite flaccid. I took it between my palms and stroked up and down his length.

A breath gusted out of him.

"Getting stiffer already," I said, and moved one hand to massage his inner thigh while my other hand worked his shaft. "Want me to suck your dick?"

He choked on a laugh. "Never dreamed I'd hear those words come out of your mouth."

"Not twenty-two anymore, Iain." I dragged my thumb over the slit on the underside of his head. When he hissed in a breath, I smiled. "You're at my mercy."

"I am." He thumped his fists down on the bed, grunting each time I frisked my hand up and down his length. "Have a little mercy, sunshine. Ahm only a man."

"Are you saying women can handle orgasm denial, but men can't?" I flicked my thumb over his cock's tip. "That would mean women are tougher."

He'd gone hard again, so I gave his balls a swift tug.

"Christ, woman," he growled. "Yer turning me into a bampot."

"A what?"

"Lunatic." A breath burst out of him when I bent to rake my tongue over the tip of his penis. "Yer driving me mad."

"Good. I like you off balance." I scooted backward and ducked my head to take him into my mouth. With one hand, I gripped the base of his shaft. I balanced myself with the other hand on his thigh as I licked and sucked, whisking my mouth up and down his erection.

He grunted and gasped, his hands fisting in the sheets, his teeth gritted.

My breasts grazed his thighs while I worked him, making my nipples go hard.

"Rae!" he shouted at the instant he came in my mouth.

Once his cock had pulsed for the last time, I sat up and wiped my mouth. "I love doing that to you."

Chest heaving, he managed only a lopsided half grin. "You did it *for* me, *mein Liebling*. For me."

"You make it sound like I did you a huge favor."

He held out a hand, beckoning me to him with wriggling fingers.

I waddled forward and stretched out atop his warm, firm body with my chin on his chest, my hands folded under my chin.

"You did do me a favor," he said, caressing my hair with one hand. "No other woman has given me that gift with such enthusiasm."

"I enjoyed it too." For about a second, I debated whether to share another small secret with him. What the heck. "I wanted to do that to you the first time around. I even sort of...researched it."

"Researched it?"

"Yeah, not long after we met. I was completely smitten with you and hoped we'd have sex sometime very soon." I sighed with mock wistfulness. "But I had no idea you'd take so damn long to seduce me. In the meantime, I read all the sex ed books in the Nackington library and bought raunchier ones over the Internet. When we finally had sex, I was too nervous to try any of the things I'd learned about, especially oral sex."

He clasped his hands over my back. "Did you try it with the men you've been with since?"

"A few times, but I didn't enjoy it. And they never reciprocated."

"You mean you gifted them with bloody fantastic blow jobs and they refused to go down on you in return."

"Exactly."

He made a disgusted noise. "Eejits. They had a bonnie, sensual, amazing woman in their arms and let her slip away."

"You should thank them. If I'd married one of those guys, we wouldn't be here together."

"We would." He whisked his hands down to my bottom. "I would've seduced you away from whatever prat you'd married."

"Hmm." I eyed him with mock suspicion. "You would seduce a married woman? I don't believe it."

The upward curve of his lips flattened out, and the lighthearted tone of our banter abruptly shifted into somber territory. "Your faith in my moral character is misplaced."

Like a hammer slammed down on my head, his statement left me stunned and confused. I stared at him for a moment, struggling to sort out what had happened. Flirtatious banter. Quips about my former lovers. He joked about luring me away from another man, and I joked about him seducing married women. Now, he told me in a grim voice I shouldn't have faith in his "moral character."

I pushed up on my elbows to gaze down at him, searching his stoic face. "Why do you keep hinting you're a bad person?"

"Because I am. They may have called me the Notorious Dr. MacT at Nackington, but I earned the title after I left you. I am not a good man."

Frowning, I kept studying his face but saw no clues to guide me. "That's bullshit. You're the best man I've ever known."

He winced ever so faintly. His hands fell away from my body. "No, Rae, I'm not."

I rolled off him and sat up. "Explain, Iain. A little mystery can be sexy, but this enigma does not fall into that category. We're sleeping together, and you're determined to make me love you again. I need the facts. I deserve that much."

He pushed up into a sitting position, groaning, and swung his legs off the bed. His feet on the floor, his back to me, he slumped forward and grasped the bed's edge. "May I ask you a question first?"

"Okay."

"How many men have you been with in your life?"

"My whole life? Eight." I inched a little closer but stopped short of reaching out to touch him, unsure if he would want me to. While I answered his question, I focused on the back of his head. "Two guys before you, my high school boyfriend and another one sophomore year of college. Five more after you including Grayson Parker, the idiot taxi driver, last year."

"My lovers have been...more numerous."

Okay, where was he going with this? "You're fifteen years older than I am. I didn't expect you were a monk before you met me, or for all the years since."

He groaned again, his head drooping. "You don't understand. The number is...significant."

The number of what? His lovers? I scooted even closer, moving to the side in hopes of catching a glimpse of his expression. It gave nothing away. What was he trying to tell me? He'd been with a lot of women? Fine, I could deal with that. He was, as I'd pointed out, much older than I was. I expected he'd had more than eight lovers in his life.

When he stayed silent for a minute, maybe longer, I had no choice. I had to ask. "Okay, how many women have you slept with?"

He mumbled something.

I shimmied on the bed until I sat cross-legged behind and to the right of him. "Iain, just tell me. How many? Twenty?"

He coughed into his fist. "More."

"Thirty?"

A shake of his head. He pointed one finger toward the ceiling.

"More?" I asked. "Come on, stop making me guess."

He rubbed his neck, scrunching his whole face. "A hundred, give or take."

"Give or take what? Another hundred?"

"No." He flashed me an irritated look. "Not another hundred."

I'd told myself I could handle whatever number he threw at me, yet his response had smacked into my psyche like the impact of an eighteen-wheeler. He was a man. A fifty-year-old man. An intensely sexual fifty-year-old man. If he'd started having sex as a teenager, a hundred women in thirty years or so wasn't all that shocking.

Why, then, was I sitting here mute and slack-jawed?

"Um," I began, striving for a calm tone, "a hundred in your whole life doesn't sound all that...excessive."

He stared straight ahead at the wall. "Most of those women were in the past thirteen years."

"I don't care. Why does it bother you?"

"Doesn't bother me." He peeked at me out the corner of his eye. "I assumed it would bother you. One day, I hope to take you home to meet my family—and my reputation there will be hard to ignore."

My initial shock had faded, replaced by a mild confusion. "Did you sleep with married women?"

"Only one, and she came to me. Her husband was neglectful to say the least. Even I wouldn't seduce a woman who belongs to someone else."

I grunted. "Stop trying to make me dislike you. It's damn confusing since you've spent three days trying to get me into bed and telling me you need me, you want me back."

"Rae, I do need you and want you. What I'm trying to say is I've made terrible mistakes in my life. Many mistakes." He bowed his head, scratching the back of it. "The worst ones didn't involve women."

"What does that mean?"

"Let's not talk about this anymore tonight." He raised his head, shutting his eyes for a moment. When he met my gaze again, he seemed to have set aside his angst. "I'll explain one day, I promise. One day soon. Just not tonight."

"Okay."

"You don't mind waiting for a fuller explanation?"

"No, I can wait. Everyone makes mistakes. So you're not perfect, neither am I." Far from it. I'd slept with him, let him say he loved me, and still I hadn't told him about Malina. Maybe I should tell him, but after his confession, tonight didn't seem like the time. Or maybe I was a coward.

Iain turned toward me partway. "I'd rather not talk about the worst mistakes, but I think I should tell you more about my sexual history. How much do you want to know?"

Good question. If this was sex, nothing more, then I didn't need to hear about his conquests. I kept insisting he had to leave next weekend, but I couldn't deny I'd developed a fondness for him. Sure, I'd grown fond of him only in the past few days. *Ugh*. I'd fallen for him thirteen years ago, fallen hard, and those old feelings kept sneaking back into my heart. Try as I might to ignore it, to pretend I could screw him and say goodbye, I had to be pragmatic about this. Since I felt...something for him, I ought to know the details about his past. He wouldn't tell me the physical details, I was sure of that. Good thing, because I really did not need to hear about all the ways he'd pleasured other women.

I sat up straighter, hands on my knees. "Tell me everything."

Chapter Fourteen

Iain

How had this happened? I sat naked on Rae's bed with her huddled naked beside me, discussing my less-than-admirable past with women. Moments ago, I'd given her pleasure. We'd forged a new bond, deeper and more meaningful than anything we'd had before. She trusted me with her body, which for most women meant she trusted me, full stop. Instead of basking in the afterglow of our first time together in thirteen years, I was struggling to explain why I'd shagged so many women.

Now, she wanted to know "everything."

I had no one to blame but myself. When I'd offered to tell her about my sexual history, I'd assumed she wouldn't want to know. No other woman, not even my ex-wife, had wanted to hear about other women. Rae surprised me at every turn.

She laid a hand on my arm. "I don't want to know the sexual details. I want to know about you. Were you sleeping around before we met? While we were together?"

"Neither." Resigned to my fate, I met her gaze. "Once upon a time, I was a perfect gentleman. I got to know a woman before I slept with her, and frankly, I didn't date much. My work consumed me, or rather, my need to use my work as an excuse to escape my home consumed me."

"Why would you need to escape?"

"That's another, much longer story." A sigh groaned out of me. Talking about my father wasn't the sort of mood I wanted tonight, but then, neither was talking about my ex-lovers. "I'd been with ten women before you. The moment I met you, I lost all interest in other women. When I lost you, I tried to pretend I was fine. Then my da got in trouble again and sorting out his mess compounded the strain until I cracked. Not proud of it, always thought I was stronger than that, but apparently, I'm weak. I gave in to the grief and self-loathing." I scrubbed my face with both hands. "I became an expert in self-destruction."

"I don't understand."

How could she? I still couldn't fathom why I'd done the things I'd done.

"Drowning my sorrows became my favorite pastime," I said. "Tried drink, but after several experiences with getting drunk at the local pub and getting into brawls, I gave up that method. Drugs never appealed to me, and I couldn't drown myself in work since I was unemployed. The only thing I could think of that might numb me for a while was sex. Turns out lasses love a man who acts like he doesn't give a shit about anything and seduces them with assurances the liaison will lead nowhere. I didn't care where we did it. Alleys, car parks, back rooms of shops, wherever. Quieting my conscience was all that mattered, and sex is excellent for eradicating thoughts."

She said nothing. Her face betrayed no hint of her feelings about what I'd confessed. Still in shock, no doubt. I'd been callous and selfish. Maybe I should've stayed away from her, but I'd pinned my hopes of redemption on earning the right to a future with her.

Rae had a child. How could she introduce her daughter to a man like me? If she knew about my other mistakes, the ones far more scandalous than enjoying a good poke with a willing woman, what would she do?

I'd fought too hard to recover from my mistakes, to become a man worthy of a woman like Rae. I couldn't give up now. I'd stay until she chased me out of the country.

She chewed the inside of her lip. "Do you still sleep around?"

"No, not like I did then. I've been with plenty of women, but only one in the past five years."

"Were you, um, dating these women?"

I'd never been ashamed of my past until I found Rae again. Whatever the locals at home thought of me didn't matter. Her opinion meant everything. If she couldn't make peace with my past, we had no future together.

"Some of them I dated," I said, "briefly. Most were flings. I married one."

"You mentioned that before. Said it was a mistake."

"It was." A sudden weariness overtook me, and I dropped back onto the bed, jostling it. Lying there, I stared at the tiny acoustic balls on the ceiling. "Julia was a sweet lass, but I had no right to marry her when I was still in love with you. I tried to be a good husband, tried to love her, but I failed. I cared for her, but not the way a husband should. We were married for three years but separated for all but seven months. She left me after I said your name during sex."

Rae winced. "Ouch."

All rights to sympathy in the matter belonged to Julia, as it should be. I'd entered into a marriage, promising to love and honor her, all the while knowing I could never follow through on those vows. No woman could fill the hole left behind by the only one I'd ever loved. Expecting Julia to save me from my own past had been unfair, to say the least.

"At first," I said, "Julia thought I was gay and shouting the man's name Ray. I told her the truth, but I think she would've preferred to keep thinking I liked men."

"I can see how that might be easier for her to handle. At least then she wouldn't have been rejected for not being good enough."

"She was good enough. The perfect wife." I glared at those confounded balls on the ceiling. "I was the unworthy one. The bastard who made false vows."

"You didn't lie, Iain. You made a mistake."

I cast her a sidelong glance. "Shouldn't you take my ex-wife's side? Female solidarity and whatnot?"

"Who says I'm not on her side?" Rae lay down facing me, her head propped up with one hand. "I see both viewpoints, that's all. And I know you. Whatever mistakes you've made, I will never believe you treated women callously. You wanted to love your wife and make those vows true. I believe you tried the best you could."

Her words penetrated my thick skull, and I couldn't help smiling. "You said you believe in me."

She seemed surprised for a moment, then shrugged. "Yeah, I guess I did say that."

Hooking a finger under her chin, I encouraged her to look at me. "Why does that fash you?"

"Fash means bother, right?"

"Yes."

"It doesn't fash me," she said. "I surprised myself, that's all. Hadn't realized I do believe in you, in the kind of man I know you are. Whatever you might've done in the past doesn't matter anymore. Maybe I would've bedhopped to drown my pain if I hadn't had other problems to worry about."

"Do you want to tell me about them?" I couldn't demand she open up to me, not after the way I'd left her.

She averted her gaze to the sheets, her fingers picking at the fabric. "I'm not quite ready to share everything yet. Is that okay?"

I cradled her face in my palm. "Of course it is. You have no obligation to tell me anything. I shared my story with you because you deserve to know."

"Thank you for understanding. And for sharing."

"Your reaction wasn't what I expected." I ran my thumb over her lips. "Maybe I don't deserve your forgiveness, but I won't reject it."

"Forgiveness?" She straightened her arm, pushing up into a semi-sitting position. "I haven't forgiven you because you've done nothing that needs forgiving. Whatever you did with other women in the past thirteen years is between you and them. It's got nothing to do with you and me."

"Doesn't it bother you? The way I've treated other women?"

"Have you forced yourself on women?"

"Of course not."

"Did you lie to them to get them in bed? Promise a rosy future? Claim you loved them?"

I huffed out a breath. "None of the above. I always made it clear we had no future, it was just sex."

"The way I see it," she said, "the only questionable thing you've done is sleeping with a married woman. But if she made the first move, I guess it's not so awful."

I experienced a twinge of guilt at her tacit forgiveness of my liaison with a married woman. Maybe I had allowed myself to be seduced by another man's wife, but I'd misled Rae about the extent of that involvement. It had been more than one night, though nothing close to a relationship. Should I tell Rae that?

Not yet. I'd told her about my bad behavior and confessing that bit might ruin what we found tonight, here in this bed. I would share the rest later.

Hosenscheisser. That's what you are, MacTaggart, a ruddy coward.

"Stop worrying," she said. "I'm okay with knowing the truth about your notorious past. You weren't a lothario who seduced hapless women into cheating on their husbands by whatever means necessary."

"I wish you wouldn't make excuses for me."

"Not excuses. I understand your pain because I went through it too." She painted wandering lines on my chest with her finger. "What happened to us back then, it was devastating. We handled the trauma in different ways. I won't judge you for the methods you chose, and I hope you won't judge me for mine."

Just as I wondered what she meant about me not judging her and considered asking what she meant, she let out a big yawn.

I sat up. "Time for sleep. I've exhausted you with sex and revelations."

She smiled. "Sex with you is a revelation."

Her statement stopped me for a moment, and I had no idea how to respond. After all her claims she would never sleep with me, she had. After all her claims she wouldn't care for me, she clearly did. And after everything I'd told her tonight, she still wanted me.

Christ, I had to tell her the truth.

I scratched my head and cleared my throat. "About the married woman I slept with. It was, ah, more than one time."

"Okay," she said cautiously. "How many times?"

Since I couldn't look at her, I focused on the dresser positioned against the wall. "Off and on for five years."

"Five years? You said you didn't have relationships with most of these women, except for your ex-wife. You made it sound like you casually dated a few of them and the rest were flings." She prodded my hip. "Having sex with one woman for five years is a relationship."

"It wasn't. Delyth wanted a lover to occupy her time while her husband was away on business, which was often."

"Uh-huh. Was this screw-and-run sex, or did you have conversations too?"

"We talked, but it wasn't meaningful conversation." When I twisted toward Rae, her sharp gaze made me uneasy. I wished to bleeding hell she'd give up this line of questioning. "You're making too much of it. That part of my life ended, so it doesn't matter."

"You're not sleeping with her anymore."

"No."

Rae shut her eyes and sighed, her bunched shoulders slackening. "All right, fine. Your past is your business, and it's not my place to criticize. I'd say we need to be totally honest with each other, but that would be hypocritical since there are things I'm not going to tell you."

"I will be honest with you, always. And when you're ready, you'll be honest with me."

"You don't have to be so reasonable all the time."

"Wasn't reasonable when I wanted to batter your friend Ben." I caught one of her fingers and lunged my head forward to pull it into my mouth, releasing it slowly. "You can tell me anything. I won't judge your past."

"My past isn't as wild as yours. But I will tell you more, eventually."

We settled into bed again, her cheek on my shoulder, her voluptuous body molded to my side. I curled an arm around her, relishing the normalcy of this moment. After years of believing I could never have her again, here I was lying in bed with Rae in my arms. When I told her about my other mistakes, I might lose this. But for now, I would enjoy it.

"Good night, Iain," she murmured, her voice already sleepy.

I kissed the top of her head. "Good night, sunshine."

Chapter Fifteen

Rae

I woke in the morning cocooned in Iain MacTaggart's body. We lay on our sides, Iain behind me with one of his muscular arms under my neck, supporting it like the best neck rest ever. His other arm draped over my belly, those long fingers grazing my skin every time I inhaled. His breaths ruffled my hair, and his hips molded to my body while one of his legs had sneaked between mine.

What a wonderful way to wake up.

Snuggling deeper against him, I kept my eyes closed and let myself revel in this feeling. It was even better than the first time we'd spent the night together, so many years ago. We had both matured and changed—in good ways, I thought, despite Iain's claims he was a bad man. How could anyone who held me like this be anything but good?

I laid my hand over Iain's on my belly, loving the solidity of him. This was no fantasy. He was here. Last night, when he'd promised to be honest with me, I'd wanted to promise the same in return. I had suffered an almost overpowering impulse to confess everything to him right then and there. Maybe I should have, but I couldn't form the words. *Guess what, Iain, you have a daughter.* Too blunt, for sure. *Hey, remember that other night when we had sex? Well, you weren't as careful about using a condom as you think.* Too obtuse. When I told him, if I told him, I'd have to be direct but somehow soften the blow.

Piece of cake. If the cake was filled with iron filings.

Guilt sucked.

Iain stirred, sighing into my hair. *"Guten Morgen, mein Liebling."*

"Does that mean good morning?"

"The full translation is 'good morning, my darling', and yes, it's German."

Since his body entangled with mine prevented me from rolling over, I squirmed until I lay on my back, his hand still on my belly. "You said the same thing the morning after that other night."

"I know." He pressed his lips to mine for a sweet, lingering kiss. "Let's take a shower together."

Clucking my tongue, I wagged a finger at him. "If we get in the shower together, we won't be getting clean. I need to get out there and do my morning chores, and I'm positive you'll delay me."

"Mmm." He nuzzled my neck. "That is my plan. You work too hard."

"Out of necessity. Animals don't understand the concept of vacation days."

"I promise not to delay you more than half an hour." He slid his hand down to my groin, cupping me intimately. "Give in. We both know you want to."

How on earth could I resist him? I'd never had any luck with that. The man was like chocolate-flavored opium. Not that I'd ever done drugs, but I imagined the high he gave me wasn't dissimilar. Orgasms delivered by Iain MacTaggart were highly addictive.

The sheep and my llama grazed for their food, and the horses wouldn't starve in the next half hour. I'd give them extra munchies to make up for the wait.

Oh, I couldn't.

He pressed his palm into my mound more and slipped his middle finger between my folds.

I moaned, instinctively rolling my hips into his touch.

"You win," I said, ending the statement with a gasp when he swirled his fingertip around my clit. "Let's take a shower."

He kissed my throat. "Wise choice."

"Because you wouldn't give up until I said yes. You are unbelievably stubborn."

"So are you." He shoved his hand between my thighs, grinding the heel into my clitoris and diving two fingers inside me. "Christ, you're so wet already. Did you wake up like this?"

"It's your fault. I had the most erotic dreams of my life last night."

"Ye need a release, then." He rubbed his growing erection against my hip. "Cannae wait for the shower."

"Me neither." I let out a long, guttural moan when he began pumping those fingers inside me.

He pushed an arm under me and flipped onto his back, taking me with him.

Sprawled on top of him, I writhed against his hand while those fingers kept up the delicious torture. I burned to feel him inside me—not his fingers, but his hard cock.

"Uh-uh," I said, sitting up and sliding off his body. "It's my turn."

He threw his arms wide. "Go on, then. My body is yours."

A hot tingle swept through my entire body, stiffening my already pebbled nipples. Having my way with Iain turned me on big time.

I flapped a hand in a *move your ass* gesture. "Get up."

Without questioning me, and with a slight smirk kinking his mouth, he pushed up into a sitting position.

"Against the headboard," I said, "please."

"Demanding and polite?" His smirk broadened into a grin as he shimmied backward to sit with his back against the headboard. "I like the new, improved Rae. Confidence turns me on, but your combination of sweetness and command is the sexiest thing on earth."

"Thank you." I leaned way over to snag a condom from the box he'd discarded on the floor last night. On my knees, I walked to him and straddled his lap, reaching down to pull his stiff cock up between our bodies. I rubbed my thumb over the damp head. "Damn, Iain, you're hard as stone."

"Entirely your fault, *gràidh*."

I tore open the condom packet and rolled it onto his shaft. Tossing the foil away, I gave his dick a long, slow stroke. When he hissed in a breath, teeth clenched, I said, "Maybe I should take it slow. Tease you first, the way you like to tease me."

"You can handle it." He grimaced when I stroked him again. "I'll *caith* before I'm inside you if you try teasing me."

"So, you *are* admitting women are tougher than men."

"Aye, if that'll get you to fuck me."

I rose onto my knees, laying my hands on his shoulders. "Is the notorious Iain MacTaggart begging me to do him?"

"Yes." He gripped my hips and bent his head back to hit me with a scorching look. "Please, Rae."

His voice was rough and sultry, like dark honey warmed by the sun.

I took hold of his cock, positioned my body, and impaled myself on him.

We both gasped. His hands tightened on my hips, and I gripped his shoulders harder. My breasts heaved with each breath I struggled to take, drawing Iain's attention to them.

He lunged his head down to swallow one rigid peak.

I threw my head back and rode him. Slowly at first, relishing the sensation of him filling me up and the weight of his hands on my hips. My breaths shortened. My pulse quickened. Faster, I moved. Faster, with more force, desperate to prolong this feeling but even more desperate to make him come. Make us both come. I wanted my orgasm to overtake me at the instant his overtook him. To join us in a physical way, yes. But more than that. More than sex.

"Oh God," I moaned, rising up and plunging down onto him again, taking him deeply into my body. More than sex? My own cries answered my question. "Oh yes, Iain, yes."

He closed his mouth over my nipple when I rose up again, suckling it fiercely, and I gasped as I impaled myself on his length once again, the hardness and heat of him intoxicating. His hands shifted to my ass, urging me to rock into his hips.

"Ah," he hissed, "Rae, ye feel so bloody good. Ahm needing ye to come, quick, before ah lose mah grip."

"I'm close. God, I'm so close."

"Harder, faster, hurry."

The desperation in his gruff voice escalated my need, and I obeyed his plea. I rode him harder, faster, and when he thrust a hand down to pinch my clit, I lost *my* grip. While my body pulsed around him, and he pinched my clit again, I wrapped my entire body around him and cried out from the power of the climax ripping through me.

He came too, shouting and burying his face against my neck, his arms latched around me.

"Rae," he said, breathless, peppering kisses up my throat to my ear. "Thank you for that."

I laughed. "Thank you? You are so weird, Iain."

He pulled his head back to look me in the eye. "You are an amazing woman. I'm grateful to have you for however long you'll have me."

My throat went thick, my mouth went dry. How long *would* I have him? I'd said he must leave by next Saturday, a week from today, but now…I didn't want him to go. If he stayed, I'd have to tell him about Malina before she came home.

Iain brushed a thumb over my cheek. "What is it? You look grim."

Did I? Grim? Well, I did feel like a giant hammer was hovering over my head, ready to slam down on me at any second. I wanted Iain. I was terrified to tell him the truth. The strength that had seen me through the worst times in my life had abandoned me now. I was once again the lovestruck college student.

"Nothing," I said, sliding off his lap to sit back against the headboard beside him. "I'm thinking about all the chores I have to do, that's all."

He tapped my nose. "That's not what you're thinking."

Dammit, why did he have to know me so well? It wasn't fair. After all these years, he should've forgotten all that stuff, and besides, I'd changed. Hadn't I? I suppressed a grunt. Clearly, I hadn't changed as much as I'd thought if Iain could tell when I was lying.

"It's about the things you won't tell me," he said. "Isn't it?"

"Yes." I hesitated, then added, "I like to think I'm older and wiser, but I don't think I've got the wisdom part down yet."

"Wisdom is overrated." He flashed me a grin. "I'm not wiser. I'm older and better."

I couldn't argue with that. He had gotten better. Sexier, for sure. More determined. More confident. And definitely better in bed.

He placed a hand on my cheek, turning my face toward him. "You can tell me anything. But I can wait until you're ready."

Oh God, why did he have to be so sincere and understanding? Naughty Iain was a hell of a lot easier to dismiss as nothing more than a sex partner for the week. But sweet, strong, caring Iain might just disintegrate my resolve.

That Iain, the irresistibly kind one, gave me a quick kiss and jumped off the bed. He stretched, affording me a spectacular view of his flexing muscles and his tight ass.

I sighed wistfully. Yes, Iain's ass made me wistful. Weird? Absolutely. But somehow, it made sense. I'd first witnessed his gorgeous body thirteen years ago, but today, his body was even hotter and more nibble-worthy than ever.

He turned in a circle, brows knitting together, and squinted at the floor.

"What are you doing?" I asked.

"Looking for my clothes."

"You're in my room. And since you don't bring any clothes when you go to take a shower, your stuff would be in your room upstairs."

"Oh." He stopped searching and stared at me for a moment, then a slow smile spread across his face. "You called it my room."

"You're sleeping there. That makes it your room, temporarily."

"Ah, temporarily. That does explain it."

His sarcastic tone suggested it didn't explain anything. He was right, of course. My slip of the tongue probably carried more meaning than I wanted to admit.

Iain gazed past the foot of the bed into space—until something caught his attention, and his brows drew together again. "What is that?"

He marched straight to the pile of books in the corner.

"Wait," I said too late, springing forward like I could somehow stop him from looking at the books and understanding what they were. "That's, um…"

My mind couldn't drum up an explanation.

Iain turned his head this way and that, examining the books without bending down to touch them. He tipped his head toward me and smirked. "Why do you have a mountain of books in the corner? They seem to all be about Scotland."

"Well, uh..." I scrunched up my whole face. "They are."

"I see." He turned toward me, his naked body no distraction from the discovery he'd made. "Why do you have so many books about my country?"

Shit. Given Iain's amused expression, I must have muttered the word aloud. The man looked far too pleased with himself. I considered lying, but what was the point? He knew me too damn well.

Exhaling a heavy sigh, I let my shoulders slump. "Let's not pretend we don't both know why I have those books. I've been kind of obsessed with your homeland."

He rested one hand on the dresser and leaned into it. "Why?"

Lie. Evade. Tell the truth. I mulled the options and realized I had only one.

"Because I missed you," I admitted.

His self-satisfied smile softened, and so did his gaze. "I missed you too. Every day."

I swallowed, but the lump in my throat wouldn't budge.

My notoriously hot lover knelt to study the books. "Travel. History. Law. Social customs. You seem to have covered every aspect of Scotland." He picked up a book and eyed me sideways. "Gaelic? Have you been pretending to have no idea what I'm saying to you?"

"No, most of the things you say aren't in that book."

He thumped the tome on his palm. "Fair useless, then, isn't it?"

"It's a primer, not an exhaustive study of the language."

Dropping the book, he moved to sit at the foot of the bed, angled toward me. "What shall we do today?"

I shrugged. "Feed the critters, clean out the barn—"

"For fun, Rae. What will we do for fun?"

"Don't know." I hunched my shoulders, smiling sheepishly. "Watch Disney movies?"

He shook his head and laughed. "You are severely lacking in adult fun."

"We don't have time for more sex. Hungry anjimals are waiting."

"Anjimals?" he said, his voice hitching with a half-suppressed laugh.

"Sorry. I really have spent too much time with a kid."

Iain sauntered around the bed to where I sat. He held out a hand, and I accepted it, letting him pull me off the bed and onto my feet.

"First," he said, "breakfast. Then, I will find something enjoyable to do that doesn't involve animals or children. Rae Everhart will have fun today." He slapped my bottom. "That's an order."

"Yes, sir."

Chapter Sixteen

Iain

My plan to make Rae have fun turned out a bit differently than I'd imagined. It began when I walked into the kitchen and opened the refrigerator door. Scanning the contents, I laid a hand on the door's top edge and bent to gaze at the near-empty shelves inside. "I wanted to cook you dinner, but you don't have any food. Need to get the messages, eh?"

Across the kitchen, Rae bent over the stove cooking what smelled like sausages. "Yeah, I need to make a pilgrimage to the grocery store."

"You remember what 'messages' means."

She tapped her temple. "Yep, got a brain and everything."

I shut the refrigerator door, leaning against it. "We're having a date tonight."

She froze, spatula in hand, in the midst of flipping little sausages. Without looking up from her task, she said, "We had sex, so now you think we're dating."

"That's right." I strolled up behind her, laying my hands on her hips, and slanted in to whisper in her ear. "Let's not repeat the same stupid mistake we made last time. We were dating then, and we're dating now." I nuzzled her cheek. "You said you missed me."

"I know, and I did." She finished turning the sausages and leaned into me, resting her head against my chest. "Fine, we're dating."

"Thank you." I kissed her cheek. "About time you admitted it."

She slapped a hand over my face and pushed me away.

I gave her bottom a light squeeze and took a seat at the kitchen table. "How often do you leave the homestead?"

"Once every two weeks or so."

"Two weeks?" I shook my head, though she couldn't see it with her back to me. "You need to get out more often. What are you hiding from?"

She spun toward me, spatula in hand. "Not hiding. Busy running a ranch and raising a kid."

Each word was punctuated with a slash of her spatula.

I raised my hands palms out. "I surrender. No need to beat me to death with your kitchen implement."

She glanced down at the spatula as if she hadn't realized she held it. Plunking it down on the counter, she said, "We'll go to town after the morning chores. Satisfied?"

"Not quite." I grasped the waistband of her jeans and hauled her toward my chair, spreading my thighs to trap her between them. "I need a kiss."

"I think you'll survive at least an hour without a kiss."

"But I won't." I frisked my hands up the backs of her thighs. "Take pity on me. You've made me addicted to your lips, your hands, your breasts, your erse, and especially your hot, slick—"

"Uh-huh, I get the picture." She slung a leg over mine and settled her bottom onto my lap, looping her arms around my neck. "Guess I better feed the beast."

I growled.

"You are such a naughty man, Iain MacTaggart."

Her lips met mine, soft and warm. She burrowed her fingers into my hair, deepening the kiss with a sweet little moan. I curled my tongue around hers, relishing the flavor of her and the sensation of her flesh against mine, the way she responded with ravenous lashes of her tongue. My Rae was a passionate lass.

She pulled away, her cheeks lightly flushed. "That should tide you over for a while."

Rae slid off my lap and returned to the stove.

After breakfast and chores, we climbed into Rae's pickup and headed into town. She'd insisted on driving because I "don't know how to drive on the right side and don't know the traffic rules." Though I reminded her I'd lived in America before and survived the wrong-sided driving experience, I could tell she was more comfortable taking the wheel herself. While she guided the pickup down the two-lane highway, I admired the scenery—the sort outside the windows and the sort sitting beside me. Rae had changed into tan pants that hugged her curves and a loose-fitting, short-sleeve blouse with a low neckline that showed off her bonnie breasts without revealing too much.

She had also done something to her hair. Curled it, maybe. I'd never understood the female grooming routine. She must've applied makeup too, but the subtle kind that enhanced her natural beauty. My God, she was stunning, even in dirty jeans and scuffed boots with her hair cinched up in a messy ponytail. With her hair down, the way it was now, she was an angel.

My gaze traveled down to her breasts.

"Uh-uh-uh," Rae said. "No hanky-panky in the truck."

"Not while we're racing down the highway at Le Mans speed."

"I never speed." She flashed me a grin. "But I'm feeling wild today."

Rae uninhibited was a sight to behold. "That's nothing new, sunshine. You ravished me with wild abandon last night and this morning."

"The ravishing was mutual."

I stared out the windows for the rest of the trip, so I wouldn't distract her from driving. Crashing into a tree was not the excitement I hoped for with Rae. Instead, I admired the rolling green hills, the wildflowers in bloom, the cattle and horses grazing in fields. The sun burned hot in the blue sky, but the air temperature hadn't caught up to it yet.

On our way to the grocery store, we passed a park where a large banner announced, "Twine Festival."

"You weren't joking," I said. "There is a festival celebrating a ball of twine."

"I never joke about the world's fifth-largest ball of twine."

Craning my neck, I tried to spot the object in question. "Don't see it."

"You can't see it from the road." She patted my leg. "I'll take you to the festival later, so you can experience the American rural life."

"I'd love to show you the Scottish rural life. You have all those books, wouldn't you like to visit the country?"

"Sure," she said cautiously, throwing me a suspicious glance.

"Relax," I said. "Not planning to abduct you. But if you and your daughter want to visit Scotland, I can take you there in a private jet. Show you my new house. Introduce you to my family."

"You're not meeting my daughter, remember? No family introductions, no holiday in Scotland. Got it?"

I realized in that moment I would never understand her secrecy about her daughter. Even before I'd shared my past with her, she'd refused to let me anywhere near her child and wouldn't even tell me the lassie's name or how old she was. I wanted to know Rae, but how could I when she locked me out of a large part of her life?

This was my penance. I'd abandoned her once, and she still didn't trust me not to do it again.

Rae steered the pickup around a corner, the grocery store visible ahead.

I stared out the window at the passing buildings, wondering if she would ever trust me.

Chapter Seventeen

Rae

Shopping with Iain was oddly…nice. We strolled down the aisles, holding hands while Iain pushed the cart with his other hand, chatting and discussing which items to buy, just like any normal couple might do. Was this what it would be like to be married to Iain? Hot sex at night, grocery shopping in the daytime, conversation in between. Since I'd never been married or had a serious relationship, except for the ten months I'd spent with him, I had no idea what the couples life would entail.

But I liked this. Shopping with him. Sleeping with him. Being with him.

No, I didn't like it. I loved it.

A shiver rushed through me, raising goosebumps on my arms. I was doing it again. Getting addicted to the insanely hot Scotsman who made me feel cherished and lusted for at the same time. Nothing else explained why I'd worn makeup and curled my hair for the first time in so long I couldn't remember how long it had been.

Iain picked up a box of cereal. "Do we want regular or chocolate Cheerios?"

My tummy did a little flip-flop. He'd said "we" like that was a thing with us. Like "we" had become a couple. Like he wasn't going to leave.

Well, he wouldn't—unless I kept to my decree and made him go.

If I changed my mind…

A sour taste crept into my mouth. Even if I wanted him to stay, I couldn't let him. Maybe if I'd told him about Malina from the start, or at least on the second day, then I could ask him to stick around and get to know his daughter. But I'd concealed the truth from him even after he told me about his womanizing past. He shared his secrets, but I held back.

He shook the cereal box in front of my face. "Are you sleeping on your feet, sunshine?"

Oh God, I really wished he'd stop calling me "sunshine." I would've had an easier time ordering him to leave if he'd stop using endearments. "Sunshine" was the worst because it meant the most to me. He'd started calling me that three weeks after we met, and I'd loved it. I'd loved him, so much.

My throat thickened.

I swallowed hard, cleared my throat, and said, "Regular Cheerios. But we need to get some strawberry Frosted Mini Wheats too for when—" I swallowed again. "For when my daughter comes home."

He dropped the cereal box in the cart. "Are you implying I'll be here when that happens?"

"No," I said too quickly and with too much emphasis. Might as well have hung a neon sign over my head that flashed GUILTY in bright-red letters. I tucked my hands under my arms. "You can't be here then, but I might as well do all the grocery shopping today."

Disappointment flitted across his face but vanished into his standard serene smile. "If it's all right with you, I'll keep a hopeful attitude toward our future together."

Warmth blossomed in my chest even as my gut twisted. Our future together? I had no idea if I wanted that.

Liar. I wanted it. I wanted him. I wanted our family, together at last, but it was another fantasy, like whatever we'd had long, long ago in a messed-up Midwestern town.

We finished buying the messages—oh yeah, I was catching up with all the Scottish lingo—and we headed to the feed store. Iain studied the bags of oats and alfalfa pellets with an adorable seriousness as if "our future" hinged on the choice of munchies for my animals. I approached the bags of alfalfa pellets and tried to pick one up.

Iain pushed in front of me. "Allow me."

"Sure, go for it."

"How many do you need?"

"Two bags."

He tossed one fifty-pound sack over his left shoulder, then tossed another over his left. He strode toward the flat shopping cart designed for feed bags and dropped both onto it. The cart rattled and shook.

"What now?" he asked.

A warm, pleasant shiver rushed through me this time. Damn, the man was strong. And sexy as hell. And…I wanted to rip his clothes off right here in the horse-feed aisle.

"Um," I said, struggling to stay coherent despite the heat pooling in my belly, "we need some oats. Two bags of that too."

I pointed to the bags of oats on the shelves.

He plucked one up like it weighed a few ounces, not fifty pounds, and chucked it onto his shoulder. After slinging another over his other shoulder, he sauntered to the cart and plopped the bags onto it. Rattle. Shake.

A tingle swept through me, settling between my thighs.

That serene smile flared into a sizzling grin. "I know that look, sunshine. It's the one that comes right before you do."

I glanced around, suddenly aware of the other customers not far away. "Shush, Iain. No sex talk here."

He chuckled softly. "You're the one staring at me like you want to be f—"

"Stop that." I rushed to him and slapped a hand over his mouth before he could say anything else that might get us arrested for public indecency. I would've known what he'd been about to say even if he hadn't told me the exact same thing last night.

I still had my hand over his mouth when he mumbled against it, "Fucked."

His eyes sparkled with humor, and I could feel him smiling.

"Sorry," I said, removing my hand. "Yes, I do want that. But not here."

"No worries." He licked his lips. "Even your hand tastes good."

Just like that, he disintegrated all my anxiety and my self-control. I threw my arms around his neck and bounced up onto the balls of my feet with my heels elevated. Tightening my arms, I brought our mouths within kissing distance.

He dipped his head closer, his eyes half closed.

I moistened my lips, parting them, and let my eyes drift half closed too. Angling closer. Breathing in his breaths. Lips tingling, every part of me hungry for a kiss.

Peripherally, I noticed movement to my left. My eyes rotated in that direction of their own accord, because I wanted nothing more than to gaze into Iain's eyes right before our lids shut and our lips met. Instead, I found myself turning my head to follow the track my eyes had taken.

Grayson Parker watched us, his lips pursed, hands on his hips.

I blinked rapidly, confused by his appearance. Though I occasionally spotted him when I came into town, we hadn't spoken or looked at each other in ages.

"There are kids in this store, ya know," he said in his Texas twang, contorting his mouth like he'd sucked on a rancid candy. "How old is this guy, anyway? Banging a senior citizen is pervy."

"My life is none of your business," I said, and dropped my heels back onto the floor, stepping away from Iain. "I can kiss my boyfriend whenever I want."

Iain's serene smile turned downright cheerful.

Yeah, calling a fifty-year-old man my boyfriend sounded odd. What else could I call him?

He may have been fifty, but he didn't look it. I wondered why Grayson assumed Iain was significantly older than I was.

"The guy's not even American," Grayson said. "And he's got a faggy name. Iain MacTaggart. Sounds like a leprechaun."

"Leprechauns," Iain said, his features and his voice turning hard as steel, "are Irish. I am Scottish. Do try to get it right, laddie."

The way he said "laddie" made every hair on my body go stiff, with a frisson of anxiety and with the warm, shivery awareness that he meant business. The dangerous kind of business. The possessive kind.

His deadly tone affected Grayson as well, who shuffled backward half a step.

"Listen, pal," Grayson said, "you can have her. She's not that great in bed, and besides, she's got a brat at home, ya know?" Grayson hooked his thumbs inside the waistband of his jeans. "Maybe a Scottish leprechaun doesn't mind raising some other dick's spawn."

A muscle twitched in Iain's jaw. His eyes narrowed. He flexed his fingers and then crooked them toward his palms. "Best watch your mouth, laddie. You're in the presence of a lady."

Grayson sniggered. "Lady? Rae-Rae here loved to get her mouth on my willy, couldn't get enough of it."

Iain blustered a breath out his nostrils like a bull preparing to gore someone. I wouldn't have been surprised if he had pawed one foot and snorted. He didn't, though he did take one menacing step toward Grayson.

My former lover seemed to have summoned a bit of nerve, and foolishness, because he refused to keep his stupid mouth shut. He slanted forward and said in a stage whisper, "You payin' her to suck you off every night?"

Christ, I'd never realized until this moment what a prick Grayson Parker was. How could I have ever liked him? With an inward cringe, I wondered how I could've ever considered introducing him to my daughter.

"Best take that back," Iain said in a voice so low and threatening that Grayson recoiled. "Apologize to the lady. *Now.*"

Every other customer in the place seemed to have vanished.

I laid a hand on Iain's arm. "He's not worth it."

"Aye, he is." Iain's fists clenched. "What'll it be, laddie?"

Grayson rolled his eyes. "Stop calling me 'laddie', grandpa. Believe me, that hoe ain't worth it—even if she does give wicked-hot blow jobs."

Iain surged toward Grayson and punched him in the gut.

My ex-lover doubled over, coughing and wheezing.

"Next time," Iain said, "I'll aim lower."

Red-faced and still wheezing, Grayson staggered away down the aisles until he veered around a corner and out of sight.

Iain's body, taut as a high-tension power line a moment ago, slackened in a heartbeat. He turned toward me, that Buddha smile on his face again.

"You didn't need to do that on my account," I said. "Can't believe I ever slept with him. I swear he wasn't such a prick when I was with him."

"He won't be that much of a prick to you ever again, I'd wager."

"You're probably right." I screwed up my mouth, struggling to understand. "Grayson and I have ignored each other ever since our break-up. I don't get why he behaved like that today. I mean, he said those obnoxious things to me when we broke up, but I assumed that was embarrassment."

"It probably was," Iain said. "Now it's jealousy. The erse regrets letting you go and lashed out as a defense mechanism. I've seen it often in weak men."

Weak? Yes, Grayson was that.

"It's not my business," Iain said, rubbing his chin, "but may I ask why you wanted that scunner to meet your daughter? You said it was a test of his commitment, but there must be more to it."

I hunched my shoulders. "Well, I asked Grayson if he wanted to meet my daughter because I had a feeling he wasn't the long-haul type. I needed to know for sure, so I tested him."

"And he failed."

"Crashed and burned is more like it."

"Mm, I see." Iain watched me with a combination of that easygoing smile and an analytical glint in his eyes. "I could extrapolate another meaning from that. You don't want me to meet your daughter because you believe I might be the long-haul sort."

Rats. I'd hoped he wouldn't figure that out yet. Hiding my secrets from him got harder and harder every day.

I tried another tactic to evade the discussion. "Why would Grayson assume you're a lot older than me? You don't look it."

"We had a conversation during the drive to your home. He made pop culture references I didn't understand, and I told him a man of fifty doesn't keep up with the youngsters."

"Youngsters?" I raised my brows. "Is that how you see me?"

"No, you are a mature woman."

The way he said it made my skin tighten. He could turn a phrase like "mature woman" into the most erotic compliment.

"You don't need to beat up my exes," I said as I walked up to him and ran my hands over his chest. "It was really hot, though. Nobody's ever slugged someone to defend my honor." I tilted my head so study his face. "You never did that before either. Back at Nackington, guys would make rude comments to me and you never punched any of them."

"Didn't need to. They were easily cowed." He cupped my face in one hand. "Besides, I was different then. I cared about pointless things like propriety. I'm not worried about that shit anymore."

I gave him a quick kiss. "I liked the old you, but the new you is even better."

He bent his head to murmur in my ear, "Let's go home and get naked."

"You read my mind."

We made it to the checkout line with no more incidents, but then Iain put his hand on my behind while I was trying to insert my credit card into the reader thingy. I shooed him away, and the blasted man backed up with his palms raised, smirking all the time.

In the parking lot, I spotted Grayson shambling toward his truck three aisles over and decided to resolve this issue right away. I told Iain to wait for me in my truck. He balked, but when I promised to reward him later in any manner he liked, he leaned against the truck's bed where he could keep an eye on me and my ex-lover.

Grayson was unlocking the door of his Chevy when I walked up to him.

"You owe me an explanation," I said. "Why did you say those horrible things about me?"

He hunched his shoulders, tucking his chin, and avoided looking at me. "Sorry about that. I kinda lost it when I saw you with that other guy. Got no call to be jealous, I know, but—whatever."

"That's your explanation?"

"Knew I made a mistake last year. When you wanted me to meet your daughter, I panicked." He scratched his forehead, his face pinched. "My girl-friend dumped my ass last week. She said I need to grow up and grow a pair, pretty much what you told me when we broke up."

Smart woman, I thought but did not say.

"Listen," he said, "I'm real sorry for the way I've acted. You're a nice person, and I've got shit for brains. Everybody knows that."

Yeah, I couldn't argue with that assessment.

I offered him my hand. "Bygones. Let's end on good terms."

"Sure." He shook my hand, holding it so loosely it almost didn't qualify as a handshake. "Goodbye, Rae."

"Goodbye, Grayson."

He peeked around me and winced. "Should I, uh, apologize to your boyfriend?"

"Oh no, I think you've said enough to Iain. Let's not poke that bear."

He nodded and climbed into his truck.

I trotted back to Iain, who said nothing but merely raised an eyebrow. I shrugged, and we got in my truck. No need to glance back. I had zero regrets about saying adieu to Grayson once and for all.

Though he pronounced it "barmy," I dragged Iain to the Twine Festival. He got into the spirit of it once we were there and even joked with a vendor selling "genuine replicas" of the giant ball of twine—aka normal-size balls of twine. As we walked away from the vendor's booth, Iain held up the replica ball he'd bought and whispered to me, "I paid five dollars for this. Could've bought one in the feed store for fifty cents."

"But this one's a genuine replica with a certificate of authenticity." I bumped my shoulder into him. "Besides, you're supporting the local economy."

"At least it's a good deed, then. When do I see the real thing?"

That's how we wound up standing in front of the gigantic ball of twine hand in hand. An older couple had offered to take a picture of us with my phone's camera. I would've politely declined, but Iain jumped in before I could speak, accepting their offer. Now, I had a photo of the two of us standing in front of the twine ball, Iain's arm around my shoulders, both of us smiling. The looks on our faces reminded me of the photo booth pictures from way back when. We looked so...in love.

Fifteen minutes later, we were having sex in my truck, parked in the secluded alley behind the public library. And I tried not to think about that photograph.

After our interlude, Iain insisted we visit a lumber yard. Ricksville may be a small town, but we had the essentials—food for man and beast, and a hardware store that also sold lumber. When I asked why he needed lumber and tools, Iain gave me his Buddha smile and said, "To prepare a surprise for you."

I'd assumed he'd cook me dinner tonight, but no. He put off our date so he could "prepare" his surprise first.

No man had ever made a surprise for me with his own two hands. I'd let him have his secrecy, and somehow, I'd work up the nerve to tell him about Malina.

Eventually.

Chapter Eighteen

Iain

We spent Monday morning tending to the sheep—or "sheepies," as Rae called them. I'd even caught myself calling them sheepies. If my cousins heard me say that, they would've harassed me without end. They knew better than to expect I'd be offended or embarrassed, though. I'd experienced too many humiliations during my formative years to take offense at anything my cousins dreamed up to insult me. And harassing each other was a MacTaggart family tradition.

After lunch, Rae retreated to her office on the second floor of the house to handle business matters. She'd told me she needed to "submit to the self-inflicted torture every self-employed person has to endure." I sympathized. When I'd been an archaeologist, I'd spent more time writing reports and grant proposals than I had in the field or in the classroom. When I told Rae this, while we were standing near the paddock fence, she had naturally latched on to the past-tense formation of my sentence.

"*When* you were an archaeologist?" She settled one hand on her cocked hip, fingers tapping. "The other day you said something about not being qualified anymore. What gives?"

"I was blacklisted."

Her hand fell away from her hip. "You were what? I thought running you out of the country was all the Bremner-Ashtons wanted. All Cece wanted. Most of her wrath was aimed at me, that's how it seemed."

"I thought the same thing."

Rae's words made me wonder what wrath Cece had unleashed on her.

Out in one of the fenced pastures, the sheep grazed. I lodged one boot on the bottom board of the fence and rested my crossed arms on the top board. In the distance, the pale and indistinct shapes of the flock milled about, and the occasional baa drifted on the breeze. Sweat dribbled down my temples, thanks to the hot weather. I lifted my fedora—my Indiana Jones hat, according to Rae—and swiped the perspiration away before resettling my hat. "I applied to positions at various universities, colleges, and even museums in the UK. None wanted even an interview. Finally, I applied to a post at the National Museum of Scotland. Someone there was kind enough to let me know why I couldn't find a new position. Whenever I submitted my CV for consideration, the recipient organization would call my last employer."

Rae made a disgusted noise, joining me at the fence. "And someone from Nackington would inform them of what a sleaze you are."

"Worse. They labeled me a sexual predator."

She jerked, and her head swung around. Her blue eyes zeroed in on me. "Are you serious? Those jackasses said that? Did they try to get you arrested?"

"No, but it had the desired effect." I stared up at the blue sky dotted with small, white clouds, unwilling to look at Rae. "Whether they believed the claim or not, no one in the academic world would risk hiring me. If the public found out a university or museum had hired a possible predator, there would've been an outcry. Even back then, those things were frowned on."

"Those bastards. I'm sorry, Iain."

"Not your fault. I'm the one who seduced a student."

"I wanted you to seduce me. Besides, we were both adults, and I technically wasn't a student anymore."

"We broke the rules," I said, turning my body toward her. She studied the ground inside the paddock. I hooked a finger under her chin and urged her to look at me. "I am the one to blame for all of this. If I'd kept my distance for another month, everything would have been different."

"You don't know that."

"I do." My gaze wandered to the sky again. "If I'd kept my lust in check, we'd both have gotten what we wanted."

Rae would have gotten what she wanted, what she deserved—a teaching career. What I'd wanted, only she could have given me. I'd waited too long to try for it and lost everything.

She chewed on her bottom lip. "Do you have any idea what I wanted back then?"

"To become a university teacher, a professor of English."

"But did you ever figure out why I wanted that?"

I kicked at the fence board. "Not a mind reader."

She bowed her head, sucking in a breath that lifted her shoulders. "I dreamed of becoming a college teacher because that's what you were. All I wanted was you."

The world around us seemed to tilt for the briefest moment. I clutched at the wooden fence, my foot tumbling off the bottom board to thump onto the ground. Unable to comprehend what she'd said, I mumbled a stupid response. "What do you mean?"

"What do you think I mean? I was in love with you, and I had a sappy romantic fantasy of the two of us becoming this academic power couple. I hadn't planned on becoming a teacher until I met you. I wanted a life with you, but instead of my perfect fantasy, I got a big fat nothing. No job, no degree, no—" She sniffled, then cleared her throat. "None of my dreams came true. That's how it goes, right? Dreams get shattered, and we move on."

She'd moved on. The fact she had a daughter attested to that. I, the *arschgeige*, had trampled through life without a care for the collateral damage. Never again. I would prove to Rae she could trust me. If she'd loved me once, she might love me again.

I'd been the hammer that shattered her dreams. Whatever the Bremner-Ashtons had done, I made the choice to stay away, to accept it, to let Rae go.

But I never had let her go. She'd been with me always, a ghost I could never banish no matter what I'd done to erase the memories. It never worked. I would love this woman until I died and even beyond death.

"I tried to find you," I said. "Cece answered the apartment phone and told me you went home, but she didn't know where that was. I had no idea of where you might be. We'd never talked about our families, our childhoods, or anything very personal. Besides, I was preoccupied with other things. I should've tried harder somehow to find you. I'm sorry."

She leaned one shoulder against the fence, facing me. "It doesn't matter anymore."

But it did. Earning her trust required more than saying I was sorry and I regretted leaving. It required reciprocation. She'd shared her dreams from long ago, she'd told me how she lost those dreams, and she had let me glimpse the pain it caused her. I needed to offer a similar confession.

One elbow on the fence, I turned fully toward her. "I mentioned I had reasons for accepting my banishment, even though it wasn't a legal action."

"It was one family of bullies and all their connections."

"Yes." A stone had settled in my gut, cold and hard. This would be more difficult than I'd imagined. My gaze shifted to the ground unconsciously, but I forced myself to meet her eyes. "My father has been in and out of prison all my life. He's what you might call a well-meaning but inept burglar."

Her mouth opened as if she meant to speak.

I held up a hand to stay her questions. "Let me explain before you say anything."

"Okay."

"When I was a lad, we never had money," I began. "Not enough of it, at any rate. Anytime things got rough, my da would resort to less-than-legal means to keep his family out of the poor house. He would break into the home of a wealthy person and steal one item of enough value to provide the money he needed, no more than that. I'm not saying he's a saint, but he did what he felt was necessary. My da had been in prison twice by the time I was ten. Ma did everything she could to keep Da in line, but he's a stubborn old fool."

Rae watched me, silent, her face impassive though her eyes seemed to shine with sympathy.

I scratched my neck. "When I was eleven, I took it on myself to intervene. I couldn't convince Da to stop, so I would approach his…ah…victims. Some I convinced not to file charges. Begged if I had to. Cried sometimes, and it was no act. I was terrified Da would be sentenced to a much longer term in prison because of his repeated offenses. Sometimes, I offered to work off the cost of the stolen item. If I found the item in our house before Da had time to fence it, I would return it to the rightful owner. I managed to keep my father out of prison for twelve years, until I left on my first archaeological excavation. It was in Germany. While I was away, Da got in more trouble and Ma pleaded with the aggrieved parties. I came home sometimes to help her keep Da in line, but not as often as I should have. It's a bloody hard job. Work was my escape."

Rae touched my arm tentatively. "I'm so sorry, Iain. That must've been awful."

A sigh gusted out of me. "The worst of it is I love my da. He's a good man, except for his one fault. To his mind, desperate times call for larcenous measures. Eventually, I took a job at a small college in Edinburgh to be closer to home, so Ma wouldn't need to look after Da all on her own. We kept him out of trouble, and eventually, he stopped burgling the neighbors. I helped with their expenses, but Da found steady work as a carpenter and everything seemed well enough. That's when I accepted a position at Nackington. I needed a break from home life and spending a year in America with a potential extension of another year sounded perfect."

I turned my gaze to the ground, unwilling to see the pity on her face. I wasn't sharing my life story with her to gain her sympathy. She needed to understand why I'd abandoned her. I didn't expect forgiveness, but at least she might understand.

Rae settled a hand on my arm where it rested on the fence. "I get why you never told me any of this before, but I'm glad you told me now."

The tenderness in her voice made me glance up.

Her smile was soft and gentle, just like her gaze. No pity. Empathy, pure and simple.

I had more to confess, though, and no idea if she would understand this part of the story.

"Three weeks after my expulsion," I said, "three weeks after I left you, my da was arrested again. After years of living as a law-abiding citizen, he reverted to his old ways. I'd lost my job, after all, and I was…behaving selfishly at the time. Concerned only with my feelings. But I told you that already. Da decided we needed more money and so he broke into the home of a Welsh businessman who'd recently moved to Loch Fairbairn, our village. The Welshman had owned mines and whatnot, earned a fortune and bought a fair lot of trinkets to display his wealth. Da stole an item that turned out to be worth far more than he thought. The Welshman, Rhys Kendrick, was not pleased."

Rae spread her fingers over my arm, sliding her palm up and down in a soothing gesture. I longed to pull her into my arms and kiss her until we both forgot what I'd been saying.

Instead, I told her, "Talking to Kendrick didn't help. He was intractable. I asked for my cousin Rory's help. He'd recently finished his traineeship, the final step to becoming a solicitor, and he was glad to intervene on Da's behalf. Kendrick would not be pacified. He threatened to file charges." I shut my eyes, the memory too clear in my mind. "Unless I did him a favor."

"What kind of favor?"

"He wanted me to authenticate an artifact for him. Though I'd been fired from my last job, I had the credentials to sign off on something like that." I rubbed my eyes with my thumb and forefinger. "Kendrick said if I did this for him, he would forget about the charges against Da."

"I don't understand," Rae said. "What's the big deal about signing a paper to say this guy's artifact is genuine?"

"Because it wasn't. The artifact was a forgery." I scrubbed my mouth with one hand. "Antiquities found in Scotland are subject to treasure trove, but this one was imported from Greece. It appeared to be a Neolithic idol, a marble statue carved in the abstract style of that period, dating to approximately five thousand BC. The real thing would've been worth over fifty thousand pounds."

"This one was fake."

"I'm not an expert on the Neolithic, but I've gained a good deal of knowledge about identifying forged antiquities. Wherever I took part in an excavation, my colleagues would ask for my opinion about artifacts of questionable origin." With Rae's hand lingering on my arm, I wanted to pull away but couldn't. The tacit acceptance of her touch meant too much to me. "Rhys Kendrick owned the original artifact but had a reproduction made. A quite good one, in fact. He planned to hold on to the original, keeping it hidden in his private vault, and declare the forgery had been stolen so he could make an insurance claim. That's where I came in. He wanted me to authenticate the replica, say it was a genuine antiquity. He bribed a man at the insurance company to seal the deal. Kendrick didn't need the money, but he seems to enjoy getting away with breaking the law."

Rae's fingers tensed on my arm. "It was an insurance scam."

"That's right," I said. "And I did it."

I looked at her then, expecting…I didn't know what. Disgust. Disappointment. Maybe I wanted her to agree I was a criminal like my father and a bastard too. I should've known better than to expect that sort of response from Rae.

She took my hands in hers and said, "You did the best you could. If anyone threatened someone I loved, I would do anything to protect them."

"The best I could do was to become an accessory to the commission of insurance fraud. Maybe that's not the right terminology for what I did. I couldn't very well ask Rory about it. This was my fault, and I've had to live with it ever since."

She clasped her hands firmly around mine, spearing her gaze straight into mine. "All my life, whenever I got frustrated with other people's behavior, my mom would tell me the same thing. Everybody's doing the best they can. Most people don't make mistakes on purpose and intentionally hurt others. The rest of us muddle along the best way we know how."

"Your mother sounds like a wise woman, but I doubt she had criminal behavior in mind when she said that."

"Listen, I know what the Bremner-Ashtons did. I was there, I went through it too." She moved closer, tilting her head back to keep her gaze trained on mine. "You did the best you could in the aftermath."

I tried to speak, but for a moment, I couldn't. When I regained my voice, it came out hushed. "Are you forgiving me?"

"No. There's nothing to forgive." She tugged on my hands. "That's what I keep trying to knock into that thick skull of yours. You've made mistakes, so have I, but we need to move on from the past and make the best of the present and the future."

Her words sank into my thick skull slowly. The future, she'd said. For the first time since I'd walked back into her life, she'd mentioned the future—not with a melancholy tone, but with certainty. And for the first time since I'd slogged up her driveway, I had a tangible hope the future she spoke of might include me.

"So," she said, lingering close to me, keeping her hold on my hands, "you saved your father from another stint in prison. That's the bright side, right?"

"Well…no." I squinted my face. "Kendrick broke his word. He filed charges, and Da was sentenced to three years in prison."

"What? Jesus, Iain, that's awful."

"Kendrick convinced the judge a repeat offender should be punished more harshly. Da was released on license, on parole, after eighteen months."

Rae got a look on her face, a fierce one that revealed her lioness heart. In that moment, she reminded me of my mother. If I were arrested, would Rae stand by me the way Ma had stood by Da all these years?

"My mother is a strong woman," I said, "but the sentence hit her hard. She went to Perth to visit her sister and ended up staying until Da was released. I couldn't blame her for wanting to escape. That's what I'd done for most of my adult life. I was no intrepid archaeologist, no globe-trotting adventurer. I had adventures because I was running away from my life." I glanced down at my hands entwined with Rae's. "That's what I did with you. I ran away because I couldn't handle it, and because I didn't want to become a criminal like my father. But I did. Kendrick filed his insurance claim, got fifty thousand pounds richer, and ever since he's held that false authentication over my head. Never speaks of it, but we both know it's there."

"That son of a bitch," Rae hissed. "Is he still blackmailing you?"

"No. I've avoided him for years, and he has ignored me. I did have my revenge, of a sort."

"In what way?"

Though I tried to shake my hands free of hers, Rae wouldn't let go. "Delyth, the woman I told you about last night, she's Rhys Kendrick's wife."

"You stuck it to him by screwing his wife? Did he ever find out?"

"I didn't meet Delyth until years after the incident with Da, but Rhys is a bully, so I'm sure she told him about us." This time I jerked my hands away from hers. "The point is that I became like my father, taking the easy way out instead of gritting my teeth and doing what's hard and painful and necessary. Maybe I could've found another way to keep Da out of prison, but I didn't even try."

"Your father did those things to protect his family. You did the same." She canted her head, scrutinizing me. "Is it such a bad thing to be like your father? Loyal to your family, devoted to protecting them? I may not agree with his methods, but I understand the need to take care of the ones you love at any cost."

Watching her face, I had an epiphany of sorts. "That's what you've done too, looking out for your family, your daughter, at any cost. You wouldn't break the law, but you've sacrificed your own happiness to provide a stable home for your child."

She barred her arms over her chest, making her breasts lift a wee bit. "Do you think I've been miserable all these years? I haven't. My life is good."

"But you want more." I stepped toward her, taking her upper arms in my hands. "You gave up on love, but you want it. Don't you?"

Rae sucked her bottom lip into her mouth. Her eyes shimmered as if she might cry. Though I longed to pull her into my arms and comfort her, I knew she wouldn't want that.

With my hands around her arms, I rubbed my thumbs in small circles. "You deserve more than a good life. You deserve to have everything you've ever wanted."

She snorted, a derisive sound, but her eyes still shimmered. "Nobody gets everything they want."

"I can make certain you get it." I leaned closer. "I've amassed a great deal of money, through legal means. I can give you everything, if you'll let me."

Her eyes narrowed. "A great deal of money? How much is that, exactly? You said you're rich, but—"

"Over ten million pounds. That's how much, exactly."

Chapter Nineteen

Rae

Are you trying to buy my love?" I asked, totally dumbfounded by his statement. Sure, he'd told me he was rich, but I never would've guessed…so many zeroes. Though a fat bank balance didn't impress me, I couldn't help wondering how he got so rich. Legal means, he'd said.

"I would never try to buy any part of you," he said. "I will never abandon you again, Rae. Let me take care of you and show you we can have a great life together."

"Take care of me?" I bristled, yanking out of his grasp. "I've done just fine on my own, for me and for my daughter. I don't need saving."

"Not trying to save you. I want a life with you."

"Iain, I don't—Shit, I don't know what to say or think. You drop this bomb on my head and expect me to bounce right back. I'm not Mrs. Buddha. I can't do that. Give me a minute, okay?"

He nodded and backed up a couple steps, granting me some space.

"Might help," I said, "if you told me how you got so rich."

"Ten years ago, not long after Da was released from prison for the last time, I decided I should make enough money so he wouldn't feel the need to steal anymore." Iain began to pace in front of me while he explained, "I worked any job I could find, but odd jobs weren't enough. That's when I realized I could support my parents and get a sort of comeuppance too."

"Comeuppance?"

He nodded grimly, walking back and forth past me. "My career was ruined with lies. Even colleagues back home, people I had considered friends, threw me away like so much trash. Maybe I could show them what a mistake they'd made and earn the money I needed for my family. Those former colleagues would regret making me a pariah."

I thrust out a hand to grasp his arm and stop him. "What exactly did you do?"

"Nothing illegal." He turned toward me. "Any items of historical importance found in Scotland are treasure trove, meaning they belong to the government. Chance finds, things discovered outside of any organized field work, are slightly different. They're still treasure trove, but the finder might be given an ex gratia payment—a reward."

"Are you saying you found artifacts and got those reward payments?"

"That's right. I wasn't involved in organized field work anymore, but I grew up in Loch Fairbairn and knew the people who lived out in the countryside. I also understood the archaeology of the region. It wasn't difficult to choose potential sites and convince farmers to let me explore their land with a metal detector, especially when I promised to share any reward with them."

The bomb-drop sensation I'd experienced a moment ago when he told me he had ten million pounds in the bank had transformed into a numb awe. "You found artifacts all by yourself and got paid for it?"

"Yes." He glanced down, hands on his hips, and peered up at me through the curls of his hair that fell over his eyes. "I've made eight finds in the last ten years. Took ex gratia payments for myself on only the first three. My cousin Lachlan was my financial adviser, and he helped me invest the money, growing it into a sizable nest egg."

Nest egg? Ten million pounds? He'd made a fortune, legally, using his intelligence, expertise, and determination. I admired him for that, but I couldn't wrap my head around these revelations.

He watched me with an anxious expression, seeming to await my judgment.

"That's amazing, Iain," I said. "You are amazing."

"Not wanting praise. No amount of money will make you trust me. What will?"

I focused on his chest to avoid witnessing the longing in his eyes. "I get why you ran away before, and I know you mean it when you say you'll never do it again. But I still don't know if I can trust that. It's not all your fault, why I can't trust you. I have trouble trusting anyone."

"Why?"

I wrapped my arms around myself and leaned against the fence. How much should I reveal to him? Listening to Iain's story, I'd at last understood why he behaved the way he did in the aftermath of our first night together. I understood, but like I'd told him, I wasn't sure it would make a difference. I had trouble with trusting people, yes, but also with trusting life itself.

How much should I reveal? I realized the answer with the sharpness and suddenness of a knife to the chest.

Everything. That's what I had to tell him.

Though I kept my arms around me, I hunched my shoulders. "My dad was never around much when I was a kid. He worked for a big company that owned a lot of resorts around the world. The job required a lot of travel, but even when he was home, he didn't have much interest in my life. He didn't even go to my high school graduation."

Iain grunted. "Can't understand a father behaving that way. My da, with all his faults, never missed an event in my life."

"My dad wasn't like that." I bowed my head while I mulled how to explain the rest. When I raised my head again, I said, "Despite his standoffish attitude, I still thought our family was basically happy. Until the summer before my senior year at Nackington."

When I paused, Iain sidled closer. "What happened then?"

"I went home for the summer break like I always did, but everything had changed." I fought the impulse to lean into Iain for a few seconds before I gave in. Why shouldn't I accept his support? He'd exposed his deepest secrets to me. I could trust him with some of my secrets. "I found out my parents had been separated for six months and they'd just filed for divorce. My mom didn't tell me because she wanted me to focus on school without any drama to distract me. I couldn't believe it. I mean, Dad can be distant, but I had no idea they were having trouble."

"Your mother wanted to shield you from it. That's what good parents do."

His warm body buttressed mine, and his gentle voice bolstered me. "I could tell there was something Mom wasn't saying. I pestered her until she told me. My dad had been cheating on her off and on for years. Whenever he went away on business, he'd have a one-nighter or even spend a week with some woman or other. He finally took up with a bimbo two years older than me. He left Mom for his new plaything."

"What a bleeding ersehole." Iain slipped an arm around me, pulling me snug against him. "I'm sorry, Rae."

"Not your fault." I let my head rest on his chest. "Meeting you was the one thing that kept me from thinking about my parents. My dad. You want to take care of me now, but you saved me back then."

"In what way?"

"Right before Christmas during my senior year, my dad announced he was moving to Hong Kong to manage one of his company's resorts there. He called me to say he was starting a new life, so I shouldn't contact him again."

"Christ, Rae..."

"Remember that day I called you to say I was sick and wouldn't be in class?"

"I remember."

Lifting my head, I gazed up at him. "That was the morning after my dad's call. I would've hidden in my bedroom for days feeling sorry for myself. But you showed up and wouldn't leave until I agreed to go to a museum with you."

"Ah, the Egyptian exhibition. You always loved ancient Egypt."

I smiled a little, remembering our trip to the museum. "You must've known I was upset about something, not really sick."

He brushed his fingertips across my cheek. "When you called, you sounded like you'd been crying. I had an idea you were upset. It wasn't my place to ask, but I couldn't let you hide in your room all day, alone. Had to do something."

"You saved me that day, Iain. You turned your classes over to your TA and spent the whole day taking care of me in a way no one else ever had." I slid my arms around his waist. "I think that's the day I fell in love with you."

Had I ever stopped loving him? No, how could I. This man had changed my life in so many ways, and I would always love him.

Iain combed his fingers through my hair. "Your father abandoned you, and then I abandoned you. Is that why you can't trust I'll never leave you again?"

"Probably. It's not only my feelings I worry about, though. I have a daughter." I peeled myself away from him and took a few steps backward. "Her well-being is my top priority. If she got attached to you and then you left—Well, I can't let that happen."

"You're a good mother. I understand your fears."

The shocking thing was I believed him. He did understand. His childhood hadn't exactly been idyllic, though his father loved him. We were both only children. Another thing we had in common. I wanted to trust he would stick around, wanted to believe it so badly. Maybe I already trusted him. Even if I did, I had another, far more snarled mess to clean up.

Malina thought her father was dead, and Iain had no clue he had a child.

Fortunately, he changed the subject. "How did you end up raising sheep?"

"Mom bought this place—" I waved to indicate the ranch around us. "— with the money she got in the divorce settlement. My parents sold their house and split the proceeds. Since they'd owned the same house for twenty years, it was worth a lot more than when they'd bought it. Anyway, Mom owns the property, but she always tells me it's my place. We moved here when I was—"

I'd been about to say *when I was four months pregnant*. Too big a clue for the perceptive man listening to every word I spoke.

"When you were what?" he asked.

Too damn perceptive, that's what he was. I floundered for a response that wouldn't give away the one thing I couldn't bring myself to tell him. "When I was looking to get away from everything. I'd grown up in that house in Iowa—with my dad. Other things happened too, and I was ready to leave. Mom felt the same way. We moved here four months after you left. Seven years ago, my mom remarried and moved to California with her new husband, Greg. He's a plastic surgeon with two kids, Ty and Zoey. Ty's in college, but Zoey's about to start her senior year of high school. My mom met Greg through an online dating site, and now they live in the hills near Malibu."

And they were very well off. Why did it seem like everybody I knew had boatloads more money than I did? I wasn't jealous, but sometimes I wondered what I was doing wrong.

"You must like your stepfamily," Iain said. "You've had them here and bought a bed for your very large stepbrother."

I smiled thinking of the Raines family. "They're good people. I couldn't have asked for a nicer stepdad, and Ty and Zoey are the kid brother and kid sister I never had."

"How often do you see them?"

"Not as much as I'd like. Last summer, we were all supposed to go to Bermuda. My daughter and I both got passports and everything, but Ben broke his arm and couldn't work for a while. I had to stay home to take care of the animals. My daughter was really disappointed we missed the trip, but I bought her an iPod and then she was over it."

Iain blew out a breath. "Children recover much faster than adults, don't they?"

"Yes they do." I stuffed my hands in my jeans pockets. "I still haven't used my passport. The thing's stuffed in a drawer in my dresser."

He braced a hand on the fence. "You sound almost melancholy about that passport."

"No, I wasn't that excited about Bermuda. I'm a homebody."

"But it's a shame to have a passport and not put it to good use." He drummed his fingers on the fence board. "When was your daughter born?"

I shook my head. "You said you wouldn't ask about her anymore."

"My curiosity won't leave me be." He glanced out at the sheep grazing in the far pasture. "I'm wondering how you built this ranch into a business while taking care of a baby."

"With help. My mom took care of the baby while I worked in the mornings, and for the rest of the day, Mom would do the ranch work. Sometimes, I would carry my daughter on my back in one of those baby-backpack things. When she got older, we would take her outside with us and both keep an eye on her."

Iain got that analytical glint in his eyes. "Your daughter is more than seven years old."

Shit, damn, and hell in a handbasket. I'd slipped up, and he'd caught on. Distracted by trying so hard not to say Malina's name, I had inadvertently given him clues to her age. He couldn't extrapolate too much from the fact she was more than seven years old. One clue wouldn't convince him the kid was twelve years old and his daughter.

The queasy feeling in my tummy disagreed.

I clutched my hands over my belly, struggling to figure out what to say.

"You've achieved so much here," Iain said. "You're quite a woman, Rae."

What could I say to that? "Uh, thanks."

He sauntered toward me and laid his hand on my shoulder, sliding it to my nape. His fingers toyed with my hair. "Will you ever trust me again?"

"A lot of shit went down after you left, some I haven't told you yet. I lost my sense of security. Took years to get it back." I stifled a moan when he began to massage my nape. "Please don't take this the wrong way, but you showing up wrecked my hard-won sense of security."

He winced. "I've dredged up bad memories for you, by being here."

"It's not your fault. Just the way it is." I clasped my hands tighter over my belly. "All my life, I followed the rules and did what was expected. Then I met you, and everything changed. I wanted you. Didn't care if it was against the rules, didn't care about the consequences. I was so in love with you back then, I would've done anything to be with you. If you'd asked me to run away to Scotland with you, I would've done it." I drew in a shaky breath, letting it out gradually. "The universe punished me for my selfishness."

Chapter Twenty

Rae

He searched my face, his mouth compressed into a slash, probably struggling to understand what the hell I was talking about. It sounded crazy. But this was how I felt, and he needed to get that.

Why? It only mattered if I planned on letting him stick around.

God, I wanted him to stay. Forever.

"Listen," I said, "I don't expect you to understand all my issues right off the bat. Even I don't completely get why I feel this way, but I want—I need to figure this out."

He rubbed a hand over his mouth. "I understand. You need more time. Take all of it you need, Rae, I'm not leaving until you make me."

I couldn't tell him to go. Having him around took me back to those days before the hurricane had slammed into us, back when we were two people reveling in the glory of falling in love. If I couldn't tell him everything, I could at least share one more tidbit that might explain my reaction to his return.

"There's another thing," I said. With his gaze steadily on me, I shrugged away from his hand and backed up to the fence. "After Cece and her family chased you away, I went home to Iowa to lick my wounds in private. Or so I thought. My Mom was very understanding once I told her the gist of what went down."

"You told her about us?"

"Not the X-rated details, but yes. I told Mom we were involved, and I told her what Cece had done to break us apart." I slumped against the fence. "Ten days later, weird things started happening. I drove into town with my mom, and while we were in the grocery store, somebody slashed our tires. The next morning, a rock crashed through my bedroom window at five a.m., and the day after that, our garage got spray-painted with graffiti saying 'bitch' and 'whore' and similar lovely things. My mom called the police, but there wasn't much they could do without any evidence of the culprit's identity. They found footprints, but they came from a popular brand of sneakers. Things like that kept going on for about a week—until I caught the culprit in the act."

I hesitated, recalling the night I'd heard a noise outside my bedroom window and peeked out to see a familiar figure there. Even now, I had trouble believing it.

"Who was it?" Iain asked.

"Cecelia Bremner-Ashton."

"What—Why would she do that to you?"

"You mean why would she stalk and terrorize me?" I huffed. "She's nuts. When I saw her skulking outside my bedroom window, she ran off. My mom called the police. They caught her fleeing the scene in her Mercedes convertible, roaring down the highway like a bat out of hell. The next morning, her father and a psychiatrist came to retrieve her. Conrad Bremner-Ashton stopped by our house to apologize for his daughter's behavior. She was 'fragile' and 'high-strung,' and I should forgive her because her fiancé had dumped her a couple months before that. My forgiveness would help her recovery since she was headed to a rehab center back home. I had no idea she'd been engaged, but I didn't give a damn. She had no excuse for the things she'd done—to me and to you. I told Conrad to go jump into a sticker bush."

Iain chuckled softly. "I'm certain he didn't appreciate your sarcasm."

"Not sarcasm. I wanted to toss him into a pit of rattlesnakes." I picked at the wood boards behind me. "Instead, I cried. A lot."

He fastened an arm around my shoulders. "I should've been there for you."

"Doesn't matter. Regrets are pointless, we can't change the past."

"No, we can't."

We stood in silence for several seconds until I started to squirm and he cleared his throat, withdrawing his arm. In bed, we were at ease with each other. The rest of the time...

I pushed away from the fence. "Isn't sex supposed to make us more comfortable with each other? Not feeling that yet."

"Can't be comfortable after the conversation we've had."

"Guess you're right. Ripping open old wounds is bound to put us both on edge."

He roved his gaze up and down my body, admiring every curve, his lips kicking up into the start of a sensual smirk. "We need to take the edge off."

The heat in his eyes and in his voice ignited a smoldering fire inside me. How he could make me so hot with one look, I had no clue. I didn't care why, only that he made me feel this way.

I moved closer and settled my hands on his hips. "Let's smooth out those edges right away."

He whipped a condom packet out of his pocket. "On the grass or in the barn?"

Laughter bubbled out of me like champagne fizz. "Do you always have a condom in your pocket?"

"*Semper paratus.* You are a randy lass. Pays to be prepared."

I plastered my body to his, linking my arms around his neck, rubbing against the hard lump inside his pants. "Hurry up and fuck me, Dr. MacTaggart. Show me how notorious you really are."

His breaths came faster and heavier even as his cock swelled. The knowledge of how much he wanted me got me even hotter, my body throbbing and tingling in all the right places. When I wriggled against him, the granite line of his erection scraped against my belly and my nipples raked over his firm chest. The fabric between us couldn't dampen the sensation, or my ravenous hunger for him.

"Please," I moaned, rising onto my toes to nibble his ear. I dragged my tongue down his throat, earning a deep groan from him. "I want it quick and hard and dirty."

"Ah, Rae, yer the sexiest—" His words choked off when I ground my crotch against his cock. "*Verdammt nochmal.*"

He swept me up in his arms and carted me into the barn. Just inside the doors, he hesitated, glancing around like he was searching for the perfect spot in which to defile me. His chin lifted, and he flashed me a smug smile. Then he carried me toward the empty horse stall and set me down on my feet, positioned to the left of the half door to the stall. Cheeks red, eyes blazing with need, he drank me in for a moment, his tongue flicking out to moisten his lips.

I reached for him.

He grasped my waist and flipped me around, mashing me to the wall with his body. "Do ye trust me, sunshine?"

"Yes," I breathed.

Trapped like this, I could see him only in my peripheral vision, only glimpses of his movements. Sounds told me what he was doing. The metallic zing of his zipper when he tore it open. The *whump* of his pants falling down to his ankles. The ripping of a condom packet.

One of his big hands slid around to my navel. He found the button of my jeans, tearing it open. He jerked my zipper down, and with both hands, yanked my jeans and panties down to my ankles. When he stripped my jeans away, his hand had bumped the cell phone hidden in my pocket. He didn't seem to notice, or else he didn't care about it. His raging hard-on might've distracted him just a touch.

"Still trust me?" he said, his mouth on my ear, his entire body covering me.

"I do."

He kicked my feet apart, grasped my hips, and drove his cock into me.

A gasp exploded out of me. The thrill of him consuming me, the pressure of his length buried deep inside, it had me shuddering with need. When he pinned my wrists above my head with one of his hands, I rocked my hips backward in a desperate attempt to take him even deeper. His body secured me to the wall, the heat of him penetrated my clothes, and his every movement flexed all those muscles against me. I rocked back again. A long, low groan rumbled in his chest and vibrated into me.

He thrust hard and fast, ruthless in his lust. I had little leverage to move or touch him, and so I gave in to the dominant man shackling me to the wall. He shoved a hand between my body and the wall, found my clit, and rubbed it with merciless vigor. A sharp cry burst out of me. His relentless, punishing thrusts drove me beyond reason, beyond thought, beyond caring about anything except him and the way he made me feel.

Wanted. Needed. Worshiped. Gloriously sexy and wild.

That finger rubbed my clit faster, harder. His cock plowed into me again and again. The scorching pleasure robbed me of breath, set my heart to pounding like a giant drum inside my chest. Whimpering cries tumbled from my lips, but I didn't give a damn. Even the wet sucking sounds every time he plowed into me barely registered in my fevered mind.

His hips pumped wildly, crushing me into the wall. His hoarse grunts escalated into shouts and roars.

My climax seized my entire body, and like a wild thing, I screamed from the pleasure erupting inside me. "Iain!"

I rode out the orgasm, my sex clenching and releasing around his shaft while he pounded into me several more times. At last, his body went rigid, and with a throaty bellow, he came inside me, his release pulsating and drawing one last spasm out of me.

We held still, bound to each other in the most intimate way, reveling in the afterglow of incredible sex. I fought for breath, and so did he. In our mutual state of speechlessness, neither of us seemed willing to move even one inch. I felt him inside me, softened but not soft. If I could've spoken, I would've begged him to never pull out, to stay with me forever.

He kissed my neck, his stubble tickling my skin.

I moaned, limp and sated beyond belief.

He shifted his mouth to my ear. "I love you, Rae."

My heart thudded, my mouth went dry.

Iain stepped back, leaving me empty and alone. He pulled up my panties and jeans, zipped them, and hooked the button. Patting my behind, he said, "That took the edge off, eh?"

The smirk I couldn't see colored his voice.

Spinning around, I jabbed a finger at him. "You can't say that right after sex and then act like you didn't say it."

He tipped his head to the side, eying me with amusement. "Say what, sunshine?"

"That you...love me."

"Ahhh, that." He gave me his Buddha smile. "Since you don't want me to say it at all, why does it matter when I say the words? I do love you, and I won't pretend otherwise. I've said the words before, and I'll say them again if I feel the need."

I was being irrational, and I knew it. Every time he called me "sunshine," I got confused. When he said those three words, I panicked. Why? *Dammit.* I knew why. I was terrified I might be falling for Iain all over again.

Falling for the man who'd left me once before? Bad idea. Falling for the father of my child who had no idea he was a father? Monumentally bad idea. Falling all over again for the only man I'd ever loved? That was dangerous.

Iain watched me with that infernally serene expression, his pants still lumped around his ankles, his half-erect penis dangling. How on earth could the man look so relaxed with his dick hanging out? He really didn't care a fig about exposing himself. Iain MacTaggart had always had no shame.

Me, I had a big old steamer trunk full of mine, like a dead and dismembered body stuffed inside that trunk and waiting to be discovered. Might was well unlock that trunk and expose my last secret.

"Um," I began in the most moronic opening I could have imagined, "there's something else I need to tell you. It's about my daughter, and it's the hardest thing of all. I, well..." Couldn't summon the words to tell him. What a goddamn coward I'd become. "It's, uh..."

He held up a hand. "Don't say it now. I can wait until you're ready."

"You keep saying that. Aren't you tired of waiting for me to grow a spine?"

"Rae, you are not a coward. Whatever it is you need to tell me, you'll say it in your own time. Moments after I fucked you up against the barn wall is not the most auspicious time to share a secret."

"Are you sure?"

"Yes."

That nausea roiled in my gut again, and my skin itched everywhere. I shoved a hand into my jeans pocket, relieved to find my phone still there and undamaged. I needed a reason to escape, so I made one up.

Yanking out the phone, I waved it at Iain. "Gotta call and check on my daughter."

Not a complete lie. I did want to check in with Malina since she'd been homesick the past few days. Needing to do that right this minute was an exaggeration.

I rushed out of the barn and left my half-naked lover alone.

Chapter Twenty-One

Iain

All the next day while I put the final touches on Rae's surprise, I wondered about her statement yesterday. She believed the universe had punished her for breaking the rules, for taking a chance and having something for herself. Loving me had ruined the life she'd mapped out for herself, for us, but did she wish she'd never gotten involved with me? I could never regret a single moment with her, no matter the consequences. Before Rae, I'd used wanderlust as an excuse to run away from my family problems. With Rae, I'd found peace.

My behavior after losing her had nothing to do with Rae. It had everything to do with my weakness and my need to punish myself for not having the strength of will to fight for her. I was fighting now. I would not stop until she told me there was no hope, until she spat in my face and threatened to call the police, ordering me to leave the premises and never return.

I paused in polishing the flat wood surface in front of me. Rae must want me to stay past Saturday. Her actions and the little things she said gave me hope for that. And when we made love, I felt the connection between us. The intimacy of it gave me a deeper peace than I'd ever known before. If I could do the same for her, she might stop worrying about the powers that be punishing her for having one thing she wanted, just for herself. She deserved that much and more.

Yesterday, she'd wanted to share another secret with me, but when she'd said it involved her daughter, I'd stopped her from telling me. She had been confused, of course. More than once, I'd asked her about the father of her child. Now that she wanted to answer my question, I wouldn't let her. In that moment, I had realized why.

Wanting to know was one thing. The prospect of learning the answer made me uneasy. I couldn't bear to hear about the man who'd given Rae a child. What if he had been the love of her life and she still pined for him? Maybe he'd died, and the loss broke her heart. Rae was the love of my life, but I had no right to assume I had ever been hers. Could I live with it if she told me I wasn't?

The better question was when had I become such a selfish coward. If Rae gave me any portion of her love, I should be grateful for the gift.

An hour later, done with preparing the bulk of her surprise, I went to Rae's office on the second floor of the house. I knocked three times on the closed door.

"Come in, Iain," she called.

I opened the door and ambled inside the room. Two tall file cabinets, containing four drawers each, abutted the far wall while cardboard boxes lay strewn about the floor. Her desk—a wooden table, really—sat against the right-hand wall. Rae slumped in an office chair, twirling a pen between her fingers while she frowned at the screen of the computer that occupied the desk. A stack of papers lay to the right of the computer. I couldn't tell what was on the screen, due to the angle from which I observed and the fact I wasn't wearing my reading glasses.

Not that I'd intended to spy. It wasn't my business.

Rae tossed the pen onto the desk and spun her chair toward me. "What's up?"

"Your surprise is done." I rested my erse on the desk's corner. "I will unveil it tonight after dinner."

She smiled. "I can't believe you're cooking me dinner. No man has ever done more than heat up hot dogs in the microwave for me."

"Try to temper your expectations. I'm no gourmet chef."

"I wasn't expecting a Cordon Bleu experience." She stretched out a foot to nudge my calf. "Why do I have to wait until after dinner for my surprise?"

"Because."

She linked her hands over her belly, elbows on the chair. "That's not an answer."

I pushed away from the desk, planted my hands on her chair's arms, and kissed the tip of her nose. "If you're very good, I might let you see your surprise before dinner."

One of her knees rose up to rub my groin. "How good do I have to be?"

"Now who's misbehaving?" I set a hand on her knee and eased it down. "Be patient is what I meant."

"Fine," she said with a melodramatic sigh. "I'll wait."

And then she yawned noisily.

I knelt in front of her, glancing sideways at the computer screen. "What have you been doing in here all morning? You're exhausted."

"Business-y stuff." She flapped a hand toward the computer. "Accounting, mostly. Updating my website too. Tedious, mind-numbing things every businessperson must do."

"My cousin Lachlan was a financial adviser before he retired three years ago. He taught me quite a bit about money matters." I squinted at the blurry screen. "Maybe I can help."

"I thought all your cousins were younger than you. How can one of them be retired?"

"From his company. He sold it when he married Erica. Today, they own a farm and sell fresh produce and milk, all organic."

Rae gazed into space. "I've been thinking about branching out into dairy sheep, but it requires a lot more work. Do your cousin and his wife make a living with their farm?"

"They don't need to. Lachlan is wealthy."

"Ohhh, that does explain it. I forgot you said you have three rich cousins." She gave me a wry smile. "Must be nice to do whatever you want and not worry about how to pay the bills."

"It is." I skimmed a finger down her jaw to her chin. "Let me help you."

"With my accounting? Sure. Go crazy with it." Her lips tightened. "But I don't want your charity."

I sat back on my haunches. "You're as stubborn as my cousin Aidan. He wouldn't accept financial help from any of us when his construction business was on the verge of bankruptcy. Eventually, he realized it's not charity when it comes from the people who love you."

"Are you going to use your cousins as examples every time I try to reject your help?"

"You could learn a great deal from the mistakes made by the MacTaggart men."

"Hmm." She watched me for a moment, her lips working as if she cogitated on a tough riddle. Finally, she shoved her chair backward, got up, and waved an arm toward the computer. "You win. Help me, Iain, please."

I did not miss the sarcastic tone of the last bit.

"All right," I said. "Since you asked nicely."

I dropped into the chair, pulled it up to the desk, and squinted again at the blurry screen. *Bod an Donais*, I was going to have to wear my glasses. In front of Rae. I'd shatter her image of me as the ageless Indiana Jones of her dreams. Ah well, she wanted to know all of me.

Clearing my throat, I pulled my glasses out of the breast pocket of my shirt and slipped them on.

Rae bent over the chair from behind, her cheek brushing mine. "You need reading glasses? A sign of your true age at last."

"My cousin Rory wears reading glasses, and he's younger than I am."

"Don't worry, I'm still half convinced you must be a vampire."

"Vampire?"

"Your eternal youth."

"Ah. No, I'm not a vampire." I turned my head to graze my lips over her throat. "But I would love to bite your neck and suck on various parts of your body."

"We'll try that later."

For the next two hours, I worked with Rae to sort out her accounting problems. She'd done an excellent job of noting income and expenses, but she didn't do well with running reports to track her progress over time. I helped her install different software that would make financial tasks easier for her, and she pretended to be impressed an old man like me knew how to use a computer.

I loved the way she teased me. It was a sign of affection. We had never been this at ease with each other at Nackington. Our relationship had changed in the best ways.

After I'd shown Rae everything I knew about finances and computers, I went downstairs to have a piece in the kitchen. She stayed in her office performing more updates on her website. I had no knowledge of that sort of thing. My cousin Evan, the technical expert, would've had more help to offer there.

Once I'd finished off one of the oatmeal muffins Rae had baked yesterday, I washed up my plate and utensils. Leaning against the sink, I excavated my mobile phone from my pocket and dialed up my friend Gavin's number.

My mobile made a rude noise.

The screen said, "No signal."

I'd called my mother from this house the other day. Suddenly, I'd lost the signal?

When I tried again, the damn device chastised me again. I stepped away from the sink and dialed one more time with the same result. No signal. I pulled out my glasses to check the screen. It showed zero bars.

"Gah," I growled, and stomped toward the door to the hallway glaring at the mobile phone in my hand.

Rae nearly crashed into me.

She yelped, and I stumbled into the wall.

"Haven't you heard," she said, one hand on her chest, "about the dangers of texting and walking?"

"Thought that was texting and driving. At any rate, I wasn't texting." I held up my mobile. "Tried to call my friend Gavin, but the bleeding thing has no signal."

"Were you standing near the sink?"

"At first, but after two attempts I moved away from it."

"You must've still been on the sink side of the table." She waved toward the kitchen table. "You have to get on this side of the kitchen for cell phones to work. It's something about the pipes? I don't know. One of those weird anomalies, I guess."

"Think I'll try it in the living room."

"Sure, you could do that." She slanted toward me, her breasts nudging my chest. "Or I could give you a surprise instead." Her fingers found the button of my pants and unhooked it. "How badly do you want to chat with your buddy?"

"Hell with Gavin."

I swept her up in my arms and carried her into the living room where she gave me the kind of surprise every man dreams of receiving. Fifteen minutes later, I sank back into the sofa and gazed down at Rae, breathing hard and feeling well satisfied. She lifted her head from my lap and licked her lips in languid swipes of that agile pink tongue. I combed my fingers through her hair, marveling at the sensual woman who'd just taken my cock in her mouth and given me intense pleasure without expecting anything in return. She continued to amaze me with her boldness in sexual pursuits—and with everything else that made her the sunshine of my world. Bonnie, clever, strong, sweet, sexy, determined. That was my Rae.

"Is it surprise time yet?" she asked, climbing onto my lap.

"Not quite. I have to cook dinner."

"Do I need to dress up for this feast?"

"If you like." I skated a hand up her thigh. "But the feast is after dinner, when I gorge myself on you."

She leaped off my lap. "How about we skip dinner, get straight to the surprise, and then move on to the sex."

I couldn't help laughing. She was adorable when she got lustful.

"Take it easy, *gràidh*." I slapped her bottom. "We'll get there, I promise."

"Better be one phenomenal surprise considering how long I've had to wait."

"You'll find out soon." I tickled her neck with one finger, rewarded by her delicate shiver. "Do you have a land line? I'd like to call Gavin in the kitchen."

"Why?" she said with suspicion. Then, she bent her head so close to mine our noses bumped each other. "Is this part of my top-secret surprise?"

"It is."

"Sorry, no land line. Too expensive."

Part of me, a rather large part, wanted to offer financial assistance. I already knew she wouldn't like that, so I kept my mouth shut.

Rae grudgingly agreed to my plans for the evening after a long and deep kiss that made her go soft in the most exquisite ways. I headed for the kitchen to prepare the meal. With my limited cooking skills, I needed advice, but I didn't want to bother Rae about it. This was meant to be an evening of relaxation and pampering for her. I called Gavin instead since he had a talent for making simple meals that satisfied both his wife and anyone who joined them for dinner. I'd enjoyed his food on many occasions.

I stayed on the opposite side of the kitchen from the sink.

"You don't need my help," Gavin announced as soon as I explained the problem. "I've eaten at your house, Iain, and you do fine. Sounds like you're nervous about your first date with Rae, that's all. Go figure. Zen master Mac-Taggart is chewing his nails over a woman."

"Not chewing my nails." But I was scraping them on the countertop. "I'll admit to being anxious, though."

In the background of the call, a feminine voice said something I couldn't quite hear.

Gavin snickered. "Jamie says it's gotta be true love if you're so desperate you called me for advice. Not sure if I should be offended by that. I'll have to spread this through the MacTaggart grapevine, for sure."

"Go on. I don't care who knows about it."

"The Zen master returns."

"Do you have any advice, or would you prefer to keep mocking me?"

"Keep it simple, man. That's the advice. Rae already likes you." He lowered his voice to a whisper. "Just don't pull a Rory and get hitched in America without telling anybody."

"I won't, since I don't have a caber up my erse."

Rory's brother Aidan had coined that phrase to describe his uptight brother. Formerly uptight. If Rory could find freedom and happiness with the right woman, I could bloody well make a meal for Rae.

Gavin and I exchanged a few more good-natured gibes, then said goodbye. Keep it simple. I could do that.

Shortly after I finished crafting our meal, I went to the living room and found Rae seated in the armchair, legs crossed, hands folded on her lap. She wore a white dress printed with a colorful, abstract design reminiscent of flowers. White shoes with modest heels covered her feet. She'd done something to her hair that gave it voluptuous waves and dainty curls that framed her face. The neckline of the dress offered a glimpse of her breasts and the plumpness of those mounds.

I stopped short, blatantly staring at her. "You are the most beautiful woman in the world."

She smiled and rose from the chair. The hem of her dress ended a few centimeters above her knees, revealing the delicate curve of her calves and ankles as well as a hint of her thighs.

"Thank you," she said. "I decided to dress for the occasion after all."

"And I'm glad you did." I let my gaze skim over her cleavage one more time before I walked up to her and pulled a strip of black fabric from my pocket where I'd stuffed it earlier. "For the sake of dramatic effect, I need to blindfold you."

"Sure."

I loved the way she answered without hesitation. She might hold on to a few reservations about me, but I'd earned her trust.

Once I secured the fabric over her eyes, tying it behind her head, she asked, "Where did you get a blindfold? Do you take one with you everywhere you go?"

"I bought it in the hardware store. It's a microfiber cleaning cloth."

"You sure were a busy beaver in that hardware store."

"Wanted tonight to be perfect. Now, sit." Once again, she obeyed without question. I told her, "Stay here while I finish the final preparations for your surprise."

The wonderful woman crossed her legs again and waited.

I ran upstairs to change into more appropriate clothing, then I transported the food to the barn, with Rae's promise to keep the blindfold in place. My surprise waited in the barn, and I'd taken the liberty of adjusting the atmosphere inside it to suit the evening's mood. Romantic, that was the mood. I meant to woo Rae.

Fifteen minutes later, I led a blindfolded Rae through the main doors into the barn. The horses, Sunny and Ariel, grazed on hay in their shared stall. Little Ariel peeked over the stall door at us, then returned to eating.

I stopped Rae just inside the doors. "I've been meaning to ask. Why is your horse called Sunny?"

She reached for the blindfold, but I stayed her hand with my own.

"Not yet," I said.

Rae lowered her hand. "Might as well tell you. I named my horse Sunny because you always called me 'sunshine.' That's his full name, Sunny is a nickname. It was, um, a sentimental thing."

"A sentimental thing?"

She let her chin drop to her chest and made an irritated noise, then lifted her face to me. "I missed you, okay? I named my horse Sunny because I missed you."

I hooked an arm around her shoulders and pulled her close. "Well, he is as bonnie and braw as his namesake."

Rae huffed. "Can we get to the surprise already?"

"Yes, right away."

I whipped the blindfold off.

She blinked several times, adjusting to the lighting, and surveyed her surroundings.

The torches I'd fashioned from tree branches bathed her in warm, sumptuous light.

"Holy cow," she said with true awe in her voice. "This is amazing."

Rae flung herself at me.

I caught her, holding her up with her feet suspended above the ground.

She crushed her lips to mine.

Chapter Twenty-Two

Rae

*I*t wasn't until I stopped kissing Iain and opened my eyes again, sliding off his body, that I noticed his clothing. I backed up a few steps to get a better view. *Holy cow.* Warmth rushed through me from head to toe, setting off a tingling sensation that settled between my thighs.

The flickering light from torches lent his skin a golden quality. He seemed to have made the torches from branches and affixed them to the walls with metal brackets. I didn't care that he'd drilled holes in my barn instead of using the overhead lights. I wouldn't have cared if he'd blown up the whole damn barn.

He stood before me like a vision from the past. A hot Scottish vision.

A kilt of green-and-blue plaid swathed his hips and hung down almost to his knees. Black-and-brown leather boots sheathed his calves from the knees down with big, bronze-colored buttons down one side of each boot. I let my gaze travel up his body, past the black belt with its big silver buckle adorned with Celtic symbols and over the sporran, a leather pouch dangling from the belt to shield his privates. The *sgian dubh*, his replica medieval knife, was strapped to his right hip. From the waist down, he looked like a medieval Highland warrior. Above the waist, he wore a sky-blue, long-sleeve dress shirt with the top two buttons undone.

When I got to his face, my jaw dropped.

He'd shaved. No more stubble. And he'd tamed his wild hair, brushing it back from his face.

My God, I'd seen him like this once before—the day he'd strode across the entire campus dressed in this exact outfit and marched into the lecture hall to the stunned silence of his students. His mostly period-appropriate attire had gone along with his lecture for the day, a discussion of the medieval clan structure in Scotland. Damn, but he'd made history sexy. I'd wanted to jump him right then and there.

Tonight, he was…breathtaking.

And I wanted to jump him.

I let myself ogle him one more time. "Is that the same shirt you wore last time?"

"Yes."

"And the boots, and the—"

"Everything is the same." He took one big step toward me. "I've kept it all for thirteen years."

I tilted my head back to meet his gaze. "Why?"

"Why did I keep this shirt?" He plucked the fabric with his fingers. "Because you liked it."

For a long moment, I gaped at him. My body had come alive the second I noticed his clothing, but my heart had swelled when I'd spotted my surprise. His outfit had distracted me, and I'd forgotten all about the amazing thing he'd made for me.

I turned around to admire his handiwork.

The back wall now featured shelves. Four of them. Sturdy, beautiful shelves. Beside the shelves, he'd installed hooks for hanging up my implements, like the shovel he'd placed there.

He came up behind me, his hands settling on my shoulders. "I would've put your tools and things on the shelves and hooks, but I wasn't sure where you'd prefer to have them. The shovel is there in case you couldn't figure out what the hooks are for."

"Oh Iain, this is incredible. Thank you."

"That's not all. You needed shelves, but the last gift is strictly for your comfort." He approached a large object covered with a tarp and snatched the tarp away. "Have a seat."

My jaw dropped again.

Iain had made me a rocking chair. The most beautiful one I'd ever seen. One with curving, elegant arms and ornate slats. Celtic symbols of swirling shapes and little squares decorated the whole rocker, and a plump, plaid cushion padded the seat.

"Where did you get that cushion?" I asked. "They don't have those in the hardware store."

"Ordered it over the Internet. The UPS truck brought it yesterday while you were holed up in your office." His lips formed a smug smile. "You didn't hear it, did you? The delivery truck."

"No." I gave him a suspicious look. "Is that why you convinced me to play music while I was working in my office? So I wouldn't hear UPS driving up?"

He shrugged one shoulder, supremely pleased with his trickery. "I also ordered this."

I followed his hand as he gestured toward the table he'd created by placing a wood plank over two columns of stacked hay bales. On the table sat a bottle of...

"Champagne?" I asked.

"We are celebrating our reunion."

Guessed we were, though I hadn't thought of it that way until he said the words. Reunion. It sounded so...romantic. Iain had always been thoughtful, but tonight he'd kicked it up a notch. Or two. Or five.

On the table lay two plates, each covered with another plate set atop it upside down. Each place setting also included a champagne flute and a glass of water along with the requisite silverware.

I pointed at the table settings. "Did you order the champagne flutes too?"

He nodded. "I took care of everything."

"What's under the plates?"

"Come and see." He moved to the table and lifted the makeshift cover off of one plate. "What do you think?"

I surveyed the meal he'd prepared, and a grin overtook me. "Macaroni and cheese?"

"Not a gourmet meal," he said, uncovering the other plate, "but it's rather good, I think. The brown bits are those little sausages you like, chopped and mixed into the dish. I've rarely had to feed anyone but myself, and I have simple tastes."

"Guess that means your wife did all the cooking." As soon as I said it, I wished I hadn't brought up his wife. Dredging up bad memories was a surefire way to wreck the romantic mood he'd worked so hard to create for me. "Sorry, I shouldn't have mentioned your wife."

"I'm not that sensitive. You can mention Julia anytime." He picked up the champagne bottle. "Yes, she did the cooking. For the rest of the evening, let's forget about everyone else and focus on each other."

"Sounds good."

He removed the foil from the champagne bottle and popped the cork with ease, then poured some into the flutes.

I wandered over to the rocking chair, running my fingers over the smooth, polished wood. He'd made me a chair. A beautiful, beautiful chair. And the shelves. And the meal. Mac and cheese was fine by me. The fact he'd made all of this solely for my benefit meant more than I could say. When I settled into the rocking chair, feeling the soft cushion beneath me, my throat constricted and my vision got blurry. I was about to cry because a man gave me a hand-made gift.

Oh, he was definitely getting lucky tonight. Very, very lucky.

He offered me his hand, helping me up from the rocking chair, and led me to the table. We took our seats opposite each other.

Iain raised his flute. "Shall we make a toast?"

"Sure." I lifted my flute too. "I can't think of anything good to say. How about thank you for all the wonderful presents you made for me and may I please fuck you all night long."

He laughed. "We'll do that later, but I had a proper toast in mind."

"Okay."

Iain gazed into my eyes, his focus so entirely on me that it rippled a hot shiver through my body. "Here's to second chances and reuniting with the only woman who has ever made me want to grow old with her and have children that will be as sweet and bonnie as she is."

He clinked his glass against mine.

Oh God. My throat constricted again, my mouth went dry, and my bottom lip quivered from the sob threatening to burst out of me. He wanted children, with me.

My champagne flute jiggled in my hand. I clapped it down on the table. Christ, I had to tell him.

Iain set down his glass and clasped both of my hands. "What is it? I shouldn't have mentioned growing old together and having bairns. I meant it as a toast to the possibility, not an assumption it would happen." He hissed a curse under his breath, maybe in German. "I didn't mean to upset you. I'm a flaming eejit."

"The problem is me," I said, "not you. Iain, you've been so good to me this past week, and I love the surprises you gave me tonight. I can't keep this from you anymore. I need to tell you something. It's about my daughter."

He leaned back in his chair, releasing my hands, his shoulders slumping. "I know I've asked about the father of your child more than once, but I had no right to."

"I want to tell you. I need to tell you."

"Wait until tomorrow." He grasped his champagne flute. "Let's enjoy tonight without any revelations or confessions. One night to celebrate finding each other again. Can we do that?"

The look on his face, the tone of his voice, they conveyed something more than a desire to avoid emotional discussions tonight. He seemed sad and a little anxious. If he suspected the truth, he ought to be angry with me. If he didn't suspect, then what was bothering him? I wanted to ask, but he'd requested a concession. After everything he'd given me, I had to grant him this one thing.

"Yes, we can do that," I said. "One night without angst."

I raised my flute again.

He raised his, visibly relaxing.

"To us," I said.

Glasses clinked. We took sips of the fizzy liquid.

And just like that, everything went back to normal.

Tomorrow, I would tell him. I had to. Keeping this secret was eating me up from the inside out, and besides, he deserved to know the truth. Once I told him, he wouldn't want to leave. I no longer wanted him to leave, anyway. But could he forgive me for keeping a secret this huge?

No more wussing out. Whatever might happen, he deserved the truth.

Decision made, I allowed myself to enjoy a torch-lit dinner with Iain. Afterward, we made our way into the house and upstairs to Iain's room. We stripped each other naked and made love, tenderly at first, then with more gusto and lots more noise. I'd discovered I loved getting loud with Iain, letting go of my inhibitions and relishing the dirty and the sublime moments in his arms. For the first time since the first time I'd been with Iain, I could envision a long and amazing future with a man. This man.

In the morning, I would tell him about Malina whether he liked it or not.

After Iain fell asleep, I slipped down to the kitchen to wash up the dishes he'd used in cooking up his mac-and-cheese masterpiece. He had offered to clean up, but I'd told him to wait until morning. I couldn't sleep, though, too wired from worrying about how to break the news to Iain tomorrow. Doing the dishes usually relaxed me. I turned on the tap and paced the width of the kitchen while I waited for the water to heat up.

On my second circuit, as I spun on my heels and marched away from the sink, my cell phone rang. I'd brought it downstairs with me in case of emergency. With my kid over a thousand miles away, I worried about her—and about how to tell Iain he had a daughter.

"Hey, Mom," I said, checking the caller ID this time. "What's up? Please tell me Malina is not still awake. It's late there too."

"She's asleep," my mother said. "I had a heck of a time getting her into bed, though. She would not go to sleep until I promised to call and ask you right away."

"Ask me what?" I halted facing the cabinets on the wall by the doorway, my gaze aimed at them but not really seeing anything. "Is Malina okay?"

"Our girl is getting more and more homesick. She wants to cut the visit short."

I exhaled out the breath I'd been holding, my shoulders slumping. "Oh, is that all. Sure, of course she can come home early. But not tomorrow. I need one day to sort out some things." Someone, actually. "Malina will survive one more day. Tell her I'll see her Thursday."

"Sorry, I—" Silence cut off her words. "— say tomorrow?"

"Are you walking around while using the phone again? Can you hear me?"

"Caught some of it. Wednesday, right?"

I groaned. "No, Mom, I said not Wednesday. Send her home Thursday. Got it? Thursday."

"You said—" Silence. "— day. Right?"

"Ugh, Mom." I whirled around and spotted the steam rising up from the sink. Racing toward it, I enunciated each syllable sharply when I said, "Thursday. Not tomorrow. Thursday."

I twisted the faucet handle, shutting off the steaming water.

Dead silence on the phone.

"Mom? You there?"

Nothing. I held the phone away from my face. No bars. My call had dropped out. Turning around, I took two steps away from the sink.

Iain appeared in the doorway, stark naked with his hair a mess. "Something wrong? I woke, and you were gone."

"Thought I'd wash the dishes, but my mom called and—" Did he really need all the details? I set my phone on the table and waved him away. "Go back to bed. I'll be right there."

"Donnae take too long." He gave me a sleepy-sexy smile. "Suddenly find I cannae sleep without ye."

How could he be so sweet and adorable while completely nude?

"Shoo," I said. "I'm coming."

He shooed.

I dialed my mom's number, but her cell went straight to voicemail. I left a message and, to be double sure, sent her a short, direct text that left no room for misinterpretation: *Come home THURSDAY.*

Then I hurried upstairs to crawl back into bed with Iain.

Chapter Twenty-Three

Rae

I woke from an erotic dream about Iain petting me in the most intimate ways to find Iain petting me intimately. I lay on my back on the bed, the sheets thrown aside to make room for Iain beside me. My body already burned with a simmering fire he'd ignited with his fingers on my sex, stroking my outer folds in slow sweeps. His thumb grazed my clitoris every time he stroked up my skin, firing a shock of pure pleasure through me.

His face hovered over mine, his gaze intent on mine. "Good morning, sunshine."

Even his voice made me hotter, wetter, while his fingers kept stroking me. I struggled to calm my uneven breaths but couldn't quite manage it. "Morning. Oh…This is the way to wake up."

"You were already slick when I touched you."

Apparently, that dream had begun before he started his sensual massage. I wriggled when his thumb grazed my clit again. "I was dreaming about you."

"Tell me." His voice had become rough, almost a growl, and his erection prodded my hip. "What did you dream of us doing?"

I undulated my body, loving the way he touched me. "We were naked. You were hard, and I couldn't resist taking you in my mouth. That cock of yours is…mm…a beautiful thing to behold—or just to hold. In my hand, between my lips, inside my body. I dreamed of devouring you, sucking and licking and pumping until you came and came and came in my mouth. Then…oh, don't stop…because it was a dream, you got hard again instantly, and I tied your hands to the headboard and rode you until we both came with the bed banging on the floor."

He stopped moving his fingers, his eyes locked on mine, his breaths growing heavier. "You want to tie me up?"

From the tone of his voice, it sounded like he might not mind that.

"Not really," I said, "but in the dream it was hot."

"That explains why you were so slick and hot when I started touching you." He palmed my groin firmly. "For the record, you can do anything you want to me. With me."

"I once dreamed I ran Grayson over with my truck, and I really enjoyed that dream." I slid my hand up his chest to his shoulder. "I'm not actually going to run him over, and I'm not actually going to tie you up."

"You don't have to." He pressed a quick kiss to my lips. "I'm trying to tell you there's no need to hold back with me. As long as you don't start whipping me, I'm interested in anything you want to try."

"Have you ever tied up a woman?"

"No." His mouth arched upward on one side. "Those tricks are for men with no imagination. I donnae need props to make mah woman come."

Whenever he started talking that way—"donnae" and "mah"—I knew he was about to ravish me good.

"You are very talented at that," I said. "At least, you're very good at making me come undone. How do you always know exactly what to do?"

"Practice and attention." He nibbled my earlobe while his hand on my groin began to move in slow circles. "No more talking."

He thrust a finger between my folds, straight down my cleft and into my entrance. The heel of his hand rubbed my clit as he pumped his finger inside me, then added another finger, thrusting and thrusting, making me writhe and pant and moan. I clutched at his shoulders. He leaned over me more, and when my mouth fell open on a cry, he covered it with his own, swallowing every sound that erupted out of me. His tongue pumped in time with his fingers, penetrating my mouth as deeply as his fingers penetrated my sex.

I bent my knees, feet planted on the mattress. My hips lifted off the bed every time his fingers plunged inside me.

Pleasure. Thick, molten, searing. It seized my body with an orgasm that squeezed sharp whimpers out of me and shot them straight into Iain's mouth. I sank my nails into his shoulders. He kept kissing me through every shuddering spasm, every desperate cry, until I fell limp on the bed.

He swept hair from my face. "Breathe, *mon amour*. Christ, ye come like a star exploding. Stunning, fiery, and all-consuming."

Dimly, I realized he'd called me his love in French. My heart warmed at the endearment, but I had more important things on my mind.

"You make me come like that," I said, reaching down to curl my fingers around his shaft. "It's your turn. Let's see if I can make you go supernova."

"Ah, love, ye make me do that every time." He rose onto hands and knees, strad-dling my body. "Maybe ye donnae want to tie me up, but ye can ride me."

"Oh God, I'd love that."

He ducked his head to seal his mouth over mine again, his erection scrap-ing my belly, rubbing its moisture onto my skin.

I moaned into his mouth.

With a grunt, he broke the kiss and flung a hand out to the bedside table to yank the drawer open. A pile of condom packets lay scattered within it. He tried to grab one but fumbled. Snarling a curse, probably in German or Gaelic, he reached for a packet but his hand shook just enough to make him fumble it again.

"Breathe, *mon amour*," I said, repeating his phrase without even thinking about what the words meant. Or maybe I tried to convince myself I didn't think about it. "Let me get that for you."

He withdrew his hand, and I snagged a condom packet.

Iain kissed me. Hard and rough, almost brutal.

My phone rang.

We both froze. He pulled his head back, rotating his eyes to the side to eye my phone on the table.

I grabbed the phone. On the screen, it said, "Mom calling."

"Gotta get this," I said, all but shoving Iain away as I swiped to accept the call. "Hey, Mom, is everything okay?"

"Everything's fine," Mom said. "We're here."

The entire world, every atom of every molecule, seemed to grind to a sud-den halt. I gaped at the ceiling, uncomprehending. "You're—where?"

"In the kitchen."

"The—" *Shit, shit, shit, shit.* A litany of that one word repeated in my brain as I sprang to a sitting position with my heart racing and cold panic flash-freezing my blood. My voice came out a touch squeaky when I said, "You're in the house? My house? Wha—How?"

"You said Malina could come home today, so we took the first flight out this morning."

"Mom, I said Thursday. This is Wednesday."

"I thought we agreed to today." She paused. "Maybe I misunderstood, what with my phone cutting in and out. Oh well, we're here now."

My pulse kept racing, making my head swim. "I texted you last night and left a voicemail. *Thursday*, not Wednesday."

"Forgot to charge my phone. It died right after I called you last night. Luck-ily, I brought my charger and got the phone working again on the drive to your place." She paused, and her voice took on a motherly note of concern. "You sound strange, Rae. Are you feeling all right?"

No, not in any way imaginable. Phone troubles had instigated a disaster. Seriously? And Iain thought it was dumb to think the universe hated me.

I sucked in a deep breath, exhaling it gradually. I did it again. And again. Iain's attention made my skin crawl, but I had no time to spare for his confusion. Scratching the top of my head, I screwed up my face. "You got Malina up in the middle of the night to take a red eye?"

"No, Malina wouldn't sleep. She was awake after I called you last night and couldn't wait to come home. Greg chartered us a private jet from LAX. We left at four a.m." She hesitated before asking, "Are you okay, baby? You sound like you just woke up, but that can't be. I know you're up every day by six."

Realization smacked me in the face. I turned my head in slow motion to look at the clock on the table.

It gave the time as eleven thirty.

For half a second, I let myself think it was nighttime—except the sun was streaming through the windows.

"Um, uh," I said in a way that did not sound at all suspicious, "I took a—a nap. Gimme a few minutes to wake up, and I'll be right there." I glanced at Iain, sitting beside me propped up with one straight arm, that serene smile on his lips. Naked Iain. Naked, aroused Iain. "Mom, don't leave the kitchen. That goes for both of you. Do not leave the kitchen under any circumstances."

"Whatever you want, Rae." The tone of her voice told me she knew exactly what I'd been doing, and it had nothing to do with catching some Z's.

Plus, I never napped.

Damn, I should've come up with a better lie.

I hung up on my mom and slapped the phone down on the table.

"What is it?" Iain asked.

My thoughts spun like a team of whirling dervishes bashing into each other. My plan to break the news gently when I told Iain he had a daughter had disintegrated. He couldn't meet her, not yet, not until I…Dammit, I had no idea what I would do.

This was his fault. He had refused to let me tell him last night and the time before that.

No, the whole huge, honking mess was my doing.

Yep, the universe had smacked me down again. I gulped against the rock in my throat, my mouth parched and my eyes burning because I'd stopped blinking. Shutting my eyes, I gave myself two seconds to regain a smidgen of composure, but no such luck.

I swallowed again and faced Iain. "My mom and my daughter are here, downstairs in the kitchen."

"Are they?" he said lightly. "I'd love to meet them."

Oh no, hell no, not like this. *Hey, sweetie, come meet Mommy's lover who does naughty things to her every day and night. And oh, by the way, he's your daddy who I told you was dead. Whoopsy! He's alive.*

I sprang off the bed, frantically snatching my pink robe off the hook on the back of the door. The door that hung wide open.

Slamming the door, I whirled to face Iain, the robe dangling from my hand. "You have to leave. Now. Right away. They can't see you, please, just—" I veered my gaze around the room, desperate for a solution to the problem. "Climb out the window, okay? Go to the barn and hide in the hay loft."

"In the hay loft?" he said with a chuckle. "Take it easy, Rae. This isn't a catastrophe."

Like hell it wasn't. "Please. Go. Hide."

He slid across the bed to swing his feet down onto the floor. "We're on the second floor, and I am not an acrobat. I can't pop out the window."

"But you have to go."

He gazed at me with sympathy, the bastard. Why couldn't he get angry like any normal man?

God, I'd really lost it. I wished for a good man to act like a dickhead.

Iain rubbed his neck, sighed, and strode across the room to me. He grasped my upper arms and spoke in a soothing voice. "One of us has their bum oot the windae, but it's not going to be me."

"Dammit, Iain, I don't have time for another lesson in Scottish slang."

"You're panicking." He kissed my forehead. "Try to relax. I was saying you're talking nonsense, and that I'm not going out the window."

I wrung the robe in my hands, chewing my lip so hard I risked drawing blood.

He took my face in his hands. "Calm down, Rae. Take a breath."

For some reason, I did what he said. I took a breath. Let it out.

"Breathe deeper," he said, his voice gentle and calming.

I drew in a deep breath, exhaling slowly, and repeated the process until my heart no longer thrashed in my chest.

He took the robe, gently uncurling my fingers to free it, and held it out for me to slip one arm and then the other into it. Thank heavens I'd left a robe up here.

Iain tied the sash around my waist.

"Sorry," I said.

"Don't be. You're allowed to have emotions, even crazed ones."

How had he known what to do? What to say? He'd calmed me so quickly I couldn't imagine how it was possible.

I glimpsed the clock. "How did I sleep past eleven? I never do that. The horses must be starving."

"They're fine. I fed them."

"You did what?"

He smiled that placid smile. "I fed them. I've helped you do it for several days, I know what they each get." He trailed a fingertip down my cheek. "You looked so peaceful and contented sleeping, so I didn't wake you."

"But I never, ever, ever sleep past six."

Iain lifted one shoulder. "Today, you did. About bloody time, I'd say. You work too hard."

Sleeping late? Not like me at all. But I'd done lots of new things since Iain waltzed up my driveway. Maybe he was right, and it was about damn time I shook up my life.

"What would you like me to do?" he said. "Other than climbing out the window."

Thanks to his efforts, I could think again. Sort of. "I'll go to the kitchen and keep them occupied. You sneak out the front door and wait on the porch. I have to figure out what to tell them. Is that okay?"

"Yes, it's fine."

I swept my gaze up and down his naked body. "Could you put some clothes on, please?"

He smiled and kissed me. "Yes, Rae, I will put on some clothes."

"Thank you."

I spun around, flung the door open, and hurried downstairs. I'd reached the bottom of the stairs when footfalls pounded down them behind me. Turning, I froze. Iain rushed to me, halting with one foot on the last step and the other on the step above, dressed in jeans and a fresh T-shirt and holding a wad of clothes in one hand.

He offered the wad to me. "You forgot this."

"Oh." I took the clothes, my outfit I'd shed in a rush last night, and hugged them to me. "Thanks."

Iain bent closer, clearly aiming for my lips.

"Mom!"

We swung our heads at the same time to look down the hall.

Malina, her eyes as large as saucers, flicked her gaze from me to Iain and back again. "Who is that?"

A thousand stupid lies careened through my mind. *He's filling in for Ben. He's the plumber. He's the UPS guy.*

I glanced at Iain, but he was staring at the five-foot-tall girl gaping back at him, the girl with golden-brown hair and pale-blue eyes and an aquiline nose.

Slowly, he turned his face to me.

And I knew he knew.

Chapter Twenty-Four

Iain

Rae's eyes flared wide, and she clutched her clothes tighter. I glanced from her to the girl, back and forth, several times, struggling to comprehend. Rae might've been simply shocked to have her daughter see us together while she was wearing nothing but a robe. I might have believed that, if not for the girl.

I studied her for a moment. The light-brown hair. The pale-blue eyes. It was the nose, however, that had rendered me speechless. Christ, the girl looked like me. A smaller, feminine version of me.

But with Rae's beauty and inner light.

Memories reeled through my mind. Rae not wanting me to stay. Rae having no pictures of her daughter on display. Rae wanting to tell me something about her daughter. I remembered the day I'd arrived when Rae had ordered me to wait in the entryway, and I'd heard noises as if she were scrambling about doing who-knew-what.

Hiding pictures of her daughter? And she'd hidden the books about Scotland.

But no, I couldn't be—this girl couldn't be—

Rae flapped her hands at the girl. "Get back in the kitchen. I'll be right there."

The girl didn't move, her wide eyes locked on me.

"Go," Rae said sternly.

The girl bit her lip and scuffed back into the kitchen.

Rae seized my shirt and hauled me into her bedroom. She shut the door, dumped her dress and shoes from last night on the floor, and rummaged in her dresser for jeans and a shirt. While she pulled on her clothes, she told me, "I know you have questions, but I have to talk to my mom and my kid. I need you to be patient and wait here. Please. I'll explain later, I promise."

Given her panic upstairs, I didn't have the heart to demand she explain right away. Besides, she'd wanted to tell me for days. She'd tried to tell me. I had stopped her every time out of a selfish fear of what she might say because I'd thought she might tell me about another man who'd been the love of her life. But now, I wondered…

It couldn't be.

Rae finished dressing and faced me, rolling her shoulders back and meeting my gaze. "That girl is Malina. Our daughter."

I staggered backward half a step. Our daughter. My…daughter.

"That can't be," I said like the most backward numpty on earth.

Rae bit her lip, just like Malina had done a moment ago. "Look, I know this is a shock. I'm sorry, but I don't have time to explain. Please, Iain, wait here. Please."

Though my mind spun its wheels, unable to find traction, I understood one thing. She was anxious, possibly on the verge of panic again, and I needed to do what she asked of me.

"I'll wait," I said. "Go, see your daughter."

Our daughter. Christ almighty.

Rae dashed out the door, shutting it behind her, leaving me alone in her bedroom.

I shuffled to the bed and dropped onto it, elbows on my knees, my head braced in my raised hands. A daughter. Mine. Ours. Why hadn't I tried harder to find her all those years ago? Why had I run away like a coward? If I'd known…

But I hadn't. She wouldn't have known either, not for a while after our night together. How many months had gone by before she'd realized she was pregnant? After everything she had endured, all the trials she'd told me about, I couldn't be angry with her.

I loved Rae. I wanted children with her.

Well, I had what I wanted. That bonnie girl belonged to me.

My mobile phone chimed. I recognized the sound of a new text message and absently dug my mobile out of my pocket to check it. Delyth.

I groaned and tapped the message to read the full text: *When are you coming home?* As if the woman had a right to keep track of my movements. We had shagged off and on for a while, but that didn't entitle her to be my keeper. Delyth was lonely, though, and Rhys ignored her except for the occasional bout of bullying and belittling her. I sympathized, but I could not communicate with my ex-lover while I was trying to win Rae's love.

Particularly not when we had a child.

Our daughter. I wanted to run into the kitchen and…do something. Hug the lassie. Tell her I was sorry for missing twelve years of her life. Tell her… *Merde*. I had no idea what to say. Stay here like Rae had asked, that's what I should do.

I deleted the text from Delyth and sat there tapping my foot on the floor.

Rae

I walked into the kitchen stiffly, my socked feet dragging. Malina and my mother waited at the table in the center of the room, Mom at the head of the table and Malina in the chair kitty-corner to her. My mother kept a hand on Malina's as if comforting her, and my daughter had her head bowed. Oh God, I'd made such a mess of everything. How on earth could I explain any of it?

Find a way, I admonished myself. *You have no choice.*

"Hey," I said, pulling out the chair beside Malina and settling onto it.

My daughter lifted her head to fix her pale-blue eyes on me. "Who is that man?"

"I'll let you two talk alone," Mom said, getting up and hightailing it out of the room.

Not that I could blame her. This was my mess, and I had to clean it up on my own. A big, stinking pile of *merde* I'd piled up with my lies.

I picked up a lock of Malina's long, golden-brown hair, wrapped it around my finger, and let it go. "That man is Iain MacTaggart. He, um…" *Spit it out, get it over with*. Better for both of us if I ripped off that Band-Aid. "He's your father."

Her unblinking gaze zeroed in on me, her eyes the only part of her body that moved.

Jesus, I wished I could've found a way to soften the blow. How did you cushion the sucker-punch shock of finding out the father your mom said died was alive and staying in your house? Maybe a smarter person would figure out the answer. A smarter person would've come up with a better explanation for Iain's absence than telling my daughter he died.

"I'm sorry," I told her. "You deserve to know the truth. I should've told you from the start, from the first time you asked me what happened to your dad. Saying he died was the easy way out because I couldn't bear to think about what really happened. I need to tell you the story, though, even if it is years too late. I'm so sorry."

"You said that already." Malina leaned back in her chair, arms folded over her chest, not looking at me anymore. "It's okay."

My head jerked back, and I stared at her profile. "You forgive me?"

She shrugged. "Yeah."

Okay, that had been way too easy. Malina had never been prone to emotional outbursts or hissy fits, but this was no normal situation.

I put a hand on her shoulder. "It's okay if you're mad or hurt. You don't have to pretend everything's all right."

"Not pretending." She hunched her shoulders, and finally, she turned her face toward me, those eyes so like Iain's focusing on my face. "You knew he was alive, didn't you?"

"Yes, but I had no idea how to find him. He lives in Scotland, and it wasn't as easy to find people on the Internet back then."

Her eyes lit up, and she twisted around to lean closer. "He's really Scottish? You didn't make that stuff up? Is the tartan I drew when I was little really his family's?"

And here came the onslaught of questions. At least the return of her enthusiasm and curiosity assured me she wasn't feigning being okay.

I held up my hands. "Whoa, cowgirl, gimme a chance to catch up. Yes, Iain is Scottish, and yes, that is the MacTaggart clan tartan. Everything I told you about him is true except for the part about him dying. What I didn't tell you is how we met and how we lost each other. That's a story you deserve to hear."

She rotated her whole body toward me, excitement glittering in her eyes. "Yeah, you were always kinda vague about that. Did he rescue you from Nazis or an evil cult, like Indiana Jones? Did you help him find really cool stuff?"

"Hold up, sweetie. I never said any of that."

"No, but you told me he was like Indiana Jones."

The trouble with kids was they took things literally. "I said he was an archaeologist like Indiana Jones, but I did not tell you he fought Nazis and evil cults. Before I met him, Iain traveled the world working at excavation sites and helping other archaeologists figure out if artifacts were real or fake. I met him in college. I was a student, and he was my teacher."

Malina listened with intense focus as I related the tale of my ten months with Iain at Nackington, leaving out the salacious bits.

When I'd finished the story, she asked, "How old is he?"

"Fifty."

Her eyes bulged. "Whoa, he's like a senior citizen."

I stifled a laugh. "Not quite."

"But he doesn't look old."

"Maybe you'll inherit his ageless genes."

She bent closer, craning her neck to scrutinize my face. "You don't look old either."

Ah yes, to a twelve-year-old, thirty-five sounded decrepit.

Malina sat back. "Did he tell you stories about cool stuff he dug up?"

"Yes." I combed my fingers through her silky hair. "If you ask nice, I bet he'd tell you all the best stories."

"Really?" She grinned. "Awesome. When school starts again, I can make everybody jealous when they hear my dad is Indiana Jones."

I knew I couldn't talk her out of proclaiming that to her schoolmates. How I would explain to their parents that my child's father whom I declared was deceased was alive and well, I had no frigging clue. Since it was no one's goddamn business anyway, a half-assed explanation would suffice for the other parents.

"Why did you say he died?" Malina asked.

Here came the hard part. How much should I share? I rubbed my forehead, shutting my eyes for a moment before I answered. "When Iain had to leave, I missed him so much it physically hurt. I didn't know if he'd wanted to leave or if he'd been forced to go. I didn't know anything except he had disappeared. When you got old enough to ask questions, I delayed as long as I could. Eventually, I had to tell you something."

She was biting her lip the way I did whenever I was confused or scared or anxious.

"Maybe I made the wrong choice," I said. "I don't know. Today, I wish I'd told you some part of the truth, but at the time, it still hurt too much to talk about your dad. Telling you he died, it was the easy way out. Of course, it didn't stop you from asking questions about him." I clasped both her hands between mine. "Everything else I told you about him is true. Everything. I'm so sorry I lied about him dying, but—"

"It's okay, Mom."

Part of me, a rather large part, couldn't accept she was accepting all of this without any resentment or confusion. Maybe she had inherited Iain's equanimity along with his hair, eyes, and nose. She certainly hadn't gotten it from me.

I raised our clasped hands between us. "You're sure you're all right about this? You're allowed to be upset."

"You never lied to me about anything else. Right?"

"I swear I have never told you any other lies."

She shrugged. "Then we're cool."

I pulled her in for a firm hug. "Thank you, sweetie. I love you so much."

Rarely did I ever say those words, but this seemed like the appropriate time for it. My twelve-year-old daughter had dealt with the situation far better than I had.

I squeezed her harder.

"Mom," she whined, "you're squishing me. And it's getting kind of weird."

"Sorry." I let go of her and smoothed stray hairs away from her face. "You are one awesome kid, Malina."

"Whatever." Her cheeks had turned faintly pink, despite her offhanded wording. She pushed her chair back and stood up. "Can I talk to him?"

"In a few minutes." I got up too, pushing my chair up to the table. "I need to explain a few things to Iain first, okay? He's been waiting for me."

"Sure. I'll hang in the living room." As she trotted out of the kitchen, she called over her shoulder, "Maybe there's something good on the Science Channel."

I watched her tromp out of the kitchen, marveling at how much like Iain she was. Not many twelve-year-old girls were addicted to science and history. She'd handled the news about her father with a calmness so much like Iain's and the maturity of someone much older.

Maturity. It was about damn time I started acting like I had some of that. Iain's return had thrown me off kilter, but I needed to get back to being me. Rae Everhart, single mom and sheep rancher, knew how to handle tough situations.

Straightening, I rolled my shoulders back and headed for the bedroom.

Chapter Twenty-Five

Iain

Hours seemed to inch past while I waited for Rae to come back, though it likely had been ten or fifteen minutes at most. I studied the braided rug under my feet, the oval one that covered the floor under the bed and spread out around it. Following the twisting paths of the colored strands in the rug hypnotized me, or maybe that was the shock of learning I'd become a father twelve years ago. Rae had our child. Alone. Not knowing what had become of me.

The door swung inward, and Rae walked into the room. She shut the door, glancing around warily.

I sat up straighter and asked, "How did it go?"

"Amazingly well." She wandered to the dresser and leaned back, her bottom resting against it, gripping its edge with both hands. "I told her everything. Well, except for the pornographic parts."

"There weren't many of those." I hadn't touched her or held her hand until the last day. When I thought back on the night when I'd asked her to stay with me, I could recall every detail—except one. "I don't remember using a condom that night."

"We didn't. I should've said something, but—"

"It was my responsibility, and I fucked it up." I grunted, disgusted with my own callous disregard for the consequences of giving in to my unbridled lust for her. "You must think I'm a right plonker the way I kept insisting I always use a condom."

"No, I don't think that. I haven't behaved very responsibly either." She pressed her lips together, evading my gaze. "Listen, I—I told Malina you died. Not today. I mean years ago when she started asking about her father, that's what I said. It was easier than trying to explain what happened, why you left, especially since I wasn't sure about the answer to that question."

"Which question?"

At last, she fixed her attention on me. "Why you left."

"You know the answer now."

What must she have thought when I vanished? She'd said once she had worried she was nothing but a fling to me, and that was why I'd run away. She had also said she dismissed the idea. Knowing the truth today didn't erase the years of wondering.

I rose and approached her, stopping at arm's length from her body. "I can see why you might've thought I died."

She shook her head. "Stop being so damn understanding. That's not why I told Malina that. I took the easy way out. By saying you died, I didn't have to answer any more questions about where you were."

"And you spared her from wondering why her father didn't want her."

"You would've wanted her if you'd known."

The certainty in her voice surprised me. She had faith in my character, no matter what I'd done before today. Rae believed in me.

I moved closer and placed my hands on the dresser at either side of her. "I know now. I'm here, and I will not leave you or our daughter. My days of running when life gets complicated are over."

She hauled in a quivering breath, and her eyes shimmered with unshed tears. "I should've told you about Malina the day you showed up. I could've told you the next day or the day after or every day since. Don't you get it? I planned not to tell you, to make you leave before she came home so you wouldn't realize how much she looks like you and figure out the truth. I didn't want to share her with you."

"You'll never convince me of that." I slanted in until our gazes were level and our mouths hovered a centimeter apart. Keeping my voice low and soft, I told her, "Something else made you afraid to let me see her. You've talked about being careful not to bring a parade of men into your daughter's life. I think you were, and still are, afraid to let me into your life. Are you worried I'll leave?"

"No." She swallowed audibly. "If you stay, Malina will get attached to you."

"Not seeing the problem. If you're certain I'll stay—"

"I'll get attached to you too. And the universe might smack me down again."

Her statement stopped me, and I studied her averted face for an answer but found none. "Nothing will ever make me leave you again."

Her sapphire eyes still shimmered, though less brightly. Her tears were drying. "You didn't want to leave last time. The universe—"

"Is not trying to punish you." I rubbed my thumb over her chin. "There's no cosmic conspiracy to rob you of any happiness."

"Being with you broke the rules, and we both got punished for it."

"There are no rules to break this time. We have a child, a family. I know you want me, for more than sex."

Her voice was almost a whisper. "I want what I've wanted since the day we met. A life with you."

"Then have a little faith, *gràidh*. You can push me away and never know what we might've had, or you can take a risk and let me in." I spread my hand over her cheek, sliding my fingers into her hair, and drew her in for a gentle kiss. "Try to believe you deserve happiness. The universe will not punish you for loving me."

She laid her hand over mine on her cheek. "I want to believe that."

I swept my lips over hers again, our noses bumping. "I know you do."

"Give me time, okay? I can't get over my fears in five minutes."

"Take all the time you need." I pressed my mouth to hers, holding her face in both hands, waiting until she opened her lips to me before I slipped my tongue inside, exploring her warm, sweet mouth with leisurely strokes. She moaned, and her body slackened. I took full advantage, lunging deep, groaning when she responded with rough lashes of her tongue. By the time we ended the kiss, her eyes had gone soft. I smiled and said, "I'm not going anywhere."

She smiled like the quiet yet strong woman I'd fallen in love with years ago, the way she'd smiled at me that day when I suggested we have a picnic, and later, when I asked her to stay the night with me. My Rae of sunshine hadn't dimmed. The light would always burn inside her.

I stepped back, though not far, and shoved my hands in my pockets. "When is Malina's birthday?"

"February fifteenth."

Sure I must've misheard, I asked, "The fifteenth? Of February?"

"Yes, the fifteenth day in the month of February."

"That's the same day I started looking for you. It almost seems like… fate." Something I had never believed in. This coincidence had me wondering if I might've been wrong to dismiss it.

"Let's not ascribe too much meaning to that." Rae drummed her fingers on the dresser's edge. "I'm sure you've noticed our daughter's name."

"Malina."

She raised her brows, nodding as if she expected me to say more. When I didn't, she said, "You're the expert on what names mean. Are you seriously telling me you haven't figured it out?"

"Figured what—" My mouth fell open, cutting off my own words. "Malina. It's the feminine version of Malcolm."

"I wanted to name her after you, but the female versions of Iain didn't appeal to me. I picked your middle name." She fingered her earlobe, glancing down at her feet. "I wanted to give her your last name, but that would've led to more questions I didn't want to answer."

"Why honor me that way at all? I abandoned you."

She wrapped her arms around herself. "You're her father, whether you were around or not."

Her answer didn't satisfy my curiosity, but I decided to accept it for the moment.

"May I see her?" I asked.

"Yes, she's waiting." Rae gave me a rueful smile. "Be prepared for questions. Lots of them. She may not give you a chance to answer before she fires off more questions, so try to roll with it."

"I don't get frustrated easily, but you know that."

"Yeah, Malina's got that easygoing quality too." She raised a finger. "Except when she's excited. Normally, she's shy around strangers. Not today, though."

My daughter shared a trait in common with me? It seemed odd considering she had never met me, but I found I liked the idea.

Rae cleared her throat. "Why wouldn't you let me tell you? For days, I've been trying to. Finally worked up the courage to do it, and you kept putting me off."

"Yes, I know."

"Why?"

I groaned out a sigh. "Didn't want to hear you'd loved another man more than me. Sounds rather narcissistic, doesn't it?"

"Not at all." Her lips quirked into a small smile. "I wouldn't want to hear about it if you had found your true love. Either we're both narcissistic or…"

"We never quite got over each other."

"Yeah." Rae exhaled a rush of air. Then she dropped into a crouch, pulling open the bottom drawer of the dresser, and brought out a small object. On her feet again, she held the item out to me. "I made this for you."

I accepted the item, realizing it was a photo album.

She flipped the cover open. "I documented our daughter's life for you, beginning with the first ultrasound."

I squinted at the ultrasound image, making out the shape of a fetus. My throat went thick.

"It's the first picture of our daughter," Rae said. "Keep going."

With a sense of unreality enveloping me, I browsed the photo album. Pictures documented Rae's growing belly and then…Rae holding our newborn daughter, smiling with pure joy though she looked tired. I'd never seen anything more beautiful. The rest of the album captured moments in our daughter's life with captions handwritten beneath them. I watched Malina grow from a baby to a toddler to a little girl, and finally, the twelve-year-old I'd seen today.

"You made this for me?" I asked.

She nodded, hugging herself again.

I offered the album to her.

"No," she said, waving it away with one finger. "That belongs to you."

"Thank you," I said, hearing an unfamiliar catch in my voice. Rae had kept a record of our daughter's life—for me. She must've hoped one day we would find each other again. She must have wanted...our family.

Rae scanned me up and down, her lips flattening. "Listen, you can't prance around in the nude anymore. We have a kid in the house, so behave accordingly."

"I've never lived with a child before."

"Use your common sense." She gave me a half smirk. "Assuming you have any of that."

"Cheeky woman."

"Guilty as charged." She reached for my hand. "Let's go. It's time to meet your daughter."

Rae

When we walked into the living room, Malina flew off the sofa but stayed right next to it. Her eyes shined with excitement, and she caught her lip between her teeth as if struggling not to erupt like a question-spewing volcano. Her shy side held her back, but I had a feeling that restraint wouldn't last long. The father she'd dreamed about had become a reality.

I led Iain to the end of the sofa, six feet away from our daughter.

"Malina," I said, "this is Iain MacTaggart. Your father."

She bounced on her toes, smacking her hands together and clasping them near her chest. In a voice filled with awe, she said, "You're really Scottish?"

"I was born and raised in the Highlands of Scotland, and that's where I still live."

Malina rushed toward Iain and stopped inches away. "Are you really an archaeologist like Indiana Jones?"

Iain opened his mouth.

"Did you ever go to Egypt?" Malina asked before he could answer the first question. "What about China? Or the Grand Canyon?" She paused for half a second. "Do you wear a hat like Indiana Jones had? What about the whip and the gun? It would so cool if you had stuff like that, but it's okay if you don't. Do they let you bring a whip on an airliner? I bet they don't. Do you wear kilts? It would be totally sick if you did."

"Well—"

"Oh! Have you seen the Loch Ness Monster? I know a loch is a lake. I read that in Mom's books. Have you never been to Russia?"

The randomness of her questions seemed to have Iain flummoxed, based on his befuddled expression and his gaping mouth.

I took pity on him.

"Malina," I said, settling a hand on her shoulder, "why don't you give Iain a minute to catch up. He's not used to the tween inquisition."

Her shoulders sagged. "All right."

Iain studied our daughter for a moment, looking a bit shell-shocked, then bent his knees to get closer to her. "I haven't seen Nessie myself, but my cousin Rory swears he did. Most everyone thinks he's having us on since he's always been a pragmatic sort, but his wife swears it's true."

"Did she see Nessie too?" Malina asked.

"No, it happened long before Rory met Emery. But if she says it's true, it must be."

"Wow." Malina squinted as if thinking hard. "Pragmatic. That means logical, right?"

"Aye."

She tilted her head to the side. "What does 'aye' mean?"

Iain's easygoing smile broadened. "It means yes."

"That's a Scottish word?"

He winked. "Aye."

"Can you teach me more Scottish words?"

Iain straightened and tousled her hair. "I'll teach you all about my home."

"Awesome!" Malina glanced at me. "Can I show him the animals?"

Rather than pointing out Iain had already met the horses, the llama, and the sheep, I nodded. "Go on. I'm sure Iain would love to get the grand tour of the barn."

Malina grabbed Iain's hand, half dragging him out of the house. He barely managed to snag his boots from beside the door where he'd left them yesterday and yank them on.

I followed them out onto the porch but stayed there while they sprinted for the barn.

My mom sat in the porch swing, legs crossed, gently swinging. She halted the swing's motion and gestured for me to approach.

Father and daughter had disappeared into the barn.

I took a seat next to my mother. "Well, the secret's out. I imagined this would be a catastrophe full of tears and accusations." I shook my head, bewildered. "But Malina's fine about it."

"Children are more adaptable than adults."

"Guess so."

Mom gave me an assessing look. "If you'd known we were coming today, what would you have done with Iain? Kicked him out the door?"

I turned sideways toward Mom, one knee bent in front of me. "I'd planned to make him leave before Malina came home, but I couldn't make myself do it. This morning, I ordered him to climb out the window and hide in the hay loft. I've lost my mind, haven't I?"

"No, baby, you haven't." Mom threw a significant glance toward the barn. "I would've called you during the drive out here, but I thought you were expecting us. I couldn't have known you and Iain would be having a roll in the hay at eleven o'clock in the morning."

"I would've picked you up at the airport."

"Why bother you? I'm capable of renting a car and driving us here. Malina and I both napped on the plane."

"This whole debacle is my fault. I lied to my daughter and kept a huge secret from Iain."

"In your heart of hearts, I know you always wanted Malina to have her father in her life—and in yours." She touched my knee. "Remember, I was there when Iain left and you were devastated. The way you talked about him, and what you didn't say, told me all I needed to know about your feelings for him. If he makes you happy, that's all I want."

He certainly made Malina happy, at least so far. That was all I wanted. She'd spent her entire life wishing for a complete family, to know her father, to have the fairy-tale ending.

My mother leaned toward me. "Do you love him?"

"Iain deserves to know his daughter, and Malina deserves to know her father."

"That's not what I asked."

I gazed over my shoulder toward the barn where Malina and Iain had walked out into the sunshine grinning and laughing. A pang lanced my heart, and I couldn't lie to my mother. "I never stopped loving him. That's why I never had much enthusiasm for dating. Partly, I wanted to protect Malina from the pain of having possible stepdads walk away from her. Mostly, I couldn't picture myself with anyone else. How did you do it? How did you move on after Dad split?"

"Don't compare our lives, Rae. Your father wanted to leave, no one forced him to do it. You and Iain were at the mercy of events beyond your control." She squeezed my knee. "I saw how the Nackington thing affected you. I was there when that crazy girl stalked you. Baby, you lost more than the man you loved. You lost your faith in the future."

I had, more than she could know. Being with Iain this past week, I'd regained some of my faith that I wasn't being punished for taking something for myself. I had a ways to go yet before I could stop worrying about the future, about losing Iain again, about how that might affect me and our daughter. For the first time since Iain had returned, I could envision my future with him.

"We didn't fight hard enough," I said, "to stay together the first time around. I know Iain doesn't want to leave me again, and he'll fight for us, for our family. But you never can predict when those events beyond your control will pounce on you."

"The answer is simple," my mom said. "This time, fight like hell."

Chapter Twenty-Six

Rae

We became a family. It happened faster than I expected, faster than seemed logical, but I'd given in to the whirlwind of emotions. Malina was happier than I'd ever seen her, which was saying a lot. Every day, the three of us did the barn chores, played games, walked the pastures, and just hung out. My mother joined us sometimes, but often she would stay in the house or on the porch to watch us or read.

I'd caught her perusing some of my Scotland books on several occasions. Though I'd owned those books for years, she had never looked at them before. I didn't know what her sudden interest in them meant.

Malina and Iain bonded instantly. They went for rides together on Sunny and Ariel, like Iain and I had done while Malina was away. They were two of a kind—smart, inquisitive, generally easygoing, and fun loving. Not that I was a stick in the mud. My energy dwindled much faster than theirs, though, and even Iain had trouble keeping up with his daughter.

Every night, we retreated to our separate bedrooms too exhausted for anything more than a quick good-night kiss. I would've loved to fall asleep next to Iain and wake up with him in the morning, but I didn't want Malina getting the wrong idea—that we were a whole family, together forever. Yeah, I was being illogical. Couldn't help it.

Three days after my mom and my daughter had arrived, I sat on the porch swing with Mom while Malina and Iain played Frisbee in the grassy area between the house and the barn. They both grinned and laughed loudly every time Iain missed a catch on purpose to make Malina laugh. While I watched, she hurled the Frisbee and Iain dived sideways, way too low to nab the plastic disk, and twisted around to hit the ground on his back. He threw his arms out, moaning in a very loud and very phony way as if he'd been horribly injured.

"I'm knackered," he complained. "I concede the match."

Malina giggled.

Iain clambered to his feet, staggering like he could barely stand, making Malina laugh more. The two of them retreated into the barn chattering at too low a volume for me to hear. Watching them together made me ache for things I'd convinced myself I could never have. A life with Iain. A family with him. I had the family part, but the rest...

"What will you do with him?" my mother asked.

"Not sure what you're asking me."

"You told me you're still in love with Iain. He and Malina are getting along famously." She turned partway toward me. "So, what are you going to do with him?"

"I haven't got a frigging clue. He lives in Scotland, Malina and I live here."

"Have you thought about moving there?"

I swerved my head to stare at her. "Leave the country? I don't know about that. Getting used to Texas after growing up in Iowa was a big adjustment. Malina's never lived anywhere else."

"If Iain's as rich as you say, he could afford to travel back and forth until you two figure things out."

Today was the day I'd planned on making him leave. Saturday, that had been my deadline.

Everything changed the moment he met his daughter. I couldn't make him leave if I'd wanted to, and I had realized days ago I no longer wanted to. Even before the abrupt family reunion, I'd known I wanted him around for longer than ten days.

Mom stretched and yawned. "I should call Greg and check in."

"Say hi for me."

"I will."

While she went into the house to call her husband, I gazed out at the pastures and rolling hills that stretched far beyond the confines of my ranch. I'd spent over a decade molding this place into a business that supported me and my daughter. Iain kept telling me I worked too hard. Maybe I did, but I'd been at this for so long I didn't know how to slow down. Besides, I had to take care of my daughter.

Unless I let Iain take care of us.

My mom had been instrumental in getting this ranch going, though I'd handled the business end of things myself. I had felt guilty for letting her lend a hand with the physical work and for letting her pay for the property and many of the repairs it had needed. I'd never been any good at accepting help. Didn't know if I had it in me to let Iain ease my burden.

Movement lured my attention back to the barn. Malina and Iain wandered out of the building, heading for the house.

When they reached the porch, Malina said, "Hey, Mom. Can I have some pop? I'm soooo thirsty."

"Go ahead. Have a couple peanut butter cookies too."

She asked Iain, "Do you want some pop? We have Dr. Pepper and Coke."

"No thank you," he said. "I'll stay here with your mother."

Malina chewed her lip, glancing back and forth between me and Iain. She asked me, "Could I call him Dad?"

The request rocked me. Literally. My foot slipped, and the swing rocked back. She wanted to call Iain Dad. I shouldn't have been surprised given how well they got along and how thrilled she was to have a cool archaeologist for her father, but surprise me it did.

I met Iain's ice-blue gaze. "That's up to your father."

He stared at me blankly.

Malina swung around to aim her earnest gaze at him. "Well? Can I?"

"I…" He hesitated, then rolled his shoulders back and regained his serene smile. "Yes, you may. I would like that."

"Cool." She grinned. "Thanks, Dad."

With that, she raced into the house.

Iain leaned against the nearest post at the porch railing. "Thank you for that."

"Whatever makes the kiddo happy. You are her dad after all."

He rested his fingertips on the railing, squinting as if studying the wood. "Does this mean I'm not required to leave today?"

I tucked my legs under me cross-legged style. "Of course you don't have to leave. Ben comes back Monday, so you won't need to help out with the chores anymore."

"What if I enjoy helping you?"

"Then I guess you can keep on shoveling shit, if that's your secret passion."

"You are my passion, Rae. You always have been."

I clamped my hands over my knees, not having a clue what to say.

When he spoke again, his tone was measured and careful. "I love you. I don't expect you to love me, not yet, maybe never again. Meeting our daughter has changed everything, for both of us. All I want is to get to know the wonderful girl you've raised. She's like you in so many ways." He crossed his arms over his chest, fidgeted, and then shoved his hands in his pants pockets. "I always wanted to show you the world, starting with Scotland. Now, I have the chance to share that with Malina too."

My mouth had gone dry, and my fingers dug into my knees. "Are you trying to ask me a question?"

"I am." He leaned back against the railing and looked straight at me. "Come home with me. Let me show you and Malina my home and introduce you to my family, the cousins included. Bring your mother too if it will make you feel more comfortable. Bring your stepbrother and stepsister, your stepfather, bring everyone you know. But come home with me for a few weeks."

Weeks. In another country. With all his relatives. Thirteen years ago, I would've jumped at the chance. Today, I got a queasy feeling in my stomach. I'd never left the United States before.

I did have a passport, though. No excuses left.

The only thing that mattered was the answer to one simple question. Did I want to go with him?

"I understand," he said, "it's a big decision. Take your time thinking about it."

He'd given me time to think about everything. Whether to sleep with him. Whether to tell him about our daughter. Always, he waited for me to be ready.

Iain ran a hand over his mouth, his focus on the floorboards. "I don't expect anything from you. I have enough space in my house for you to have your own bedroom."

The anxiety on his face, the earnestness in his voice, those things proved to me I knew the answer to my own question. Did I want to go with him?

Oh God, yes.

I leaped off the swing, sending it reeling, and marched straight up to him.

He slowly lifted his gaze to mine.

"Oh Iain," I said, bracketing his face with my hands. "I love you. Let's go to Scotland."

He'd stopped blinking, stopped breathing, and stared at me for the longest moment before asking in a halting tone, "Are you sure?"

"Yes."

I rose onto my tiptoes, wrapped my arms around his neck, and crushed my mouth to his. Neither of us deepened the kiss, and I let myself simply enjoy the pleasure of his lips on mine, the warmth and softness of his skin, the scent of sweat and man surrounding me. He slipped his arms around me, his big hands spread over my back.

We broke the kiss but lingered close enough our lips nearly touched.

Perched on my toes, I toyed with a lock of his hair. "Why did you say you have space for me to have my own room? We've been sleeping together here."

"Not since Malina came home."

My finger went still, his silky hair coiled around it. "Did you think I stopped crawling into bed with you because I don't want to anymore?"

He made a face reminiscent of a shrug.

I tapped a finger on his mouth. "I didn't sleep with you because our daughter has been exhausting us both on a daily basis. She's calming down now, what with the novelty of having a dad wearing off. That means I might crawl into your bed tonight."

"You can be fair certain I won't be crawling into your bed."

I'd been sharing my bed with Mom since neither of us could tolerate the air mattress in the other guest room.

"No threesomes?" I said with a teasing smile.

He feigned a shudder. "Not the mother-daughter sort."

I began twirling his hair around my finger again. "So, you have tried threesomes."

"Once." He sighed heavily and with great sarcasm. "Making two women happy is too much bloody work."

"You could've done a three-way with a woman and a man."

His disgust was genuine. "Och, no. I'm a womanizer, which means women only."

"I'm not a man-izer, but it is men only for me."

"My womanizing days ended a long time ago." He pulled me snugly against him, his palms drifting higher up my back. "And now it's you and only you for the rest of my life."

A shiver stiffened the hairs on my arms and nape. I had the weirdest feeling he was about to ask me to marry him, and I had no idea how I might answer.

"Relax," he said. "I'm not proposing marriage. Yet."

He winked and smirked.

"Maybe later, then," I said, and wondered why the heck I said it.

Iain's mouth opened.

Desperate to end this discussion, I covered his mouth with mine.

The front door opened with a click and a faint squeak.

"Mom and Dad are kissing!"

Our daughter's exclamation made me jerk my head around to look at her.

She was grinning, holding the screen door halfway open.

My mom came up behind her and smiled at us.

I smiled too. So did Iain. The four of us stood there smiling and not saying a word for several seconds before I realized Iain and I had news to share.

Reluctantly, I gave up the firmness and warmth of his body to face Malina and my mom. With Iain beside me, I slipped my hand into his. He curled his fingers around my hand, and I gripped his too.

"Guess what," I said. "We're going to Scotland."

Malina shrieked.

Chapter Twenty-Seven

Iain

The house became a frantic flurry of activity for the rest of the day. Rae's mother had decided to come with us, and she and Rae rushed around making plans for our departure.

The three ladies all had passports, but they needed to pack and make arrangements. Rae's mother had brought her passport because, as she told me, "It's like my gold card. I never leave home without it."

Rae called Ben, and he offered to come back a day early so we could leave for Scotland tomorrow. I'd called Rory to arrange for his jet to fly in Sunday morning to retrieve us at the Austin airport.

My family was coming home with me. *My family.*

In one week, I'd gone from a single man who did what I liked when I liked to a man with a daughter and the woman I loved by my side. I'd stuffed my belongings back into the duffel bag, though I'd kept a few condoms out in case Rae made good on her suggestion of crawling into bed with me tonight. Even if she did, we might both be too knackered for sex. Didn't hurt to be prepared, though.

While packing, I took out the old velvet ring box and flipped up the lid. The diamond glittered as brightly as ever, untarnished by thirteen years in a box. When I'd told Rae my side of the story of that day when our lives fell apart, she'd wondered why I took so long to get to my office that morning. I'd sidestepped the question. The truth was, I'd visited a jewelry store to buy this ring.

I'd meant to ask Rae to marry me.

She had wanted a future with me, and I'd longed for the same thing. After all the years that passed since that day, I shouldn't have a second chance. But Rae had given me one, and she sensed I wanted to ask her a vital question. She'd guessed the truth, though I had quickly assured her I wouldn't ask today. "Maybe later, then," she'd said.

Maybe later. If I waited for the right moment, she might give me the answer I prayed to hear.

After dinner while the lasses washed dishes, a task they'd refused to let me help with, I went out on the porch and called my parents' house. Earlier today, I'd broken the news to them about Malina. This time, I had different news to share.

Ma answered, sounding cheerful as ever. "How are ye, *mo luran?*"

"Ma, I'm too old to be called a baby."

"You'll never be too old, unless ye somehow grow older than me."

No point in arguing with my mother. I got my stubbornness from her and my foolishness from Da. "I'm coming home tomorrow—with Rae and Malina. Rae's mother is coming too."

"Och, Iain! I'll meet my granddaughter." Her tone turned sly when she added, "And the woman who stole my boy's heart. I'm sure she's braw and bonnie. About bloody time I got to meet her."

My mother never said the word bloody except in reference to the red bodily fluid. For her to utter the word now meant she was more excited than she'd ever been before.

"Easy, Ma," I said. "Rae is intelligent, determined, and a wonderful mother. You'll love her."

"Da is having drinks at the pub with Niall and your cousins." She made an excited little noise. "He'll be so pleased to hear this news."

"Tell him not to nick anything in celebration."

"Oh, donnae tease your da. He hasn't broken the law in years."

Because I'd made certain he didn't need to ever again. I had worked hard to acquire enough money so I could support my parents in comfort. I could support Rae and Malina too, if Rae would let me.

I said goodbye to Ma. For the rest of the evening, I lounged on the sofa with Malina while Rae relaxed in the rocking chair I'd made for her. They were watching a movie about teenage girls having absurd adventures, accompanied by music so cheerful it made my ears ache. Rae's mother sat in the armchair enjoying the film. When I'd called her Mrs. Raines earlier, she had insisted I call her Cheryl. She even joked that maybe I should call her Mom. Considering she was only seven years my senior, I couldn't quite bring myself to call her that.

Though the ladies watched the TV, I watched my daughter and Rae. I had a family of my own. A daughter. I'd missed twelve years of her life, but I meant to make up for it in any way I could. Though we'd started the process of getting to know each other, I wanted more time with her. Much more time.

At ten o'clock, Rae told Malina, "Bedtime."

Our daughter rolled her eyes and moaned. "Aw, Mom, it's Saturday."

"Yes, and I let you stay up an hour later." Rae flapped a hand. "Off to bed."

Malina moaned again. "I'm not a baby, I'm twelve. I want to talk to Dad more."

"Nice try," Rae said, getting up and grasping Malina's hand to encourage her to get up too. "You can talk to Dad tomorrow. It's bedtime. You can get yourself in bed, Leenie, or I can tuck you in."

"Ech, don't use that baby name." Malina rose stiffly as if she were a hundred years old. "You're so embarrassing, Mom. None of my friends get tucked in anymore."

Rae patted the girl's bottom. "Scoot."

Our daughter shuffled off to her bedroom. A few minutes later, I heard the sink running in the bathroom.

Rae flopped onto the sofa. "I'm so not looking forward to the teen years."

I claimed one of her hands. "You won't need to endure it alone."

"Sure you can handle it?"

"Don't worry about me. I'm Indiana Jones, remember?"

"You may wish you had a bullwhip when Malina goes from tween to teen."

The conversation went on from there while Rae and I discussed what it might be like to raise a teenager, and later, I answered her questions about Scotland. She had almost as many questions as Malina had asked me today, but I didn't mind. Eventually, Cheryl excused herself to go to bed. Rae and I talked for an hour longer about nothing in particular. She told me about the nastier side of Texas wildlife—rattlesnakes and scorpions and Africanized bees—and I pretended to be terrified to make her laugh. I loved that sound, the melodic and sweet tones of her laughter. Her eyes sparkled too, and her cheeks dimpled.

Rae and I said good night in the hallway at the door to the room she currently shared with her mother. Soft snoring issued from the other side of the closed door. Our good-night kiss was tender and lingering, though I hungered for more. She must've been exhausted, but she didn't look it.

Once Rae had gone into her bedroom and shut the door, I made my way upstairs to the guest room. I brought out the ring box again, fingering the brilliant stone.

A beautiful, wonderful woman loved me. Rae loved me.

What a lucky bastard I was.

Sometime later, I was lying in bed trying to sleep but having no luck. Tomorrow, I would bring my family home to the Highlands. Rae would meet my parents and my cousins, my aunts and uncles and my friends. I'd need to limit how many of them I'd introduce Rae and Malina to at one time so they wouldn't get overwhelmed. The MacTaggarts, particularly my cousins, could overwhelm even the toughest sorts. The MacTaggart sense of humor might prove confusing to Rae and Malina.

Two family members at a time. Yes, that sounded right. If I could convince my relatives.

A soft creak made me glance across the moonlit room at the door.

It eased inward little by little, and a shapely figure sneaked inside, shutting the door as slowly as it had opened.

Rae couldn't have seen my smile as she skulked toward the bed. Lying in the bed's center, I linked my hands under my head on the pillow and waited. Her white nightie seemed to glow in the moonlight.

When she reached the bed, she pushed the nightie's straps off her shoulders and let it fall to the floor. She lifted the sheet and crawled under it, dropped to her belly, and slithered closer.

"Hmm, is that a ghost?" I murmured.

"Yes, I'm a spirit about to possess you."

I lifted my arm so she could nestle against me with her head on my chest. "You already own my heart, what else of me are you going to possess?"

She yawned loudly. "If I weren't so wiped out, I could think of lots of ways to do that."

"We have plenty of time for that later." I bent my head to inhale the scent of her hair. "Can't wait to make love to you in Scotland."

"Do I have to scream your name with a Scottish accent once we're there?"

"I think your normal American voice will do fine."

"Mm, good. I suck at accents."

She wriggled, nestling closer, and slung her leg over mine and one arm across my chest.

I pulled the sheet over us both, relishing the feel of her warm, supple body. "Good night, Rae."

"Good night, Iain," she mumbled.

Oh yes, I was the luckiest bastard on earth.

I woke in the morning with Rae still draped over me, her breathing shallow and regular, a sign she was asleep. Reluctant to wake her, I lay there enjoying the simple pleasure of waking up with the woman I loved. She smelled of sweet soap and woman, two of my favorite scents, especially when combined.

Rae moaned and stretched her lithe body against me. "Good morning."

"Mm, it is a good morning when I wake up with you."

She lifted her head, propping her chin on my chest. "We're going to Scotland today. I bet Malina is already up and bouncing around like a manic bobblehead toy."

I glanced at the clock on the table. "It's only six thirty."

"Trust me, this is like Christmas and her birthday all wrapped up in plaid with sparkly bows on top. She'll be awake." Rae puckered her lips, her brows lowering. "Why hasn't she woken us up yet?"

"She probably expects to find you in your room."

"Right." She laid a hand on her forehead and groaned. "I bet she woke Mom up, and Mom had to stop her from running up here to look for me."

"Let's check." I grabbed my mobile off the table and dialed Cheryl's number, which she'd given me a few days ago. When Rae's mother answered, I asked, "Hope I didn't wake you."

"No, Iain, I'm already up." Her tone suggested she wasn't entirely pleased with that fact. "Malina is hopping around like a jackrabbit and wants Scotland-shaped pancakes for breakfast. I don't even know what shape Scotland is."

I laughed. "I wouldn't recommend trying to replicate it in pancake form. Too complex, with all those lochs and inlets. Not to mention the islands."

"That's what I thought." She must've held her hand over the phone because the shout that followed was muffled. "Malina, no Scotland pancakes. Regular ones." To me, Cheryl said, "Will you and Rae be joining us for breakfast?"

I glanced at the naked woman draped over me and said, "Not immediately. We may... sleep a little longer."

"Pancakes won't be ready for half an hour or so."

"Brilliant. We'll be down in half an hour."

Disconnecting the call, I set down the phone and folded my arms around Rae. "Your mother is taking care of Malina. We have half an hour to ourselves."

Rae dragged her tongue up my chest. "What should we do?"

"Play."

She licked her lips. "I'd love to play with you. Don't move a muscle."

"You have plans?"

"Absolutely." She slid her entire body on top of me, her hands on my shoulders and her mouth on my neck. She nibbled my flesh. "I want to eat you up."

"Shouldn't we be quiet?"

"Mm-hm."

I hissed in a breath when she sank her teeth into my shoulder. "Cannae be quiet if ye keep—ah. Doing that."

"But I'm having so much fun."

Helpless to resist her sultry voice and her writhing body, I surrendered. "Do what ye want, but donnae blame me if I'm noisy."

"No blame, only pleasure."

She licked and nibbled her way down my chest, coiled her tongue around my nipples and sucked them, and swirled her tongue in my naval. I sank my fingers into the pillow, restraining my lust even when she moved lower and her silken hair brushed my cock. She ran her tongue over the head in one long, slow stroke, and I choked back a grunt.

Rae shimmied ever lower, massaging my inner thighs, kissing my skin, her breasts rubbing against me and her taut nipples scraping me. When she reached my knees, she gave me a saucy smirk and lunged up to swallow my cock.

"Fuck, Rae," I muttered, my teeth clenched.

The wicked woman sat back on her heels. "Good idea. Fuck Rae. I like it."

I gaped at her, barely able to breathe from the need hardening my cock even more.

She swayed her hips, and her breasts wobbled. "Well, are you going to do what you said?"

Unable to speak, I growled instead. Then I sprang up, grabbed her around the waist, and spun us around. I tossed her onto the bed. She landed with a bounce and a squeak that had not come from the bed but from her rosy lips. "Careful what ye wish fer."

She spread her thighs, revealing the pink, glistening flesh there.

I shoved a hand between her legs, feeling how slick and hot she already was. "Have another erotic dream about me?"

"Every night." She arched her back, lifting her breasts. "It's been days since I had you inside me. How much longer do I have to wait?"

"No more waiting." I snatched a condom off the table, ripped the foil apart, and sheathed myself. "Time to fuck Rae."

She caught her bottom lip between her teeth.

On my knees between her legs, I lifted her hips and sank into her body. The way she writhed and gasped drove me mad, but I pumped into her at a measured pace. Her body rose up when I pushed inside her and dropped back down when I withdrew, making her breasts bob and jiggle, those nipples jutting up and begging to be devoured. I released her hips and bent to capture one rigid, dusky pink peak, suckling and nibbling at it until she clutched my head and swallowed a moan. When she bucked her hips, I hissed in a breath.

"I need you," she whispered. "Please, Iain, make love to me."

With my cock still inside her, I planted my hands at either side of her body and gazed down at her flushed face. *Make love to me*, she'd said. For the past ten days, I'd fucked her. Today, she needed something more, something to show her what she meant to me. I laid my body on top of hers, careful not to crush her.

I kissed her. Slowly. Tenderly. I slipped my tongue into her mouth and explored her with leisurely strokes, even as I moved my hips, taking her body while I took her mouth, every stroke of my tongue in time with the thrusts of my cock. Her hands settled on my upper back, her fingers kneading, and she bucked her hips every time I pushed inside her, our movements in sync, almost as if we'd become one. I loved the feel of her, I loved the scent of her, I loved her passion and her sweetness and that sharp wit. I loved everything about this woman.

Her neck arched, pulling her mouth away from mine. She whispered to me between her gasps of pleasure, but I couldn't focus on her words. I dipped my head close to her, my cheek alongside her cheek, and words tumbled out of me.

"Rae," I said on a groan, lunging deeper into her wet heat. "Rae, my sunshine, *mo chridhe, mon amour.*"

Her fingers dug into my back. She locked her legs around my hips and threw her head back, her mouth falling open as her entire body went rigid.

"Come for me, *gràidh.*" I pushed the words out between my clenched teeth, the pressure to let go mounting inside me, throbbing in my cock. "I love ye, Rae, marry me."

The instant I spoke the words, her orgasm swept over her. It wrenched her body and her face, but it glowed from within her, the indescribable glory of a woman on fire with passion and unbridled pleasure. Hushed, gasping cries escaped her lips.

I plowed into her hard and fast once, twice, coming on the third and final thrust. I buried my face in the pillow beside her head, squelching my shout.

We lay there, me on top of her, for a while. Seconds. Minutes. I had no conception of time while enjoying the sensation of her body beneath me and her breaths ruffling my hair. I kept my face in the pillow, letting out the longest groan I'd ever made. Being with Rae was nothing like shagging all those other women. She brought out something in me no one else ever could. My sentimental side. I wanted to mumble idiotic things to her about how much I loved her hair, her eyes, her lips, the look on her face when she came, and the sound of her gasps. I wanted to wax poetic about the scent of her arousal and the slickness of it. I could've compared her vagina to a summer's day, plagiarizing Shakespeare to make my point.

She'd turned me into a dafty, and I didn't mind at all.

Rae was more concerned with something I'd actually said.

When I rolled off of her, lying on my side next to her, she gave me a slightly peeved look. "Tell me I was hallucinating and you did not just propose to me during sex."

I shrugged one shoulder. "Does it bother you?"

"Not sure. I'm still recovering from the orgasm high."

"Well then." I snaked an arm across her belly to grasp her hip. "I take it back. It's too soon."

She punched my arm. "You don't get take-backs on things like that."

"Consider it a preview of the romantic proposal I'll give you later." I kissed her shoulder. "You'll have plenty of time to think about your answer."

"I—" A noise erupted out of her, something between a groan and a growl. "You are insane, do you know that?"

"Yes, but it's part of my charm."

She tried to scowl at me, but the expression quickly softened. "What am I going to do with you?"

"Anything you like, sunshine." I caught her around the midsection and rolled onto my back, pulling her on top of me. "Anything at all."

"Tempting, but we have a super-excited preteen waiting for us downstairs." She climbed off of me and off the bed, snatching up her nightie and, to my dismay, covering her body with it. "Rise and shine, Dr. MacT. We're fleeing the country today."

Rae flashed me a grin and fled the room.

I crawled out of bed and pulled on my clothes, all the while wondering what she might've said if I hadn't taken back that proposal. My hand reached for the ring box like it had a mind of its own. I ran my thumb over the worn velvet.

What might she have said?

Chapter Twenty-Eight

Rae

The leather seats in the GulfStream jet molded to my bottom, soft and comfy, the epitome of luxury travel. How could I ever go back to commercial flights after this? We hadn't left the runway yet, but already I loved this jet, the one owned by Lachlan MacTaggart but most often used by Rory MacTaggart and currently loaned out to Iain MacTaggart. According to Iain, his cousins were as rich as he was, though Lachlan might've been richer. Evan MacTaggart sounded like the richest of all. I had to admit I felt a twinge of jealousy. Never in my life had I been able to afford this kind of luxury.

"Enjoying the leather?" Iain asked.

I suddenly realized I'd been petting my seat. Linking my hands on my lap, I told him, "I'm not used to this. Buying a newer used sofa is big excitement in our house."

"You won't need used furniture anymore. I can buy you the best of everything."

And here we went again. Ever since leaving the ranch, Iain had repeatedly mentioned that he could buy me anything I wanted or needed. I kept telling him I didn't need fancy crap, and I didn't feel comfortable taking his money. We didn't argue about it, but we did keep circling back around to the topic.

It had all started with Ben.

The poor guy came home to a madhouse, with Malina so excited she could hardly stand still, regaling Ben with stories of her awesome dad and the awesome things we would see in Scotland. Ben had already agreed over the phone that he would stay at the ranch full-time until we returned from our vacation. The money issue reared its ugly green head when I offered to pay Ben a little extra for the trouble.

Iain had pulled me aside and asked, "Can you afford to pay him extra? You said you don't have the money for full-time help."

"Chill out. I'll tap into my savings to cover the cost."

"Would that be the money you're saving for Malina's college tuition?"

"Yes. I'll make it up later."

Iain locked his arms over his chest, making his biceps bulge even larger. "I will pay for Ben to work full-time."

"No, I can handle it."

"Either that," he said, "or I will pay for Malina's education. She is my daughter after all."

"Let's not talk about this right now."

Grudgingly, he'd let it go.

Until we climbed into the limo he'd insisted on renting to get us to the Austin airport. Malina and my mom sat on one side of the limo while Iain and I occupied the opposite seat, with at least eight feet between us and them.

Iain had leaned in to whisper into my ear, "Let me pay Ben's wages. Please."

"Taking your money makes me uncomfortable." I crossed my legs, uncrossed them, and crossed them again. "But if you insist on doing something, you can contribute to Malina's college fund."

"I'll gladly do that, but I want to help you too."

"That's not necessary. I'm fine."

For two seconds, I thought he might give up. No such luck.

"Listen to me," he murmured into my ear, "I worked hard to make enough money that I could take care of the people I love. That includes you, Rae."

Thankfully, our daughter intervened.

Malina clapped her hands and said, "Let's play 'I spy.' I can start." She bent forward, peering out the shaded window. "I spy a horse. No, maybe it was a cow. How fast are we going? I think the driver must be speeding because everything's zooming by in a big blur."

Iain hadn't brought up the money thing again until now.

He sighed and slouched back in his seat. "You're stubbornly determined not to let me take care of you in any way. I don't understand."

"Try to, please." I slouched in my seat too. "I let my mom buy me a ranch. I felt weird about it, but I let her do it because she really wanted to. She won't even let me pay rent. When my old truck broke down for the umpteenth time, she insisted on buying me a spanking-new one. I talk the big talk about being independent, but I've really been living off my mom all these years."

He made a frustrated face. "What is wrong with accepting help from the people who love you? Besides, I know you've run a business by yourself and done well. I've seen your account books, Rae. You made the business profit-able all on your own."

"I *had* a good business, past tense. The wool market is dwindling, thanks to microfiber and other modern synthetics."

"That's nothing you could control, and it doesn't negate what you've built through hard work and dedication."

I let my head fall back against the seat. More cushy leather cradled it. My gaze wandered to the ceiling. "I've lived alone for a long time. Just me and Malina. I can't go from single mom to...whatever this is without any adjust-ment period."

"Are you saying you might accept my help later?"

The hope in his voice spurred me to look at him. I had to be honest—with myself and with him. "Maybe."

He sat forward, his lips curling upward a touch. "That's enough for me."

"I am letting you whisk us away to Scotland on a spiffy private jet."

He nodded. "I can be patient and wait until you're ready to let me be a part of your family."

A part of my family? I glanced over at Malina, who lounged on a leather sofa on the opposite side of the plane. Seated sideways, she had one knee bent in front of her and the other leg dangling off the sofa, her foot swinging. Her gaze stayed glued to the view outside the little windows.

"When are we taking off?" she asked.

"Soon," Iain said. "Have you flown before?"

"Never." She bent forward, studying something outside. "My first plane ride is on a way-cool jet taking me to Scotland. My friends will be soooo jeal-ous." She threw me a pointed look. "I could text them the news if I had my own phone."

"You don't need a phone."

"But it's for safety."

"Uh-huh," I said. "Somehow kids like you survived childhood before the invention of the cellular phone. And I don't want you having access to who-knows-what on your phone. It's the same reason I won't let you sign up on social media or look at the Internet unsupervised."

She rolled her eyes and moaned. "Mom, you're such a stick in the mud."

"I can live with that."

Malina's eyes got bigger, and I could practically see a light bulb popping on over her head. She veered her attention to Iain. "Dad, would you buy me a phone? Pretty please?"

"Clever lass. Nice try, but no. I agree with your mother."

Surprised, I eyed him with a new appreciation. He was taking to his fa-therly role better than I'd expected. And I wasn't saying that only because he'd backed me up on the phone issue.

My mom emerged from the rear of the plane where the bathroom, bedroom, and kitchen lay. She dropped onto the sofa near Malina.

I waved at Mom. "You sure were in the bathroom a long time."

"Fixing my face and hair." She moved her hands as if coiffing her curls. "That is one splendid bathroom. I don't think I'll ever be able to stand commercial air travel after this."

"Yeah, me neither."

The jet engines powered up, their whine drowning out any conversation we might've tried to have. Before I knew it, we were lifting off the runway so gently I hardly noticed the change. The jet reached altitude not long after and leveled off, the engine whine subsiding.

Iain rose and stretched, letting out a phony yawn. "I could use a lie-down. How about you, Rae?"

Of course he wanted to get me into the bedroom. The man had a one-track mind.

"No, I'm fine," I said, because I knew if he got me into a private room, we would wind up naked and moaning. What kind of example would that set for our daughter?

Iain strode around the little table between us and bent over my chair, his hands lighting on the arms. He murmured, "Come with me, Rae."

Oh yeah, he meant "come with me" as more than an invitation to walk back to the bedroom.

"There's a child on the plane," I whispered.

"We will be back there—" He nodded toward the hallway. "— and she will be up here."

"And what if she figures out we're not napping in there?"

"I'm sure our daughter won't be irreparably traumatized by the idea of her parents having sex."

Gazing into his pale eyes, I knew I was being ridiculous. "You're right. But really, we had sex this morning."

"I seem to recall a certain American lass seducing me three times a day or more. And then there were the times you threw me down on the sofa and put your mouth around my—"

"I remember what I did. And I enjoyed doing that to you."

Leaning in closer, he pressed his lips to my ear. "We can have a poke or talk, whichever you prefer. But I would like some time alone with you before we land in Scotland and the rest of the MacTaggarts descend on us."

"Descend? That sounds really welcoming."

He kissed my cheek. "Don't worry. I told Lachlan to make sure they won't overwhelm you. My extended family can be...exuberant."

"Great. People I don't know are going to exuberantly descend on me."

"If you're anxious, I can help you relax."

Yes, he definitely knew how to accomplish that.

I laid a hand on his chest and pushed until he backed up, then I hopped up and said, "Iain and I are going to take a little nap."

"Okay," Malina said, once again fixated on the view outside the windows.

My mom gave me a knowing smile. "Have a nice nap."

Iain took my hand and guided me down the hallway and into the bedroom, shutting the door behind us. "How should I relax you?"

He looped an arm around my waist, tugging me close, and nuzzled my neck.

"You could answer a question for me."

"Not what I had in mind." He dragged his tongue up my throat.

I couldn't stop my body from melting into him. Even as my head fell back and he kissed, licked, and nibbled his way back down my throat, I asked, "Will I be running into your ex-lovers in your hometown?"

He froze, letting out a long, deep groan of frustration. "Do we need to discuss that now?"

"You'd rather wait until one of them ambushes me on the street?"

Iain hissed a breath out his nostrils and straightened. "None of my former lovers will bother you."

"Not even Delyth, your five-year fling?"

"Delyth is my past. You are my present and my future."

"I know, but she does live nearby, right? Don't most of your ex-bedmates live in and around Loch Fairbairn?"

"Yes." He pinched the bridge of his nose between his thumb and forefinger, squinting his eyes. "I can't do a thing about that. They live in the area. I don't socialize with any of them, not even Delyth. I've been honest with you about my past, and I thought you accepted it."

"I do, but I'd like to know what I might be walking into." I flumped down onto the bed. "Not strictly for my sake. I don't want Malina to hear rumors about your notorious past. She already worships you, and I'm not sure how she'd deal with any of this."

He flumped onto the bed beside me. *Bod an Donais.* I didn't think of that."

"You said your exes won't be a problem. Are you saying that's not true?"

"My former lovers won't bother us." He blustered out a breath, and his shoulders sagged. "But there are a few men in the village who have no fondness for me. They like to blether about my past indiscretions."

Gossiping men. Who knew.

Iain covered his face with his hands. "I'm sorry, Rae. I should've thought of that and...I don't know. Warned you sooner. Or not brought you to my home." He snarled a curse in German under his breath. "I'm no father to be worshiped."

"Hey." I peeled his hands away from his face. "You are a wonderful father. You're patient and kind and not afraid to roll in the mud just to make your daughter laugh. Plus, I know you would do anything to protect her. That's the kind of man you are."

"A flaming erse with a past no mother would want her child to know about."

I grasped his face in both hands and made him look at me. "You are a good man, Iain."

"But the rumors—"

"Whatever happens, we will deal with it as a family. Got it?"

He stared at me for several seconds, then straightened and nodded. "Agreed. We do this together."

"Good." I jumped up and started unbuttoning my blouse. "I think it's time you made me a member of the mile-high club."

"That I can do."

He flung out both arms to snare me in them, yanked me to him, and flipped us both over so I lay on my back with my knees hanging off the bed. He landed on top but released me and knelt between my legs. With deft fingers, he unbuttoned my blouse and jeans.

"Grab a pillow," he said. "You may need to muffle your screams."

A hot shiver rippled through me.

I grabbed a pillow.

Chapter Twenty-Nine

Iain

We reclined on the bed side by side, spent and exhausted in the best way. I picked up Rae's hand, twining our fingers. She sighed, a contented sound that gave me an ache in my chest. Now that I had her, I would do whatever it took to keep her because I could never go back to living without her. We were a family—me, Rae, and Malina—and MacTaggarts fought for the ones they loved.

I brought her hand to my mouth and kissed her knuckles one by one. "*Mo chridhe*, you are the most precious treasure I've ever found."

"Wow," she said, "Iain MacTaggart is gushing. Never thought I'd see the day."

"Because you think I'm too manly for it?"

"No, not at all. But you aren't exactly the kind of guy who spouts romantic phrases." She bumped me with her hip. "Dirty ones, for sure. But not romantic stuff."

"More comfortable with dirty than romantic." I lifted my arm, she cuddled against me, and I settled my arm around her shoulders. "How do you feel about meeting my family?"

"If I can handle you, I'm sure I can handle them." She propped her chin on my shoulder. "Don't be surprised if Malina clams up. She gets nervous around strangers."

"She's never seemed it around me."

"That's different. You're her father."

"But Malina had never met me until a few days ago."

"True, but she felt like she knew you." Rae drew little circles on my chest with one finger, focused on the task. "I told her all about your exploits as an archaeologist, all the stories you told me, and I told her she has your eyes and hair and nose. I also showed her the scarf you gave me, the one your mother made from the MacTaggart clan tartan. Malina took all that information and created a fairy-tale fantasy about the perfect family. Us."

"Do I live up to the fantasy?"

"Oh, Malina thinks you're the cat's pajamas. She worshiped you from day one."

"Worshiped?" I mulled the concept but couldn't make sense of it. A child worshiped me. My child. "Not certain I deserve it."

"You do." Rae slid her hand up my neck to cover my cheek. "I worship you too, in a different way. You're very, very worship-worthy."

"I think you're having me on."

"Nope, it's true." She trailed her fingertips over my mouth. "I was infatuated back in college, and I thought I got over that, but I realize now I will always have an irresistible, incurable addiction to you."

"You're not alone in that." I moved my hand to her rump. "I worship you, Rae, and I'll prove it to you every day for the rest of my life."

She fixed her deep-blue eyes on me, the light sparkling in them, lending them the appearance of faceted jewels. For a moment, neither of us spoke. Something had passed between us, something strong and indescribable, and I wouldn't interrupt it.

Finally, Rae spoke. "Ask me again."

"Ask you what?"

"You know what." She pushed up on one arm, her breasts waving in my face. "Ask me again, Iain. It's time."

I knew bloody well what she meant, but I needed to do it right this time. So, I jumped off the bed and ran to my bag where it slouched on the floor against the wall. Rae watched me with keen interest, shimmying to the foot of the bed. I dug out the item I needed and returned to the bed, offering her my hand.

"Up," I said. "Doing it right this time."

She accepted my hand and slid off the bed and onto her feet. Standing before me, she glanced at both our bodies in turn. "Is naked the right way to do it?"

"For us it is." I dropped to one knee, raised the ring box, and flipped up the lid. "Rae, my sunshine, *mo chridhe*, I've never loved anyone but you and will never love anyone else. Will you marry me?"

"Yes."

I slipped the ring onto her finger.

We both grinned.

Rae held up her hand, admiring the ring glittering on her finger. Her eyes shimmered with moisture as she took in a shaky breath.

The box in my hand caught her eye, and her brows knit together.

She tapped a finger on the box. "Why does this look old? Is the ring an antique?"

"Not officially," I said, turning the box in my hand. "You wanted to know why it took me so long to go from your apartment to my office that day. I stopped at a jeweler's. I meant to ask you to marry me, but I never had the chance."

"What?" She stopped blinking, her lips parted. "You wanted to marry me then?"

"Of course I did."

She clasped a hand to her chest. "Oh my God, Iain, I had no idea."

"You were never a fling, Rae. Never. From the moment we met, I wanted a life with you."

Her eyes shimmered again with gathering tears. She held a hand to her mouth and sniffled.

I pulled her into my arms and kissed her until she sagged into me and moaned.

"Are you happy?" I murmured against her lips.

"Yes, very." She wrapped her arms around my neck. "I love you, Iain. You're the only man I've ever loved."

"Do you think our daughter will be happy?"

"That we're getting married?" Rae gave me a look that implied I must be a nutter to ask the question. "Be prepared for squealing and clapping, possibly dancing and hopping too."

"Glad I can make the lasses in my life happy."

She twirled a lock of my hair around her finger. "What does *mo chridhe* mean? You've called me that three times."

"It means my heart. That's what you are, the missing part of my soul."

"There you go again, spouting poetry."

I peeled her arms away from my neck. "Time to get dressed, sunshine. We have to tell our daughter the good news."

A few minutes later when we told Malina, she did squeal and hop up and down. My ears rang for several minutes after she finished expressing her joy with a series of shrieks.

I had Rae. I had our daughter. I had everything I'd wanted.

Assuming Rae survived meeting the MacTaggarts.

Rae

We had barely exited the jet and stepped off the air stairs at the Inverness airport when four adults and a small child rushed up to greet us. The adults consisted of an older couple and a younger couple, with the younger woman pregnant and holding the hand of the little boy who looked to be no more than a few years old. The boy had the same pale-blue eyes as Iain and the man who held the younger woman's hand.

The older couple approached us first.

"Meet my parents," Iain said. "This is Angus and Glenna MacTaggart. Ma, Da, this is Rae Everhart and our daughter, Malina."

Glenna MacTaggart seized me in a bear hug, blubbering words I couldn't make out. Maybe she was speaking Gaelic, or maybe she was simply overcome with emotion. She kissed my cheek, tears spilling down her face. "We've waited so long to meet Iain's Rae. We didnae know your name until this week, but we always knew there was a lass he'd loved a long time ago."

"I'm, uh, pleased to meet you too, Mrs. MacTaggart."

"Call me Glenna." She grabbed me for another fierce hug. "Ahm so happy to meet ye."

I introduced my mom next. The two mothers hugged, then my mom hugged Angus.

Malina hung back, peeking around me at the strangers smiling at us.

Angus MacTaggart gripped my hand, shaking it fervently. "Welcome to the family, Rae. We couldnae be happier Iain finally found the right lass. For a time there, he was going through the lasses like—"

"Da," Iain said firmly. "Don't frighten the woman I'm going to marry."

"I'm fine," I said. "Not like you haven't told me all about your past with the ladies."

Glenna clasped her hands in front of her mouth, more tears running down her face. "Och, Iain, did ye say you're marrying Rae?"

"That's right," Iain said, looking harried as his father clapped him on the back. "Rae accepted my proposal on the flight from America."

Malina set a hand on my arm and whispered, "Do I have to say something?"

I put an arm around her shoulders and pulled her up alongside me. To Iain's parents, I said, "This is Malina, your granddaughter."

Malina's eyes went wide when Glenna dragged her in for a fierce hug, crying and blubbering again. I understood her emotional state. If I'd found out I had a grandchild I had never met, and that my fifty-year-old son had finally found the love of his life, I might behave the same way. Hell, I'd cried when I accepted Iain's proposal. Women reserved the right to blubber under such circumstances.

Angus shook Malina's hand, hesitated, then pulled her in for a hug. He lifted the ninety-pound preteen off the ground like she was a toddler, and she giggled and grinned. Angus stood a few inches shorter than his son, but despite his pot belly, he possessed the MacTaggart strength.

"My granddaughter," Angus said to the younger couple behind him. "Can ye believe it? I thought Iain would never settle down with the right woman. When he stopped skipping all over the planet, I was happy. But I never imagined—"

"Da," Iain said. "Why don't you set Malina down? She's twelve years old, not a newborn baby."

"I don't mind," Malina said.

"Relax," I told Iain, coming up beside him. "Let them be. Everyone's happy."

But my fiancé looked oddly anxious.

I hooked my arm under his and leaned into him.

The younger couple came forward. The man with Iain's eyes offered me his hand.

"Lachlan MacTaggart," he said. "Pleased to meet you, Rae. I thought Iain would stay a bachelor forever, but when we heard he'd found you again, Erica and I knew he'd be different."

I wasn't sure I wanted him to be different with me. I liked him the way he was.

Of course, Lachlan probably meant Iain had stopped sleeping around. That change I did welcome.

The pretty brunette holding Lachlan's hand let go of her husband to shake my hand. She said with an unmistakable American accent, "I'm Erica, Lachlan's wife. And this is our son, Nicholas."

A squeal drew my attention to Malina, who was now perched on Angus's shoulders.

Smiling, I turned my attention to the little boy huddled against Erica's legs. I knelt in front of him and said, "Nice to meet you, Nicholas. I'm Rae."

I held out my hand.

Nicholas stared wide-eyed at it for a moment before he slipped his tiny hand into mine.

A few minutes later, we had all piled into a limousine. Malina elected to sit between her new grandparents, which didn't upset my mom. She knew how exciting it must be for Malina to meet a new branch of her family. I sat between Iain and my mom while Lachlan, Erica, and Nicholas occupied the seat that lined the side of the limo. My mom moved onto the seat with the younger MacTaggarts to chat about lord-knew-what.

Iain stretched an arm across the seat back behind me. "How are you adjusting to my boisterous family?"

"Don't worry so much, I'm fine."

"You haven't met the rest of my cousins yet."

I elbowed him in the side. "You make it sound like I'm going to the Roman Colosseum to be eaten by lions."

"No, but you will be subject to Aidan's roguish behavior and Rory's odd sense of humor."

"Trust me, I can handle it."

For the entire journey to Iain's house in the countryside, he remained tense, not at all the unshakable man I'd gotten used to seeing. What was he really worried about? That I might run into one of his ex-lovers? I could handle that too. He had met one of my exes, and we survived that—though Grayson Parker might have a different perspective on the encounter. Since I wasn't likely to punch Iain's exes, I decided that wasn't the issue. Unless it wasn't exes plural he worried about, but one ex in particular.

Delyth Kendrick.

Or her blackmailing husband.

Possibly both.

I put those thoughts out of my mind as we pulled up in front of Iain's house. The two-story home featured multiple gables on the second floor and windows everywhere. Painted a dusky shade of pale rose, the house looked like it had been plucked straight out of the past and plunked down here in the present day. Flowering bushes lined the front of the house, and a path made of small, round stones led up to the concrete pad at the front door.

My soon-to-be-husband insisted the rest of the family hang back while he showed me and Malina his house. He unlocked the door, pushing it inward.

Then he scooped me up and carried me across the threshold.

Malina giggled and hurried in after us.

Once he'd set me down, Iain spread an arm wide, indicating the short hallway in which we stood. "The grand tour, milady." He winked at Malina. "Pardon me. Miladies."

The grand tour stunned me. The house had been outfitted with country-ish furnishings and decor, everything from an overstuffed sofa clad in flower-print fabric to four-poster beds in all eight bedrooms—yep, eight bedrooms—and finally the library stacked with books that looked old but well cared for. Most of the titles referenced history or archaeology. No surprise there.

In the kitchen, I admired the farm sink and curving faucet. "Iain, this house is gorgeous. But I have to admit I pictured you living in, um…"

"A messy house?" he offered with a smirk.

"Yes. Sorry."

Malina was busily examining the contents of the massive refrigerator, oblivious of our conversation.

"Don't worry," he said, coming up behind me to rest his hands on my hips. "I'm not offended. In fact, I did live in a messy house for many years. I bought this one three months ago. For you."

I jerked my head around to peek up at him. "What? Why would you buy a house for me when you hadn't even found me yet?"

"Hopeful anticipation." He pulled me back against him and murmured into my ear, "I didn't want the love of my life sleeping in a pig sty. Bachelors tend to grow lax with their house cleaning. Well, all except my cousin Rory."

"Why didn't you clean up the house you had? Buying a new one seems like an extreme solution."

He linked his hands over my belly, his chin on my shoulder. "I wanted us to have a fresh start in a new house. Though technically, this is an old house. I had it renovated by my cousin Aidan."

"You said Aidan is roguish, but he fixed up this house like a pro."

"A man can be both a rogue and a hard worker."

I leaned into him, laying my hands over his. "I'm well aware of that, being engaged to a notorious rogue who builds me incredible furniture and wrestles with my sheep."

"A reformed rogue," he corrected. "I'm yours and only yours."

"You better believe it."

Chapter Thirty

Rae

Iain kissed my cheek and left to retrieve the family members waiting outside. While Malina played with Nicholas in the drawing room—oh yes, the house had one of those—and the adults hung out in the dining room, Iain pulled me into another, smaller room. It housed a fancy wooden desk, a fancy leather executive chair, and naturally, fancy wooden file cabinets. A window behind the desk overlooked blooming rose bushes.

"This," Iain said, "is your office."

"My office?" Was I going to live here? We hadn't talked about living arrangements, and honestly, I'd been too overwhelmed by getting engaged and meeting his family to consider the ramifications. We were getting married. Changes would be required.

"You're getting anxious," Iain said. "Why?"

He had relaxed more and more the closer we got to his home. Our home? Sheesh, he lived on another continent across a wide ocean from where I'd raised our daughter and built a business.

I took a deep breath and let it out slowly. "We have a big decision to make. Malina and I live in Texas. You live here. Uprooting my entire life is a daunting prospect."

"We could spend summers here and live in Texas the rest of the time." He took my left hand, sandwiching it between his. "I will do anything for you. Tell me what you need."

"Time to think. This is all happening awfully fast."

He glanced down at the ring sparkling on my finger. "Do you regret saying yes?"

"No." I placed a hand on his cheek. "I love you, Iain. I want to marry you, but for today, let's not talk about where we'll live. Let's have fun meeting your multitude of relatives and worry about the rest later."

"When do you want to meet the rest of the multitude? I asked them to wait until I call them."

"Might as well make the call. The more the merrier, eh?"

Grinning, he brought out his phone and dialed.

The rest of the MacTaggarts arrived fifteen minutes later.

Malina and I waited on the pebble path in front of the house while our new family members filed past to greet us. Aidan and his very pregnant wife, Calli, came first with their one-year-old daughter. As Iain had warned me, Aidan had a roguish sense of humor, but I couldn't help liking him. Calli was a sweet redhead who knew how to handle her husband. Niall and Sorcha MacTaggart approached us next. These were Iain's aunt and uncle, parents of the large brood that included Lachlan and Aidan. Both of them hugged me and Malina. Finally, Rory and Emery walked up the path to us. If I'd thought Calli looked very pregnant, Emery looked like she might pop out her twins any second.

Emery hugged me as best she could with her outrageously swollen belly.

Rory hugged me too, but he seemed distracted by his wife's condition. Iain had told me Rory went through three disastrous marriages before meeting Emery and that he'd always wanted children but thought he would never have them. Now, the wife he clearly adored was bursting at the seams with two babies. I couldn't blame the guy for being tense.

By the time everyone left, we had an open invitation to visit the home of every MacTaggart, including the castle of Dùndubhan. Rory and Emery owned the castle, but Rory's sister Jamie and her husband, Gavin, lived there and ran a museum that occupied a good portion of the building. It sounded intriguing, especially since Iain had helped design the exhibits.

Malina and my mom had gone into the sitting room to watch UK television, which thrilled Malina.

"This is so weird," she said with a grin. "I love it."

Iain and I wandered into the kitchen for a piece—of the blueberry tray cake Emery had brought us, though she freely admitted she'd hadn't baked it because Rory wouldn't let her do anything more strenuous than walking. Mrs. Darroch, their housekeeper who did double duty in their home and at Dùndubhan, had whipped up the yummy treat.

Seated at the kitchen island across from Iain, I stuffed another mouthful of blueberry goodness into my mouth. Around the food, I said, "This house is huge."

He half rose from his stool to brush crumbs away from my mouth with his thumb. "Sorry, sunshine, I can't understand you. How rude to speak with your mouth full."

"It's your fault." I swallowed and downed a mouthful of milk from the glass beside my plate. "First, you get me to swear out loud. Then, you get me to have sex anywhere and everywhere. It's only natural I start talking with food in my mouth, setting a terrible example for our child."

He shoved a forkful of cake into his mouth. "Might as well both be terrible examples."

I set down my fork and folded my arms atop the island. "Like I was saying, this house is enormous. You have enough rooms to put up a soccer team."

"When you're among the MacTaggarts," he said, twirling his fork in the air, "best talk about shinty, not football. And by the way, football is the proper name for the sport you mentioned."

"Ugh, let's not argue semantics. America and Scotland are different. End of story."

He got a mischievous gleam in his eyes, set his fork down, and leaned back in his stool chair. "It's different because Scotland is right, and America is wrong. You even drive on the wrong side of the road."

"Emery said if you teased me about driving over here, I should remind you that it's called the right side of the road for a reason." I slanted forward until my breasts pushed against my arms. "Driving on the right is right."

"Perhaps," he said slowly, "but that doesn't explain football. Americans carry the ball, they don't move it with their feet."

I threw my hands up in surrender. "I never watch sports, except figure skating. Let's talk about something else. Like where everyone will sleep tonight."

He stabbed his fork into the cake, tearing off a piece. "We sleep in the house, naturally."

Still teasing me. Two could play this game.

While he chewed his bite of food, I sat back and said, "In the house? Okay, then you can sleep on the sofa in the sitting room."

He pointed at me with his now-empty fork. "Excellent idea. You can sneak downstairs to crawl onto the sofa with me. Your screams will be muffled by the floors and walls between us and the upstairs."

I shook my head, sighing. "You are incorrigible."

"There are eight bedrooms, Rae. Have your pick."

"So," I said, running my fingers along the island's edge, "I guess we're sleeping in separate rooms."

He smiled—not his Buddha smile, but a wide one that exposed his teeth. "Ah, I see the problem. You can't stand a night without me."

"You're joking, but it's true." I leaned into the island, gazing at him with honest-to-goodness wistful longing. "I've missed spending the night with you since Malina came home. I want to share a bedroom with you, but I'm worried about what the kid will think."

"She's twelve, as she keeps reminding everyone, not a baby." He reached across the island to lay a hand on my arm. "We've had this discussion before. Our daughter will not be irreparably traumatized by knowing her parents are sleeping together. Besides, we are engaged."

"You're right, I know. I'm being silly." I bit the inside of my lip. "It's just that I've kept my love life secret, to protect her. It's hard to break a long-term habit."

Iain slid off his stool and strode around the island to me. He lifted me off my stool, setting me down on my feet, and wrapped his arms around me.

"We're a family now," he said. "You don't need to protect Malina from that. I will never leave you again, no matter what happens."

"I know that."

He kissed my forehead. "Rory would never let either of us be deported, and believe me, when Rory MacTaggart is on your side you have no worries."

"Good to know." After meeting his cousin, I could believe it. Rory was sweet and tender with his wife, but when he talked about how a vengeful Englishman had tried to cause his baby sister anguish by having her fiancé deported, I heard the steely edge in his voice. He had set things right with his solicitor skills and connections. If Iain or I should have any legal issues, I had no doubts Rory would intervene and succeed.

Wow. I had a lawyer in the family.

Even though Iain and I weren't married yet, every member of the MacTaggart clan had treated me like family. They'd welcomed Malina with open arms, and I was grateful beyond words for that. I'd never seen my daughter happier.

When she found out Iain and I would share a room, she grinned and hugged us both.

Yeah, she was traumatized. I gave myself a mental slap. How dumb I'd been worrying about this. Finding out her parents would be sleeping in the same bed had thrilled her. Her lifelong dream of a fairy-tale family had come true.

My long-lost dream had come true too. I was marrying Iain MacTaggart.

Chapter Thirty-One

Iain

The next day, I woke in my new favorite way—with Rae's backside tucked against my front, my arm draped over her hip, listening to the whispering of her breaths. After all the years of wishing for this very thing to happen, I finally had it. I had her. My fiancée. I slid my arm up to her waist, nuzzling her neck while she slept on, her breaths shallow and even. She smelled of powder and tropical shampoo, and she felt like heaven. But this was real, not a dream.

This was *real*.

I had slept while curled up against the naked, lush body of the only woman I'd ever loved. Every night from here on, I would sleep with her.

Rae stirred, moaning as she stretched her entire body from her face down to her toes. She twisted her head around to aim a sleepy smile at me. "Morning."

"Good morning, *mo chridhe*." I caught her face in my palm and kissed her. "What should we do today?"

"I'd love to see that castle. Malina's excited about it too."

"Dùndubhan is a museum, but it's closed on Mondays. A private tour should be simple to arrange." I kissed her again, more deeply. "Anything you want, you can have."

She flipped onto her back, running her fingers over my cheek. "Your stubble's getting longer and scratchier."

"I'll shave."

"Just like that? I didn't mean you had to—"

"I shaved for you for our first date the other night." I scraped my cheek on her breast, making her laugh. "I told you, I'll give you anything you want."

She folded her hands over her belly. "But what do *you* want? I'd like to know."

"You've given me what I wanted—you and our daughter."

"Come on, there has to be something else." She tapped a finger on my chest. "Don't be shy. Tell me your heart's desire."

"You are my—"

She snorted. "That doesn't count."

I reached for her breast, determined to distract her from this line of questioning, but she caught on to my tactic.

Rae got up to sit cross-legged and set her hands on her knees. "No sexing your way out of answering this time. Tell me what you really, really, really want."

Since she gave me no choice, I sat up too. "I don't expect you to give me everything I want. Even I'm not that selfish."

"You are not selfish at all. In fact, you've made it damn hard for me to do anything for you."

"All I wanted was you."

Rae made an irritated face. "Mission accomplished. What else do you want?"

Her tone had become sharp. She wouldn't give up until I confessed, but I worried how she might react.

"I know what you're thinking," she said. "You're worried I'll freak out. I won't. Trust me. Whatever it is, you can tell me."

"You have mind-reading skills, eh?"

"Getting naked and naughty with you for a week taught me a lot about how to read you."

"The unintended side effects of bloody brilliant sex."

"Mm-hm." She slanted toward me. "Just say it."

I shoved both hands into my hair and scratched my scalp vigorously, then blew out a breath. "I want to have a baby with you."

"We have one. She's sleeping down the hall."

"She's twelve. I missed...so much with Malina." I swallowed hard but couldn't knock loose the rock inside my throat. "I want to have a baby now, with you."

"Oh." Her eyes had gone large, and she'd stopped blinking. "I, uh...That's a big deal."

"I realize that, which is why I didn't mention it before."

She nodded cautiously, her lips clamped between her teeth.

"Forget I said it," I told her, bowing my head to scratch the back of it.

A silence fell between us, and I worried I'd shocked her despite her vow she could handle whatever I told her. She had already given birth to a child, raised our daughter alone, and I expected her to go through another pregnancy to satisfy my egotistical need to be there from the beginning. I'd missed twelve years of Malina's life because of my own selfish fears.

"If you'd known about Malina," Rae said, "you would've been here. I believe that."

Christ, she really could read my mind.

"Not divining your thoughts," she told me. "I know how guilty you feel about not being here all those years. Like I've said before, regrets are pointless. We need to move forward and make a new life together."

"We will."

She clapped her hands down on her knees. "A baby could be the perfect way to do that."

I gawped at her, frozen in mind and body. She couldn't have said what I thought she'd said.

"Yes, Iain," she told me. "I'm saying we should have a baby. But honestly, I might be too old to get pregnant."

Joy swelled in my chest, but I managed to speak with a calm tone. "You're not too old. My Aunt Sorcha gave birth to her sixth child at thirty-eight."

"Yes, it can happen. I don't want you getting your hopes up only to find out my eggs have shriveled up into little raisins."

"I'm older than you. My sperm might've shriveled."

A laugh burst out of her, and she slapped a hand over her mouth to squelch it. "This is the weirdest conversation we've ever had."

"It might be." I took hold of her hand. "Are we trying, then?"

"Yes, I'd love to have a baby with you. Again."

I glanced at the door, thinking of what lay beyond it. "How do you think Malina will feel about this?"

Rae patted my cheek. "Honey, she will be over the moon."

Catching her hand before she could pull it away, I said, "You called me 'honey.' You've never applied an endearment to me before."

"The first time around, I was too embarrassed to say anything like that. This time, I had to get used to you again." She spread her free hand on my chest, over my heart. "I'm accustomed to you now."

She'd repeated what I had told her the day I arrived at her ranch. I'd said we needed to get accustomed to each other again.

"Hmm," I said. "You told me that would never happen."

"I've been known to be wrong on occasion." She rested her hands on her knees again and fixed me with a serious look. "Tell me why you were so anxious yesterday."

Rae

I waited for a response while Iain casually stretched out on the bed with his hands linked under his head and one knee bent. His expression was pinched. Only Iain MacTaggart could manage to look embarrassed and sexy at the same time.

"Come on," I said, nudging his thigh with my knee. "Don't clam up on me. I agreed to going through another pregnancy for you, so the least you could do is explain to me why you got anxious the minute we stepped off the plane yesterday. You didn't relax until we pulled up here at your house."

"Our house."

"Yes, our house." I nudged him again. "Quit procrastinating and tell me."

He grumbled. "Several reasons."

"Such as?"

"My father, for one." He squirmed, his face pinching more. "I know he's stopped his thieving ways, but only because I earned enough money to keep him and Ma comfortably. If anything should happen, if I should lose the money somehow, he might...start up again. I don't want you and Malina to have the shame I've had all these years."

"We Everhart women are tougher than you think. And your father seems like a sweet man."

"He is, but if he feels the financial noose tightening, he will return to his old habits."

"You don't know that for sure." I lay down beside him, holding my head up with my hand. "Besides, we are family. You, me, and Malina. Families stick together no matter what, which means you will never lose us."

He snaked an arm around me. "I know you mean that, but there are other issues that might change your mind."

"Nothing will change my mind about you."

"Listen to me, Rae." He let his forehead fall onto my shoulder, holding it there for a moment, then raised his face to me. "I've told you about my past, but the fact is most of my former lovers live in Loch Fairbairn or in the vicinity of the village."

"You told me your ex-lovers won't be a problem, but there are a few men who might gossip about you. I can handle it."

"That's true." He screwed up his face. "As far as I know. But there's Delyth, and I'm not certain how she'll react to you."

"You said it's over, you broke things off with her."

"It is but, ah..." He covered his face with one hand, then scrubbed that hand through his hair. "She has been texting me."

"Texting?" I pushed up on my straight arm, staring down at him. "Why didn't you tell me?"

"I assumed Delyth would give up. She's a lonely woman, and I thought she was having trouble letting go but would get over it soon enough."

"She didn't, did she? You should've told me, Iain. When was the last time she contacted you?"

"Yesterday on the jet. You and Malina were playing checkers with your mother, so none of you heard the chime when the text arrived. I was on the opposite side of the plane."

"What has she been saying to you?"

He groaned with all the humiliation of a man sentenced to wear a pink dress for a month. "She says she misses me and when am I coming home."

Though a cold sense of betrayal swept through me, I kept calm with an effort. "What did you say in response?"

"Nothing. I've ignored her."

"Dammit, Iain, you told me it was over with Delyth."

"It is," he said through gritted teeth.

A dozen choice words, nasty words, popped into my mind—but I bit them back. His revelation had knocked me for a loop, but I honestly couldn't believe he had kept this from me for any reason other than embarrassment. His ex-lover couldn't let go. Not a problem I'd ever encountered, so I had trouble processing the information.

He hadn't informed me his ex contacted him. Men had perpetuated a myth that only women were ever irrational and emotional, but guys reacted that way all the time. Case in point, Grayson Parker and his "deadbeat dad's castoff" comment. Instead of admitting he was ashamed of his fears of getting into a relationship, he'd lashed out at me. Iain would never react that way, but he had found his own irrational method of dealing with his persistent ex.

I paused for a moment before speaking again. "Did she have any reason to believe you might get back together with her?"

"We weren't together, not the way you're implying." He slapped both hands on his forehead. "Christ, Rae, I donnae know why she's doing this."

"Are you sure you broke things off with her? I mean in a firm, final way. No wiggle room or wishy-washy language."

He pushed up on his elbows, frowning at me. "You think I led her on?"

"Men can do that without meaning to."

"Not me."

"What exactly did you tell her when you ended things?"

He fidgeted, clearing his throat, and scrutinized the corner of the room. "I told her it was the last time."

"The last time? As in the last time you would sleep with her?" When he nodded, I growled out a sigh. "That's not an un-vague blow-off. That's the kind of thing people say when they really mean 'I want to keep fucking you but I'm feeling guilty about it.' Not the thing you say to end an affair once and for all."

"I was ending it once and for all."

"But you didn't tell her that." I rubbed my forehead, feeling the first twinges of a headache. "Iain, you need to tell Delyth the cold, hard truth. As long as she thinks there's hope, she'll be miserable wondering when you might show up again."

He sat up, his knees bent in front of him, and let his arms fall over his knees. "I didn't mean to lead her on. What I said seemed clear enough to me." He drooped his head, shook it once, and lifted his face to aim a sad look at me. "But I see you're right. I'm sorry, Rae, I never meant to drag you into the mire of my past."

"I'm not leaving you, if that's what you're thinking." I touched a finger to his furrowed brow. "Stop worrying. I know you'll deal with the Delyth situation now that you realize what a goof you've been about it."

"You can call me a dickhead, I deserve it. *Bod ceann*, if you want to use the Gaelic."

"Not calling you either of those." I lashed my arms around him. "We're in this together, but we have to be honest with each other. No more keeping secrets because you're embarrassed."

"Aye, lesson learned." He cupped my face in one big hand. "You are an extraordinary woman, Rae Everhart."

"Better get used to calling me Rae MacTaggart."

"I don't expect you to take my name, not after the way I left you."

"Long, long ago in another life. I'm over it, and of course I want to take your name." I leaned into his touch, loving the warmth of his callused palm on my cheek. "You know, Malina asked me yesterday if she could change her last name when we get married. She wants to be Malina MacTaggart."

His eyes widened. "She...wants that?"

"Yep. We're a family, remember?"

A smile stretched his lips little by little, finally splitting into a wide grin. "Shall we start trying, then?"

"For a baby? Sure, but I'm on the pill so it might take a while before I'm fertile. Even if I stop taking the medication today."

"We could practice trying for a baby."

"Practice? That sounds like a lame excuse for having lots of sex."

Iain palmed my breast. "When did we start needing an excuse?"

"Never."

He pulled me down onto the bed, and we got started on practicing.

Chapter Thirty-Two

Iain

After two vigorous attempts at practicing for making a bairn, Rae and I wandered downstairs to the kitchen intending to make breakfast. We'd gotten out the required bowls and utensils along with the waffle maker. I hadn't known I owned one of those until this morning. My cousins Jamie, Catriona, and Fiona had stocked the kitchen for me. The American Wives Club had handled other tasks in the house like picking out furniture and drapes my future wife might like.

Rae and I had gathered the food items necessary for whipping up waffle batter when our plans took a different turn. We ended up standing at the island—Rae leaning against it and me leaning into her, kissing each other with great fervor—when our daughter's voice squealed from the doorway.

"Mom and Dad are kissing again!" she shouted as if this were important news to shout through the house.

The voice of Rae's mother echoed from down the hallway. "That's nice, dear."

"Hurry, Grandma, so you can see it."

We had already stopped kissing by then, but Malina grinned at us like she was waiting for us to start up again.

That was when I noticed the mobile in her hand.

She held it up, aimed at us. "Do it again so I can make sure I got a good picture. The first one might've been blurry."

I raised one brow. "You're photographing us?"

Rae squinted at our daughter. "Where did you get a phone?"

"Borrowed Grandma's."

As if on cue, Cheryl Raines appeared behind Malina.

"Mom," Rae said, "you gave her a phone. You know the policy."

"It's not her phone," Cheryl said, "it's mine. She claimed she wanted to take pictures of the flowers outside. Instead, she snuck in here to take some candid-camera shots."

Malina hunched her shoulders, raising her hands with the phone clutched in one palm. "Not my fault Mom and Dad make out where anybody can see them."

Rae wriggled away from me, planted her hands on her hips, and speared our daughter with a sharp look. "What are you planning to do with photos of me and your father kissing?"

"Put them in my scrapbook." Malina's voice took on a wounded tone as she pouted slightly. "I've been cheated. I never got to see my parents getting gushy and act disgusted."

I braced a hand on the island. "You didn't seem disgusted."

She rolled her eyes and huffed. "Can I take pictures or what?"

Rae pointed a finger at Malina. "Only for your scrapbook. I don't want to find pictures of us on Facebook."

"Mom," Malina said with a long-suffering tone, "Facebook is for geezers. Instagram is where all the cool kids go." She pouted again. "But you won't let me on there."

"Oh yes, your life is ruined because you haven't seen selfies of people with cartoon cat faces pasted onto them."

Malina rolled her eyes again. "Like I would do something soooo lame. I'd pick a sheep face."

She stated it as if everyone should have known mature children do this.

Rae glanced at me, her lips curving up in an exasperated but affectionate smile.

I scratched my chin, then told our daughter, "What about a compromise? You vow never to post any pictures of us online or share them with anyone without our permission. In return, we'll give you a picture worthy of your scrapbook."

Rae's attention swerved back to me, her eyes wide.

I winked, then asked Malina, "Is it a deal?"

She hopped on her toes. "Yes, yes, yes."

"Get your camera ready."

Malina raised the phone, its tiny camera aimed at us.

I grabbed Rae, dipping her backward, and kissed her.

Our daughter giggled. "Got it! Thanks, Dad. That's super gross."

She didn't sound disgusted. In fact, she sounded thrilled.

I returned Rae to her feet.

My sunshine touched her lips, seeming dazed for a moment before she smacked my arm. "You really are incorrigible."

"You knew that thirteen years ago."

"But it's more pronounced these days."

I waved toward the ingredients we'd gathered on the island. "Shall we make waffles?"

Malina answered, hopping on her toes again. "Yes! Yes!"

Rae caught my gaze and murmured, "Should we tell her yet?"

"Why not?"

"Kiddo," Rae said, moving toward Malina, "we have some news."

Our daughter clapped her hands and bounced on her toes. "Are you pregnant?"

"What? Why would you say that?"

Malina shrugged. "You and Dad sleep in the same bedroom. Cammie's parents have separate rooms because her dad snores really loud, and they only sleep in the same bed when they're getting pregnant."

"I'm not pregnant," Rae said. "Yet. We're trying to have a baby."

Our daughter shrieked. "That's awesome!"

Rae held up her hands as if trying to calm our child. "It may not happen. I'm older and—"

"Yeah, I know, you're way old." Malina shrugged again, abruptly calm. "It'll be cool if this happens and I get a baby sister or brother. I'd be the boss, right? And I won't have to, like, wash diapers or anything?"

"They have a little thing called disposable diapers these days, not like back in the Stone Age when I had you."

"Mom," Malina said with that exasperated tone and an eye roll, "Dad's the one from the Stone Age. He's *fifty*." She said this with an exaggeratedly shocked expression. "That's, like, soooo old."

I scratched my cheek. "Yes, I suppose it is. But then, I am a vampire according to your mother."

Her eyes flew wide. "Are you really?"

"No," Rae said, shaking her head at the pair of us, "your father is not a vampire. Look at his teeth."

Malina nodded thoughtfully. "Yeah, they're not pointy."

Cheryl, who had lingered in the doorway, staying out of the fray, at last spoke up. "Are we eating breakfast today, or is this a Scottish fasting holiday?"

Rae and I set about making waffles while Cheryl and Malina set the table in the dining room. Rae had just poured a serving of batter into the waffle maker and closed its lid when I came up behind her and sank my teeth into the exposed flesh of her shoulder.

She laughed.

I licked the spot I'd just bitten. "Still haven't taken you up on the offer to practice my vampire skills on you."

"There's been plenty of sucking."

"Yes, but—" I nipped her earlobe and whispered, "I want to fuck you while I bite your neck."

A laugh spluttered out of her. "That statement is simultaneously hot and silly."

"We'll try it tonight."

"You are so weird."

I slapped her bottom. "Must be a side effect of that ageless potion I swallowed years ago."

"Whatever you say, Dr. MacT."

"That does sound like the name of a mad scientist."

Our daughter arrived then, determined to help with the waffles. I didn't get the chance to sink my teeth into Rae again or show her what a mad Scottish scientist could do. After breakfast, I offered the ladies a treat.

"It's time," I announced, rising from the dining-room table. "I'm handing my wallet over to the three of you. Let's go shopping."

Malina shrieked. Cheryl whooped.

Rae leaned in and murmured in my ear, "You do realize you just handed your credit card over to a twelve-year-old."

"That's right, she's twelve," I said in the same tone our daughter used whenever she spoke the phrase, the one that implied the word twelve was a synonym for "mature adult."

Rae laid a hand on my shoulder. "I hope that card has a limit."

I pecked a kiss on the tip of her nose. "Limitless."

"You're either brave or completely insane."

"Or both."

Malina jumped up and down. "Let's go!"

Rae

Iain really had no idea what he'd let himself in for, giving a preteen access to virtually unlimited funds. He kept control of his credit card but paid for whatever our daughter wanted. I drew the line at an Aston Martin. She couldn't drive yet, for one thing. For another, she only wanted that particular car because she'd seen Lachlan MacTaggart's Aston Martin yesterday. He had informed her James Bond used to drive one of those, and Malina had instantly wanted her own.

"No way," I said for the umpteenth time as we exited a quaint clothing shop in Loch Fairbairn. "Not even when you're thirty."

"Come on," she whined. "Dad said I could have anything I want."

Iain emerged from the shop, having paid the bill, and clasped my hand.

"Dad," Malina said, "tell Mom I can have an Aston Martin."

He tousled her hair. "Afraid not."

She huffed. "You said I could have anything."

"Anything your mother says is acceptable."

"Man, that's not fair. Parents ganging up on me." She feigned a pout and pointed a finger at me. "You're supposed to be on my side because you're, like, racked with guilt over not being around for so incredibly long."

Racked with guilt? From what website did she get that term? I didn't recall ever saying that when I was twelve.

"You missed my whole childhood," Malina said to Iain.

I poked her arm. "You're twelve, kiddo, which means you're still a child."

"Mom." Her exasperation was real, but her fake pout faded. "You're such a fuddy-duddy."

"Ahhh," Iain said, smirking, "that is the fate of parents, isn't it? To become old and boring."

Boring? Not Iain, not ever.

He bent to press his lips to my ear. "Not you, sunshine. You will always be exciting and young."

"You better hope I stay forever young to keep up with your appetites."

I said it too softly for our daughter to hear.

My mom, however, was exiting the shop and overheard my statement. She gave me a knowing smile.

Did I have a smile like that? I never felt particularly knowing when it came to my kid, but maybe I did the knowing-smile thing unconsciously.

Probably not.

The four of us ambled down the sidewalk admiring the adorable village where Iain had grown up—well, where he'd gone to school. He'd grown up on a farm outside the village, though not the place where his parents currently lived. Iain had bought them a brand-new house a few years ago. Though I knew he'd bought them a house to keep his father from pilfering things, I also knew he would've bought them a house anyway, even if his dad hadn't been a bumbling burglar.

Loch Fairbairn was lovely. Most of the buildings were historic, restored to their original glory, but others had been constructed more recently in a similar style. This ensured the village had a cohesive feel evocative of the olden days. We passed right in front of the law offices of Rory MacTaggart, and when Iain saw a light inside, he asked if we'd like to stop in and visit with his cousin. Malina loved the idea, of course. She had told me earlier she thought everything and everyone Scottish was "awesome beyond the awesomest." She told me Iain's cousins—her first cousins once removed, or whatever—were "so not cringey at all." That was high praise in kid speak.

It turned out Rory and Emery were both in the office. After hanging out with the solicitor and his wife for a while, we meandered toward the town square. Stone buildings surrounded a grassy area while the sidewalks here featured stone paving. More shops, all as picturesque as the square itself, lined the streets.

"Got an idea," I said. "You three take off so I can do some secret mommy shopping."

Iain eyed my belly. "Mommy shopping?"

"Not pregnant yet," I said with mock sternness.

"She wants to buy us presents," Malina explained.

"Ah, I see," Iain said. "Should we do our own secret mommy shopping?"

"To buy presents for Mom?" Malina beamed at the idea.

"Of course."

"Extra awesome, Dad!"

"I agree," my mom said. "Since Rae won't spend Iain's money, we have an obligation to do it for her."

The three of them marched off to buy me who-knew-what, and I ambled down the stone-paved sidewalk past the cutest shops I'd ever seen. I veered into one that looked promising. After buying gifts for Malina, my mom, and Iain, I strolled out onto the sidewalk again.

My phone rang, and I stopped to answer it.

"Whose money are you spending?" Iain said in that sexy rumble. "Better be mine, _gràidh_."

"I did notice one of your credit cards had mysteriously made its way into my purse."

"Did you use it?"

Since he would find out anyway when he got the bill at the end of the month, I admitted, "Yes, I blew your dough like a grifter on speed."

"Glad to hear it. What changed your mind?"

"I knew you wouldn't stop pestering me to burn through your savings until I'd made at least a minor effort to do that."

"Good." His voice became muffled and indistinct like he'd held a hand over the speaker. After a moment, his voice became clear again. "Our daughter has grand plans for my bank account. Most of them involve spoiling you."

"Me?" I sounded shocked, which I was. "What happened to buying her an Aston Martin?"

"You vetoed the idea, and Malina says you are 'too uptight to treat yourself.' That is a direct quote from an expert."

"Uh-huh." I shook my head, though he couldn't tell. Malina and Iain had lots of fun together, but I hadn't expected today's fun to involve buying things for me. "I better go. Got more secret shopping to do. What say we meet at the little restaurant on the square in fifteen minutes?"

"It's a date." He lowered his voice to a sultry whisper. "Malina's wrong, though. You are nothing close to uptight."

"She's a kid. To her, uptight means I wouldn't let her go bungee jumping."

We said goodbye, and I turned to go left down the sidewalk.

A dark-haired woman stared at me from no more than five feet away.

I stared right back, unnerved by the stranger's attention.

The woman's green eyes darted as if she were embarrassed to be caught watching me. Her fair skin seemed paler in the shadows cast by the building beside us. When her hand floated up to her long, slender throat, I spied impeccably manicured nails painted a deep shade of crimson.

"Oh," she said, daring to look at me again. "Please excuse me. I wasn't following you. I saw Iain and then…you."

She knew Iain? Her accent wasn't Scottish, though. Not American either. I'd heard an accent like this before, on a British TV series. The character had been Welsh.

Cold spiked through me. A Welsh woman who knew Iain.

The woman touched her throat again. "I shouldn't have followed you, but I had to know. Are you the one he flew to America for?"

The bags I'd been carrying slipped from my fingers, plopping onto the sidewalk.

I swallowed against a sudden tightness in my throat. "You're Delyth Kendrick."

Chapter Thirty-Three

Iain

Malina, Cheryl, and I had just walked out of a shop when I glanced across the street and saw it. Saw them. Rae and Delyth. I stopped, paralyzed for a moment too long.

"Who is Mom talking to?" Malina asked.

Your mother is speaking to the woman I fucked regularly for five years. That would not be an appropriate thing to say to my daughter even if it was the truth. I opted for a version of the truth unlikely to scar Malina's psyche. "That's an old friend of mine."

"Old friend?" Cheryl said, sounding as if she knew the term friend was a euphemism.

"Yes." I met Cheryl's gaze. "Why don't you take Malina into the restaurant and find a table while I go over there and fetch Rae."

"We'll do that."

Malina balked. "But I want to meet Dad's friend."

"Another time," I said. "Go with your grandmother."

Though Malina gave me a wounded look, she let Cheryl guide her toward the restaurant.

As soon as they disappeared into the building, I raced across the street to Rae. When I reached the two women, they were smiling and laughing.

I stopped beside Rae, but my gaze flicked between her and Delyth. What was going on here? I'd expected to find Rae angry or hurt or both and Delyth crying about the way I'd ignored her for nearly two weeks. Instead, the women seemed to be enjoying themselves.

Rae hooked her arm under mine, her hand curled around my inner elbow. She smiled at me when she told Delyth, "Iain's afraid you'll turn into a psycho stalker. Maybe we should put his mind at ease."

Delyth turned a sweet smile in my direction. "Rae explained what happened. I'm not angry with you. I'd always known if you found your lost love, our time together would end. You couldn't stop talking about her even though you wouldn't say her name. You're a lucky man to have a second chance at love." Delyth's face darkened with a sadness I'd witnessed too many times on her bonnie face. "Not everyone finds it once, much less twice."

What was I meant to say to that?

Rae touched my ex-lover's arm. "Take care, Delyth."

"You too, Rae. And you as well, Iain."

"Thank you, Del," I mumbled, incapable of stringing together any more words.

As Rae led me across the street, she said, "I like her. She's a sweet lady."

"She is."

"But she seems very sad." Rae glanced up at me. "It's her husband, isn't it?"

I nodded. "She could leave him, her family has money and would take her in, but she won't. He can be charming when it suits his purposes, but he bullies and belittles her every chance he gets. Rhys also cheats on her often, everywhere he goes, sometimes getting women pregnant solely to spread his seed far and wide like a medieval king looking for an heir. He pays off the women and never sees them again. Never sees the children either. Why Delyth stays with him, I can't understand."

"Yeah, I don't get it either. That's not our business. I wish her well, but you and I have our own life to think about."

"Life?" I wrapped my arm around her shoulders. "As in one shared future?"

"Duh. Of course that's what I meant." She poked me in the side. "We're getting married."

We hopped onto the sidewalk. "How long an engagement did you want?"

"Not long. Very, very short. Like maybe two weeks at most."

"Two weeks?" I pulled us to a halt outside the restaurant's door. "Doesn't give me much time to organize the elaborate ceremony and reception you deserve."

Rae let out an exasperated groan. "I don't give a rat's ass about elaborate. All I need is to marry you. Keep it simple, Iain. Don't overdo this because you think I want a fancy wedding with all the bells and whistles."

"But you deserve—"

She slapped a hand over my mouth. "Nothing fancy. Nod if you understand."

I nodded, smiling against her palm.

My wife-to-be removed her hand and kissed me. "Good boy. You get a treat when we get home."

"What sort of treat?"

"Oh, it might involve lingerie and whipped cream and you biting my neck."

I swung the restaurant door open. "My favorite sort of treat."

I knelt at the foot of the bed admiring the masterpiece laid out before me—the work of art known as Rae Everhart, the mother of my child and soon to be my wife. The warm light from the bedside lamp painted her nude body with shades of liquid gold, accentuating every curve and dip. Her rosy nipples swelled up from her lush breasts, which rose and fell with her breaths. She held one knee bent, her foot flat on the bed. With her arms above her head, she toyed with her hair and licked her lips.

"Well?" she said. "Are you planning to bite me or what?"

A can of whipped cream sat on the table. Rae had worn the lingerie she'd bought, but it hadn't lasted long. I'd stripped her seconds after she walked out of the bathroom dressed in nothing but sheer black panties, the tiniest I'd ever seen, and a sheer black bra that lifted her breasts. How could she expect me to see her in that and not rip it off her edible body?

She smiled as if she knew my thoughts. "We did the lingerie thing, sort of, which leaves the whipped cream and neck biting. Have you lost your enthusiasm for it?"

"No, I'm deciding which part of you to devour first."

Her gaze flicked to my cock. "I know which part of you I'd pick."

"You'll have your turn later."

I walked forward on my knees until I straddled her thighs, then I reached for the whipped cream. Rae gasped when I sprayed some onto her nipples.

"That's cold," she said, right before her lips parted in a naughty smile. "I like it."

"Let me warm you up." I bent to lave one nipple, lapping up every speck of cream before shifting to the other breast. I relished the way her breaths quickened when I swirled my tongue around and around her stiff peak. I groaned deeply. "This is the sort of dessert a man needs."

"Don't use up all the whipped cream. I have plans for it too."

I sprayed more cream in a line from her collarbone down to her pubic bone, stopping just shy of the hairs there. "Donnae worry. There's another can of it in the refrigerator."

"Oh good. Oh…"

She arched into me as I licked and nibbled my way down her body, diving my tongue into her navel again and again until not one molecule of cream remained there. She moaned, wriggling her hips. It seemed impossible, but my cock shot harder. I loved her responses and how easily I could excite her, how easily I could drive her to come. She wouldn't come for me yet, though. I'd make certain of that.

I stretched my fingers over her mound, teasing the hairs until she gasped again. "Do you really want me to bite you?"

"Do anything you want. I love it all, I love you."

"But ye donnae mean *anything*. Ye must have limits."

"Not with you." She reached down to slide her fingers into my hair. "I know you would never hurt me, so I'm down with whatever you want to do."

I concentrated on whisking my fingers through the curly hairs of her mound. "But I did hurt you. I seduced and abandoned you, never tried to find you until this year. For more than a decade, I was shagging other women while I dreamed about you."

She stroked my scalp with her fingertips. "Iain, what is this? Post-engagement jitters? We've already talked about that stuff, and I told you it doesn't matter. Regrets are pointless."

"Rae, I've been with more than a hundred women. Only a few meant more to me than a one-off fling."

"You told me this already." She sat up and scooted backward to lean against the headboard. "I thought we were done with the 'I'm a rotten bastard' thing. What gives?"

I sat too, my knees bent in front of me. "Delyth."

Rae's brows crinkled. "What about her? Is she still texting you?"

"No, it's well and truly over. I called her and explained. She understands." I stared at the wall, unwilling to meet Rae's gaze. "You met Delyth. You spoke to her for…I don't know how long."

"Five minutes, tops."

"You like her. She liked you too."

Rae observed me for several seconds like she was figuring me out, but she'd done that a long time ago. "Are you worried I'll become best friends with Delyth and she'll tell me all your dirty little secrets? I already know what a naughty man you are and how notorious you are for bed-hopping with the local ladies. I doubt there's anything Delyth could say that would shock me, and besides, I don't discuss sex with anyone except you."

I scrubbed a hand over my face. "Am I being a fucking eejit?"

"No, you're being the man who promised to fuck me but who hasn't followed through yet." She stretched out one leg to tap her big toe on my upper arm. "Seeing Delyth knocked you for a loop, didn't it?"

"Seeing you with Delyth did that."

"Because she's the woman you had an affair with for five years."

"It wasn't that way. Not an affair."

Rae prodded me with her toe again. "For her, it was. I think you're feeling guilty because you inadvertently led her on. You keep thinking you need my forgiveness, but you don't. It's time to forgive yourself."

I scrubbed my face again, trying to wipe away the sins of my past. Rae was right. She had never thought less of me because of my past or for leaving her to raise our child alone. She had always seen things in me I never could. Maybe it was time I looked at myself through her eyes, trusted in her opinions the way she trusted me in everything, and let go of the past.

"How long have you been wallowing in guilt?" she asked. "According to your cousins, you're an easygoing, happy guy. This self-flagellation routine must be recent."

"Yes, it is."

"And it started when you found me in Texas."

"Before that. When I decided to look for you." I couldn't look *at* her now, though I sensed her studying me. "It's not your fault. I don't know why this happened."

She made a dismissive noise. "It's obvious."

I turned my face to her. "What is?"

"Why you feel guilty since you decided to track me down." She gave me a look that suggested I should have known the answer and made an exasperated noise when I clearly didn't understand. "I used to think you were not like any other man on earth, but it turns out you're exactly like the majority of males on the planet in at least one way. You don't understand your own feelings. Won't examine them. Won't talk about them. That's how you lunkheaded men get yourselves into these messes."

Another man might have gotten irritated, but I found myself smiling. "You're sexy when you're insulting me."

"Not insulting you. It's a simple biological fact that men are morons when it comes to feelings."

"I love you. Is that moronic?"

"Now you're being facetious." She folded her arms under her breasts. "Another evasion tactic. I know why you're acting this way, but I want you to tell me."

"Only a woman would say that. And only you could make me want to ravish you for saying it."

"And only you would be amused by it." She lowered her arms. "Tell me, Iain."

No wonder I loved her. She was the only woman I'd ever known who wouldn't let me quip my way out of a serious discussion.

Resting a hand on my knee, I told her. "My guilt isn't about Delyth or my wife or my da. It's about you. I ran away instead of fighting for you, and in the process, I cheated myself out of thirteen years I could have spent with you and our daughter."

Her gaze stayed steadily on me, though she said nothing.

I shut my eyes, exhaling a long breath before I looked at her again. "I hurt you. I hurt our daughter. I thought I'd finished with punishing myself, but seeing you again brought it all to the surface. You're right, I need to forgive myself, but I don't know if I can."

"Let me give you a jump start." She crawled on hands and knees to me. "I forgive you. The past belongs in the past. It's time to focus on the future, our future, and move on. I love you, Iain Malcolm MacTaggart, and you are not getting away from me again."

"Not planning to." I latched an arm around her waist. "You've always made me feel I could do anything as long as you're beside me. That includes forgiving myself. I'm ready to move on—with you and with Malina." I glanced down at her belly. "And the brother or sister we'll be giving her."

"Better put in more practice, then."

I rose to my knees.

Her attention snapped to my cock waving in her face. She licked her lips.

"Lie back," I told her.

"Mm-mm. Not this time." She snatched up the whipped cream and sprayed a dollop on the tip of my cock.

"Want a cherry too?"

"Nope." She scraped her tongue over the head. "I like an Iain sundae. If only we had some caramel sauce…"

I plunged a hand into her hair, tilting her head back. "It's still my turn, sunshine."

She shook her head. "Not as long as I'm right here in position."

Before I could speak, she clasped her hand around the base of my erection and began pumping in easy strokes. Her delicate mouth closed around the head, and her tongue lapped at the slit on the underside.

"Christ," I hissed. "Yer a sexy devil, but ye better stop or—"

She took me deeper in her mouth, licking and suckling, while her hand kept stroking me.

I gave in and let her have her way. Resisting Rae had never been easy, and I had no reason in the world to deny her anything. Her agile tongue tormented me, her soft lips glided over my skin, and her hand pumped in a firm, steady rhythm that had me grasping the back of her head and groaning. I tried not to thrust into her mouth, but *bod an Donais*, she was making my cock throb, and I lost all semblance of control, pushing forward every time she sank my length into her mouth with her tongue flicking and her hand stroking.

Christ, the noises she made. Hungry little grunts like she couldn't get enough.

I clasped her head in both hands to stay her actions.

She blinked up at me, eyes glazed with lust, lips pinker and still sealed around my cock.

I brushed a lock of hair from her eyes. "Time to feed the vampire."

She sat back, peeling her mouth away from my flesh, and swiped her tongue over her lips, letting out a throaty moan. "I was really looking forward to you coming in my mouth."

"Later." I rubbed my thumb over her bottom lip. "Lie down."

She obliged without another word. This woman honestly trusted me and would go along with whatever I wanted to do with her. If she could place all her faith in me, I owed her the courtesy of trusting myself.

"From now on," I said, "no more guilt."

"About damn time."

I lay down alongside her and splayed my palm on her belly just under her breasts, gliding my hand down little by little. My cock grazed her hip. Her eyes were half closed, her lips parted. I let the heel of my hand come to rest over her mound, slipped two fingers between her slick lips, and pushed my middle finger down to tease her opening.

Her back bowed up, her fingers clenched the sheets.

Watching her face, drinking in her responses, I massaged her folds and dived my finger inside her sheath, over and over, until she was thrashing and making desperate noises. When her body went rigid, I stopped.

She gaped at me, struggling to catch her breath, the blush of arousal coloring her cheeks. "You can't stop."

"But I did." I ran my hand down her inner thigh. "Only for a moment."

The saucy woman reached down, clearly meaning to rub herself to climax.

I caught her hand. "Uh-uh-uh."

The scent of her lust wafted over me, the most intoxicating combination of sex and woman spiced with a sweet and musky aroma that deepened my hunger for her. I anchored one knee between both of hers and nudged her legs apart. She raised her knees and let them fall wide apart.

"So eager," I said, taking hold of one ankle.

"I get that way when you don't let me come."

"Donnae worry, ye will come." I slung her leg over my shoulder and thrust into her, driving as deep as I could go. "When ahm wanting ye to."

She gasped and hooked her other ankle behind my erse. "More, oh God, more."

I thrust fast and deep and hard, making her body bounce and her breaths shorten into grunts and sharp, whimpering cries. When I slapped my hands onto the bed at either side of her shoulders, she gripped my arms so tightly I winced. Didnae care. Didnae think about anything. Nothing but her and the sweat dribbling down between her breasts, the way her pupils dilated, the slight puckering of her lips as she huffed out panting breaths. My cock pulsed with the need to come, but I couldn't let go until she did.

"Yes, Iain," she moaned. "I'm so close."

"Aye, love, I know." I lunged my head down to her neck, to the tender spot where her shoulder met her throat, and sank my teeth into her flesh.

She sank her teeth into my shoulder.

I shouted, fucking her harder than I'd ever fucked a woman before.

Her body clenched around me, squeezing again and again. She screamed into my shoulder, her cries muffled, and her nails dug into my arms.

With my mouth latched onto her neck, I jerked my hips back to pull out until only the head of my cock touched her. I sucked in a breath and slammed into her, coming so hard I bellowed against her throat. My heart pounding, gasping for breath, I thrust twice more, slower each time, until I'd spent myself inside her lush body.

I eased her leg off my shoulder and collapsed onto the bed beside her. "You are remarkably flexible."

She blew out a breath, fanning herself. "Have to be to handle a man like you. And wow, that neck-biting thing was even hotter than I imagined it would be. I can see why women go for vampires."

"Happy to sink my teeth into you anytime." To prove I meant it, I gave her breast a gentle bite.

"Need to recover from this time before we do that again." She laid a hand on her reddened cheek. "Whew, that was a workout."

"Never met another woman who would let me bite her. Not that I tried to..."

"I trust you, Iain. You can do anything to me, and you don't need to hold back. I can handle whatever you throw at me."

She meant it, I knew that. Whether I took her hard or made love to her delicately, she enjoyed it as much as I did. How could I have worried she wouldn't accept my past once she was confronted with the harsh reality of it? Meeting Delyth hadn't fazed her. Knowing how many women I'd been with didn't faze her. Rae understood me, accepted me, and loved me no matter what.

"Your work isn't done yet," she said.

"Making love to you is never work." I swept my gaze up and down the length of her body, taking a moment to appreciate her breasts and the flushed skin on her chest. "What did you have in mind?"

"Somebody needs to trot his hot self on down to the kitchen and get us a snack."

"Would you like me to call Lachlan so he can do that?"

"Ha-ha. I need nourishment before the second course."

I pushed up on one elbow, giving her the look she called my Buddha smile. "Who would you be referring to, then?"

She danced her fingertips over my lips. "You've got a PhD. Figure it out, Dr. MacT."

"By second course, I'm assuming you mean we should eat and then go to sleep."

"Eat, yes…after our snack." She caught my lower lip between her teeth, sucked gently, and set it free. "The Professor of Fuckology ought to know what I'm talking about. I mean, you did all that research with the village women."

For a heartbeat, I thought she might be annoyed. But no, my sunshine really had made peace with my past. "No more research. I want you to teach me."

"Me? That's crazy."

"No, it's necessary." I skimmed my fingers down to her mouth. "I want to know every way to give you pleasure."

She sealed her lips around my finger, releasing it gradually. "I'd like that. But I want to learn every way to make you pop your cork too."

"It's a deal."

She caught my fingertip in her mouth again, swirling her tongue around it while she aimed those lustrous sapphire eyes at me.

Christ, this woman could make me hard in an instant.

Rae feathered her lips over mine. "Are you going to feed me or what?"

"Anything for my sunshine."

Chapter Thirty-Four

Rae

For the next week, our little family explored the village and the surrounding areas, meeting friends and neighbors as well as more cousins and other relatives. Iain took us through Ballachulish, the town where his favorite cousins had been born and raised, to visit the home of Lachlan and Erica MacTaggart. Malina played with their toddler son while the adults chatted. Iain's closeness with his cousins seemed odd to me because I'd never met most of mine, and I hadn't gotten along with the ones I had met.

When I mentioned this to Iain, he told me, "Now you have good cousins, a great many of them. MacTaggarts are loyal and stubborn, so you'll fit in with us fine."

"But they're not my relatives," I said.

"Not blood relations, but you are part of the family." He kissed my cheek and winked. "Best get used to it, love. You've joined the cult and can't escape."

"Hmm. Does this cult involve sex rituals?"

"Naturally." He pulled me close. "I'm a vampire, after all. I expect you to offer your body to me for nightly rituals."

"I always knew you'd corrupt me."

"Well, if you'd rather we keep to the missionary position…"

"Oh no. You owe me thirteen years' worth of hot, naughty sex."

"Whatever my sunshine wants."

I'd gotten used to him calling me "sunshine" even in the presence of other people. No one seemed to care or think it was strange. When we visited Aidan and Calli's home, Iain's impish cousin declared, "At least I finally know why

Iain kept talking about needing more sunshine. I thought he wanted a tan or was getting vitamin D deficient."

Yes, all the MacTaggarts were snarky.

We spent as much time as possible with Iain's parents, and he relaxed more every day that we saw them. Angus showed Malina his carpentry workshop and regaled her with stories of Iain's youth and his first, less than successful attempts at woodworking. I showed Angus a photo I'd taken of the rocking chair Iain had crafted for me.

The man cried. He slapped a hand over his eyes and wept.

I didn't know what to say, so I patted his arm.

Malina was in the far corner inspecting shelves her grandfather had made.

"Forgive me," Angus said in a hushed voice, swiping at his eyes with his shirt sleeve. "Donnae mean to weep like this. The last time I was—away for a wee spell, Iain swore he'd never build anything again. He didnae want to be like me in any way."

I glanced out the doorway of the woodworking shed to where Iain entertained my mom and his mom. Glenna was smiling broadly as she'd done every time I'd seen her. The woman was thrilled to have Iain home and to have a grandchild. Yesterday, she'd asked if I minded if she called me her daughter. What could I say?

"Please do," I had told her. "I'd like that."

She cried and hugged me.

Now her husband had cried in front of me. Because he'd thought his son hated him. Because Iain had sworn never to be a carpenter like his father. I knew Iain could never have meant those words. He'd said them out of pain and fear.

Iain caught me watching him and smiled.

And I smiled back.

Turning to Angus, I said, "Iain doesn't feel that way. Every time he talks about you, it's clear he loves you very much."

Like a true man, he looked abashed, head bowed. "I caused him so much trouble, the way he worked so hard to keep me out of prison. He thinks I don't know what he did for me, but I do. A father should take care of his son, not the other way round."

"Iain told me he would do it all again. He has no regrets about helping you."

Angus's head popped up. "He said so?"

"Yep."

Though I was pretty sure Iain wouldn't mind what I'd told his father so far, I decided not to confide that Iain felt guilty for not being able to stop Rhys Kendrick from sending Angus to prison. These two had enough guilt between them. Maybe one day soon they'd have an honest talk and work through it all. If I gave Iain a tiny push in that direction. Meddling sounded like a bad thing to do, but Emery MacTaggart swore it could work if done right. Maybe she would give me some pointers. I had no experience with butting my nose into someone else's business.

Then again, Iain and I shared a life these days which made his business mine too.

"Glad you're in the family," Angus said. "You and Malina."

"We're glad too." I gave Angus a quick hug and a peck on the cheek, then waved to Malina. "Let's go see what your dad is up to, hey?"

Later, once we were alone in our bedroom, I told Iain what I'd shared with his father. "Do you mind what I said? I didn't think you would, but if I overstepped, tell me. I won't do it again."

"I'm not angry." He didn't even pause in undressing but flashed me a wry smile. "Shouldn't have let you spend time with Emery."

As I pulled my shirt off over my head, I made a sheepish face. "I'm sorry. The words came out before I realized what I'd said. Your dad looked so sad, I had to do something."

"I am not angry," Iain repeated. "Though I should've been the one to tell him."

"Like you ever would have." I shimmied out of my jeans. "You'll be happy to know I did not share with Angus how guilty you feel for the Rhys thing."

"Thank heavens your blethering has limits," he said with a smirk.

"You should talk." In my underwear only, I anchored my hands on my hips. "A certain someone told my mom I felt guilty for taking her money all these years."

"What's the problem? It's true."

He was right, and I doubted my mom had been surprised to hear it. We all meddled in each other's lives out of love, not a desire to cause trouble.

One day, the four of us headed out onto Iain's land for a picnic. Yes, he owned enough acreage to qualify as a farm or ranch, if he'd wanted to do something like that. I might've thought he purchased land as a means of making life in Scotland more attractive to me—except he'd bought this place before he found me and discovered I ran a sheep ranch. Maybe kismet had played a role. I'd never believed in that sort of thing before, but so much about our relationship, from how we'd met to the fact we were both only children to the way he'd found me again, seemed like more than dumb luck.

Were Iain and I meant to be? It sounded dumb, but it felt right. After all, he had started his search for me on Malina's birthday. After everything we'd both been through, we deserved a little kismet. I decided to accept fate might've lent a hand. Why not? Crazier things had happened.

The remains of our picnic lay scattered on a plaid blanket on the ground. My mom and Malina had wandered a ways off, though not too far, to pick wildflow-ers and generally enjoy the scenery and this beautiful, sunny day. Iain and I picked up the lunch remnants and stowed them in the cooler, then we lay on our backs side by side.

The sun warmed my face and glowed behind my eyelids as I lazed there amid the grass and flowers. Iain's hand found mine, and we linked our fingers. The ease and comfort of our new relationship seemed odd when I compared it to our ten months of hands-off behavior at Nackington. I loved our dynamic now, but I wouldn't have changed our past if I could. Iain had been a gentleman then, and despite his claims to the contrary, he still was one.

"I have a question to ask you," Iain said, his voice as relaxed as my body.

"What is it?" I asked sleepily.

"Do you want a church wedding or something less formal?"

My eyes sprang open, and I smacked his leg. "Told you already, noth-ing fancy."

"A church wedding doesn't need to be elaborate." A rustling indicated he'd moved, and given the shift in his hand position, I suspected he'd rolled onto his side. "You haven't answered my question. I'm trying to plan our nup-tials, but you're not telling me what you want."

"Too sleepy." Since I realized the stubborn man I planned to marry wouldn't give up until I gave him an answer, I yawned, stretched, and sat up. Gazing down at him where he lay on his side, I said, "No church required, unless that's what you want. A backyard ceremony would be fine with me."

Iain sat up too. "Would that be our backyard? Because there's also Dùn-dubhan, a beautiful spot for a wedding. Rory and Emery had their second ceremony there."

Oh yes, I'd been given the gist of the story of Rory and Emery's rocky road to love. It involved a quickie ceremony in a magistrate's office in Colo-rado, followed by Rory whisking Emery away to Scotland where the solicitor's mommy insisted on a real wedding. Their union had started out as a marriage of convenience to convince his family to stop pestering him to find a wife. It seemed all the MacTaggart men had taken a long and bumpy road to true love, from Lachlan's insistence he wanted only a fling with Erica to Calli's green-card marriage to a man she didn't love and her fears of getting entangled with Aidan, and finally to Rory and Emery.

And now, Iain and me.

Our bumpy road was the longest by far. Thirteen years, nearly fourteen counting the ten months of our medievally chivalrous courtship.

I shifted around to sit cross-legged facing Iain. "Our backyard. Well, tech-nically, it's yours. But I would love to marry you here."

"Sounds perfect." He bent forward to give me a quick, sweet kiss. "But this is *our* home. Which reminds me, we need to discuss living arrangements."

Though I'd known this topic would come up again, I had preferred to avoid thinking about it. I wanted to be with Iain, I planned to marry him very soon, but I had no idea whether I wanted to move here.

He crooked a finger under my chin, his thumb rubbing over my skin. "I will do whatever you want."

"I know." I gnawed on the inside of my cheek, contemplating the options. "Should Malina and I move here? Or should you move to America? Or do we spend summers here and the rest of the year in Texas? I could use a little input from you."

He lowered his hand to settle it over mine on my knee. "Whatever you—"

"Stop that." I grumbled and shut my eyes for a second. "Stop being so damn reasonable. I need to know how you feel about the options. Saying you'll do whatever I want is sweet, but it's not fair to you. We are a couple, Iain, which means we make decisions together."

"I suppose you're right." He scratched his chin, squinting his whole face. "I have no experience with a genuine relationship."

"You were married before."

"Julia let me have my way in everything."

I considered him for a moment. "If you were king of the castle in your first marriage, why are you being so wishy-washy with me?"

His gaze flitted here and there before settling on me. "I don't want you to leave me."

"We've been through this already. You are stuck with me for the rest of your life, stuck like superglue."

"In that case, about our living arrangements…"

"Uh-uh." I poked his chest. "You express an opinion first this time."

"All right." He rubbed his cheek, averting his gaze. "I would rather live here."

"Me too." I spoke the words without thinking, which must've meant they were the honest truth. Moving to another country scared me, but Iain had a wonderful life here with his parents and his cousins. As much as I longed to join that life, I couldn't shake all my doubts in thirty seconds. "I have my animals to consider. And there's my business. And there's—"

"None of that is an insurmountable obstacle." His mouth tightened in a closed-mouth smile. His eyes glinted in the sunlight. "We have sheep in Scotland, you know."

"Sure, but the horses and Lily—"

"Can be moved here. I've already asked Rory about that, since he's done work for farmers and ranchers. I'm sure we could bring Sunny and Ariel here—and Lily too, of course."

He winced faintly when he mentioned the llama.

I slapped his chest with the back of my hand. "Sure you want to commit to a life with Lily? She is madly in love with you."

He gave a melodramatic sigh. "I'm used to women falling for me at first sight. It's a burden I've had to bear all my life."

"All those women will have to find another man to pine for. You're taken, for keeps."

"I am, for certain." He grinned. "Does this mean you'll move here?"

"Need to talk to Malina first, but I have a feeling she'll be on board."

Ten minutes later, when I asked Malina how she would feel about emigrating to Scotland, she screamed and jumped up and down. Her scream segued into whooping while she waved her arms in the air. Once she'd calmed down a little, I let her know the horses and Lily could come with us. She flung herself at me for a big hug that nearly cut off my air supply. Once she let me go, Malina raced to Iain and suffocated him too.

My mom watched all of this while smiling, lines crinkling around her eyes. On the hike back to the house, Mom and I hung back so Iain and Malina could have more father-daughter bonding time. We walked fifteen or twenty feet behind them, giving us as much privacy as we were giving them.

I took the opportunity to talk with my mom. "How do you feel about this move? We'll be an ocean and a continent away."

"Don't worry about me." She bumped her shoulder into mine. "I've never seen you this happy before. You or Malina. I want you two to have everything you want, and what both my girls want more than anything is that man."

She nodded toward Iain.

"You sure you're okay with it?" I asked. "We won't be able to visit as much."

Cheryl Raines made a dismissive noise. "Iain has access to a private jet. I'm sure we'll get to visit each other as much as we want. Besides, I know how to send email, and Ty can show me how to do video calls. He does that all the time with his friends."

"Yeah, I guess the Internet really has made it impossible to get away from your relatives."

"As long as you and Malina are happy, that's all I care about. The rest will work itself out."

I believed her. I believed Iain too when he assured me later in the day that the jet he shared with Rory and Lachlan would be available to the Everhart women whenever we needed it. If necessary, he would buy us our own jet. Everything seemed possible, and more than that, a reality.

The next day, Iain waltzed into the kitchen with a big smile on his face.

I shut the refrigerator door, a can of pop in my hand. "You sure are happy today."

He had his phone in his hand. "Emery is in labor. Lachlan says Rory desperately wants to growl at the doctors and nurses, but Emery made him swear he wouldn't be an ogre. We're hoping Emery delivers soon, or else Rory might renege on that promise. He's in a state."

"Aw, the poor guy is worried about his wife. It's sweet." I sauntered toward Iain and set my pop can on the island. "Will you be Mr. Buddha Smile when I'm in labor? If I get pregnant, that is."

"I'll be calm and collected, naturally."

The way his mouth hiked up at one corner suggested he was fibbing.

He pulled me into his body, sliding his hands down my back to my ass. "I'll probably need a tranquilizer then as much as Rory does today."

For some reason, I liked hearing that. His unflappable side could be a huge comfort, but the depth of his feelings for me gave me a warm glow in my chest.

That glow lasted one more day, until I took a solo trip into the village to pick up some groceries. Iain had let me drive his Range Rover, just to prove he trusted my left-sided driving. I was stashing the groceries in the backseat when a shadow distended over me.

I glanced back over my shoulder.

A tall bruiser of a man inspected me with a coldness that made my skin itch.

Keeping the car door between us, I said, "May I help you?"

"No, Rae Everhart, you may not," he said in an accent I recognized as Welsh, like Delyth's.

"I don't believe we've ever met."

"You know my wife." His smile was nothing close to merry as he thrust out a hand to me. "Rhys Kendrick. We need to have a chat."

Chapter Thirty-Five

Rae

I have nothing to say to you." I couldn't stop myself from staring at Rhys Kendrick, the man who had imprisoned Iain's father and threatened to do the same to Iain. Part of me wanted to run, but a larger part needed to confront this man. Stupid, for sure. Though we were on a public street, no one else was around. I should've climbed into the Range Rover and driven away. Instead, I found myself intrigued by Kendrick—not like I was attracted to him, but in the way a person might be intrigued by a nature show about mountain goat rams doing violent battle with their horns.

Rhys Kendrick seemed more like a bull, though. His stocky body wasn't as muscular as Iain's, but Kendrick had the bearing of a man who knew how to use his bulk to best advantage. He wasn't fat either, but simply…large. Very large. Tall and broad and undoubtedly strong. His square jaw and tough nose, along with his wide mouth and squinty eyes, gave him the appearance of a street fighter. The kind nobody messed with. He wore a crisp suit, gray-blue in color and tailored to fit his frame. The juxtaposition made him even more imposing.

I straightened, rolled my shoulders back, and glared at him. "What do you want?"

Kendrick's mouth twisted up in a half sneer. "I heard Iain MacTaggart was marrying an American, and I thought you should know the kind of man you're involved with."

"There's nothing you can tell me about Iain that I don't already know." Like that Iain was ten thousand times the man Rhys Kendrick could ever hope to be. A good man, a good father, a good son. Kendrick neglected his wife and got his mistresses pregnant just to spread his seed far and wide like a medieval king looking for an heir, as Iain had phrased it.

Yeah, that was gross every time I thought about it.

Kendrick leaned against the Range Rover. "He's been fornicating with my wife for five years."

I shrugged one shoulder, aiming for an aura of cool indifference. Not sure I achieved it, but I gave it a try.

My new friend raked his gaze over me, what he could see through the car door. "I hear MacTaggart got his end away and left you with a child to care for on your own. He ran home and set about defiling every woman in this village while you were struggling to provide for his child."

Got his end away? I decided that meant sex.

Though I opened my mouth to correct his misconceptions, I realized I'd have to share private information with this creep in order to do that. Town gossip might've clued Kendrick in to the general story, but the only people who knew everything would never gossip about it. Why the hell should I care what this man thought, anyway? I knew the truth. My knee-jerk reaction to defend Iain would only cause more trouble. I had to stay quiet.

But I really, really wanted to lambaste this jerk.

My fingers gripped the door harder, making my knuckles ache.

"I know Iain better than anyone," I said calmly, "and nothing you say will change my opinion of him."

Kendrick picked at his teeth with one fingernail like he had something stuck in there. Wiping his finger on his impeccable jacket, he said, "The man you're going to marry is a thief and a forger."

"I know what you forced him to do, so you can cut the crap."

"Forced him?" Kendrick smiled like a hyena circling a carcass. "You're referring to the false authentication. Did Iain claim that's the only illegal activity he has ever engaged in?"

Keeping my mouth shut seemed like the best course. I ought to leave, but something made me stay put and listen to this man. Morbid curiosity, I supposed. What lies would he invent about Iain? I didn't have to wait long to find out.

"Dr. Iain MacTaggart," he said," has been stealing artifacts for years. How do you think he became so wealthy?"

"He told me all about that. I trust Iain's version, not yours."

Kendrick scoffed. "I imagine he claimed to have legally discovered the artifacts and gotten his honest reward from the government. It's a fairy story, and I have the proof."

"Bullshit."

He reached inside his suit jacket to withdraw a manila envelope, folded in half, from an inside pocket. "Here is the evidence. Look it over, think about it, and call me when you want to know more of the truth about the man you're marrying."

Kendrick set the envelope on the Rover's hood and tramped down the sidewalk away from me.

I regarded the envelope warily for a long moment, then I grabbed it and drove home.

Iain

Rae stomped into the kitchen where I was browsing the food selections in the cupboards. She dropped her purse on the floor and climbed onto a stool at the island, slumping her shoulders. Her hair, which had been sleek and wavy when she left, looked unkempt like a strong wind had buffeted her.

There had been no wind here, so I doubted there had been a gale in Loch Fairbairn.

Before I could ask what had happened to her, she shoved her fingers into her hair and whisked them around, upsetting her locks even more.

That explained her tousled hair, but not her emotional state.

"What's upset you?" I asked, moving to sit on the stool beside her.

She worried her lip, setting an elbow on the island and supporting her chin in her palm. "I debated whether to tell you, but we did promise to be honest with each other. Really, it was nothing. Don't go Vengeful Iain this time, like you did with Grayson."

A knot coiled in my gut. She was afraid I'd get angry and hit someone. Who and for what reason, I had no idea. Rae knew I wouldn't do anything of the sort unless someone threatened her or shouted vulgar insults at her the way her ex-lover had done.

The knot cinched tighter.

"It's all right," I said. "You can tell me. No violence unless absolutely necessary, you have my word."

She straightened, smoothing her hands over her thighs. "I met your nemesis."

"My nemesis?" I said with a slight laugh. The idea was ludicrous. "I have a nemesis? Interesting. Should I be wearing a cape?"

"No, but you would look really hot in one." She almost smiled, but the expression died a swift death. "I met Rhys Kendrick."

The floor and the entire earth beneath me seemed to drop away, leaving me wobbling on a stool in the void. Kendrick, that bastard, had approached Rae and—What?

I bent toward Rae, laying a hand on her leg. "Tell me what he did."

"What he did? Nothing much." She strapped her arms around herself. "He was pretty chatty, though."

"Tell me what happened." My jaw had tightened, and I struggled not to grind my teeth. If Rhys had hurt Rae in any way, emotional or physical, I'd beat him bloody.

She hunched her shoulders. "He was obviously trying to shock me, but it didn't work at first. I mean, I already knew you'd been indiscriminate in choosing your lovers. So, when Kendrick told me 'Iain defiled every woman in the village' it wasn't the shocker he expected. He seemed to think I don't know you slept with Delyth for five years. He did know some personal details I never told anyone outside our families."

"What did he know?"

"That thirteen years ago you took off suddenly and left me alone and pregnant."

I winced inwardly at the reminder of my worst mistake. It was just like Rhys to use my less-than-admirable behavior in an attempt to drive a wedge between me and Rae. But how the hell did he know about my flight from America? He could've guessed Rae had been pregnant at the time since I'd brought both her and our twelve-year-old daughter home with me. As for the rest...

Rae placed her hand over mine on her thigh. "Relax, I'm not upset about what he said. It was his attitude and physical presence that unsettled me. I don't know what his game is, but he clearly wants to rock our boat."

"Can't understand how he knew I left America suddenly."

"Did you tell Delyth?"

"No, I—" A conversation I'd had with Delyth months ago sprang to the front of my mind. "Not long after I asked for Rory's help in finding you, Delyth asked why I was on edge. The search for you wasn't going well, and I was starting to think it would fail. The investigator hadn't been able to track you after you went home to Iowa. Eventually, he discovered your mother had bought property in Texas, but it took time to uncover that fact since she'd changed her last name."

"Yeah, she went back to her maiden name after the divorce. Then she remarried and changed her name again."

"The investigator found that out, but it took months." I tried to pull my hand away, but Rae wouldn't let me. "During those months, I was a wee bit tense. Delyth noticed. When she asked, I...may have explained more than I should have. It was a stupid thing to do. I already knew Delyth would tell Rhys anything I told her, otherwise he would punish her for keeping secrets."

"Does he beat her?"

"No, nothing physical. Rhys prefers mental torture. Delyth never discussed the details, but everyone in the village has witnessed his behavior at one time or another." My jaw tensed more when I recalled the two instances I'd witnessed. "He rarely shouts, but he enjoys belittling people, especially his wife. I once saw him berate her on the streets of Loch Fairbairn, calling her everything from a stupid bitch to a raving whore, all because she smiled at a waiter and thanked him for serving their meal."

"I had a feeling he was that kind of man."

"He's a right bastard." I took a long, slow breath and said, "I'm sorry. I shouldn't have discussed you with Delyth. Whatever Rhys knows, it's my fault."

"No it is not." She swiveled her stool toward me. "Rhys is an asshole. That's his fault, not yours. Delyth shouldn't have told him, but I can see how a sensitive woman like her could cave under that kind of pressure. The only one to blame is Rhys Kendrick."

How could I go on blaming myself? Rae's logic and the intensity in her voice made it impossible. If she didn't blame me, I had no reason to feel guilty anymore.

We did have a problem, though.

"You shouldn't go into the village alone again," I said. "Not until I deal with Rhys Kendrick."

"How are you planning to do that?" She gave me a look that implied my statement had been barmy. "He told me something else too. I don't believe it, but I need to hear your explanation."

The knot that had begun to unravel snapped taut again.

"What is it?" I asked.

"Rhys claims you're a thief and forger, that you've been stealing artifacts for years and burying them in the countryside so you can 'discover' them and get a big reward."

I jerked as if she'd swung a cricket bat at my face. A thief and a forger? That was exactly what I'd spent my life trying not to become. My one and only slip had been when I let Rhys bully me into falsely authenticating his artifact. Rae knew this, and I knew she believed me, not Rhys Kendrick.

"That's not all," she said. "He gave me his so-called evidence."

Rae bent sideways to grab her purse and drop it onto the island. She dug inside its main compartment and brought out a large envelope.

She slid the envelope across the island toward me. "I haven't opened this. No amount of evidence provided by Rhys Kendrick is going to convince me of jack shit. I know you. I trust you. Whether you want to open that envelope is up to you."

"I'd rather not," I admitted. "But I ought to see what Rhys has concocted to implicate me."

Picking up the envelope, I unhooked the metal prongs that held it shut and opened the flap. I contemplated the envelope, dreading what might lie inside it. Rhys was the worst sort of *bod ceann*, but he was intelligent and cunning, not to mention ruthlessly determined. If he resolved to destroy me, he would do whatever it took to achieve his goal.

Rae clasped my hand. "We'll look at it together. No matter what's in there, it will never change the way I feel about you. Never. Understand?"

Despite the cold prickling my skin, I felt my lips tick up. "I would never question your commitment, *gràidh*."

She kissed my cheek. "Smart man."

I tipped the envelope, and its contents slid out onto the island. A sheaf of papers fanned out across the smooth surface. I picked up one sheet, then another, and another, skimming the information each held.

A Gaelic curse hissed out of me on a harsh breath.

"What is it?" Rae asked, leaning closer to peer at the papers.

"Rhys has fabricated evidence that shows every discovery I made in the past ten years was a fraud." I slapped the papers down. "Besides documentary evidence, he has testimony from three individuals who claim to have worked with me to defraud the government. According to these documents, I led a ring of criminals specializing in antiquities fraud. I would instruct my cohorts to acquire illegal artifacts which I would then bury on the property of an unsuspecting landowner and claim to have discovered them in situ. Sometimes I would give the landowner a portion of the reward to make the scheme appear legitimate. The rest of the money was split between me and my cohorts."

"But you can prove you kept all of your cut of the reward."

"Rhys has thought of that too." I snatched up a sheet, flapping it in the air. "Apparently, I've been acquiring and selling artifacts on the black market as well, using the treasure-trove finds as a cover."

"That's insane. Nobody will believe that nonsense." Rae grabbed the paper I held and scowled at it. "You documented everything you found, in writing and with photographs. If you had been sneaking onto other people's land in the dead of night to bury artifacts so you could 'find' them later, your photos would show disturbed earth, right?"

I slouched against my stool. "You haven't read the document that explains how I would bury the artifacts and wait until the grass had grown over the spot again before coming back to discover the thing again."

"Don't you do that."

"What?" I swept my hand over the island, scattering the papers. Some fluttered to the floor. "Admit I'm buggered? Rhys is clever and ruthless, and he has the underworld connections to get forged papers that say anything he likes. Papers that will convince anyone, even the authorities."

Rae seized my arm. "Don't you dare give up."

"Fighting is pointless. Rhys has an ace he can play at any time, one I can't refute."

"The forged artifact you authenticated."

I nodded, my focus tethered to the papers strewn across the island. "I committed a crime. Rhys doesn't mind being exiled from the UK he since owns a home in Thailand where he can most likely bribe his way out of any extradition. He can testify himself about what I did for him."

"There were extenuating circumstances."

"Helping my foolish old da is no excuse."

Rae jumped off her stool and thumped her fist on the island in front of me. "You do not get to give up. We are family now, you and me and Malina. If you don't give a shit what happens to you, then give a shit about what happens to us. Fight for us, Iain. For your family."

I swung my gaze to hers, stunned by the ferocity in her voice. This woman would do anything for the ones she loved, and she would never give up without a fight. A spark of hope ignited inside me, a spark borne out of the love and trust Rae had gifted to me in spite of the past.

"Listen up," she said. "I gave up thirteen years ago. I let the Bremner-Ashtons bully me into running away and not fighting what they'd done to us. Maybe I would've lost the battle anyway, but I didn't even try. I will never make that mistake again. And neither should you."

"You never broke the law, Rae."

She slugged my arm without much force. "You have a frigging lawyer for a cousin. Talk to Rory. I'll go with you."

The spark grew into a flame, the warm and golden light of Rae—of my sunshine.

What else could I do? I hopped off the stool and pulled her into my arms. "We will fight. Together."

"Damn straight we will."

"I love you, Rae, more than ever."

And then I proved I meant it, kissing her like the world would cease spinning if not for our lips fused to each other. She was certain we could fight Rhys and win, and because she believed, I had no choice but to believe it too.

Chapter Thirty-Six

Rae

To put Iain's mind at ease, I did not go out alone the next day. Iain accompanied me into town, along with Malina, though my mom stayed at the house. Glenna and Sorcha MacTaggart, Iain's mother and his cousins' mother, arrived when the three of us were heading out. The moms had lots of secret planning to do for the wedding, and I had resolved to find a dress today. With only a handful of days to go until the wedding, I had to get the task done.

The three of us planned on exploring Ballachulish and Glencoe, winding up the sojourn in Loch Fairbairn. According to Iain's cousin Jamie, Loch Fairbairn was the perfect place to find the perfect dress, so we decided to make it our last stop. I looked forward to seeing the village and Loch Leven as well as visiting Lachlan and Erica at their farm again. Malina was excited to spend more time with their cows, their dog, their garden, and of course their son, Nicholas.

We drove over the bridge that separated Loch Leven from Loch Linnhe, Malina and I marveling at the scenery. In Texas, we didn't have mountains rising up around glassy lochs or roads with numbers painted on them. We saw cows, and though we recognized those animals, Malina got excited about them anyway. The lochs and villages gave way to fields and woods. Iain turned us around and drove back toward the bridge to take us in the other direction toward the village of Ballachulish. It occupied one side of Loch Leven, Iain told us, away from the bridge. South Ballachulish sat near the bridge and North Ballachulish resided on the opposite shore, a fact that confused us Americans. The town of Glencoe lay beyond the village of Ballachulish. We would make our way there too, but ever the professor, Iain insisted on driving sedately to point out historical landmarks and features.

"The name Ballachulish," Iain told us, "is *Baile a' chaolais* in Gaelic. It means settlement on the strait. There used to be a slate quarry here that employed many people. If you watch, you'll see a large slate slab with the village's name on it that was put up to honor the village doctor who served the quarry workers more than a hundred years ago."

Malina popped her head between the front seats. "What was the doctor's name?"

"Lachlan Grant."

"Just like our cousin Lachlan."

"That's right, though your cousin wouldn't want to hear that." With a mischievous smile, Iain added, "He likes to think he's the only Lachlan that matters."

We made our way past Ballachulish and Glencoe, heading for Lachlan and Erica's home. Their farm lay on the side of a hill that overlooked Loch Leven and the villages surrounding it, the waters a dark stain on the landscape. Maybe my mind went straight to darkness and stains because of my encounter with Rhys Kendrick yesterday. Though I enjoyed our family day out, my thoughts kept boomeranging back to Iain's nemesis. The forged documents. Rhys's threatening demeanor. If he implicated Iain in the crimes he'd invented…

And what about the crime in which Iain was in fact implicated? Would Rhys actually flee to Thailand strictly to get Iain?

Delyth called Iain while Malina was getting a lesson in gardening from Lachlan and Erica. Their son played in the grass nearby under Erica's watchful gaze. Iain and I had moved a short distance away into the shade of a tree.

When Iain's phone rang, he glanced at the caller ID and told me, "It's Delyth."

"Better answer, then."

"You don't mind?"

"She's your past. I've made peace with that."

He answered with a terse hello, clearly not wanting to deal with his ex-lover today. His features tensed too as his eyes narrowed and he listened to whatever Delyth was saying. After a minute or so of grunts and "mmm" noises, his expression relaxed a bit. "It's all right, Del. I don't blame you for telling Rhys. He would've found out one way or another. The man is relentless. No, I'm sorry, I can't do that anymore. Aye. Goodbye."

Iain hung up and looked at me.

"Everything okay?" I asked.

He scratched his jaw. "She wanted to meet with me, just to talk. Delyth is in a state, the way she always gets when Rhys is in town, but I told her I can't see her anymore."

"I heard."

"She said she understands why, and she wishes us both well. Delyth likes you very much."

"You feel guilty for not being there for her, don't you?"

"For too long I acted as her private therapist." Iain took my hand, his gaze squarely on mine. "I have a family now, and I will not leave you here so I can comfort another man's wife. Delyth is an adult. She needs to deal with Rhys on her own. He is her problem, not mine. I suppose that sounds callous."

"No, it sounds practical. I like Delyth, but she's the one who married Rhys and refuses to leave him. Neither of us can be her therapist." I hesitated for a moment, considering everything I knew and had deduced about Iain's relationship with Delyth. "I'm glad she had you for those five years. She clearly feels affection for you and gratitude too, and I know how good you are at soothing a woman's fears."

He stopped blinking, probably stopped breathing too. His lips parted, but he said nothing.

"Don't worry," I told him. "I'm not jealous of the woman you slept with for five years, even though you refuse to admit it was a relationship."

Iain swallowed, his Adam's apple jumping. "Maybe it was, but I didn't love her. We were friends who, ah..."

"Screwed now and then?"

"Yes."

Thinking of him screwing Delyth brought back a litany of things he'd told me about her. Yesterday, he had said in a roundabout way he'd still been sleeping with her after he started the search for me. Well, he'd mentioned having conversations with her after that and how she'd noticed he was tense. Maybe it shouldn't have mattered anymore, but I was gripped by a sudden need to know.

"Iain," I said, speaking carefully, "when was the last time you slept with Delyth?"

He scrunched his mouth, turning his face away, and mumbled something.

"Speak up," I said.

With another hard swallow, he answered my question. "Eight days before I found you."

I drew my head back, sure I must've misheard him since he was still mumbling a little. "Eight days?"

He nodded, grimacing.

Glancing over my shoulder, I assured myself Malina and her cousins were still too far away to hear our conversation. I stepped close to Iain, angling my head back to stare at him until he met my gaze. "I thought you were desperate to find me and win me back."

"I was." He tugged at the collar of his shirt, his focus shifting away from me and back again. "It was looking like I would never find you. The months of waiting and wondering had turned me into a nutter, on the inside at least. I warned you I've never been a monk, and Delyth was a familiar port in the storm."

My knee-jerk response was to be offended, but I restrained the impulse. We hadn't been together at the time, and I believed he had honestly not known whether he would ever find me again. If I'd spent months searching for him, expending untold resources in the process, how would I have felt? Exhausted. Stressed out. Despondent.

That's how I'd felt after he disappeared thirteen years ago.

At least his honest answer explained why Delyth had continued texting him. Not only had he failed to definitively end their sexual relationship, but he'd continued sleeping with her until mere days before he took off for America.

"If I had known," Iain said, "I would find you soon, I'd never have gone to Delyth that night. We hadn't slept together in months, not since I decided to look for you. That day, I'd gotten a message from the investigator saying he still couldn't track you. He might've had a lead, but it sounded less than promising. If I had realized…"

He shut his eyes and shook his head.

This man loved me. What else did I need to know? He would never jeopardize our relationship, our family, by cheating on me or lying to me. I understood how he could've forgotten to mention he'd been with Delyth eight days before he showed up on my doorstep. Things had gotten a little crazy after that. If he had thought of telling me, he would've been afraid I'd give him the boot if he did confess. Did he worry about losing me even now?

"Iain, look at me."

"Don't forgive me for this."

A rude noise snorted out of me. "Get over yourself, Dr. MacTaggart. I'm not a starry-eyed coed anymore, and you're not my insanely hot teacher. We are adults in a committed relationship. I'm not so petty I'll hold a grudge because you slept with another woman before we got together."

He cracked his lids open, peering at me through his lashes. "You aren't angry?"

"No." I thumped my loosely fisted hand on his chest. "I'm not leaving you either. You are stuck with me till death do us part."

"We haven't said our vows yet." The tiny upward tick of his lips assured me he was coming out of his guilt coma.

"In six days, we will. But you've been mine exclusively since the day you waltzed up my driveway and announced your plan to win me back."

"That is true."

"And the same goes for me." I linked my arms around his neck. "I'm yours exclusively, whatever comes, whatever Welsh assholes try to break us apart. I'm with you, Iain Malcolm MacTaggart."

He pulled me into him, dipping his head to claim my lips.

"Eeee-ew!" our daughter hollered as Iain's mouth slid over mine. "Mom and Dad are kissing again. That is soooooooo gross."

I twisted my head around to shout back, "If it's too gross for you, stop watching."

Malina grinned.

Not long after that, we piled back into the Range Rover to head for Rory and Emery's house on the North Ballachulish side of Loch Leven. Though Rory kept his office in Loch Fairbairn, he went there only on occasion these days. As a semi-retired solicitor, he preferred to hang out with his wife and their new babies, a boy and a girl. Iain had called Rory yesterday to ask for his help in getting me and Malina family visas, the first step in a long journey to becoming Scottish citizens. We were uprooting our lives, and Malina seemed as certain of our decision as I was.

The Everhart women had fallen head over heels for Iain MacTaggart.

Rory, the overprotective husband and new father, allowed us five minutes with Emery and their days-old twins. After that, he ushered us out of the living room and into his home office for a meeting about visas and immigration laws and other fun topics. Rory offered to handle all the paperwork for us so we could focus on the wedding preparations.

Despite my insistence we both wanted nothing elaborate, I had a feeling the mothers would overdo it somehow. I couldn't blame them. According to Catriona, who had visited us at our home last week, the epic love story of Iain MacTaggart and his true love had become the sole focus of the Loch Fairbairn grapevine. With that kind of hype to live up to, the three mothers handling the arrangements would have a hard time resisting the urge to go all out.

By the time we got to the dress shop in Loch Fairbairn, it was late afternoon. By the time I'd bought a dress, Malina had announced she was "totally starved, like about to die." We'd eaten lunch with Lachlan and Erica, but that had been hours ago. My stomach was growling too. Iain took us to his favorite restaurant and introduced us to some Scottish foods, but only the yummiest ones that wouldn't tax our American taste buds.

While Iain paid the bill and Malina headed for the restroom, I went out to the Rover to start up the engine. The weather had taken a chilly turn, and I wanted the Rover's heater going strong as soon as possible.

I had just opened the driver's door when a familiar and unwanted figure came up beside me.

Rhys Kendrick clapped a hand on the Rover's roof, penning me between him and the door. "Have you studied the documents I gave you?"

"Didn't need to. I know it's all bullshit."

"He authenticated a forged artifact."

I knew that part was true, but I also knew Rhys had backed Iain into a corner to get him to do it. Betraying Iain by turning his father in to the police had been a vengeful move. I couldn't understand his need for revenge against a man who'd done nothing to him. "Why did you betray Iain after he did what you wanted? You didn't know him."

"Knew of him," Kendrick said, his lip curling. "Everyone in Loch Fairbairn knows about the intellectual lothario of the village and how the stupid bitches in this place adore him."

Well, at least that made a certain sense. Simple male jealousy had spurred this whole thing.

"Tell me," I said, "why did you let Iain screw your wife for five years?"

One corner of his mouth twisted into a half smirk, half sneer. "He did me a favor in that respect. Delyth's sexual tastes are...pedestrian. She's a passable trophy to wear on my arm, but I lost any desire for her long ago. Iain can have her." Rhys's smirk gave way to a full sneer. "Maybe he'll have you both at the same time."

Baiting me, that's what he was doing. I would not fall into that trap.

"Go home," I told Kendrick. "Your crappy little frame-up won't fool me."

"Maybe it won't." He pitched toward me, his breaths blowing in my face. "But I think the police will be very interested in the evidence I've collected. And if all else fails, I'll provide testimony in relation to Iain's forgery."

"You'll go to jail too."

"My jet flies very fast. I'll be in Thailand before they have a chance to arrest me."

My God, this Neanderthal really would flee the country to stick it to Iain.

"Sure, you could do that," I said. "But if you do anything to hurt Iain or me or my daughter, you will have one pissed-off American to contend with."

He sniggered and bent his head inches from mine. "Am I to be frightened by a waif? I've dealt with the Russian mafia and the South American cartels. You do not bother me in the least."

"You haven't seen me angry," I snarled. "I may be physically smaller than you, but I've got a weapon you will never have."

He regarded me like I was a dimwitted loon. "What might that be, waif?"

I supposed "waif" was the softest insult he could lob at me, though he seemed to think it was a terrible slur. I squared my shoulders and glared straight into his beady eyes. "I'm a MacTaggart."

Rhys Kendrick cocked his head, eying me with an unsettling interest.

Maybe I was a loon, considering what I did next.

I stamped the heel of my boot down on his foot, surprising him enough he stumbled backward into the Rover. I ducked sideways and slammed the car door into him.

He grunted, and his eyes flew wide, as the full force of the impact struck him.

Yanking the door open, I surged forward and rammed my knee into his groin.

Rhys Kendrick howled, partly rage, partly agony. His features contorted, his face flushed red.

"Mom!"

I whirled around. Iain was holding our daughter back, though she struggled to get free, determined to rush to me. I backed away from Kendrick, who had doubled over gasping.

"What the—" Iain began, but stopped when he spotted Rhys Kendrick. "Rae, are you all right? What's the bastard done to you?"

"Nothing, I'm fine. He's a mangy dog who snarls a lot, that's all."

Kendrick rose into a hunched standing position, breathing hard, his face a deep crimson. He hurled a slew of words in another language—Welsh, I supposed. "This isn't over."

He hurried away down the sidewalk in a bowlegged gait.

The mangy dog did not glance back.

"Whoa, Mom," Malina said with awe in her voice. "Did you, like, kick that guy's you-know-what?"

A slow smile spread over Iain's face. "I believe your mother did. She's a force to be reckoned with."

"Yeah. A force for good."

"Naturally. If she ever turned to the dark side, we'd all be in trouble."

Malina rushed forward to seize me in a bear hug. "You're awesome, Mom."

"Uh, thanks." I wasn't sure I'd set a good parental example today, but then, self-defense was an important lesson to learn. "Don't ever do anything like that unless you're in danger."

"Yeah-yeah, I know," she said in an exasperated tone as she finally let go of me. "I am twelve, you know."

Of course. Being twelve explained everything.

When we arrived home, Malina volunteered to go to bed early. Apparently, the excitement of our big sightseeing tour coupled with visiting relatives and concluding with a violent climax had left our kid exhausted. Malina went to her room, and Iain and I retired to our bedroom.

The encounter with Rhys Kendrick had been disturbing, but it had left me oddly wired.

"Should we talk about Rhys?" I asked while undressing.

"Later." Iain stripped off his shirt. "I'm feeling an overpowering need to make my wife-to-be come hard and fast." He shed his jeans. "Several times."

I couldn't argue with that plan.

Chapter Thirty-Seven

Iain

For the next five days, we forgot about Rhys Kendrick and his threats. We focused on our upcoming wedding, though we didn't have much to do for it other than choose our clothing for the day. Our mothers and Aunt Sorcha wouldn't tell us a bleeding thing about the ceremony except to assure us it would be, as Sorcha put it, "less than a royal wedding but more than a civil ceremony in a magistrate's office." Rory's mother would never let him forget how he'd wed Emery in America without even telling his family until after the deed was done. She'd had her revenge with the elaborate wedding and reception at Dùndubhan three weeks later.

Christ, I hoped the matriarchs wouldn't turn this into a carnival in my backyard.

Our backyard. I'd already asked Rory to help me change the deed so Rae would own the property too once we were married. Everything I had would become hers and vice versa.

Three days before the wedding, Malina announced she wanted to change her last name to MacTaggart. Rae had already confided this to me, but I acted sufficiently surprised to please our daughter. She went on to barrage us with questions. Did I need to adopt her so she could change her name. Would it be "massively weird" for me if she did. My brain began to go numb at all her questions, and I found myself staring at Rae while she deftly answered every one of our daughter's queries. Rae had spent twelve years with Malina. Naturally, she knew how to handle the lassie.

I had so much to learn about my daughter.

By the next day, two days before nuptial Armageddon, I was getting antsy about the entire affair. Ma refused to share any details no matter what I said. Rae refused to show me her dress, citing "tradition and bad luck, you hopelessly silly man." I loved it when she teased me, and even when she jokingly insulted me, but I couldn't concede the point.

"We've had our life's share of bad luck," I pointed out. "Seeing your dress won't cause a calamity."

My wife-to-be, wearing only a very small nightie, sat down on the bed near where I lay. She clucked her tongue, shaking her head. "No sneak peeks. Don't care how much you pout."

"Not pouting. Men do not do that."

"Oh please. Men are the biggest pouters of all."

"Not me."

"Maybe not most of the time." She stretched a hand out to finger my lip. "But you're coming awfully close to it."

I punched my pillow and dropped my head onto it. "Blame our mothers. They won't tell me a damn thing about the wedding."

"Oh, poor Iain. He doesn't know everything, and no amount of research will help. I'm surprised you haven't hired a private investigator to ferret out the details."

I shifted uncomfortably on the bed. "I considered it."

Laughter exploded out of her. Loud, snorting laughter. Eyes watering, she slapped a hand over her mouth.

The woman I loved offered no sympathy—and neither did any member of the MacTaggart clan or the Everhart family. My irritation about the wedding secrecy incited Lachlan to laugh heartily when I asked if he had any insight.

"Forget it," he said once his guffaws had ended. "You'll have to wait for Saturday."

I may have grumbled or possibly growled.

Lachlan smiled. "Never thought I'd see the day Iain MacTaggart was anxious about anything."

"This is not anxiety. I don't like not knowing what the mothers are up to."

"Is that what you think is fashing you? Ask Rae. She'll know what you're really on about."

The night before the wedding, when Rae chased me out of our bedroom, I took Lachlan's advice.

"Shoo," she said, pushing me through the open doorway into the hall. "We can't sleep together the night before our wedding."

"We're not virgins."

"Tradition and bad luck, remember?"

"Never knew you were so superstitious."

"I'm not usually. But I'm nervous about this whole wedding thing and clinging to superstitions gives me something else to focus on."

"Hmm, I suppose that makes an odd sort of sense." I leaned against the doorjamb. "Lachlan thinks I'm anxious. No idea why he believes that."

"Because you are anxious." Rae mimicked the face Malina made whenever her parents exasperated her. She mimicked Malina's exasperated voice too. "Double duh. It's only, like, totally obvious to everyone who's not you."

I couldn't help smiling. "Is it?"

"Yep." She leaned against the jamb too, bringing our faces within kissing distance. "You're having a conniption about the top-secret wedding plans because you're anxious about tying the knot again. With me. Because you have this pointless guilt complex about what happened many, many moons ago on another planet."

"The planet of Nackington?"

"It was a weird place. Might as well have been another world."

I rubbed my neck. "Maybe I do worry you'll regret this."

"And that," she said, punctuating the words by poking her finger into my chest, "is known as wedding jitters, aka cold feet. You do it on a grand scale, but it's completely normal."

"Is it normal to worry I'll be arrested at the altar?"

Rae spread her warm palm on my chest. "For you, yes. But we can't worry about what Rhys might do. We need to live our lives and deal with whatever might come our way together."

"The evidence he contrived—"

"Shush." Her finger sealed my lips. "I do not want to talk about Rhys Kendrick until after our wedding and our honeymoon."

"Honeymoon?" I feigned ignorance, but she was clearly not fooled. "Was I meant to organize that? I thought we didn't need a honeymoon since we already have a child."

"Come off it, Iain. I know you wouldn't shirk the one and only wedding duty you have."

"I also had to help my groomsmen choose accessories for their kilts. And I got you this." I excavated a small velvet pouch from my pocket and offered it to her. "A wedding gift, and a Scottish tradition."

She accepted the pouch and loosened the drawstring, peering inside. Her jaw slackened. Head down, she peeked up at me.

"You can touch it," I said. "It won't explode in your hand."

Rae brought out the silver brooch, laying it on her palm. She traced the shape with one fingertip—two entwined hearts topped with a crown—and then flipped it over to study the pin affixed to the backside.

"A brooch?" she said, looking up at me.

"It's called a luckenbooth. The crown represents Mary Queen of Scots, and the hearts represent our love." I closed her fingers around the brooch. "This is the same luckenbooth my father gave to my mother before their wedding."

Rae bit her upper lip. "Did you give this to, um…"

"Julia? No, I never gave her any sort of luckenbooth."

"Why not?"

I bowed my head, scratching the top. "I knew when I married Julia I was making a mistake that would hurt us both. Being a selfish *bod ceann*, I did it anyway. You know the story. Giving Julia a token like this seemed…wrong."

"You are not a dickhead." Rae lifted onto the tips of her toes to kiss the crown of my head. "Everyone makes mistakes. After what you've been through in your life, with your father and the Nackington thing, I understand why you married a woman you didn't love. A safe choice must've seemed very attractive. Stop beating yourself up over it. Tomorrow, we'll be married and have a fresh start."

Only a few months ago, a fresh start would've seemed impossible. Thanks to Rae, I believed we could have a second chance and that I might deserve one with her.

I stole a kiss from her soft, sweet lips. "You are a remarkable woman, Rae."

"You don't have to butter me up anymore, I'm a sure thing." She held up the luckenbooth. "Is it okay if I wear this tomorrow?"

"Yes, I'd love it if you would."

"I have something for you too. Almost forgot." She dashed to the dresser and brought out a package wrapped in tissue paper. She dashed back to me and held out the package. "Your wedding gift. It was your mom's idea. Well, half of it was. She said it's tradition."

Taking the package, I carefully removed the delicate wrapping.

"A shirt?" I said.

"I know you're wearing a kilt, not a tuxedo, but Glenna said the wedding sark is an old tradition where the groom pays for the bride's dress and she buys him a shirt." Rae tapped the shirt I held balanced on my hand. "I picked pale blue to go with your eyes—and your kilt."

When I cleared my throat and shifted my weight from one foot to the other, something hard moved inside the shirt. I unfolded the fabric, revealing a picture frame. The photograph inside it was of me, Rae, and Malina. I had one arm around Rae's shoulders and the other arm around Malina's. We were all smiling, the picture of a happy family.

"Angus took that photo," Rae said. "Remember? The first time we all went to your parents' house for dinner."

I did remember. Da had insisted we pose for a picture.

With my free hand, I pulled Rae close. "Thank you, sunshine. It's the perfect gift."

"Glad you like it." She drew her head back, out of my reach, when I tried to kiss her. "None of that until tomorrow, Mr. MacTaggart."

Somehow, I tore myself away from her tempting body and retreated to one of the guest rooms for the night. I didn't see Rae again until the wedding.

The mothers had done a spectacular job with the decorations. I had taken up my position in the garden on the right side of an arched arbor covered with flowers and greenery, with silver ribbons laced through them. The minister had taken his post directly in front of the arbor. Aidan, Rory, and Lachlan stood by me as groomsmen, but Gavin Douglas was best man. My cousins hadn't minded since they knew what a large role Gavin had played in my decision to find Rae. Jamie, Fiona, and Catriona waited on the other side of the altar, a trio of bridesmaids, but the maid of honor hadn't arrived yet. She was performing double duty today.

Rows of white chairs filled the garden, with the requisite aisle between them, and a crowd of MacTaggarts occupied most of the chairs. The Everhart clan was represented by Cheryl, her husband Greg, and her two stepchildren. Greg's chair sat empty since Rae had asked him to walk her down the aisle. Her father had been invited but declined to attend. I knew his decision hurt her, though being a strong woman, she refused to let it spoil our wedding. She'd had years to get used to the idea her father wanted no part in her life, and though she might never shed the vestiges of that pain, she had moved on.

We were moving on, together.

The music began, a lovely tune played by a single violin.

Malina made her way down the aisle carrying a bouquet of daisies and heather. She tossed the flowers one by one until she reached the altar.

I winked at her.

She grinned and hurried to her position at the head of the line of bridesmaids. The maid of honor had arrived.

The solitary violin fell silent.

I straightened and fiddled with the neck of my shirt, the one Rae had chosen for me. The color did match the tartan of my kilt perfectly as Rae had said. My palms grew clammy, but I tried not to think about the gravity of this moment. I loved her, she loved me, and—

The fiddle launched into the wedding march.

Movement lured my attention to the far end of the aisle—and the breath caught in my throat.

Rae floated down the aisle like an angel on a cloud, her arm linked with her stepfather's. Greg Raines smiled down at his stepdaughter, then nodded to me. Rae wore a blissful smile as she proceeded toward me, her pale-blue dress swishing around her knees and the luckenbooth pinned over her heart. Sprigs of purple heather had been woven into her hair, the auburn locks kissing her shoulders.

My chest tightened. I tried to swallow, but my throat had constricted too.

She took her place beside me, and we faced each other before the altar.

I scarcely heard a syllable the minister spoke, and I recited my vows by rote without a conscious thought for what I was saying. The vision of Rae had stunned me. She was beautiful, perfect, as glorious as the sun in the sky. My sunshine, that was Rae.

My wife.

We kissed, and the garden erupted with whoops and clapping.

Rae rose onto her tiptoes, slanting in close to whisper in my ear, "Breathe, Iain. The hard part's over. This time, you married the right woman."

As if by her command, I hauled in a deep breath and exhaled it slowly.

Bagpipes revved up, playing a boisterous tune. Rae had requested the pipes, and as usual, I could deny her nothing.

I let Rae lead me out to the front lawn where the reception would soon begin. I was married. Again. Rae had been right as usual.

This time, I had married the right woman.

Chapter Thirty-Eight

Rae

The ceremony had been beautiful. The three MacTaggart moms might've gone a touch overboard, but in a tasteful manner. My plans for a low-key wedding hadn't lasted long once I realized how many relatives Iain had—much more than his six cousins. I wondered how many MacTaggarts were running around the Highlands because it sure seemed like half the region's population had gathered in our garden.

Okay, it might not have been quite that many. A lot, though.

My family seemed pitifully small in comparison. And yeah, my dad had turned down his invitation, citing "business obligations." Any remnants of interest he'd had in my life evaporated the day I told him I was pregnant and had no prospects of marrying the father. Maybe his refusal to attend my wedding should've bothered me more, but I'd gotten used to his indifference. Besides, I had Iain and Malina, not to mention Mom, Greg, Ty, and Zoey. My family.

Couldn't forget the MacTaggarts either. I had acquired an army of relatives.

Half an hour after we said our vows, Iain and I were dancing on the well-manicured lawn. Tavish Brody, the groundskeeper at Dùndubhan, also worked for Iain these days tending to the garden and lawn of our new home. The mothers had wanted to erect an actual dance floor but decided that would stretch the "nothing fancy" guideline a little too far. Instead, all the women in attendance were invited to kick off their heels and dance barefoot. This made me considerably shorter than Iain, but I didn't care. The feel of the grass between my toes was heavenly.

With my arms around Iain's neck and my cheek on his chest, I swayed with him to the slow, romantic tune played by the solitary fiddler. My eyes drifted shut, and my thoughts wandered back to the moment when I'd walked down the aisle toward Iain. He had been a sight to behold in his blue-and-green kilt with those slender orange lines shot through it. The shirt I'd bought him matched the blue of his tartan like I'd known it would. The colors of his clothing brought out the ice blue of his eyes, though the sunshine we'd been gifted with today made his irises glitter like jewels. He'd brushed his hair back and shaved off his morning stubble. When our eyes had met, a sharp pang had lanced my chest. Not a bad feeling. A very, very good one. After so many years, I'd finally gotten my wish.

I'd married Iain MacTaggart.

"Don't fall asleep," he murmured, his hands linked at the small of my back. "We still have our wedding night ahead of us, and I've got plans for you tonight."

"Wake me when we're in bed."

"Isn't that the wrong way round? You're meant to fall asleep once you're in bed, not while you're dancing with me."

With some effort, I opened my eyes and raised my head to gaze at him.

He wore that casual smile again, but this time, I knew it signified genuine contentment.

"Okay," I said. "If you insist, I'll stay awake."

Wreathed in his arms, I glanced around the reception. Malina was dancing with one of Iain's cousins, Evan MacTaggart, whose mother was Angus's sister. I'd asked Iain how Evan's last name was MacTaggart when his mother was a MacTaggart, but he'd only shrugged. Evan dwarfed my daughter, but considering the way she kept laughing and grinning, he knew how to enter-tain a twelve-year-old girl.

Earlier, I had shared a dance with Evan and learned a smidgen about him. He owned a corporation—not a mere company, but an international corporation—and had earned an unspecified fortune by the age of twenty-nine. His unusual eyes captured my attention, with their dark-blue rings en-circling gray-blue disks so pale they almost appeared silver. Even his eyeglasses couldn't obscure the striking color of his eyes. His eyes combined with his blonde hair and sweet face, as well as his affable personality, lent him the aura of an angel in disguise. It didn't mesh with my preconceived idea of a corporate tycoon.

When I asked Evan how he pulled off the feat of becoming very wealthy at such a young age, he lifted one shoulder and said, "Hard work, luck, and the help of some generous people. Your husband being one of them."

"What exactly does your company do?" I asked.

"Design and manufacture electronic devices for personal and business security and surveillance. We also create the software that runs those devices."

"Everything you said flew right over my head."

He smiled. "I doubt that. Iain swears you're the cleverest woman in the world."

Before I could get any nosier, Iain cut in on our dance.

Now, ensconced in my husband's arms, I glimpsed the cardboard box my mom had placed over the remains of the wedding cake. A number of sneaky MacTaggarts had tried to steal an extra piece. Cheryl Raines was having none of that. She'd announced the rest of the cake was for the bride and groom, and anyone who touched it risked losing a finger.

She'd been half kidding.

With Iain's warm, solid body around me, I couldn't keep my eyes open even as he turned us in a slow circle.

"You're nodding off again," he said.

"It's your fault. If you want me to stay conscious, better stop being so warm and cuddly."

"Cuddly?" he said with a laugh. "Lucky for you I'm not one of the sensitive MacTaggarts."

"One of the things I love most about you." I willed my lids to part. "Might wake me up if you kiss me."

"You think so? Best give it a go, then."

He lowered his head and touched his lips to mine.

"What the bloody hell are they doing here?"

The shock in Lachlan's voice made my eyes spring open.

Iain swung his head around to glance toward the driveway, but I couldn't see around his big body.

He halted mid twirl, tension stiffening his every muscle.

"What is it?" I asked, and hopped up onto my tiptoes. I still couldn't see past his shoulder.

His expression turned grim. "The police are here."

The fiddler stopped playing, and everyone turned toward the driveway. Iain rotated sideways, giving me a full view of the sight that had snared everyone's attention.

A police car had rolled to a stop in front of our home.

Iain released me and plodded toward the two policeman who climbed out of the car. He moved like a man on his way to death row, his steps heavy, his shoulders slumped. I hurried after him. When I jumped off the lawn onto the gravel drive, the rocks bit into my feet but I didn't give a damn.

My husband halted in the driveway, a few yards from the police car.

Panting, I caught up to him as one of the officers approached.

"Iain MacTaggart?" the young man asked.

"Aye, that's me," Iain said without inflection.

"We need to bring you in for questioning."

Iain stood there like a statue, silent and stone faced.

"Questioning for what?" I asked.

The young man's gaze flicked to me. "Are you Mrs. MacTaggart?"

"Yes. What are you claiming Iain has done?"

"We've received evidence suggesting Mr. MacTaggart may be involved in theft and fraud concerning illicit antiquities."

Rhys Kendrick had done it. He'd provided the authorities with his fake evidence implicating Iain in falsifying treasure-trove finds to get the rewards.

A coldness rushed over me. I couldn't move, frozen there as motionless and silent as Iain, numb down to the very atoms of my being.

"Please, sir," the young cop said. "Come with us to the station. We won't need to handcuff you if you come willingly."

My husband shot me a quick, bleak glance. He let the policeman usher him into the backseat of the car. The officer who'd spoken got into the driver's side while his companion got in on the passenger side.

As the car drove away, I stared at the back of Iain's bowed head while the car rolled down the driveway. The world had stopped. Time had stopped. My brain refused to register the event, leaving me adrift in a great, yawning void.

Malina sprinted up to me, tears streaming down her cheeks. "Why did they take Daddy away?"

I pulled her into my arms and fought back my own tears. I could not cry. I would not cry. Our daughter needed me to be strong, and so did Iain.

Hugging Malina to me, I spoke in a surprisingly even voice. "It's all a big mistake, I'm sure. We'll get your dad back soon."

My mom and Rory MacTaggart came up beside me. Angus and Glenna followed close behind.

I would've expected Iain's mother to be crying or visibly upset in some other way, but she and Angus both evinced a strength and composure I couldn't muster.

Glancing over my shoulder, I noticed the rest of the guests hanging back, each appearing uncertain if they should approach us.

"Don't worry," Rory said. He wore a determined look that was reflected in his voice. "I will sort this. Iain will be home very soon."

"He will," Glenna affirmed like she'd stated an irrefutable fact.

Emery strode up to us with Aidan close behind. He pushed the stroller that held Emery and Rory's new twin babies.

"You're leaving," Emery told her husband in the form of a command, not a question.

He nodded sharply. "I have a client who needs my services."

Aidan spoke up. "Calli and I will take Emery home with your bairns."

"Thank you." Rory kissed his wife and jogged to their Mercedes.

My mom threw an arm around me as we watched Rory drive off, headed for the police station. Malina still hugged me tight. The three of us lingered there in silence until the Mercedes vanished from sight.

"It's that man, isn't it?" Mom whispered near my ear.

"Yes," I whispered back. "It has to be."

Rhys Kendrick. That goddamn fucking bastard.

Our guests filed by, moving toward their vehicles, each casting me a sympathetic look. Even Lachlan and Aidan seemed uncertain what to say to me, so I excused them with a polite goodbye. Every member of the American Wives Club stopped to touch my arm or squeeze my shoulder.

When Emery had her turn, she leaned in to say, "Rory is ruthless when the situation calls for it. My husband will not let anything happen to his favorite cousin."

"I won't let anything happen to Iain either." The fierceness in my voice surprised me, but I realized the instant I spoke the words I meant it. Whatever I had to do to protect my husband, my family, I would do it.

Emery gave me a quick hug, careful to avoid the twelve-year-old clinging to me. "We're all one big family now, and family sticks up for each other."

She left with Aidan, and my mom said, "I like these MacTaggarts."

Evan MacTaggart waited until the other cousins and wives had left before he walked up to me, Malina, and my mom. He offered me a business card. "If you need anything—and I mean *anything* at all—let me know. My private number is on the back."

I accepted the card but barely glanced at it, mumbling a thank-you.

"You may not need it yet," he said, "but keep in mind I have more money than Lachlan, Rory, and Iain combined. It's yours anytime. I owe Iain a debt, in more than money."

My eyes flew wide for a heartbeat, but then I blinked swiftly. It didn't help clear the shock from my brain. This man didn't know me, yet he would give his fortune without hesitation. When he'd informed me he had more money than his wealthy cousins combined, it hadn't sounded like bragging. It was a simple statement of fact.

Evan touched my arm. "Remember what I said. Anything you need."

He spoke those words with a quiet intensity that convinced me of his sincerity.

With that, Evan MacTaggart walked away.

Mom watched his departing, muscular figure and nodded with appreciation. "I take it back. I don't like these MacTaggarts. I love them."

"So do I." My throat thickened, and I coughed to clear it. "But I love one most of all, and I will not let one son of a bitch destroy my family."

Malina's head popped up. She aimed her large eyes at me. "Mom, you swore. I've never heard you do that before."

"Special circumstances." I kissed the top of her head. "Don't you start swearing."

"When is Dad coming home?"

"As soon as I can break him out of jail."

Though I said those words in a joking tone, I really would have orchestrated a jail break for Iain. If I couldn't stop Rhys Kendrick, I might have to resort to desperate measures. Living on a Caribbean island with my husband and daughter, or in Switzerland or wherever, suited me fine. A life on the lam beat a life without my family.

Fortunately, I didn't need to plot our great escape.

I left Malina with my mom and Iain's parents. Though Glenna had cried when Iain brought me and Malina home to Scotland, she stayed amazingly stoic in the aftermath of Iain's arrest, as did Angus. With my child safely cared for by her grandparents, I raced to the police station to see Iain as soon as they would let me.

A window of glass or plastic, I had no idea which, separated us when we were allowed to see each other. He looked haggard but sat tall and proud in his chair on the other side of the transparent barrier.

"They told me you wouldn't speak," I said.

"Not much I can say."

"I understand the problem, but Rory and I are going to figure this out." The problem was that Iain couldn't deny only the fabricated charges levied by Rhys. If he failed to mention the false authentication and later Rhys Kendrick produced evidence of it, Iain would be guilty of lying to the police. If he admitted to the one crime he had committed, they'd be far more inclined to buy into the falsified evidence Rhys had already produced. It was like swimming in quicksand. Whatever he said, he might be dragging himself deeper into the quagmire.

"Stay strong," I said. "Rory's sure we can get you out on bail in the morning."

"When Rory says he can do something, he will do it." Iain placed his left hand flat on the glass, and his wedding ring glinted in the harsh fluorescent lights.

I laid my left hand on the glass. Our rings would've touched if not for the barrier between us. "You are not going to prison. That I guarantee."

His jaw set, he tilted his head to the side and contemplated me with narrowed eyes. "What are you plotting, *mo gràidh*?"

"Not sure yet."

"Stay away from Rhys."

I leaned closer until my nose grazed the glass. "I won't make any promises I may not be able to keep. I trust you one hundred percent, and you need to trust me all the way too. Can you do that?"

He nodded. "I trust you, Rae, completely and without reservation."

My heart swelled at his declaration. It somehow meant more than when he'd said he loved me. We were partners, in every way, for the rest of our lives.

"Whatever you're doing," he said, "be careful."

"*Semper paratus*, remember? I won't be going into this alone or without a plan A—or plans B and C." I pushed my chair back, preparing to stand. "I'll see you tomorrow, at home."

We said our goodbyes, and I hurried out of the Loch Fairbairn Police Station, swerving right to make a beeline for Rory's office in the village. I tried not to worry about what might come next. All I could do was deal with the facts I had at the moment. I hadn't told Iain my idea for handling Rhys because, first of all, the plan wasn't fully formed yet. Second, I didn't want him to be an accessory or whatever they called it over here.

Whether Rory would go along with my plan, I had no idea. Even if he couldn't help me, I knew he would never rat on me.

The law offices of Rory MacTaggart stood dark and apparently empty, but when I tried the doorknob, it turned in my hand. Inside, I crossed through the ever-vacant reception area lit only by the ambient light filtering in through the windows. The door to the inner office hung partway open.

I knocked on the door.

"Come," Rory said.

Squaring my shoulders, I took a deep breath and marched into his office.

Rory reclined in his leather executive chair behind his large, wooden desk. His computer and a framed photo of his wife occupied prime positions on the desktop. His chair was tipped back slightly, and he seemed to be relaxing rather than slaving away on legal matters.

Well, he was semi-retired—at forty years old.

He waved for me to sit in the chair on this side of the desk.

I perched my butt on the seat but couldn't make myself lean back into it. Hands on my thighs, I said, "Thank you for meeting me here."

Rory tipped his chair forward so it was level and rested one arm on the desk. "You've been to the police station to see Iain."

"Yes."

He tapped a fingertip on the desktop. "You understand why he can't say anything. We will get him released tomorrow, but I have no doubt the charges against him will stand unless we can expose Rhys Kendrick's evidence as a fabrication."

"I understand that too."

Rory set both elbows on the desk and steepled his fingers. "When we arranged this meeting, you mentioned having a plan."

"Before I tell you about that," I said, "I need to know if what I tell you is confidential. Iain is your client, but—"

Rory silenced me with one raised finger. "Give me a coin."

"What? All I have is American money."

"Doesn't matter." He held out one hand, palm up. "Give me a coin. Any will do."

I dug my wallet out of my purse and laid a dime in his palm.

He closed his fingers over it. "You are now my client. This coin is my retainer."

"Um, Iain's rich. We can afford to pay you more than ten cents."

Rory relaxed into his chair again, turning the dime between his thumb and forefinger. "I spoke to a constable earlier. He says they'll have no choice but to charge Iain."

No surprise, given how well Kendrick had framed my husband.

I slid my butt backward until I bumped into the chair's back. "I have an idea of how to sort this out, but I need help."

"You can count on me and every last MacTaggart."

"Thank you, but there is a problem." I gripped the chair's arms. "This could be illegal, and it might be a little...risky."

I'd promised Iain I would be careful, and I intended to keep that vow. To save our family, though, I had to take risks.

"Risky?" Rory said, his fingers ceasing their movement, the coin caught between his thumb and forefinger. "What precisely did you have in mind?"

Acid boiled in my gut, rising up into my throat. *Now or never.*

Shifting uncomfortably in my seat, I dived in. "I spoke to Delyth, Rhys's wife, right before I went to the police station. She definitely feels her husband has gone way too far this time, and she's willing to help. With a few MacTaggarts for backup, I might make this plan work."

"You have yet to explain the plan."

"I'm banking on one fact I've learned from experience. Bullies are braggarts and cowards at heart."

I dug a business card out of my pocket and stared at the phone number scrawled on its backside. Evan MacTaggart's number. I hadn't called him yet, but his vow to help in any way he could echoed in my mind. Something else echoed through my thoughts too, the words my mother had spoken on the day Iain learned he had a daughter. I had confided to her that Iain and I had both given up without a fight thirteen years ago and how much I regretted surrendering to the Bremner-Ashtons.

This time, she'd said, *fight like hell.*

"My plan is simple," I told my solicitor. "Rhys Kendrick is going to confess everything."

Chapter Thirty-Nine

Rae

I sat up straight in a fancy, high-backed chair with my hands clasped on my lap, trying to appear calm and unperturbed by the situation. Whether my act worked or not remained to be seen. I had to make this convincing, despite my lack of training in the dramatic arts. I had to do it for Iain, for Malina, for our family. We hadn't found each other again after all these years only to let another jackass bully tear us apart.

My host perched his ass on the edge of the massive mahogany desk six feet away from me. Rhys Kendrick had accepted, without hesitation, my offer for us to meet and discuss the Iain situation. I'd implied there might be some benefit to him, hoping he would assume I meant money or whatever the hell this guy really wanted.

The room, Kendrick's study, measured larger than my living room back in Texas. I'd gotten used to the large rooms in the home Iain had bought for us, but even those paled next to the cavernous spaces inside Rhys Kendrick's palatial home. I didn't use the term palatial as a metaphor. Kendrick had bought an old castle, one far larger and less friendly than the one owned by Rory and Emery MacTaggart. Dùndubhan struck me as a homey castle, but maybe that effect stemmed from the way it had been decorated. Even as a museum, Dùndubhan had a friendly air about it. On my visits there, I'd never felt uncomfortable.

Of course, the MacTaggarts were much more likable hosts than Rhys Kendrick.

Here in the gloomy study, lit only by the small lamp on the desk, I kept fighting off the urge to scratch my arms or hug myself. The dark-wood walls seemed to close in around me despite the largeness of the room. A globe of the earth perched atop a four-foot-high stand near the only window—one of those multi-paned ones that stretched from three feet off the floor up to within inches of the ceiling. The window featured a sill wide enough to serve as a bench. A fancy rug, probably Persian or whatever was chic these days, spread across the floor from behind Kendrick's desk to beyond where I sat. Outside the windows, darkness cloaked the world.

My host had left the door partway open. If I needed to run, I had to hope I was faster and more agile than the bulky man in front of me.

"You wanted to talk," Kendrick said.

"That's right."

My ear itched a little, but I resisted the impulse to scratch. The tiny earpiece I wore didn't show, though I'd worn my hair loose so it would cover my ears just in case. Evan MacTaggart had provided the tech to make this mission possible, but my backup army included Lachlan and Aidan too, as well as Gavin Douglas. I prayed Delyth would keep up her end. Everything depended on it.

My husband should've been released on bail today, but Kendrick had pulled every string he could grasp in his grimy hands to keep Iain in jail. Rory was supposed to join Operation Save Iain, but he'd been delayed by the struggle to get bail for Iain.

We couldn't wait any longer.

I cleared my throat. "Mr. Kendrick, I understand you have issues with my husband, but I hope we can reach a mutually beneficial agreement."

Rory had dictated those words to me before we left home. He believed a businessman like Kendrick would fall for that kind of bait. Since I had zero experience with filthy-rich creeps, I took Rory's word for it.

"Call me Rhys," my host said. "We shouldn't be formal considering your husband used to roger my wife, and for all either of us knows, he may still be rogering her."

He might have used a word for sex I'd never heard before, but the meaning was clear. "Thought you didn't care about that."

Kendrick's mouth crimped. "He may have done me a favor by entertaining Delyth, but I won't thank him for it."

"What do you want, Rhys?" I emphasized his name, though I hated the familiarity of being on a first-name basis with this man.

"Equitable compensation."

"Haven't you got enough money?"

Kendrick's lips twisted into a nasty sneer. "I have more than enough money. What I want is compensation of a...baser nature. Tit for tat, as they say."

My stomach flip-flopped, because I had a pretty good idea of what he must want.

A voice in my ear hissed, "Get out of there. Abort the bloody mission."

I recognized the voice as Lachlan's. Since I couldn't respond directly, I leaned back in my chair and told Kendrick, "Are you suggesting I sleep with you?"

"What else have you to offer?" He raked his gaze over my body. "If not the obvious."

Shit. What else indeed?

This time Evan spoke into my ear. "Keep him talking. Appeal to his arrogance the way we talked about. Men like Kendrick love to have their egos massaged. He'll talk if you make him comfortable."

How the hell was I supposed to do that? Everything our little group had discussed earlier fled from my brain. Keep him talking. I could do that.

I'd worn a short skirt Emery lent me, along with knee-high leather boots and a low-cut sweater. According to Emery, men got dumb when faced with a sexily clad woman.

To test the theory, I crossed my legs.

Kendrick's attention snapped to my exposed thigh. He slid his tongue across his lower lip.

God, I hated this so much I had no words to describe it. Seduction had not been a part of the original plan. Honestly, I'd expected Kendrick to want...I don't know. Something else. I was supposed to get him talking, get him to admit he'd faked the incriminating documents, and get it all on audio thanks to Evan's devices.

I glanced down at my cleavage, pretending to brush lint off my sweater. Tucked inside my bra, I glimpsed the flat, pea-size microphone. Its white color blended in with my bra, so only someone who knew it was there would spot it. I really hoped I didn't need that camouflage. If Kendrick got close enough to peer into my cleavage, I might not be able to stop myself from kneeing him in the groin again.

Suck it up and do this for Iain.

Not that he would appreciate me seducing Rhys Kendrick—or even flirting with the cretin. I would not, under any circumstances, kiss or fondle or screw Kendrick. And he would get no chance to do any of that to me. Teasing, that was as far as I would go.

But only if absolutely necessary.

"I might consider your request," I said, "if you offer something of sufficient value in return."

Kendrick bent one knee, bracing his foot against the desk, and rested a hand on that knee. "The police have the evidence. It can't be rescinded."

"You could tell them you found out your source gave you false information."

The bastard chuckled. "Why on earth would I do that? Watching Iain rot in prison will be a pleasure I can enjoy for years. When he's released eventually, he will be bankrupt and alone."

"What makes you think he'll be alone?"

"A woman like you won't stay with a convicted criminal."

I had no clue what kind of woman he assumed I was, but I had a feeling his vision of me would not be complimentary.

"Maybe you're right," I said. *Like hell* was what I thought. "Maybe I should give up on Iain. I gave him another chance in spite of the way he abandoned me before. Can't help wondering if that evidence is real. Iain did authenticate a forged artifact for you. Who knows what else he might've done once he realized how easily he could dupe the experts."

Kendrick squinted at me. "What did Iain tell you about that?"

"Not much." I uncrossed my legs, then crossed them in the other direction. My skirt rode up a little higher, snaring my host's attention. "Only that he did it for his father, or so he says."

"Angus MacTaggart," Kendrick said with disgust. "That man is the stupidest criminal on the face of the earth. Like father, like son."

I ran my fingers along the neckline of my sweater. "How did you get Iain to authenticate that fake artifact? He's awfully stubborn."

Finally, I'd uttered one true statement.

"Yes," Kendrick agreed. "I'd hoped he might give in quickly, but it took a good deal of pressure to make him crack. Iain's father is his greatest weakness. No matter what the old fool does, his son wants to protect him. The burglary turned out to be a blessing in disguise." His lips curved in a nasty smile. "I made a fortune from claiming that artifact was stolen, thanks to Iain authenticating the reproduction as the genuine article."

"Because you promised not to file charges against Angus if he did." I bent forward just enough to give him a glimpse of my cleavage. "That was very clever of you, Rhys."

I relaxed back into my chair, feigning an ease I did not feel.

Kendrick smirked, puffing up a little at my compliment. "Iain is as daft as his father. He believed I wouldn't report the theft to the police or tell them Angus had been the burglar. Iain signed the authentication document two days before I spoke to the chief superintendent. I turned Iain MacTaggart into a criminal like his father."

Eureka. He'd admitted to blackmailing Iain into aiding in his insurance fraud. I didn't know if we could use that bit, since it incriminated Iain, but at least it meant Kendrick's tongue had loosened.

Now for the rest of his confession.

"Those documents you gave me," I said, adjusting my position to make sure his focus stayed on my body, "they're very convincing. It takes a smart man to figure out how to make stuff like that."

He puffed up a bit more. "Forging documents is easy when you have the right connections."

Lachlan's voice whispered in my ear. "That's enough, Rae."

But it wasn't. Kendrick hadn't quite admitted to forging the documents. I needed a clear-cut confession that left no doubts about his guilt.

Time to step up my game.

I rose slowly, languorously, to give him a good, long look at my body. I sashayed to within an arm's length of him. "I'm very impressed, Rhys. You're so much craftier than Iain."

He sucked in a breath when I trailed a finger down my neckline and dipped it briefly into the gap between my breasts before sliding it back up.

"I'd love to know how you did that," I purred.

Kendrick coughed, shifting position as if his groin pained him.

"Smart men turn me on."

He exhaled a ragged breath, his gaze glued to my cleavage. "It was simple. I contacted a man I know in Russia who's well known for his forging skills. I paid him a hefty sum to concoct those documents to make it appear Iain had defrauded the government and the museums that bought the artifacts he found."

"But he didn't defraud anyone. Those finds were genuine."

"Yes. That was the best part of—" Kendrick froze, his focus swerving to my face. His gaze sharpened on me. "You conniving little bitch."

Chapter Forty

Rae

The soft, menacing tone of his voice shot a cold electrical current through my veins. I tried to back away, but he shackled his hands around my upper arms.

"Iain MacTaggart may be stupid," he growled, "but he found a cunning wife, didn't he? Or maybe his irritating cousins invented this scheme for you."

Since he'd caught on, I saw no point in denying it. "This was my idea. I love Iain, and I will do anything to save him from your machinations."

"You will fail."

I winced as his fingers squeezed my arms. "I've already won. You confessed everything, all because I let you peek down my blouse. Who's the bloody fucking eejit now?"

Using words Iain might've spoken struck me as highly appropriate.

Kendrick dragged me into his body, caging me between his massive thighs with my breasts mashed to his ironclad chest. With his face inches from mine, he hissed, "You overestimate the cleverness of your plan, you stupid cow. You are alone." He yanked me closer, his breaths hot on my skin. "You're mine."

I jerked my head back and shouted, "Storm the castle!"

Cued by the trigger phrase we had agreed on, my saviors burst through the door.

Aidan and Rory MacTaggart stampeded into the study followed by Delyth, who jogged up behind them. The trio stopped halfway between the door and the desk.

"Sorry I'm late," Rory said, a big sword grasped in his hand. "Had a client meeting."

Relief flooded through me, but a frisson of worry slithered beneath it. Rhys Kendrick's hands and body still restrained me.

My solicitor aimed his steely gaze at Kendrick and thumped the flat side of his sword's blade on his palm. "Let her go, Rhys. It's over."

Kendrick sniggered, eying the sword with disdain. "This isn't the Middle Ages, Rory. I can snap her neck before you take one step."

As if to prove his point, he yanked me around to face the MacTaggarts and latched one arm around my midsection, lashing my arms to my sides. He closed his hand around my throat in a loose hold.

Peripherally, I noticed movement outside the window. Kendrick and I stood sideways to the window, though, and I couldn't tell what I'd seen.

Rory thumped the sword on his palm again. "We have your confession recorded, and we have multiple witnesses to corroborate it."

He glanced at Aidan and Delyth.

Kendrick scoffed. "My wife would never betray me."

Delyth looked a bit sick, but she raised her chin and rolled her shoulders back and took one step forward. "You've gone too far this time, Rhys. I'll tell the police everything I know about you."

I managed to turn my head a smidgen, enough to glimpse the real fear in his eyes. Whatever his wife knew, it must've been far more damning than what he'd done to Iain.

Kendrick squeezed my throat.

His grip choked me. I flailed to get free of him, but his arm bound me to his body.

An unholy bellow echoed through the open door.

Rhys froze, his fingers loosening.

A figure barreled across the room toward us.

Iain slugged Kendrick in the face so hard his jaw smacked into my head. Phantom stars burst before my eyes.

Another blow jolted me and Kendrick. His hand fell away from my throat. My legs gave out, and my knees struck the floor. My hand flew to my throat. I shut my eyes, dazed, struggling to catch up with this turn of events.

Scuffling. Grunting.

Whack.

A pair of strong hands thrust under my arms and lifted me up. One cold finger pressed into my throat at the pulse point.

"She's alive," Rory said. "You can stop beating on Kendrick, Iain. He's going nowhere, and your wife needs you."

I heard someone panting. Feet shuffling. Heavy breaths in my face.

My lids parted of their own accord, revealing Iain before me.

Rory, who held me upright against his body, handed me over to my husband.

Iain clinched me tight. His breaths fluttered my hair. "Christ, Rae, what were you thinking?"

Aidan spoke up. "Don't blame her. We all agreed to this plan."

"You agreed to my wife seducing Rhys Kendrick?" Iain snarled.

"I wasn't going to screw him," I said.

One big hand caressed my hair. "I know, *mo gràidh*. But you took a dangerous chance. He could've killed you."

Iain's voice broke on the last two words.

"You're missing the point." I raised my head from his chest to gaze up at him. "We got his confession. I saved you."

"I know." He looked miserable about it.

"You saved me too."

"Wish you hadn't needed saving."

I laid a hand on his cheek. "You're my hero."

"And you're mine."

He kissed me, soft and gentle.

Someone cleared his throat.

Iain scrunched his brows at the throat-clearer, and I twisted around to get a view of that person.

Rory tipped his sword at Rhys Kendrick. "Someone want to ring the police?"

"They're on the way."

We all glanced at the doorway where Evan and Lachlan had appeared. Evan had spoken those words.

"Gavin's outside," Evan told us, "waiting for the police."

Lachlan arched one brow at Rory. "Do I get my sword back? Or are you meaning to reenact Robert the Bruce's victory at Bannockburn later tonight?"

Rory pushed past me and Iain, settled a foot on Kendrick's chest, and placed the sword's tip against the man's throat. "I have use for it yet, Lachie. You'll have it back tomorrow."

I noticed Delyth huddled in the corner to the right of the door, her hands clutched over her belly and her color a bit gray.

Raising on my tiptoes, I whispered into Iain's ear, "You should go say something to Delyth. We couldn't have done this without her cooperation. And she did it for you."

"Me?"

He did not whisper, and the gaze of every other MacTaggart in the room veered to us.

I waved toward the door. "Maybe some of you should go wait for the cops to show up."

Aidan grinned. "Aye, Lachie, we should. Rae and Iain want to make out in front of the villain, and they need less of an audience."

Rory rolled his eyes. "Go man the front door, Aidan. We all need a break from you."

Lachlan and Aidan strode out of the room.

Evan ambled to the huge window and perched on the ledge.

I pulled Iain toward the globe on a stand, away from Kendrick and Iain's cousins. Hands on my hips, I said, "Why did you practically scream when I asked you to talk to Delyth? You've slept with her, for heaven's sake."

"You said she did this for me."

"Why is that a shock?"

He tugged at the crew neck of his T-shirt. "What did you mean by that?"

"Oh lord, Iain. Do you honestly not realize the answer?" At his clueless look, I let my head fall back and gusted out a sigh. "She's in love with you."

His eyes bulged. He rocked back like I'd waved a vial of anthrax at him. "What the bloody hell are you on about? Delyth and I had sex. We never had feelings for each other."

"Maybe you didn't love her, but she is definitely in love with you." I settled my hands on his shoulders. "Why do you think she kept texting you? Saying she missed you? And for Christ's sake, Iain, why else do you think she would risk everything to help clear your name? She told Rhys he went too far this time." I gave him a gentle shake. "She meant because he hurt you."

Iain's head rotated in slow motion. He stared blankly at his former lover. "What—I—What are you expecting me to say to her?"

"Just be kind. Thank her for helping. It's not that difficult."

He fisted his hands, then slackened them. "I'll...try."

"I'd go with you, but I think it's best you do this alone."

"Probably is."

"She'll be leaving the country, Iain. Her family moved to Canada years ago. She told me they've been begging her to leave Rhys for a long time, and she's finally ready to do it. Once she's told the police everything and shown them where Rhys hides all the damning evidence, she'll be gone for good."

He gave a sharp nod, straightened, and strode across the room to Delyth.

I returned to where Rory had Kendrick pinned to the floor.

The prone bastard spat in my direction, but it landed on his own hand. "Delyth will never betray me."

"She already has," I said as I crouched over him to glare into his eyes. "You should never have gone after Iain. He's got too many people who love him, people who will do anything for him. You've got nothing and no one."

Kendrick tried to lift his head, but the movement only made Rory's blade nick his skin. A tiny bead of blood rolled down his neck.

"I wouldn't move if I were you," Rory said in a deadly calm voice. "Unless you're wanting to lose your head."

Across the room, Delyth dabbed at her eyes while Iain touched her arm. Given his earnest expression and her emotional state, he must've done what I'd suggested. He must've told Delyth how much he appreciated her help.

One last issue needed resolving.

I grasped Kendrick's chin. "Tell me where you hid the proof Iain authenticated a forged artifact."

He spat toward my face, but once again it landed on him instead.

"You will tell me." I smacked him hard. "Right now."

"No need for violence," Iain said from behind me. "Delyth told me where to find what you're looking for."

We retrieved the evidence from a drawer in Kendrick's desk. Evan produced a lighter from his pocket and set the papers ablaze, dropping them into a trash can where they burned to ash.

The noise of a siren echoed outside, and multicolored lights flashed over us through the window. The police had arrived.

A little while later, we all observed as the cops hauled Rhys Kendrick away in handcuffs. He'd gotten downright belligerent about being arrested. Iain had his arm around me the whole time, but once the police car departed, he turned me to face him.

"Why did you do this?" he asked somberly.

"For you, Iain. For us." I bracketed his face with my hands. "I knew the day Malina was born I would do anything to keep her safe and happy. When you came back into my life, it didn't take long for me to realize I'll do the same for you. Whatever it takes, for you and for our family."

"I wish you'd let me in on the plan."

"You were in jail, and I hadn't come up with a real plan until after I talked to you. There wasn't time to share the details."

"Rory got me out two hours ago." Iain folded his arms around me, our foreheads touching. "He told me everything and brought me along. Bloody hard to stay back while you were so close to that bastard Kendrick. Rory threatened to bash me with his sword if I tried to interfere. Apparently, he has complete faith in you. All my cousins do."

"Sorry I scared you, but I did what I had to do."

"I know. What you did was brave. Reckless, but brave."

"Do you forgive me?"

He raised his head, his lips forming a grateful smile. "For years, I've had a hammer hanging over my head, never knowing when it might crash down on me. You took that away. I'm free because of you."

We both knew he meant more than being freed from jail. The threat of exposure, of being convicted of insurance fraud, had evaporated. Ahead of us lay nothing but open road and a journey we would take together, for the rest of our lives.

Chapter Forty-One

Rae

The month whizzed by in a flurry of activity. Rhys Kendrick remained in jail, locked up with no one to visit him. Delyth would stick around until his trial to testify against him. Rhys, being a braggart and an arrogant ass, had let his wife witness the majority of his dastardly doings, assuming she would never have the nerve to betray him. He'd been dead wrong.

On this beautiful day, I didn't care about any of that. I was running down the long hallway of our house, naked and laughing while a kilt-clad man pursued me. Our daughter had gone to Glenna and Angus's house for the weekend, and my mom had flown home to California yesterday. We had the whole house to ourselves, enabling our long-delayed honeymoon without any worries. I could rest easy knowing Ben had taken over running the Texas ranch, which my mom and I had given him as a gift. He loved the sheep and would take great care of them.

A different kind of animal had my undivided attention today.

My feet slapping on the wood floor, I glanced back to grin at Iain.

The tartan draped over his shoulder hung down to his knees in front and back, and with every wide step he took, I glimpsed his erection waving.

"Cannae get away," he called from a dozen feet behind me. "Ahm claiming my husbandly rights, wife. Yer body belongs to me."

The statement would've sounded sexist if not for the big grin on his face.

He ran faster, his long legs carrying him ever closer. A callused hand grasped my hip.

Squealing like a teenage virgin, I swatted his hand away and veered into the kitchen.

Iain caught me at the island. He slapped the tartan around my body, spinning me around and around until I was trapped by the fabric. With both his arms, he bound me to his naked, muscled body. The stiff line of his cock pushed against my belly.

"Got ye," he murmured, breathing hard from our race down the hall.

"You win," I said, breathless.

He released the kilt, and it slid off my body to pool around my feet. "Time for my wife to service my needs."

"Yes, my lord." I closed my hand around his erection. "How may I serve you?"

"With a good, hard fuck, that's how."

I grinned again, but then rubbed my arms. The cooler air in the kitchen had raised goosebumps on my skin.

My husband picked up the kilt and spread it over the island behind me. He hoisted me up by the waist, plopping me down on the tartan, then wrapped the plaid fabric around my shoulders and over my lap. It covered most everything—on me. Iain remained jaw-droppingly nude.

Iain rested his hands on the island at either side of me, leaning in.

Despite the seductive Highlander fixated on me, his eyes and his expression hot with lust, I found my curiosity rearing up. Besides, I needed to recover from my long-distance sprint from our bedroom upstairs.

I splayed my palms on his chest. "Tell me more about Evan."

My husband groaned. "I thought we were about to fuck, not talk about my cousin."

"We will, in a minute." I hooked my ankles behind his ass, drawing his erection between my thighs. "How rich is Evan?"

"The lad is worth over a billion dollars."

"Billion?" I swore my mouth fell open far enough a small bird could've flown in there. "How does someone so young get that rich?"

"Evan is ruthlessly determined, always has been. He would never misuse anyone to get his way, but he knows how to convince people to agree. That's why I lent him two hundred thousand pounds to start his company. I suspect he talked other people into lending him even more."

"Do you think he's bent the rules to do it?"

"I have no idea," he said on a sigh. "Evan keeps himself to himself. He was very shy as a child. Outgrew it later, but he's a hard man to get to know. Maybe it's because he has never known who his father is."

That statement piqued my curiosity. "How come he doesn't know?"

"His mother, my aunt Aileen, would never tell anyone. She gave her son her last name and no clues to go on."

At least Malina had known about her father, everything except his name. Evan had grown up with a giant blank spot in his family tree.

"Evan told me he owes you a big debt."

Iain frowned. "He owes me nothing. Evan paid back the money I lent him three years later—with interest."

The heat of his cock, the way it rubbed against my inner thigh, made me forget all about the list of questions I wanted to ask about Evan. I needed my husband inside me. The rest could wait for another day.

"Enough talking," I said, taking his dick in my hand. "Time to put this to work."

"About bloody time."

He flipped the plaid fabric away from my body, grasped my hips, and thrust into me in one smooth motion. I gasped at the sensation of his hardness wedged inside me, filling and stretching my body. He began to move, the rhythm slow and sensual, his hips rocking back every time he breathed in and plunging inside me with every exhalation. I gripped him with my legs, my ankles locked behind him, and flung my arms around his neck to hang on for the ride.

Iain kissed my throat, my shoulder, nipping along the way. My breasts rasped against his firm chest, and the light stubble he hadn't yet shaved off this morning scratched on my cheek. When he bent me backward, laying me out on the island, he bent down to capture a nipple in his mouth. As he laved and suckled it, his stubble rubbed against my sensitized skin. I moaned and grasped his head.

All the while, he kept up the measured pace of his thrusts.

This was making love. This was a bond nothing and no one could shatter.

Both hands on the island, bracketing my hips, he raised up to push inside me with more force, his pace quickening with our breaths. I cried out when he lunged his head down to pinch my nipple between his teeth. He shouted when I tightened my inner muscles around his cock.

Faster, harder, he consumed me with every thrust. My body froze in that glorious moment before the climax, but Iain got there first. He plowed into me, the hot jet of his release pulsing inside me. Even as he kept coming, he shoved a hand down to rub my clit—and I came like a wild thing, screaming and pounding my fists on the island, my body thrashing beneath him.

Iain fell on top of me, his head on my chest.

By the time I'd floated down from the outer reaches of the solar system, he'd caught his breath. My chest still heaved, though, my body sizzling from the pleasure he'd wrung out of me. We lay there, our bodies entangled and his softening shaft buried inside me, for several minutes without speaking. Then,

Iain slid an arm under my body to lift me into a sitting position. He tucked the kilt around me.

"Have a surprise for you," he said, feathering a kiss over my lips.

"Where is it?"

"Right here." He thumped his chest.

"I don't get it."

He held my palm to his chest. "You are married to the newest professor of archaeology and Scottish history at the University of the Highlands and the Islands."

The import of his words took a few seconds to sink in. When it finally did, I threw my arms around him and showered kisses over his entire face. "That's wonderful! Oh Iain, I'm so happy for you."

"It's part-time, but I think that's a good place to start."

"Absolutely." I smacked a big kiss on his lips. "I'm so proud of you, honey. Going for a teaching job again must've been nerve-racking."

"My brave wife inspired me." He hugged me close, nuzzling my nose. "I decided if my wife can take on a man like Rhys Kendrick, I can call a few old friends and acquaintances to see about a job."

I wriggled forward until his penis was wedged against my groin. "Time to celebrate."

A slow, sly smile spread his lips. "With whipped cream *and* chocolate sauce."

"On one condition." I snaked a hand down between us to grasp his blossoming erection. "This time, I get to have an Iain sundae."

He grinned, swept me up in his arms, and ran all the way back upstairs. Only then did he realize he'd forgotten the whipped cream and chocolate sauce. Not long after he returned from gathering our provisions, we were enjoying our desserts.

What else did we need? Each other, our daughter, our new home, Iain's new job.

Fully satisfied, I left my slumbering husband in bed, wrapped his kilt around me, and wandered to the window. Outside, a flock of sheep grazed in the newly fenced pasture—a new flock we'd bought a week ago. Sunny, Ariel, and Lily hung out nearby.

Oh yes, we had everything and more.

Epilogue

Evan
Six months later

Snowflakes drifted past the windows, but inside Iain and Rae's home, the atmosphere was warm and welcoming. Their daughter, my cousin Malina, stared at me from across the table. Malina had been studying me for ten minutes, ever since I took a seat at the table. Rae sat in the chair beside me, her swollen belly hard to miss even with the loose shirt she wore. Iain had taken the chair beside their daughter.

The lass would not stop asking questions.

"Why do you wear glasses?" she asked, squinting at my eyeglasses. "You could get contact lenses, you know. Why don't you do that? Mom doesn't like it when Dad wears his reading glasses because she can't see his eyes very well. Does your girlfriend mind your glasses? Do you have a girlfriend?"

Before I'd walked into the dining room, Rae had warned me I might endure the "tween inquisition." It meant, according to my cousin's wife, the child liked me. I'd asked what the bloody hell "tween" meant. Rae informed me the term referred to children on the cusp of becoming teenagers. Malina would turn thirteen in a few weeks, on February fifteenth. That was also the day last year when Iain had started his search for Rae, his long-lost love. They thought the coincidence had meaning, and though I didn't believe in fate, I wouldn't contradict them. They had something I couldn't understand.

Love, I supposed. The real, long-lasting kind I'd always dismissed as a myth.

"Well?" the wee Malina insisted. "Do you?"

Since I'd forgotten which had been her last question, I opted to answer them all. "My eyes won't tolerate contact lenses. I don't know if women care about my glasses since I don't have a girlfriend and never ask for anyone's opinion of me." I raised a hand when Malina opened her mouth. "I don't date. My work takes up ninety-five percent of my time."

"What do you do the other five percent of the time?" she asked.

"Sleep." I waved a hand to indicate our group seated at the table. "And visit with family when I have the chance."

"What about your friends?"

"I don't have friends."

Malina's brows drew together, and her lips parted. "That's, like, so incredibly sad."

"Evan has friends," Iain said. He winked at me. "The American Wives Club."

Erica, Calli, Emery, and Rae made up the American Wives Club, with Gavin Douglas as an honorary member. His official title was the Original American Husband. Apparently, the wives assumed Fiona and Catriona would someday marry American men. Emery, my cousin Rory's wife, had declared that "whoever they marry, their guys will be honorary members." Heaven help those gents. They'd have no idea what they were getting into with the MacTaggart women.

Were the MacTaggarts destined to marry only Americans from here on?

Destiny. What a steaming pile of shit.

Rae laid her arm on the table, angling toward me. "The American Wives Club has its next project all picked out. We voted and everything. Even Gavin agreed with us."

I loved the American women, but honestly, they needed a better pastime than harassing every unattached man in the family.

"Guess what?" Rae said with a knowing smile that made me squirm in my seat. "It's you."

"Excuse me?"

She tapped her finger on my chest. "You, Evan MacTaggart, are our next project. We're steadfast in our determination to help you find a wife."

"An American wife."

"Doesn't matter where she's from. We want you to be happy."

I made a rather rude noise. "I'm quite content with my life. Work is all the commitment I need, and women are nothing but a distraction and a nuisance. They should find kitchens to haunt, not men with better things to do."

Had I hoped to put her off the idea with that chauvinistic statement? If I had, I should've known better. Rae, like all the American wives, could not be put off a path once she chose it.

"You're not fooling me," she said, shaking her head. The weight she'd gained since becoming pregnant had made her even bonnier and had lent her a very motherly air. "I know you're trying to shut me up. I'm not that easy to cow. Just ask Iain."

"Don't need to. It's obvious from the way he caters to your every desire." My slight smile may have given away the fact I was teasing them both. I didn't like conversation, as a rule, but over the past six months Iain and Rae had become...friends? No, I didn't have or need friends. They were my family.

Iain spoke up. "When you meet the right woman, you'll gladly do anything to make her smile."

Pleasing a woman did not matter to me. Pleasuring a woman, now that was a task I did enjoy.

Slouching in my chair, I glanced around the room. "Will there be actual food at this family dinner you invited me to?"

"Absolutely," Rae said.

The second she started to rise from her chair, Iain rushed to her side to help her. They gazed at each other with undeniable affection. More than that, though. Their love was clear on their faces and in the way they interacted. I'd never known that sort of intimacy with anyone.

And I didn't want or need to. My business would be my legacy, not children, and my company provided all the satisfaction I needed. No females required.

Except when I had an itch that needed scratching.

Iain and Rae left the dining room, headed for the kitchen.

Malina folded her arms on the tabletop. "So, I heard you went to Paris six months ago. That sounds awesome."

"Aye." Rae and Iain had to be maniacal fiends to leave me alone with their inquisitive daughter.

"What was it like? Did you meet cool people?" I must've seemed irritated, because she gave me an exasperated look. "Did you at least see the Eiffel Tower?"

Memories blasted through my mind. The Eiffel Tower lit up in the Parisian night. A cafe with a perfect view of the landmark.

A woman with long, raven hair and striking green eyes.

My throat went dry. I swallowed, fighting to shake off the memory.

"Yes," I said, my voice suddenly rougher. "I saw the Eiffel Tower."

Thankfully, Iain and Rae returned then. He was pushing a metal cart laden with various kinds of food in various type of containers.

"Dinner," Rae announced brightly. "Who's hungry?"

"Me!" Malina said, clapping her hands.

I was hungry, but not for the meal my cousin and his wife had prepared. I craved something I could never, should never, have. The woman in Paris. The

American woman. The one whose name I'd never bothered to ask because she meant nothing more to me than a quick shag.

Stifling a groan, I pretended to care about the sumptuous meal my friends—my *family* had made for me. All through dinner, my thoughts kept traveling back in time to a sultry night in Paris and the sensual woman in the cafe. I knew nothing about her—not her name, not where she lived, not even what she looked like naked. I didn't know a damn thing except what it felt like to take her body.

Rae nudged my arm. "One day you'll fall in love and then everything will make sense."

"I don't plan on falling in love. I'm not built for it."

"Unless you're a psychopath, you're built for it." She leaned in to lock her gaze on me, her deep-blue irises sparkling. "You are not a psycho."

She might change her mind about that if she found out what I'd done, the things I'd learned about myself, and what I was capable of.

But that was a story for another day.

Evan MacTaggart returns in *Insatiable in a Kilt*.

LOVE THE

Hot Scots

SERIES?

VISIT

AnnaDurand.com

TO SUBSCRIBE TO HER NEWSLETTER

FOR UPDATES ON FORTHCOMING BOOKS IN THIS SERIES.

Anna Durand is an award-winning, bestselling author of sizzling romances, including the Hot Scots series. She loves writing about spunky heroines and hunky heroes, in settings as diverse as modern Chicago and the fairy realm. Making use of her master's in library science, she owns a cataloging services company that caters to indie authors and publishers. In her free time, you'll find her binge-listening to audiobooks, playing with puppies, or crafting jewelry.

She'd love to hear from you! Contact Anna via her website at AnnaDurand.com.

Made in United States
North Haven, CT
03 October 2023

42328534R10169